Swimming to Atlantis

Swimming To Atlantis

a novel

CHARLES J. HEBERT

Autumn Books

Published by Autumn Books, an Imprint of Pontalba Press, 4417 Dryades Street, New Orleans, Louisiana, 70115

First Edition

Designed by Stephanie Stephens

Library of Congress Cataloging in Publication Data

Hebert, Charles J.
Swimming to Atlantis: a novel
ISBN 0-9653145-0-2
I. Title

For Lisa, Jordan, and Taylor

ACKNOWLEDGEMENTS

I owe many people a large serving of gratitude for their aid and support in helping to make this book what it has become:

First, my family, especially my wife, Lisa, who has been my biggest supporter, and without whom this book would never have been written. She is my biggest inspiration, and has taught me nearly everything I know about falling in love.

My mother, for her unfaltering love for me and support of my endeavors though they may not always meet with her total approval. And to my brothers and sisters: Vickie, Ricky, Jill, Mona, Angie, Theresa, Diane, John, Mandy, and their families, who comprise one of the largest support systems in the free world. Thanks for many a reading and comment.

I owe a special debt to two great English teachers: my dear friend Arlie Parker, who let me believe I was good enough and who's every suggestion (which were many and brilliant) I incorporated into my effort, and Mandy Martinez, for much needed literary guidance at precisely the right time.

Also, three English teachers of my past to whom I owe the development of my writing skills: the late Mrs. M.E. Blanchard, Ms. Catherine Cormier, and Mrs. Charles Gary.

Norena Barbella for putting me in touch with all the right people and for opening doors that otherwise would have remained firmly shut.

John Hebert for all of his encouragement, time, effort, and assistance, technical and otherwise.

A very special debt of gratitude I owe to my editor, Winter C. R. Neil, a true professional who is always directly on point, says only what need be said, and who is truly a pleasure to work with.

My other great friends, especially Clint Williamson, the first to ever read my manuscript, and whose support was determinative of my going forward; and Chuck Venezia, who could be an editor himself if he ever chose to give up his day job.

To the professionals who first believed in me and never gave up on me: my agent, Sandra Martin, Publisher/Writer Frank DeMarco, and that future big name in Hollywood, Producer Sam Okun.

Tim Look and Craig Henry, my two pseudo-agents responsible for hooking me up with Wayne Porter and Pontalba Press.

Mike Fenzel, who in the end was right about a lot more than I initially suspected.

Three attorneys: Herbert W. Christenberry, Jr., my legal mentor and much more, Joe Regard, who handled my copyright, and Edward J. D'Antoni, you know why, Edward.

Ben Jones for his magnificent artwork, and Debe and Terry Jones for their contributions, as well as the rest of the RWE gang; Mary Ellen Johnson and Christine Holmes, for reading and reviews.

And last, but certainly not least, I would especially like to thank my new friend, Wayne Porter, for his courage in publishing new authors and works outside of conventional genres, based upon his love of literature more so than the bottom line. Here's to you, Wayne, hoping you don't go bankrupt in the process.

PROLOGUE

THE WALK FROM PARISH PRISON to the busy streets of the Central Business District is long and hard in the suffocating summer heat. Unfortunately, the route is familiar.

Having emerged from the depths, convinced he is more fish than man, Christian Waterman, eldest son of Lord Dog Waterman, come to deliver the message of his people, joins the swelling ranks of the homeless upon the dirty streets of the City that Care Forgot. Awaiting his opportunity, he ceaselessly searches for the single individual that he knows will act as a conduit for his message to this world.

"Ba bluh bah bub bub bu ba." In native tongue, he gives thanks to his father for having answered his prayer, for having influenced the kind young district attorney into directing his release from the confines of the iron cell in which he had found himself. He moves relentlessly forward, stopping only to collect a sheet of cardboard from the garbage bin of a twenty-four-dollar-a-night motel. He is drawn to the skyscrapers, to the place where he now knows that he must wait. Slowly he trudges, fading away, already invisible to most, blending into the great backdrop that is the city.

IRONY. THE IRON BARS OF A PRISON CELL. I never considered the possibility that one day I might be standing on the "wrong" side of them. Facing a lifetime behind them, and for what? For nothing more than being alot stupid and perhaps a little arrogant. I knew then and I know now that I could not survive it.

My Mom's favorite saying has always been, "If life hands you a lemon, make lemonade." Growing up it seemed as though she never missed an opportunity to sling it in my direction. Whether I had a bad game, turned in a poor test score, or had gotten turned down for the prom, the solution was always the same – make lemonade. I suppose it was her way of teaching me determination, insuring me that as human beings we can always prevail in the face of adversity, but I was young and to me it was just one of those silly old things your parents say that you pay no attention to. Besides that, I never got it. It always seemed so disgustingly optimistic, so overly simplistic. Life just wasn't like that, not all lemons got made into lemonade. It never really applied to me anyway because from the beginning life had handed me lemonade, but somehow I managed to make a lemon. Mom never had a saying for that.

Forged in greed, here is my story.

First, let me begin by saying that any sympathy that I may have hoped to garner in the telling of this is immediately lost as initially I reveal, as I must, that I am an attorney. It probably will not help to condition that with the revelation that I am not the stereotypical arrogant, greedy, snobby, horse's ass member of my profession, but I feel compelled to declare it anyway. At the risk of sounding arrogant (which is, of course, what I hoped to avoid), I must say that I have always basically been a pleasant person. I was never overly concerned about money. I just always figured it would come, and I was always fair with my clients. On occasion, I represented people without compensation and, despite pressure from the firm, never over-billed. I had entered law school with a certain degree of compassion for my fellow man and I had somehow managed to graduate with that compassion in tact. This I accredit to my parents.

Mine was a spectacularly uneventful childhood. Raised in the marshlands of Southwest Louisiana in a settlement more accurately described as a village than a town, only when it was too late would I begin to appreciate the wonders and advantages that had been afforded me early in life.

Hackberry, Louisiana was a place devoid of cable television, the nearest movie theater was forty minutes to the north, and the closest thing we had to a shopping mall was Gibson's Discount Center. With a perpetual blizzard on the picture tube as the only distraction, my days, depending upon the season, were instead filled with a gumbo of outdoor activities: catching fish and crawfish, hunting ducks and deer, and playing pick-up games of football and baseball with most of the other kids in town. At night the swamp would come alive with the high-pitched chirps of a million insects joined in by the baritone grunts and groans of lonely bull gators and the distant chank-a-chank of Eric Toussaint and his boys playing their Cajun music from the back porch of the Holler Inn or the Rumboogie Lounge, depending upon which night of the week it happened to be. With so much color and beauty, so much going on, so much life to experience, only a spoiled brat could have been bored. And boy, was I bored.

Born the only child of two very hard working parents, neither of whom had attained a degree past high school, their greatest goal was to make my life easier than their own had been. As they struggled to give me more and more, I soon came to the realization that there was always more to be had. I took advantage of the situation, as any teenager would have, but it came with a price. Certain things were expected of me in return: excellent grades, politeness at all times, and church every Sunday. Both of my parents were devout Catholics and other than the little problem I had developed concerning the coveting of worldly goods at that time in my life, I, for the most part, kept all of the other nine commandments.

When you are young, life takes so long in coming. Looking back it's as though it were all but a single moment. My Dad was a fisherman and trapper, always up before the sun, trawling for fish and shrimp half the year and trapping fur-bearing mammals, mostly nutria, to make ends meet the other half. Mom took odd jobs sewing clothes and watching neighbors' kids so their own mothers could work, religiously saving half of everything she earned to pay for my college education. Although I was later to earn a scholarship that paid all of my tuition and room and board at L.S.U., Mom still gave me the money, sending it to me in increments of two hundred dollars a month. Two hundred a month, earned and saved a dollar at a time. I ended up spending most of it at the Cotton Club on weekends, breaking a couple more of those Commandments along the way.

Thanks to the great sacrifices of my parents, and my ritual cramming sessions, I graduated from business school and was able to proceed on to the Tulane School of Law in New Orleans. Law school, as it turned out, became somewhat of a religious experience for me. Prayer had become a necessity. For the first time in my life I was really challenged and it took every bit of determination I had to see my way through.

I see now how law school transformed me. I grew, matured. My life calmed down a lot. Most of the wilder aspects I left behind and I began to become more cognizant of my roots, to move ever-so-slightly back toward the values that I had learned as a child. Had it not been for law school I might have lost them forever, continued to grow away from the lessons my parents had tried to teach me. Fortunately I held on, for as I would later learn, when life was at its darkest the principles that my parents had sowed within me were to be my saving grace.

Now, don't get me wrong. I didn't arrive in New Orleans with a Bible in my hand and I certainly didn't leave it toting one either. Believe me, I did more than my share of partying on Bourbon Street, dancing in Fat City, and throwing up at Mardi Gras. It's just that at the same time I was again going to church (almost every weekend) and was at last trying to make at least some attempt at resolving the great conflict of my life, balancing my desires in the material world with attaining entry through those Pearly Gates. In other words, I was going to be the man to finally find a way to get that damned camel through the needle's eye.

I received my law degree just before the market tightened up and got a job with Keating & Fabacher, a small downtown firm that had a general practice specializing in nothing. My parents had expected me to return home to Hackberry, or at least to the larger nearby city of Lake Charles, but after my graduation I just could not bring myself to do it. New Orleans has a way of growing on you. The city had charmed me and I had fallen in love with it: the action, the mansions and oaks, the food, the street cars, the people, and the history. I was part of something big there, something significant that could not be found in a road stop like Hackberry or even the larger but relatively unknown Lake Charles. I was meant for something bigger than that, I knew it, and that something was to be found in New Orleans.

My best friend and apartment-mate in law school, Theodore Wilhelm Woodson, whom everyone simply referred to as "Bip," also decided to remain in New Orleans after graduation and was hired as a junior prosecutor with the District Attorney's office. We renewed our lease and together we were going to conquer the legal world.

Bip was what Tulanians referred to as a "trustfund baby." His grandparents had died with enough money to keep him in a comfortable lifestyle for as long as he lived. Knowing Bip, however, they had wisely placed the money in trust until he graduated from high school. Bip's grandfather, having had no formal education yet having still managed to make a fortune in oil, figured a high school diploma was all that his grandson would need to make it big in the world.

By the time Bip was a junior in college, half of the money was already gone and he was well on his way to spending the other half. Knowing that something had to be done, he reasoned that doctors and lawyers generally made the most money, but that law school required less time and effort. He ended up at Tulane with me.

Bip seldom spoke of his parents. I gathered that there had been a divorce, but he hinted once that one might have killed the other. He had made the inference after a night of heavy boozing and when I prodded him for more information he gave me such a distant and frightful gaze that I never again brought it up. He did speak very lovingly of his grandfather, however, voicing disappointment only over the fact that the old man had not made more money before dying.

I say that Bip and I were apartment-mates, but as a practical matter he and I also shared the apartment with whatever girl I happened to be dating at the time. At that point in my life I was still breaking the really fun commandments, and was going through quite a succession of girlfriends doing it. It seemed that just as one would get settled in I would find another that I liked even better and Bip and I would be moving box loads of the old one's possessions out one day and the new one's in the next. I must admit that Bip was very understanding about all of this, although when I finally settled down with Betsy, who was to end the procession for four years, I knew he was relieved.

She had been named for her adoptive grandmother but despised the name. "Betsy is an old lady's name, like Ethel or Mabel," she complained.

I loved teasing her about it. "No, it's perfect for you. Betsy's arguably the worst hurricane ever to hit the Gulf Coast." Of course, this always failed to amuse her.

Anyway, in order to avoid the possibility of anyone thinking that she may have been any older than her actual twenty-three years, Betsy insisted upon being called simply "Bets." It was fine with me, and seemed to suit her: simple, harsh, and to the point.

From the very beginning Bip liked Bets almost as much as I did and he commented once or twice that I was lucky to have found her before he had. They immediately hit it off and soon the three of us were inseparable. Bip and Bets became best friends and Bets and I lovers. At least that's how it started out.

Bets was, by everyone's assessment, a great girl. Thin and pretty, with a nice personality, she had a sternness about her that let you know she would not be taken advantage of. Never a real leader, she was, however, someone you could always count on to meticulously carry out whatever role she had assigned herself. She didn't drink, didn't curse, didn't talk bad about anyone, and insisted on easing into our sexual relationship. I, on the other hand, did drink, did curse, talked bad about almost everyone, and unwillingly resolved myself to getting through a few months of mere foreplay while waiting for her to submit to our mutual carnal desires. I just attributed her resistance about our relationship to her history.

Bets had been abandoned as a child, left on the steps of a local rectory. Her adoptive family was Catholic, respected in the community, and she seemed to take her religion more seriously than I took mine. She was not prone to speaking of her past, other than the occasional mentioning of various accomplishments that she had achieved "in her struggle," and she never expressed any interest whatsoever in finding her biological parents. You see, they were her struggle, or at least they were responsible for it, and she convinced herself that she was better off having never known them. Yet, no matter how hard she tried to hide the damage that their deserting her had inflicted, after a while it became evident that it affected her deeply.

At the time it seemed little more than a quirk in her personality, something to be accepted and tolerated, made up for by her many other wonderful qualities. But in retrospect I must wonder. You see, Bets possessed an uncanny knack of detaching herself from others' hardships. I recall reading a story to her from the newspaper once about a construction worker whose head had been flattened by a steamroller. She laughed. Actually, laughed is an understatement. She was practically rolling on the floor, so entertained by the thought of a man with a perfectly flat head that she could not see the tragedy in it. Subsequent stories about a woman cut in two by a malfunctioning elevator and a woman who witnessed a window-washer falling past her 40th story office on his way to a grisly death invoked similar reactions. Still, other than that, she seemed just like the girl that Mom would someday have wanted me to marry.

Bets had moved in with me after we had been dating for about a month. She maintained her separate apartment, mostly for appearances sake, and by the fourth month, only a little over schedule, we finally consummated our relationship. I will never forget that night.

We had been out to dinner with Bip at Venezia's, an Italian restaurant in Mid-City, and Bets' favorite. As soon as we got home Bip retired to his dark bedroom with its king-sized bed and big-screen television, and Bets and I headed off to bed. I was in first and watched as she entered from the bathroom wearing a silky, green negligee that I had never seen before.

"What have we here?" I remember asking slyly, all the while eyeing the points of her nipples holding the sheer material away from her body.

"I thought you might like this," she said, pulling the covers away from me and climbing on top.

"I do," I answered, smiling, feeling her through the silk.

"I don't mean the teddy," she said as she deftly worked her hand and joined us, sending my head into an immediate spin and my body into convulsions of pleasure. Whether it was love, or anticipation, or a combination of the two, I don't know, but from that point on everything and everyone that I had experienced before dulled in comparison. I was convinced, after that first time, that she was to be the last woman I would be with for the remainder of my life.

Slowly, however, the magic that we experienced that night and countless nights afterward began to fade. Bets definitely grew less and less interested in sex and initially I thought it might be that we had become like an old married couple, our senses dulled by overexposure to one another. But then Bets began dropping hints about our tying the knot and I began getting the impression that she might be holding back on me, pressuring me to give her a ring so that our sex life could return to the stratosphere.

Whatever the reason, things just weren't the same and I began to get the feeling that the time was approaching for Bip and me to move some more boxes. The problem was I didn't quite know how to break it – to either of them.

Well, that is pretty much the entire supporting cast: the fool, the roommate, and the cute little redhead with the Kansas smile, Kool-aid mom mannerisms, and the new "penises off" policy. The only thing lacking in this cast of characters is the star.

That summer the plight of the homeless in New Orleans had noticeably worsened. Daily, it seemed, new members joined the ranks of the pitiful beggars that roamed the streets, asking for money from each passerby. They became familiar, almost like old friends that you could count on being in the same place at the same time each day, greeting all as they passed, asking for a little extra change. We, the more fortunate, began referring to them irreverently by nicknames related to their appearances or mannerisms. There was "Johnny Carson," a man of about forty years that walked with a limp. You would swear he was Johnny Carson in rags. And "The Moaner Lisa," a pitiful older woman wrapped in a grey shawl who sat on the sidewalk behind a cardboard box, constantly moaning, only raising the volume as anyone approached. And then there was "Booger-flipper," who you would probably just as soon not hear about. Suffice it to say that his pleading for cash came with a threat attached.

But for all of the Carsons and the Moaners, all those to whom I tossed a quarter or handed a dollar, not one of them, in any way, shape, or form, was any match for the "Man From Atlantis," as we would later dub him. He was one of a kind. Although not apparent at first, everything about him set him apart from the rest. Even his stench was different, and it was his stench that I noticed first.

It hit me like a ton of bricks.

I remember the day very well. It was August, and it was hot. Not that the heat is anything unusual for New Orleans in August, nor that the fact that it was hot triggers my memory as some extraordinary event related to the moment, but I do remember that it was hot. I had just finished a hearing in the District Court (I couldn't tell you what it was about) and was walking the short block-and-a-half back to my office in the Energy Centre. I had managed to work up a sweat crossing the street; not that I am a sweaty person by nature, nor am I overweight, but the combination of heat and humidity and the stillness of the air all made it impossible to do anything but sweat.

That is when it hit me. With the power of a baseball bat swung full-force into both nostrils, it stopped me dead in my tracks and nearly keeled me over. The smell of raw fish and sewerage, rotting flesh, urine, and vomit all in one. Reeling backward, my hand instinctively flying to cover my nose, I took one small gasp of the putrid air and plowed forward, growing dizzy for lack of oxygen by the time I reached the door.

Pulling with all my might I swung the door open with such force that I feared it might shatter. Quickly stepping inside, I immediately grabbed it from the opposite side and pulled it closed with equal force. Safely within the building I gasped for air. Pausing for a moment, I took in a second breath, then a third, and glanced back toward the source.

Against the building's outer wall, with a huge, nearly toothless smile, his shoes and clothes covered with slimy black soot, and with his greasy grey-black hair pulled into a pony tail behind his head, sat the filthiest, most disgusting excuse for a human being that I had ever laid eyes upon. He sat there, his booming voice calling something out to me that was made inaudible by the distance and the glass. I did not dare open the door, because I knew what he wanted. Like the rest he wanted money, only I was not inclined to give him any. I did not wish to encourage his setting up shop on my front doorstep, and did not want to have any responsibility toward the hundreds of people who daily would have to make their way past him to get into my building. I was not going to contribute to this problem.

I turned and walked away, ignoring his call, thinking I could just put him behind me, close my eyes and make him disappear. What I did not realize was that he and I were on a collision course, a collision course with destiny – my destiny. I had no idea, no way of knowing, that one day this filthy man was going to make me filthy rich and lead me to the very brink of death. Had I known I might have reacted differently. Instead I just walked blissfully away taking in all of the cool, clean air my lungs could hold.

TWO

FROM THE FIRST DAY THAT I LAID EYES ON HIM my life seemed to have changed. Things began happening and what I like to call the "luck factor" in life took on a new dimension in mine. You see, although I am a firm believer that we are basically in control of our own destinies, I dare not discount that very real and intangible factor in life known as "luck." Its existence cannot be denied – some people have lots of it and others have none. For some it is very good and for others it is very bad. Some people are lucky to have around, while others appear to bring mayhem.

He affected mine. From that day forward, it seemed, I was to have either great luck or terrible luck, depending upon factors related to him, but which I did not discover until some time later.

By the time I made it to our offices on the fourteenth floor (actually it was the thirteenth floor but that number was conveniently skipped on the elevator key pad) I had regained my composure. There were eight attorneys in the office, two named partners, two junior partners, and four associates. I was second to last on the list, having been there for a relatively short amount of time.

Unlike many of the larger firms around town, the atmosphere at Keating & Fabacher was much more relaxed. The associates were not trying to stab one another in the back and we all got along very well with one another, that is, with one glaring exception. His name was Jeremiah Ryan St. Roch Hayes, and he was hired two years after my having joined the firm. J. Ryan, as he was known, had so many names that he chose to forego his given name, Jeremiah, for the initial J. He did not particularly like the name Ryan, but he adored the St. Roch and thought that Jeremiah was too long to couple with R. St. Roch Hayes. And, of course, he could not leave the initial out altogether lest anyone be unaware that he had four names.

On occasion J. Ryan did find it in his best interest to go by Jeremiah. Every Jewish client we had knew him as Jeremiah, as did the young woman (or women) that he was bedding during any given week. And, of course, he did make certain that he was known as "Mr. Hayes" to all of the maids, janitors, and guards working on the building's staff.

In a few words, J. Ryan was the pompous asshole that Tony D'Ensina, the junior partner for whom I worked, strove to be. Under Tony's school of thought, however, J. Ryan had no basis to act as such as his father had only recently become a millionaire, making him one of the "nouveau riche" that are so loathed by the real "old money" families of this southern bastion of aristocracy.

Tony was a completely different creature. He was a nice guy trying his best to be a snob. I worked most closely with Tony, who was ten years my senior and whose accumulated knowledge of the finer points of the law was surpassed only by his molecular knowledge of every movie made between the years 1940 and 1973, and many after that. In law school he had studied for exams in front of his television set, accounting both for his wealth of movie knowledge and for his habit of weaving the storyline of a particular motion picture into just about any legal discussion that he participated in. That morning, after I had relieved myself of my briefcase, I went directly to Tony's office to discuss a case that Mr. Keating had assigned me the evening before.

"We're defending Petrology in the Mississippi River contamination suit," I began speaking as soon as I crossed the threshold of his office.

"If George Bailey had jumped into the Mississippi, he and Clarence would both have developed lymph cancer and it wouldn't have been such a wonderful life after all," Tony responded.

"Huh?"

"*It's a Wonderful Life*. They could never have made that here."

"You're right," I answered, finally catching on, "we don't get any snow."

"Well, the EPA seems to grant whatever variances they want with regard to this particular type of situation. I think they gave Oceanic Disposal a variance for the same activity that they're denying Petrology. Not that they could legally do it for Oceanic, but it would turn the heat up if they had granted that particular variance for one and charged the other."

"No kidding!" I responded enthusiastically.

"You ever see the movie, *Cat on a Hot Tin Roof*, with Paul Newman? Burl Ives was incredible in that."

Other than movies, Tony's big topic of discussion was the social scene.

He spoke as though from a pedestal, looking down on people who, once described, usually fit my description. They were people that he could never in a million years associate with, yet at times I got the idea that I was one of his closest friends. Of course, I was an office friend, never invited over for dinner or any of the parties that he threw for others on a comparable social level.

Tony had descended from old money, which in New Orleans at least, is much more valuable than the newer variety. However, most of the fortune had been spent before Tony reached manhood. He had a lot of fond memories of that old money, a lavish childhood and an expensive adolescence, for which the family was still paying. Though he earned a comfortable living and surrounded himself with expensive family heirlooms, it just was not the same as the good ole days when his family had ordered limousines for dinner and a movie and escaped the New Orleans heat by spending summers in the family home on the Mississippi coast. He wanted most out of life to be a Kennedy or a Vanderbilt. I guess we all have our fantasies, but Tony's required reincarnation.

After learning more than I ever wanted to know about Burl Ives' film and song careers, I returned to my office and worked diligently. After lunch with a friend from law school I beat my secretary, Margo, back to the office for the fifth time in two weeks. Her tardiness was uncharacteristic so I knew that something was going on with her, but I did not ask. I figured it had to be personal and that it was not my place to be nosy, at least not until it became more of a problem.

I did not leave the building again until the end of the day. Although I had a Jeep at home, the cost of parking in the Central Business District was prohibitive, so I usually opted for public transportation, or Bip's generosity. Most days Bip called and volunteered to pick me up on his way home from the District Attorney's office. This was somewhat of an inconvenience for him, as their offices were near the criminal court building in midtown and ours were near the civil courts downtown. Still, nearly every day at 5:30 he was waiting for me and saved me a ride home on the bus.

I left my desk a 5:15 to meet Bip downstairs. By the time I exited the building, the filthy man and his stench had vacated the premises. I hoped that he had found it unprofitable there and had ventured on to greener sidewalks, though in reality he had probably left to be first in line when the dinner bell rang over at the mission down the street.

On my way to Bip's shiny, black BMW I glanced over to see the soot-stained piece of cardboard marking the spot where the beggar had been sitting. My heart sank. This could mean only one thing – he would be back.

"What are you looking at?" Bip asked as I sat in the car.

"Nothing," I responded, "just that piece of cardboard over there."

"Where?"

My jaw tightened. Bip was at it again. He had this irritating habit which bugged the shit out of me. If you told him one little piece of information, he had to find out all about it. It wasn't enough that I was looking at a stupid piece of cardboard, now he had to see it. Next he would want to know why I was looking at it, and if I got into the homeless guy topic there would be questioning all the way home. I was not up to it, and I answered a little abruptly.

"Just over there, it's nothing."

He glanced over toward the sidewalk and then took off. "My, aren't we a little testy? Have a bad day?"

"No. And I am not testy," I answered petulantly. I could see it coming, now he would want to know everything about my day. It had been exhausting. I had worked hard and was tired and hungry and did not feel like delivering a report. Why couldn't he just drive me home in silence? Maybe I should have taken the bus.

"Yes, you are testy. But that's all right," he responded, injured, keeping his grey eyes focused on the road.

Now I started feeling guilty. I was tired, and perhaps I was being a tad irritable, and he *had* been kind enough to drive over and pick me up. The least I could do was provide pleasant company for the ride home.

"How was your day?" I asked after an appropriate silence, in a much more friendly tone of voice.

"It sucked. I had a trial and the jury turned two little criminals loose on our streets tonight."

"What kind of case?" I asked.

"It was a rape. These two 'little dudes' broke into a house and raped a 27-year-old woman at knife point. A neighbor saw them coming out, called the police, and they were caught about two minutes later. One of them even had her blood on his underwear."

"And you lost that case, Hamilton Burger?" I chided.

"It's not my fault. Their attorney got up and started saying how these poor children had come from broken homes, and they were raised in an environment where there was violence around them day and night, and how they were the true victims. Then he said that there must have been two other perpetrators that broke into this woman's hundred thousand dollar home and ripped off her $50.00 pair of Victoria's Secret panties. It made me sick."

"What's all that got to do with the case?"

"Nothing!" he proclaimed loudly. "Not a damned thing. But you should have seen all those old women up there in the jury box shaking their heads, 'yea, you right, I know where they comin' from', them poor chirrens...'" He said the last part in what he thought sounded like a Black dialect.

"And they let them go?"

"Yeaaaa!" he shouted.

"So they're out on the street tonight?"

"Well, I don't know, but if they don't get out tonight they'll be out tomorrow."

"What ever happened to justice?" It seemed so unfair.

"Justice? What's that? We haven't had justice since they stopped slinging ropes over trees."

"Yah-volt, heir Hitler!" I responded, now as disgusted with Bip's prejudice as with the jury's verdict.

"I'm serious. They should move executions to the Superdome and sell tickets. They'd make plenty to build more new jails and I guarantee you it would get the message through."

"How about burning crosses in the projects?"

"You think I'm kidding."

"No, I know you're not, and it's pretty scary."

"More scary than those two little rapists roaming the street tonight? What if they hit our neighborhood?"

"I don't think I'd be their type," I shot back.

"No, they'd just blow you away and take turns on Bets."

"What about you? Where would you and the rest of the SS be?"

"In a pool of blood beside you, while they attacked your girlfriend."

"I think they'd have to kill her too."

"Why?" he asked.

"Because I doubt they'd propose marriage and that seems to be the key to her drawers," I answered.

"She's still holding out on you?"

"You know how she is, once she got this marriage bug up her ass it's all she thinks about. You know what she told me last time I tried?"

Bip shook his head no. He had a big grin on his face.

"'Just think how much better it will be on our honeymoon,'" I mocked her.

He laughed.

I was relieved the subject had changed, as Bip's stories usually depressed me. Most of them were funny, in a dark sort of way, but they all usually involved some sort of miscarriage of justice, some breakdown in the system that was supposed to be in place to protect us. Only my sex life was an even worse topic with Bip.

"Well? Does she still do the other stuff? I mean everything else but...right?"

"Yea, Bip, just like last week when you asked me," I answered impatiently. It had been some time since Bip had coaxed a young maiden into his bed and I got the feeling that he was somehow living vicariously through my sex life, what little of it there was. Hell, there was barely enough there for me and I hated to think about what he did with the information. Although Bip had money and material things, he was not the best looking thing you had ever seen and he had begun putting on a little weight. The car and money were good for a date or two, but he had not yet hooked up with that beautiful little gold-digger out there that he knew was just dying to go through his trousers to get to his checking account.

"There you go, getting testy again," he whined.

"I am not," I defended.

"Yes you are. Ever since I asked you about that piece of cardboard."

"Would you get off the cardboard already?" I said, annoyed.

"See," he said in a smart tone of voice, "something about that cardboard is bugging the shit out of you."

"Oh, something's bugging the shit out of me all right, but it's not the cardboard."

"Yes it is," he insisted.

"Who the hell are you, Bippo the Magnificent, mind-reader of the world?" I answered, moving from testy on to angry.

"I might be."

"Yea, I bet."

"Or I could be an alien, the real Bip body-snatched one night in Alabama while you were asleep, and whisked away to Alpha Centuri," Bip laughed.

"Fuck you!" I knew he was making fun of me. Bip's mind was one-dimensional. He was a fact person, never testing the boundaries of reality set by those like him who could believe only what they could see with their own eyes and touch with their own hands. The Alabama comment was a perfect example. He had misinterpreted it from the very beginning and no matter how much I tried to explain that to him, it always came back to this – his teasing me about space creatures.

I did not speak another word for the rest of the ride home.

THREE

BIP OWNED A BEACH CONDO in Orange Beach, Alabama, right near the Florida/Alabama border. We spent many a weekend there throughout the year, as much in the winter as in the summer, because Bip liked the "solitude" of the deserted sands. It was not a very big place, just one bedroom, but there was a nice pool and beautiful beaches. Bip always took the bedroom and Bets and I sacked out up front, closest to the beach and the sound of the waves, on the foldout couch in the den area. Bets and I lived on the beach and at the pool while Bip made appearances when there was nothing on television that demanded his attention. All of the trips were pretty much the same old routine, all except for the last. There must have been something in the stars that weekend.

It was a few weeks before the day that I first saw the "Man from Atlantis," and we didn't get out of New Orleans until just before midnight. Bip drove the entire three hours to the shore and Bets stayed awake to keep him from falling asleep. She was much better at keeping her mouth running continuously, and I had just finished a week-long trial with Tony in Federal Court that had not allowed me much time for sleeping.

Since they both stayed up most of the night while I snoozed in the back seat, I was the first to rise that morning. I decided to take a walk along the beach, and let them catch up on their rest.

The morning was hot, but the sand, not yet warmed by the sun's flames, was cool beneath my feet as I strolled aimlessly down the shore. I must have walked for miles, just taking in the sights and enjoying the respite from the hecticness of everyday life, while the cool water of the Gulf of Mexico crashed on my feet and then withdrew in the same endless repetition that it has practiced since the dawn of time. The beach was relatively empty, save for a few pockets of spunky kids dragging tired-eyed parents toward the brine. Time melted away as I was lured into thoughts of doubtlessly deep meaning that I can no longer specifically recall.

I smelled it before I heard them, heard them before I saw it, and had a pretty good idea of what it was from the very beginning. It was rotting and the buzzing of the flies above it droned in my ears from several yards away, attesting to their numbers. Once light grey, nearly silver, its skin had been darkened by the sun and by the forces of its own decomposition. The long, pointed nose gave it away immediately, a porpoise, huge in comparison to what I thought a porpoise should be, but with its bottom half completely missing, the victim of a propeller or a shark. It was half-buried in the sand, just at the water's edge, obviously deposited there during a higher tide.

A strange feeling took hold of me as I gazed into its dead eyes, a feeling of sadness and remorse, as though it were human and had known me. I remember thinking how intelligent they are, how playful and good-spirited, and to see one like this, up close and lifeless, filled me with such a sense of loss that I knew there was only one thing I could do.

Positioning myself above the animal, I dropped to my knees, the air around me sizzling with the noise of a thousand frightened flies simultaneously taking flight. They were not suspended for long, and about half of them chose to light on me rather than the corpse as I struggled to dislodge it from its sandy grave. Holding my breath, I heaved with all my might, pushing harder and harder as it refused to yield, using every ounce of my strength until it finally pulled free, emitting a suction-cupped sound as I pried it suddenly from the sand and fell onto its gooey underbelly, the skin of which had been eaten away by sand crabs.

"Eeeehhhh!" I exclaimed, my chest and arms covered in its putrid, rotting flesh. The stench was unbearable and the flies were all over me – I was breathing them in and spitting them out, they were in my ears and nostrils, my eyes. Still, I regained my balance and continued the trek to the sea, rolling the poor creature. It became easier and easier as the depth of the water increased and finally floated it and carried it out to the sea.

Flies still swarming around my head, I immediately sank, disappearing beneath the waves, rubbing my body on the sand below, desperately trying to get it off of me. I thrashed around in the salty waters, wanting to be cleansed, then suddenly realized the danger of making such a commotion offshore while reeking of dead porpoise. So I surfaced and scurried for the shore.

A strange sort of feeling overcame me. I was happy, and I felt good inside, good about myself, as though I had done some great deed. It was the kind of feeling you get by gratuitously helping someone in real need, a feeling that you cannot buy, that you have to earn.

The walk back to the condo seemed to take about half as much time as the walk out had. Fearing that the odor about me might offend the masses that would shortly be gathering on the beach, in the lobby, and in the elevator, I hurried toward the room and the shower. Bip's place had two bathrooms but only one had a shower, and you had to pass through his bedroom to get to it.

As I entered the foyer from outside, Bets was emerging from Bip's room wrapped only in a towel. She was using part of the towel to dry her wet hair and did not notice me at first. When she did, it startled her.

"Geeeezummmmmm!" she exclaimed with a jump.

"Hey," I responded, smiling meekly.

Bip's head appeared from around the corner, checking to see what had frightened Bets.

"Where have you been?" he questioned, coming into full view. He was dressed in his normal nighttime attire, a pair of boxer shorts.

"I went for a walk on the beach."

"What's that smell?" both Bip and Bets said at the same time.

"What smell?" I responded, kissing Bets on the cheek as I passed them on the way to the bath.

"Damn! You smell like a shrimp boat," Bip continued.

Bets shrunk away, held her nose.

"Where's my toothbrush?" I called back to her. "I have to get the flies out of my teeth." Still smiling as I closed the door, I pulled off my swim trunks and climbed into the shower.

I took a long, hot shower, the vision of the dead porpoise still fresh in my mind. Finally I felt clean again and emerged to explain to them what had happened.

"You touched it?" Bip asked.

"You could get a disease," Bets added.

"Touched it? I fell inside of it," I said proudly.

"Eeeeewwww. And you kissed me?"

Bets and I hung out at the pool most of the rest of the day, our bodies bronzing under generous doses of low-spf lotion. She looked fantastic in a bikini, her ample but firm breasts suspending her top above her chest as she lay on her back, her hard legs pulled up to reveal her tight, round buttocks. I instantly became nostalgic for the old days, remaining horny pretty much the rest of the afternoon. By bed time I was fit to be tied.

Despite my good deed of the day and my hours of yearning, I was not the recipient of any special reward once the lights went out. Bets was not really in the mood, but was good enough to do just enough to keep me from losing my mind. She used her hand where I'd have preferred an orifice. She referred to her little maneuver as "walking the dog." Since the whole marriage thing had come up, she had held the leash in her left hand sometimes, her right hand most of the time, even in her mouth once or twice, but the dog had been banished from the kennel and despite all of my futile attempts, it was not coming inside without a collar.

Her duty done, Bets rolled over and fell asleep. My mind wandered. I loved her, I knew I did, but marriage was a huge step, one I was not sure I was ready for – regardless of the price I had to pay. I planned on marrying only once, and forever was a very long time, so I had to make sure that all of my wild oats had been sowed. Hers too. And I needed to be absolutely certain that she was the one. Filled with angst now, I could not fall asleep.

It was while I was lying in bed that I first noticed the lights. They were just flashes at first, out over the Gulf, like heat lightning somewhere off beyond the horizon. I turned my head to the plate-glass windows and watched as the dancing lights grew in frequency and intensity, bouncing from one side of the night sky to the other and back. They were pretty, entertaining, and seemingly harmless. Then they were upon me.

Flash after flash, red-yellow-blue-green, like flares going off in the room, they blinded me. Actually, they scared the shit out of me. I heard nothing, but saw the lights. I turned to wake Bets and then they were gone.

"Bets! Bets!" I woke her anyway, thinking they might return.

They never did.

A week afterward I picked up one of those tabloid gossip rags at the checkout in the grocery store that reported several people on the beach in Pensacola had seen and been accosted by UFO's. I merely offered the article as evidence that I may have witnessed a phenomenon, not as proof of life on other planets, yet Bip and Bets from that day forward branded me as "a believer" and tormented me with tales of aliens, Big Foot, the Loch Ness Monster, and three-headed babies.

That is why Bip's comment pissed me off so much. It was his way of calling me a fool, telling me that my arguments had no merit because I was some kind of weirdo who believed in aliens. I don't know what I saw that night. I don't really care anymore because, you see, compared to the events and revelations that were to follow, the idea of little green men buzzing in their spacecraft over the Florida panhandle does not seem all that unrealistic after all.

FOUR

THE DAY AFTER I HAD FIRST SEEN HIM, I was aboard the downtown express bus by seven in the morning, nodding off as I attempted to read the newspaper. Each time I began to doze I would have a dream that lasted just until my head fell and woke me. The first time I dreamt I was broke and jobless. I was on the Mississippi River bridge, looking into the raging waters below, and it was snowing. I kept saying over and over again, "I have to jump, I have nothing left." Just before I took the leap Tony appeared in a pair of white long-johns and told me something about my disgrace not being the end of the world, that there was so much more to live for. I jumped anyway, but awoke just before hitting the water.

The next dream was about Bets. I came home and she was in bed with Bip's two young defendants, having intercourse. I stood there in disbelief – she was enjoying herself. I walked up to the bed and she saw me and started laughing. One of the kids had a face that looked just like Bip's, only black. I woke as the bus came to a stop, and I began the trek to my office.

I don't know how much my imagination played into it, but the stench was there at least a block away. Walking from the bus stop, I had been thinking about my last dream. Something about it really disturbed me. I wasn't sure whether it was the fact that Bets was making love with someone else or whether it was that one of them had Bip's face. Whatever it was that was bothering me, however, was immediately wiped from my mind when the smell reached my nose. Although I could not see him yet, I knew he was close.

As I neared the entryway to my building, I spied the tip of a blackened tennis shoe protruding from a cove formed between the architectural ripples of the building's design. Holding my breath and looking in the opposite direction, I made my dash for the door.

"Morning, Sir!" his great voice boomed.

I continued walking.

"Sure could use a po-boy today!"

I ignored him. Perhaps he was speaking to someone else. Not a moment too soon I reached the door, obviously in need of some serious conditioning because my lungs felt as though they were going to burst. As my hand made contact with the door, his tone changed. He sounded almost angry, and his words became inaudible.

"Blub bu ba be deeb a du be el bu bub."

I swung the big glass door open with all of my might, smiling as the cool air inside hit my face. Exhaling, I let go of the handle only seconds before the door shattered into a million pieces. I had opened it too swiftly and with too great a force, it slammed into the doorstop, twisted, and exploded.

Mortified. That is the only word to describe how I felt. For a moment I forgot all about the man outside – glass was everywhere, people were looking, and all was silent. It seemed as though even the traffic outside had stopped to see what had happened, as if the attention of the entire world was upon me and my small disaster. Then it erupted. It began with a beautiful young woman standing near one of the elevators. This loud "Baaaa Haaaa" sound came from deep inside of her and she began laughing uncontrollably, then she was joined by others and my humiliation was complete. I stood there for a second, my face burning, wondering how I could have been so idiotic. Holding my breath, running to the door, breaking it in my rush to get inside because of some bad smelling guy outside – what was I, a moron?

I was in a daze, as if everything was in slow motion. I saw the security guard leave his post, heading slowly toward me with his "Incident Report" notebook in hand, and I felt something on my shoulder. It was a hand, extended, no doubt, in sympathy. Slowly, I turned, turned toward the kindness being offered to me in my time of need, toward the nice individual who had extended a compassionate hand to the leper in the doorway, turned to see the black, slimy glove sympathetically patting the shoulder of my $400.00 suitcoat. The stench was upon me.

Instinctively I pulled back, putting a foot's distance between myself and this man. He stood there smiling, his teeth decaying, his gums swollen, his stench everywhere.

"This man bothering you?" the security guard asked.

The man's smile disappeared. I said nothing.

"You okay?" he continued.

"Yea, I'm fine."

"I knew this would happen," he said, looking toward the man. "I knew you were trouble the first time I laid eyes on you. I'm going to have to call the police."

"What for?" the man asked.

"Criminal trespass, criminal damage to property," the guard responded.

"But...," I interjected.

"That's all right, Mr. Jordan, I'll handle this. Just go on to your office, I'll take care of everything."

I stood frozen. I knew that I was responsible for the damage, but this would solve my problem. Surely he would now move on, and if he went to jail he would be fed, and they would make him shower and give him some fresh clothing. Allowing him to take the blame for the door might just be the best thing that ever happened to him.

"No, I did it," I said instinctively, snapping out of my daze, coming forth with the truth.

"What's that?" the guard asked.

"I pulled it too hard and it broke," I responded, finding it increasingly difficult to breathe. "He didn't do anything, he was just making sure I was okay. Let him go. I'll take care of it."

"The honesty is appreciated," the beggar told me. He smiled again and I smiled back at him.

"I want you out of the building," the security guard demanded harshly.

"I will leave your building," he responded, taking a step backward. Continuing to face me, he made a large sign of the cross in the air, then turned and walked out.

"We'll have to bill you for this," the guard informed me. He seemed disgruntled, disappointed that I had not allowed him the pleasure of having the man arrested.

"Sure," I responded, "go ahead and charge me for this defective glass. You're just lucky someone wasn't seriously injured."

"You said you pulled it too hard," the guard replied.

"Defective design too," I shot back. "Look at how this doorstop is placed, of course it broke. I think I may have gotten a small shard in my eye, can you see anything?" I used my hands to spread apart my eyelid and presented my eye to him for inspection.

He looked my eye over very carefully.

"I don't see anything," he said. "I'll have to speak to the building manager about this."

"Let me know where to send the optometrist bill," I added, turning toward the elevators.

"You'll have to take it up with the manager," he called behind me.

I did not respond.

"Damn, that bum sure stinks," I heard him comment as I walked away.

Although he was right, I did not give him the satisfaction of knowing that I agreed with him.

FIVE

THE NEXT COUPLE OF DAYS WERE UNEVENTFUL. Bets and I went to dinner and a show one night, stayed in and rented *The Outlaw Josie Wales* on video the next. That is one of my all-time favorite movies. I love that old Indian guy that becomes his sidekick. Tony would know the guy's name, I'm sure, and could tell you a half-dozen other movies that he has been in. I wonder if he's still alive? Bets fell asleep thirty minutes into the show.

Nothing eventful happened at work either, and the man and his piece of cardboard had both gone away. Just when I thought it was for good, he made his reappearance.

It was Friday. At first I thought it was just my imagination. The stench, not nearly so bad as it had been, assaulted my nose just before I reached the new glass door of my office building. Simultaneous with his smell arrived the sound of his voice, "Morning Mr. Jordan."

I froze. He was here and he knew my name. Where did he get my name? Why was he back?

Awkwardly I turned and looked at him. His clear, blue eyes beamed at me as he smiled his rotten-toothed smile.

"Sure would like a po-boy today!" he boomed.

I just stood there, perplexed, his smell not bothering me as much as it had in the past.

"Where have you been?" I asked. It was none of my business and was much too conversational, but it was something I wanted to know.

"Tulane and Broad," he replied, referring to Central Lockup and the Criminal Courts Building.

"For what, for the door?"

"No," he answered, still smiling. "Sleeping in the street."

"Sorry," I said, not knowing what else to say.

"It's okay," he responded with a small grin, "got a shower and three squares a day."

"Not too bad," I said more cheerfully.

"Yes it is. You ever been in jail?"

"No." My smile evaporated.

"Then you don't know yet."

"What's your name?" I asked, embarrassed, changing the topic.

"Christian Waterman, eldest son of our Lord, Dog Waterman, Savior of Ba blub do. My friends call me Flipper."

Obviously he was insane.

"Glad to meet you Flipper. I'm Andy," I said hesitantly, playing it by ear. Stupid. I should have thought it all the way through and gotten the hell out of there.

"Nice to meet you Andy," he put out his right hand for a shake. I detected a slight accent but could not place it. Maybe Caribbean, one of the British islands.

Hesitantly I grabbed his hand, weakly I squeezed. His big paw tightened around my hand and he shook it violently. Refusing to let go of it he repeated his name, "Christian Waterman. My *friends* call me Flipper."

He stressed the word "friends" as though to let me know that I was not yet one of them.

"All right, Christian," I said, my hand still trapped. We were beginning to attract the attention of passersby. Perhaps it was the still-present, yet less offensive odor.

"Andy," he repeated, showing me his teeth.

"Yep," I said, trying to wrest my hand loose. "I hope you have a nice day."

"You too," he answered, tightening his grip. "Andy," he repeated, "thought it was Jordan."

"Oh no, that's my last name," I explained. "Andy Jordan."

"Andy Jordan," he repeated after me.

"Yea, I guess I should go," I said, trying to politely pull my hand back.

"Andy Jordan, you wouldn't happen to have a little change so I could get me a po-boy today, would you?" he asked.

"Sure," I said, realizing it was the only non-violent way of getting my hand back, "I have some in my wallet."

He immediately released my hand and I reached for my back pocket. I was smiling, not wanting him to think it was such a big deal, not wanting him to have to be embarrassed about having to beg. I opened my wallet and saw that all I had were two five-dollar bills. With no alternative, I quickly snatched one out and placed it in his waiting hand.

"Oh," he said, joyfully, "thank you very much." He reached in his back pocket and pulled out a wallet that he had fashioned out of cardboard and tape. He opened it and placed the five inside with several other bills whose denominations I could not distinguish.

"I better go," I repeated, "have a nice day."

"May the peace of my father be with you," he responded, quickly replacing the wallet in his back pocket and then making a large sign of the cross in the air.

"Thank you, you too," I answered, quickly turning and walking away.

"Morning Sir!" I heard him tell another passerby as I opened the glass door. "Sure could use a po-boy today."

I did not touch another thing with my right hand until I had thoroughly washed it in scalding water in the fourteenth floor men's room. Then I walked down the hall to my office. J. Ryan joined me before I could sit down.

"Morning, Jordan," he started.

"Hey Jay."

I used to keep a pair of Ray-Bans on my desk, so I could put them on to feel cool, not temperature-wise, but personality-wise. It really sounds stupid now, but it was a real confidence boost for me to go in, put on my sunglasses, and play the cool young attorney. Now it makes me want to throw-up.

Anyway, J. Ryan walked over to my desk, grabbed my Ray-Bans, plopped himself down in one of my two client's chairs, and propped his feet on my desk. As soon as his feet hit the desk his mouth started moving.

"Remember that young chick I told you about on Friday? Julie, the one with the big...," he began motioning his hands in front of his chest as though he were holding two basketballs there and rolling them against himself.

"J. Ryan, would you get your feet off my desk? I just tipped the maid ten bucks to polish it."

"Come on man, you want to hear this. Let me tell it," he said, feet still planted firmly on my desk top.

I shook my head, let out a small groan, and sat back for the duration. I was going to hear it whether I chose to or not.

"Remember the girl..."

"Yes, yes, I remember..."

"With the big...," he started rolling his hands again.

"Tits! Yes, I remember, the basketball tits!"

"Torpedoes," he replied.

I frowned.

"We went out Friday night, or at least we started to. I went to pick her up and she had told me that she lived on the Avenue."

"Claiborne?" I tormented him, knowing it could only be St. Charles.

"No, St. Charles, you asshole. Now listen, she gave me the address, right? So I go there and it's about the biggest fucking place on the street, you know the one with the white columns and the ivy, it's on a triple lot."

"Sure," I lied.

"I couldn't believe it, that's Mark Sampson's house, you know, the Sampson, Notterly, Guidry & Stein Sampson. The guy must be forty-five, no older, and has more money than God."

"I thought you were agnostic," I interjected.

"Just let me tell it," he replied in an irritated tone.

I decided I should just shut up and listen. I started sniffing my hand, thinking I could still detect a little of the odor, only halfway listening to J. Ryan. He had a way of rambling through a story, providing you with heaps of useless facts and personal observations and keeping anything worth hearing until the very end. Knowing this, one could tune him out for the most part, listening periodically for something remotely interesting, and then finally tuning in completely as the punch line arrived.

"I couldn't believe it. So I parked the ride..."

I hated how he referred to his car as "the ride."

"...on the street out front and walked right up and rang the doorbell. It's one of those 'Ding, ding, DONG, DING, dong, DONG' kind of bells that sounds like each bell rings in a different room. Very cool."

I rolled my eyes. He was as insane as the homeless guy.

"So I'm like expecting this butler guy in a tuxedo or something to come up to the door, but when it opens, guess who it was?"

He didn't really want me to guess.

"Sampson!" he immediately declared.

Just as I had suspected.

"He opens his own door."

"You think he wipes his own ass?" I couldn't resist.

"It shocked the hell out of me," he went on, ignoring my jab. "You can imagine, I was speechless."

I nodded, smiled, and began to think about the approaching weekend.

"We just both stood there for a second."

I guess Sampson was speechless as well, seeing J. Ryan at his door. "Then he says, 'Can I help you with something?' I wanted to say,

'Yea, like a job' but I kept my cool and just asked for Julie."

"Smooth," I said.

"You know it," he responded, cockily. "So he guides me through this huge mansion to a little room in the very back of the house and he tells me to wait there and he'll get her. Now this is all getting really weird. The room has nothing but a couch and mirrors – mirrors all over the walls. I start thinking, 'Ole Sampson must like looking at himself.' So I sit on the couch and look at myself in the mirror. I was wearing my Dior..."

"Does this go on much longer?" I interrupted.

"Yea, but you won't believe it."

"How about the abridged version? I'll probably believe that."

"I felt as though I were being watched, it was eerie, man, I'm telling you. Then I thought, 'two-way mirrors.' I got up and went over to one of the walls and put my face against it and brought my hands up to block the light to see if I could see through it, you know how you can do that in the supermarket where they have those two-way mirrors to look for shoplifters?"

"J. Ryan!" I pleaded.

"Okay. Well they must have had the light off in the other room because I went to each wall and looked but I couldn't see anything, unless they were in the room above me. Anyway, I know they saw me because when Julie walked in she had this big grin on her face and wouldn't tell me what was up."

"Maybe she was just happy to see you."

"She was. She nearly attacked me. I mean the girl was all over me in a matter of seconds and her huge," motioning, "were bouncing all around, hitting me in the face and shit."

"She took them out?"

"Yea! It's weird I'm telling you."

"Jay, it might be nice, but it's not weird."

"Sure it's weird, 'cause I know her old man was watching us."

"What are you talking about?" I was really beginning to get irritated.

"Through the mirrors, I know he was watching."

"You are the most paranoid son-of-a-bitch that I have ever met. What makes you think he was watching you?"

"Because I could feel it. And because she didn't want to go anywhere else. I said, 'Hey baby, not here, your old man might come in, lets go to my place,'" and she wouldn't do it. And she kept looking up at the ceiling and trying to get my pants unzipped. But she made sure not to block the view from the ceiling."

"So what did you do?" I asked, trying to move the story along.

"I popped her a good one," he responded putting a fist into the air then pulling it down quickly.

"You're kidding," I said, astonished. "J. Ryan, they might have had a camera."

"I know. So what? I'm not the sicko here, it's Sampson. He and the old lady are probably watching it now, my ass popping up and down..."

"All right, all right, that's enough."

J. Ryan was smiling broadly.

"I hope you never have a trial against him," I said.

"Why?" he asked, still smiling. "I don't give a shit, what's he going to do?"

"Just might be a little awkward."

"Not for me it won't, maybe for him. I'll probably tell him something about it, get him a little stirred up."

"Yea, right."

Just then Margo buzzed in over the telephone intercom. "Andy?"

"Yea?"

"Mr. Fabacher wants to see you."

"Okay," I said, immediately standing up.

"What did you do?" J. Ryan kidded. Fabacher was the managing partner and we associates did not have much contact with him.

"Nothing. Mark Sampson probably gave him a call this morning and he wants to know what I think about you."

"No," J. Ryan said, more seriously, his smile disappearing.

"Sure, they're big golfing buddies. Actually, I think Fabacher's son was engaged to one of Sampson's daughters."

"You're lying."

"Gotta go," I said, heading out the door.

"He wouldn't do that. He wouldn't want your opinion. You're just a peon like me."

"You're right. He'll probably just fire you on the spot when he finds out," I said, leaving the room before J. Ryan had a chance to respond.

The meeting with Fabacher turned out to be nothing at all. He just wanted to know about some of my billings and then he told me what an excellent job he and Mr. Keating and the two junior partners thought I was doing. He also said they thought I had a bright future with the firm. This was all very uncharacteristic of Mr. Fabacher, who was usually so self-absorbed that he did not acknowledge anything positive about anyone else. The mere fact that he did not fire you was acknowledgment enough for a job well done. Needless to say, his recognition of my efforts really made my day.

That night was even better.

Bip picked me up as usual and then we got Bets at her job in a dentist's office uptown. She was his receptionist/bookkeeper, preferring the bookkeeping part over answering the telephone and ushering frightened patients into the back. It was not her life's ambition, but the money was good enough, considering that I was covering most of her day-to-day living expenses.

We all went to dinner together at the Acme Oyster Bar in the Quarter. We ate at the bar, drinking Bud Lights, and talking about our day. Just as we were finishing, Bip made some comment to Bets about her conservative dressing style and she got surprisingly upset with him.

"What are you trying to say?" she insisted.

"Nothing. Just that you dress a little conservatively," he answered nervously, knowing he had pissed her off.

"What's wrong with what I have on?" she continued, referring to the bibbed, ankle-length, dress she was wearing.

"Nothing," he insisted, "it's nothing bad, I dress conservatively too."

"What? You think I should dress like a floozy to go to work? Maybe I should just let Dr. Bonin lay me out on the chair."

"Whoaaa," I finally interjected. "Has he proposed?"

"Not funny," she turned vehemently toward me.

"I'm just kidding, y'all. Lighten up."

"He's right. I'm sorry," Bip said.

"You will be," she replied.

"Come on now," I said, growing concerned that she might stay mad at Bip for a long time which could make things very awkward for us around the house.

"Let's go," Bets demanded, standing.

Bip picked up the check, in part as an apology, I'm sure, although it was not uncommon for him to buy us both dinner.

The ride home was silent. Bip and I sat up-front while Bets stewed in the back. The only time she spoke was to ask me to tell Bip to stop at a K&B drugstore along the way for tampons. After she had gotten out of the car, Bip gave me a knowing look and we both broke down laughing. "You have great timing," I said.

Bets had lied. She had not gone in for tampons, but for condoms. She handed me one when we got home and told me that she needed to be close to me that night but had missed a couple of days of taking her pills. I, of course, was elated.

Despite the annoyance of the rubber sheath, it was great. She had been right about one thing – the wait had made it much more spectacular. I had to keep telling her to quiet down or Bip would hear, but she didn't seem to mind. I didn't really either.

Bets was unusually affectionate all night, and I really felt as though our relationship was making a turn, at least as far as her perception of it went. I had been having doubts about us but that night went a long way toward convincing me that I had been wrong. She had finally given in, it seemed, to her desire for me. She'd be back on schedule with the pills and the condoms could go out the window. I had outlasted her. The final wall of resistance was caving in and the Huns were at the gate.

SIX

THE FOLLOWING MORNING I HAD A HEARING scheduled so I woke and dressed early. The only clean suit I had was made of wool, which is suicide to wear in the summertime, but the buildings and bus would be air conditioned and I would just have to bear the short walks to my office and to the courthouse. As usual, I read the morning paper on the ride in. I had learned early on in my bus-riding career that an opened paper discouraged others from sitting next to me and was a great way of avoiding eye contact which would otherwise have required my moving over to accommodate someone eyeing the seat. My luck from the previous day must have been holding out because by the time the bus had departed from the final stop, mine was the only seat with an empty one next to it.

The humidity seemed to have dissipated somewhat overnight, and the four block walk from the bus stop was rather pleasant for that time of year. When I neared my building I heard Christian“s booming voice, “Morning, Sir!,” “Morning, Ma'am!” As I approached, I reached into my pocket for a quarter, ready to toss it to him as I sped by. Just at the moment I expected to make eye contact with him, a car pulled up and motioned him over. He walked to the curb and received a folded up bill from the passenger's side. Slyly I sped up and walked behind him as though I had not noticed that he was there. Deftly, I scurried inside the building. Not until the door had almost fully closed did I hear him address me.

“Morning, Andy Jordan!”

I dared not look back and acted as though I had not heard him. It was bad enough that he knew my name, but he didn't have to go yelling it for all to hear. The guy was a pest and I was glad I had not given him the quarter. I doubted that I'd ever give him money again. Ignoring him, that was my plan, acting as though he did not even exist. By the time I reached the elevator I had put him completely out of my mind. He was a dead issue.

The remainder of the day went downhill from there from there.

First, I lost my hearing. I don't even know what went wrong. It had been a sure thing, a motion for summary judgment before Judge Windsor Clark. Fabacher had practically single-handedly gotten him elected and our client deserved a dismissal. Keating was so sure of a victory that he went on to a breakfast meeting and let me argue it alone. I dreaded his returning to the office.

When I got back from court I found that Tony was on a rampage. After $20,000.00 of billings, the president of Petrology spent the morning screaming at him, threatening to take his case to another firm, and demanding an explanation as to why we had not achieved any results. Tony had me go through the entire file with him, explaining everything that "we" had done.

J. Ryan kept bothering me, so finally I broke down and listened to his cute little story about how he thought he had contracted herpes only to have his urologist tell him that it was merely a raging case of jock-itch. I was spared from hearing more on the topic when Mr. Keating summoned me into his office for an explanation as to how I could have possibly lost on the motion. He explained to me how he had already told our client that the matter would be resolved that day, and made me tell him word-for-word how the hearing had progressed. At the conclusion of the meeting he demanded a fifteen-page memorandum detailing the case, which was to be on his desk by the end of the day, and informed me that until further notice I would not be allowed to make any more court appearances without another member of the firm present.

By late afternoon the humidity had once again descended upon our fair city and Bip called to tell me that he was leaving work early, i.e., I would have to catch the bus home. I worked the rest of the day on Mr. Keating's memo and delivered the finished product to his office personally at 6:15. He had gone home an hour earlier.

I did not get out of the building until 6:30, and the last express pulled out from my stop with me running toward it half a block away. This left me with no alternative but the streetcar; the slow, loud, standing room only, non-air-conditioned, sweating-in-my-wool-suit streetcar.

I arrived home just before 8:00 p.m. and found a note left by Bip and Bets letting me know that they had waited as long as they could for me, but had finally broken down and gone to get something to eat. A notation at the top showed that the note had been written at 7:45. I guessed they had made up.

After putting a peanut-butter, jelly, and bologna sandwich into my belly, I brushed my teeth and decided to call it a night. I turned in early and was asleep before Bip and Bets returned. The day had been a real bear and I could not afford to have another one like it any time too soon.

By nature I am not a superstitious person. Of course, I don't go around walking under ladders or opening umbrellas in the house, and I have been known to knock on wood on occasion, but a black cat walking across my path or the breaking of a mirror does not ruin my day. However, it did not take long before I came to realize that on the days I gave Christian money and received his blessing things went well for me, and that the exact opposite effect was achieved on the days when I did not and he mumbled his curses in my direction. Still, for a long while I would not afford it much importance or significance, rationalizing it all as coincidence, which I do believe in. No man could possibly control my destiny, affect the outcome of my day. No man other than myself that is.

Be that as it may, after one particular day when I had given Christian a dollar bill, and a subsequent meeting with the EPA officials resulted in the granting of a variance for Petrology, I never left the house without first making sure that Christian's dollar was in my pocket. The Petrology matter had made me a hero at the office, as it insured us a large, wealthy, controversial client and it absolved me of any and all past wrongdoing. That dollar to Christian had been the best money I had ever spent.

Looking back, it is difficult to say exactly what I believed at the time. Perhaps it was that, somewhere in the back of my mind, I believed he had some control over the positive and negative forces of nature. I think we all do to some extent, and that by receiving Christian's blessing I would be put in a positive frame of mind and receive a sort of confidence boost which would result in my having a better day.

After a while he definitely began to have some sort of hold on me. I started seeking him out to give him money, to receive his blessing. I needed him to get those positive vibes going. Five bucks a week – big deal. Voodoo or not, it was well worth it. I couldn't afford to take any more chances.

Despite my new ritual, nothing I did seemed to change things with Bets. We had hit another plateau, doing basically the same things that we had been doing before, with a night of "safe sex" thrown in every week or two just to keep it interesting. I started seeing it all as very hypocritical and self-serving on her part, this pseudo-abstinence gig. I felt like a damned fish dangling from the end of her hook. Sooner or later she would devour me or I would have to swim free.

My life had become routine. Routine with Bets and routine with

Christian. His part had become so easy and so clean. I'd tell him hello and he'd tell me he sure could use a po-boy and I'd hand him a dollar. That was it. Bingo. Done for the day. I was happy and he was happy and things went great.

Then, one morning, it all suddenly changed. Things got really weird. Then they got downright frightening.

SEVEN

THE FIRST TIME IT HAPPENED WAS ON A MONDAY. I remember this because Bip, Bets, and I had just returned from a weekend on the beaches in Florida. Wanting a change of scenery from Orange Beach (meaning more young women in skimpy swimsuits), Bip had rented a room at the Holiday Inn on a crowded beach and drove us down in the Beemer. As a result, I was really tan that morning and feeling great.

I always made certain that Christian's dollar was in the front right pocket of my pants. It saved time. I could have it in hand and give it to him in passing without having to stop and make conversation. Having it in my right hand also saved me from having to shake his as I was paying him off. Like two runners in a relay, we had the motion down to a science and never had a miscue where either of us dropped the bill.

This day was different, though. Christian was in his usual spot, gave me the usual "Morning Andy," but he failed to hold out his hand for the exchange. Consequently, I appeared a little ridiculous, passing by with money held out, and his not accepting it. I stopped.

Christian showed me his teeth and finally held his hand out. He was toying with me, I could feel it. I handed him the money and bade him a good morning.

"I love the Florida panhandle this time of year," he told me.

"Yea, it's great," I replied, realizing that he must have recognized my tan and figured that I had spent the weekend on the Florida coast.

"Lots of porpoises," he continued.

"Really?" I feigned interest.

"Yes. Very intelligent and playful creatures, you know."

"So I hear," I said, the vision of the half-eaten porpoise at Orange Beach coming back to me.

"They mate for life. Don't give up until they find the right one."

"Is that so?" I said, turning to leave."I'll see you later."

"Some people are like that too, you know," he continued, holding me there with this conversation. "Maybe a little blow job here, let you rub on them there, perhaps even let you use a rubber every now and then, but they don't really give it all up until they know you're the right one."

I was so embarrassed about his talking to me in public about blow jobs and rubbers that the significance of the moment was lost to me. Only later did I realize that he was somehow inside of my head. Granted, the Florida panhandle was the most logical guess, but how could he possibly have known about my relationship with Bets? I went on to work, with his blessing, but in the back of my mind I knew that something was awry.

The following morning Christian was not around. This did not really bother me, because as long as I had taken care of him the last time that I had seen him, everything worked out fine until I saw him again. This superstitious stuff was starting to eat at me anyway and it would have suited me just fine had I never laid eyes on him again. He was gone on Wednesday and Thursday as well, so I did not see him again until that Friday.

The morning had started out all right. I had left Bets in bed and Bip was just getting up as I opened the door to leave. Bets had walked the dog the night before (I forget which hand) but we were getting no further. Something was definitely missing in our relationship, and I'm not sure that it was the sex. I thought I loved her, but I wasn't sure that I was really *in* love with her. Perhaps it was the sex thing, but I think it went deeper than that. Sex was a symptom rather than the illness. When it got down to our basic personalities and desires, we were very different, and neither of us had made a move to become more like the other in quite some time.

Christian's return brought with it the return of his stench. And it was as bad as ever.

"Morning, Andy," he yelled happily to me.

"Good morning, Christian," I replied, attempting the handoff.

Again he did not reach for the money. I contemplated throwing it at his feet, but that would look as though I were contemptuous of his situation, belittling him by throwing money at him, merely giving him a payoff for his goodwill. I knew him too well by then to do that. It was then that I first realized that, at least to some degree, he had become a friend. I stopped and waited for him to speak.

"Perhaps you should call me Flipper now," he said with a smile.

"Okay, great," I replied, touched that he now considered me a friend.

"And how is the little porpoise?" he asked.

"What?" I asked, confused.

"Your little lady friend. Surely you have one," he explained.

"Yea, sure, she's great," I replied.

"What is her name?" he asked.

"Bets," I answered.

"Short for Betsy?"

"Yea." This surprised me because Bets could be short for a lot of things.

"She giving you what you want?"

"Yea, we're really happy." I was both embarrassed and annoyed that he was asking me all of this.

"Come now, is she really?"

"Yea, really," I said, holding the money out again, ready to make my exit.

"Perhaps you should call me Christian," he said, his smile fading.

"Sure, whatever you prefer," I answered, throwing the dollar at his feet.

"My friends call me Flipper," he said sternly, "and friends do not lie to one another. Ba ba bee bub blu blu blu bloo."

I was immediately filled with angst and regret. What would happen now? I needed to salvage the situation.

"Look, you're really getting personal here," I pleaded my case.

"Isn't that what friends do?" he asked."Why is it that you cannot confide in me that you are unhappy? And why is it that you care whether this crazy man lets you call him Flipper or not?"

"Look, I am happy. I mean, I could be happier, but I can wait."

"Wait for what?" he asked.

"You know," I didn't want to say it, not out there on the street, not with his stench around me, "like the porpoise, to be the one."

"You are not an honest person, perhaps that is why. You should try honesty. Tell her how you feel, even if it is that she is not the one. Bring her roses and to dinner with wine, plenty of wine, and tell her. If you cannot do it honestly, it isn't worth having."

I picked up my dollar and he put his hand out to take it.

"Sure," I said, handing it to him. "That sounds good."

"You try it, Andy Jordan," he said as I turned to walk away. "And you call me Flipper," he called behind me.

"Thanks." Smiling, I waved at him then went inside to my office.

I had mentioned something to Margo about her taking too long at lunch and she had corrected the problem, taking exactly one hour each day. But she began coming in later in the mornings. That morning was no exception and she came rushing past the receptionist fifteen minutes late.

Unfortunately for her, Mr. Fabacher happened to be walking the halls just then and stopped her. I was getting myself a cup of coffee at the time and heard the ensuing conversation.

"Miss Ricalde," he scolded her as a principal would a tardy child, "don't we pay you for eight hours a day?"

"Yes, sir," she replied nervously.

"Yet you haven't been giving us our full day's worth for some time now, have you?"

"Mr. Fabacher...," she began to apologize, but he was not finished with her.

"No, you haven't. You've been working your own hours as of late, haven't you?" he continued. That is when I decided to step in and emerged from the kitchen.

"Margo!" I said, as though surprised to see her. "You're back already?"

She looked at me in confusion as Fabacher snapped his attention away from her and to me.

"I didn't think the cleaners opened until 9:00. You did bring my suits in, didn't you?"

She nodded nervously.

"Your suits?" Fabacher questioned.

"Yes, sir. I've been so busy lately with this Petrology business that I haven't had time..."

"Mr. Jordan, this is your secretary, not your servant. She is not here to run your errands and I am certainly not here to pay her to run them for you."

"Yes, sir, Mr. Fabacher," I said sheepishly.

"I was about to chide her about being late, but now I see that it is you who are responsible."

"Yes, Sir. It won't happen again. I promise you."

"It better not," he concluded, giving us each one last stern look before navigating further down the hallway.

Margo later tried to explain to me why she had been repeatedly late, something to do with her invalid grandmother, but I wouldn't allow it. I did, however, extract a promise from her that it would not happen again.

It turned out to be a very good day.

On the way home that evening I got Bip to stop at a florist and asked to borrow his car. He was a little suspicious about my motives but kindly allowed me both requests. I told him he could use my Jeep if he needed to go anywhere.

I still had not told either Bip or Bets about Flipper. They were both much more conservative than I and neither believed in handing money out to the "alleged homeless." Telling them that I had made a habit of giving Flipper a dollar on every occasion that I saw him, and that doing so improved the outcome of my day, would have subjected me to a persecution the likes of which have not been seen in modern times. They were already suspicious because of the Orange Beach incident, but at least they had no clue that my sanity was going.

Bets was thrilled about the flowers. I should have thought of that much sooner. We went out for dinner, to the Eiffel Tower restaurant, which was housed in the actual structure that at one time was the cafe atop the Eiffel Tower. As the structure had aged, it could no longer support the restaurant and it was sold off. As so many other misfits have before, it had eventually made its way to, and found acceptance in, New Orleans. The decor and ambiance were wonderful and the French cuisine quite good.

We began with a bottle of champagne. Bets was not much of a drinker, but I figured that if I started out in a festive spirit it would have more effect. It apparently worked because after we had finished the first bottle she insisted that we order another. In the years that we had been together, this was the very first time that I had ever witnessed Bets drink more than a single glass of white wine. She was normally a control type person, always maintaining control over her mind and body, until now – she was getting soused.

On the way home I suggested that we stop for coffee and a chat. We went to P.J.'s, an upbeat coffee house only a few blocks from our apartment. Bets did not drink coffee so she just had water while I ordered an espresso.

"Bets, sweetie, we need to talk," I began.

"Sure," she said, sipping her water.

"We need to talk about us," I continued.

I could see the concern growing in her eyes as she put her water down and sat attentively, like a child being scolded.

"What about us?" she asked.

"Where we are going." This seemed to relieve her somewhat and then it hit me that she probably thought I was working my way toward a proposal. "We don't seem to be communicating very well lately and we seem to have grown apart," I quickly added.

That put the concern back into her gaze.

"What do you mean?"

"We just don't seem close."

"What do you mean?"

"We're hardly even affectionate anymore."

"What are you really saying?"

"Look at us, we just exist."

"It's sex, isn't it?" she asked.

"No, it's not sex," I lied.

"Is that what this is all about? Go out to dinner and get me drunk, bring me flowers? Give me an ultimatum?"

"Nobody is giving anybody any ultimatums," I swiftly backpedaled.

"Could have fooled me."

"All I said is that we're growing apart," I dug in at my fall-back position.

"Yea, and you know just what will bring us together again, don't you?" She read me like a short story.

"No, that's not it at all. I don't want sex." What was I saying? "I just want to be happy."

"I thought we were happy."

"We are."

"Oh, we're happy but we're not close. We're just existing but we're happy. Are these the things that make you happy?"

"Look, I'm just trying to be honest."

"Then be honest, for Pete's sake," she demanded.

She was right. I wasn't being honest.

"I don't know anymore whether you are the right person for me." I just blurted it out. I was tempted to look away from her so as not to see the pain on her face, but I couldn't, I had to look her in the eye for this.

"You don't excite me. I love you but I don't know whether I am in love with you. And I don't know whether you are in love with me. We're like an old couple, existing because we have a history together. Sex isn't the disease, it's the symptom." It seemed like the proper place to work that back in.

Bets remained silent. A tear traced a path down her cheek and when I went to wipe it away, she pulled away from my outstretched hand. We just sat there for the longest time, looking at one another. She didn't cry anymore, but I could see the agony on her face. Finally she spoke.

"Can we go home now?" she asked.

"Sure," I said.

We left P.J.'s and drove the short distance home in silence. I followed Bets up the stairs and unlocked the door.

"Would you mind sleeping out here?" she asked me as we passed the couch in the den.

"No. That's okay," I responded. I felt so terrible, it was the least I could do.

As she walked away, the weight of my words and actions finally began to sink in. What had I done? I had been honest, at least I thought I was being honest, but it may have cost me one of the best relationships that I had ever had. I did not know whether Bets was right for me or not, but until someone better came along and proved to me that she was not, how could I know that losing her would not be a great mistake? I was sad, very sad, yet, somewhere inside of me, I knew that I had done the right thing. I had opened up, let out all the secrets, and if it didn't work out now it would not be my fault. There was a kernel of happiness somewhere inside of me and I knew that once the storm had settled and I had seen its worst, I would be the better for it.

Surprisingly, it did not take me long to fall asleep. I remember having had a turbulent dream, though I cannot recall any of the specifics. Something bad was happening when I awoke.

My eyes opened and I saw a figure over me, descending upon me. Disoriented, not certain of where I was and then realizing that I had fallen asleep on the couch in the front room, next to the glass door, I thought that someone had broken in and was going to execute me. I had to fight back. Then I recognized Bets' tongue.

She had come to me in the night, unable to sleep, mournful, scared. When we woke the next morning, in my bed, her sorrow had gone, as had the condoms and her year of resistance. She had realized that we were right for one another and she had convinced me.

I must admit that initially I felt somewhat guilty, having used Flipper's clairvoyance to break down Bets' resistance. It was almost as though I had resorted to some sort of "black magic" to get her to submit. But as time progressed, no more than a day or so, and as I realized that she had no regrets and that I had only been honest about my true feelings, the guilt quickly subsided. I had basically told the truth and it had paid off. I owed Flipper one, a big one.

EIGHT

FLIPPER COULD TELL THAT THERE WAS SOMETHING different about me on Monday. Perhaps it was the smile, or the whistling. I was happy and it was obvious.

"Morning, Andy!" he began, as usual, holding out his hand.

I stopped, not yet pulling the dollar out of my pocket. He moved his hand back down.

"Good morning, Flipper."

"Did you have a good weekend?"

"The best," I replied honestly, recalling the passion.

"So you were finally honest."

"Yes," I responded. "How did you know it would work?"

"The truth always does. We are all alike, we mammals," he responded.

"Yea, but how do you know all of this? Like about me and about Bets?"

"Andy," he answered, "I need a new pair of shoes."

I looked at his shoes, a pair of old, once-white canvas shoes, now nearly black and with holes exposing the bottoms of his feet.

"Okay," I said, "what size do you wear?" How could I say no? Actually I felt embarrassed that I had not thought of it before.

"I need them now," he insisted.

"It's 8:30, I doubt anything is open," I said.

"One of the stores on Canal Street would be open by the time we got there," he countered.

"Okay," I responded, just a bit reluctantly, calculating how long the journey would take. "Let's go." Even if I wound up a little late and met Fabacher in the hallway, it was a very small price to pay for the happiness that he had brought me.

He picked up his piece of cardboard, rolled it up, and put it under his arm. We began the trek to Canal Street.

"So, is she the right one?" he asked.

"You mean Bets?"

"Sure," he said, possibly mocking me.

"I think she is," I answered, smiling.

"You think? Don't you know?"

"Yes, she is," I told him.

"Obviously she knows that you are," he said.

"We're right for each other," I added.

"So when is the proposal?" he asked.

"The proposal?" I said, a little frightened.

"Sure, Andy. She mates for life, she has mated with you, you must make it for life."

"We don't need to rush into anything."

"What rush, four years?"

"How did you know that?"

"What, four years?"

"Yea, how did you know we have been together four years?"

"Didn't you tell me?"

"No, I didn't."

"Then I must have sensed it."

"Sensed it?"

"There are many forces out there, Andy Jordan. Many things you know nothing about."

"What, you have ESP or something?"

"Or something. Is it to be a large nuptial?"

"There is no wedding. Not yet."

"But there must be. You've been joined."

"You don't understand. That's how it is these days. We've both been 'joined' before."

Flipper looked shocked and a little confused. We continued walking, but did not talk for a while. I was freaking out a little. There was no way for him to know all these things about me. Someone had to be telling him all of this, someone who really knew me. But who? And why? Nobody that I knew could possibly have known about Bets, could have predicted that the way he did.

Then there was the possibility that he was telling the truth.

"Really, how do you know all of these things?" I finally asked as we reached Canal Street.

"If I told you, you would not believe it," he replied.

"Why not?" I asked, crossing the street as the "WALK" sign illuminated.

"Because you are logical. Because you have been taught not to believe in anything that you perceive to be unreal."

"Well, I know you are real."

"But you don't know who I really am."

"Your name isn't Christian Waterman?"

"Yes it is."

"Then I know who you are."

"Not really," he said.

We reached the store and walked in.

I would not say that the clerk was especially happy to see us enter his store. As soon as Flipper's odor reached him he made a sour face and put his hand to his mouth. I immediately walked toward the back, trying to make it all as quick and painless as possible. The store was notorious for inexpensive shoes and I felt as though I was getting off cheap. I located a pair that matched the ones that he was wearing. The price tag read $4.95.

"Here you go," I said, pointing, "what size do you wear?" Then I looked as his feet. "Those look pretty big."

He ignored me and walked on to a separate aisle. I followed him to the dress shoe section, and watched as he laid his hand upon a pair of loafers that were described by a nearby sign as "Shark Skin."

"I like these," he said.

I looked at the price tag. $32.50!

"I thought you might want a pair like you already have," I suggested, hoping to sway him back to the cheap section.

"No, shark skin. I like these."

"Are those your size?" I asked, hoping they were out of his size.

"They should fit," he responded, handing them to me.

The shoes were enormous. They looked as though it took a shark a piece to make them.

"You should try them on," I prompted, "they look big to me."

"I don't have any socks," he responded.

"There are some on the wall over there," I said, pointing to a sign which read "Stretch Socks – One Size Fits All – $1.50 per pair." At that price I could afford to be generous. "Get a couple of pairs," I urged him.

He walked over and picked out three pairs of various colors.

"This will do, thank you," he said, holding the box of shoes and the socks while motioning for me to leave.

"Wait," I said, "let's try them on before we pay for them." There was still a very good possibility that they did not fit.

He walked the short distance over to me, a serious look now upon his face, took my arm and led me to the back of the store, near two chairs equipped with those padded metal sloping fronts to rest your foot on while trying on a prospective pair of shoes. He sat me down in one chair and he took the other.

Leaning over to me, he whispered in my ear, "If I were to take off my shoes right here then I would be forced to tell you exactly who I am. And a man of your intelligence and belief systems might not want to believe such a thing. I think one day you might be the human I should confide in, but now is too early."

I might be "the human?" What was he, an alien? I immediately began reassessing my situation – and my sanity. I liked the guy, I really did. We had even become friends in a strange sort of way. He had changed me, he had interrupted my life and had changed my routine. The transformation actually went deeper than that. I had become somewhat superstitious and it had, surprisingly, all been for the better. But this was getting to be just a little too much to handle.

I was an up-and-coming young attorney. I could not afford to have a friend like this. What had I been thinking? And his odor, his odor didn't even really bother me anymore. But, by the looks on the faces of those who we passed, I knew it was still there. Now he was calling me a human, obviously insinuating that he was something other than this. I couldn't figure him out and I couldn't afford to. He was obviously homeless due to some mental disorder, probably released by some mental institution onto the streets, literally. He frightened me. He somehow knew about me, saw into me, and he was crazy. The combination was just too dangerous for me to continue the weird relationship that I had fallen into. It had to end. I had to make a break.

"Okay, fine," I said, "don't tell me who you are and don't try them on. But you're getting the canvas shoes. I'm not buying the most expensive pair of shoes in here for a..." I stopped myself.

"For a what?" he asked.

I clammed up.

"For a dirty, homeless man who will probably just trade them in for a bottle of wine?" he finished the sentence for me.

I remained silent, staring into his eyes as though that were, in itself, answer enough. It had to be, because it was the only response I had.

Then he softened. "It was a great gesture of kindness on your part. I should not have expected that you meant to buy someone such as myself a pair of shoes that a man of your status would wear. Please accept my apologies."

"I don't pay that kind of money for shoes without trying them on first," I finally said, finding a position that I thought I could defend.

"We're losing ground here aren't we, Andy?"

"I don't know what you're talking about. I really need to get to work. Let's just get the damn shoes. You don't have to try them on, and we can get out of here."

"You think I'm crazy, don't you?"

He didn't have to have E.S.P. to know that.

"You are wrong. Ignorant and uneducated," he insisted. "I am just foreign to you and you do not understand."

"Foreign? What are you, French?"

He laughed, then became very serious.

"No. Atlantin."

"At-what'n?"

"I am from Atlantis."

"Georgia?" I asked. "I wouldn't call Atlanta foreign."

"You are not listening. I am not from Georgia."

"Atlantis," I repeated. "You mean as in the place that slid into the sea?"

"Yes. We are a sub-sea species."

I smiled, I just couldn't help it. I nearly laughed, but I had halfway expected him to say something like that, so I was able to contain it.

"Your species?"

"Yes, sub-sea," he answered.

"Like a mermaid?" I asked, convinced more than ever that he had lost his mind.

"Somewhat. Very astute observation, Andy. That is probably where the legend originated. There have been sightings of my people throughout the course of history, and mermaids were a good way for your people to rationalize them."

He was much worse off than I had suspected. Apparently, so was I. There I sat, a lawyer, after nine o'clock in the morning, without having yet been to work, in the back of a shoe store, with a smelly, crazy man claiming to be of a sub-sea species, for whom I was about to buy a pair of shark skin shoes. How far had I slid?

"Look, Christian...I mean Flipper, you can have the shark shoes, we'll go pay for them, and then we'll get out of here." I said this calmly, as not to upset him, as I secretly began plotting how I would begin coming and going through the parking garage in the back of the building, avoiding this loon until he finally moved on. I would buy him the shoes, make him happy, get his blessing, for what it was worth, and never see him again. It was the perfect plan, the best of both worlds, the solution to my problem. No one ever had to know about this.

"No," he responded, "I will try them on. But you watch, Andy Jordan, and you just remember that it was you who wanted this."

"No, really, you don't have to..." I continued, anxious to get away. However, he held up a hand and stopped me, then lifted a foot to his chair and began untying his lace.

I watched as he untied his left shoe, wondering what he was talking about, wondering what could possibly be so significant about trying on a pair of shark skin shoes, wishing I had never met him. Then his shoe was off, and I knew.

Dumbfounded. That is the word that I must use to describe the initial effect that it had on me. I had never really considered the origin of the word "dumbfounded" before, but must now conclude that the "dumb" part does not relate to intelligence but to the ability to speak. I lost that ability, albeit temporarily, as his foot unfolded before my eyes.

Now, I've heard of people born with all types of deformities, extra digits, extra sexual organs, webbed feet. I even once paid money at the Louisiana State Fair in Shreveport to see a man whose fingers had all grown together into a single, flabby mass, except for his thumbs, which were also big and flabby, and which looked a lot like the meat inside of a lobster's claws.

Christian Waterman's feet, however, were not so much a deformity as they were a freak of nature. His feet were much more akin to flippers, like a frog's, than they were to any human foot that I had ever laid eyes on. I am not speaking of "webbed feet," although they were webbed. it's just that they were not really feet. When one thinks of a human with webbed feet, one thinks of small pieces of skin connecting each toe, giving a webbed appearance. Christian's actually unfolded, being much wider at the "toes" than they were at the heel.

"Andy, I am what I say I am," he finally said.

I looked at him, my mouth open.

"I know it is hard for you to understand, but I am from Atlantis."

"But it's a myth."

"Precisely why it has remained a secret," he countered.

"How do you breathe?" It seemed to be the obvious question.

"Ha!" he laughed, "We breathe above and below water." He tried on one shoe, folding his foot up before placing it inside of the sock.

"You can breathe underwater?"

"Brine," he answered. "Freshwater I cannot breathe. It is poison to my lungs."

"You breathe saltwater?"

"Correct," he put on the other shoe in a similar fashion.

"If I had saltwater here, you could breathe in it?"

"Not a bucket, no," he responded. "I can't make saltwater into oxygen, but I can process the oxygen out of highly oxygenated brine. I can breathe in the ocean."

"What about a lake, like Lake Pontchartrain, could you breathe in it?"

"Yes, probably so," he responded, standing to try out his shoes, smiling his snaggle-toothed grin.

"So you're telling me that if we were at the lake you could go under the water and stay there a long time before coming up?"

"A lifetime," he answered.

I was cross-examining him. The feet had thrown me. I mean I was not really beginning to believe him, but I had an irresistible urge to prove him a liar on the spot. I needed to know that he was a liar, that he was not what he purported to be, that he had no control over me or my destiny, that he was just a crazy street person with webbed feet.

"They fit!" he declared excitedly .

I looked at him. He was smiling through his rotting teeth, like a child with a new toy.

"Good," I said, "let's go."

"I'll put them back in the box," he said, sitting to take them off.

"No!" I pleaded, "go ahead and wear them out of the store. I'll just bring the box up to pay."

"Okay," he answered.

The clerk was more than happy to check us out quickly and did not question my bringing the empty box up for payment. My American Express card would not clear through his scanner for approval, not because of any problem with my credit, but because of a busy line or something. After two attempts the stench must have gotten to him because he said, as politely as he could, "Just forget about it," and he allowed me to sign the voucher.

Once outside I began walking as fast as I could. I was late for work and anxious to get to the office and away from Flipper. I saw why his friends called him that. He tried to keep up with me, but was soon lagging behind.

"Andy Jordan," he finally called, "slow down a bit."

I closed my eyes, clenched my teeth, and slowed my progression.

He caught up with me and grabbed my arm. We stopped.

"Andy, I am dying."

I felt immediate relief. I know it sounds really cold, but he was dying, he would be gone some day, and I could actually go to work through the front door like normal people.

"I won't be here much longer," he continued.

"What's wrong with you?" I asked, attempting my best to sound compassionate and concerned.

"I need to explain."

I didn't really want to hear it – I was late and there would be hell to pay back at the office if something came up that I was not there to handle. I did not want him to die, but he was interfering with my life. In my view he had a dirty, miserable little existence, even if he did seem content with his situation. He was only happy because he was crazy. Wouldn't death be preferable?

"I don't have much time."

"It will only take a second. Hear me out. A dying man." There was a desperation in his voice, an urgency.

"I am Christian Waterman, eldest son of our Lord, Dog Waterman, Savior of Atlantis, Ruler of the Seas, Master of the Oceans. I have been sent here to proclaim to the world the truth of the existence of our society, to let all know that Atlantis is real and that it is in dire need of the cooperation of the rest of the world. Your greed and consumption, your misplaced values that put profit above your fellow man and your world are clouding the waters, polluting the air, killing the fishes, and killing yourselves. You are killing us and it must stop."

"Oh my God," I uttered aloud. Webbed feet or not, this man was loony toons. Bub-a-dee, bub-a-dee, bub-a-dee, that's all folks!

"Listen to me," he pleaded.

I didn't think I had a choice, so I heard him out.

"I have been here almost a year. A year is all I was given. I cannot live in your world for more than a year and I cannot go back if I do not accomplish that which I have come to accomplish. I will die. I will die within the month and you are the only human that has a chance to help me."

"Me? Why me?" I pleaded more than asked. He was making me the center of his made up little universe. This was dangerous.

"In all the time that I have been here you alone are the only person to take any interest in me at all. Others have helped me, given me money, but none has desired any involvement with me beyond that."

If only he knew how much I desired no involvement with him.

"You are a special person. Look, it is a legend in Atlantis that when an Atlantin is devoured by a shark that he returns as a human, to walk upon the earth until his return to the sea. I believe you to be such a man."

I smiled. "No way. I'm Catholic. We don't even believe in reincarnation."

"But you believe in mating with females outside of the bonds of holy matrimony? Don't hide behind a religion you do not even follow. There is so much you do not understand. You don't know, the shark has your spirit, you must get it back from him."

"Look, this is just a little too weird for me," I pleaded, "couldn't we just forget about this?"

"Then I shall die."

"Come on," I responded, "nobody's going to die. I thought you were going to tell me that you had cancer or AIDS or something like that. Nobody dies from not telling the world they're from Atlantis."

"No one but Christian Waterman," he responded.

"Look, why don't you just go on *Oprah* or something and tell her about it. If you showed her your feet I'm sure she'd put you on. When you get your chance, make your pitch and tell the world, then you can go jump in the ocean and swim back to Atlantis."

"What's *Oprah*?"

"A television talk show. They do things like that."

"On television?" he asked.

"You do know what television is, don't you?"

"Yes, I do," he responded.

"Well, they might do it. You could start locally, get on *The Angelique Brown Show* and they might pick you up nationally."

"*The Angelique Brown Show*?"

"Yea, Angelique Brown. She's like the local Oprah."

"Will it be seen around the world?" he asked.

"Not *Angelique*, but if you get on *Oprah* you'll be seen nationally, and probably in Germany and Japan or something. You might even get on Jay Leno and then you would get world coverage for sure." Of course, I knew he had a snowball's chance in hell of getting on *Angelique Brown*, let alone Leno, but if I could just steer him in the right direction I could get him out of my life.

"Okay," he answered, "I'll do it. Television."

"Good," I responded, resuming my journey to the office.

"How soon can we do it?" he asked, following along.

"We?" I asked rhetorically. "I can't be involved. I'm a lawyer."

"So?" he questioned.

"I just can't." I couldn't tell him that the reason was that being associated with such a wacko would certainly mean the end of my career. Boy, wouldn't Fabacher love that? I could just see *The Angelique Brown Show*, "And now, local attorney Andrew Jordan, of Keating & Fabacher, would like to introduce the audience to his latest client, a man who has feet like the Creature from the Black Lagoon and insists that he's from Atlantis. Of course, just last week you probably saw him, and smelled him, on the street begging for money. No, he's not Booger-flipper, he's just plain old Flipper.

Let's give a warm welcome to..."

"You have to help me, nobody else can," Flipper pleaded.

"Look," I began to explain...then the perfect excuse popped into my head, "I can't do it. I work for a law firm. I can't have outside clients. If I were to help you promote this, it would have to be on a professional basis, which means that you would have to pay the firm a hundred twenty-five dollars an hour for my time. And on top of that they would probably want a five thousand dollar retainer. I can't do it outside of the firm and I can't do it without charging you or I would lose my job. Honestly, I would really like to help you, but it wouldn't be fair to you. I'm sure you could never afford it. All you have to do is go down to the T.V. station and tell them your story. You can do it yourself."

Flipper looked bad. His smile disappeared and he seemed depressed. He looked as though the world were crashing in all around him. He looked like a man who had just been handed a death sentence.

NINE

FLIPPER DISAPPEARED. Initially I thought he may have wound up in jail again, but then I started worrying that perhaps he had gone to the hospital or had possibly even died. Not that I would have been responsible or anything, but, as the days passed, the guilt that I felt at having been so pleased by his announcement of impending death increased.

Bip flew to Atlanta that Thursday evening to attend a great-aunt's funeral. I drove him out to the airport and along the way he explained that she had been his mother's mother's sister. She had fallen in the bathtub at the retirement home where she had been living. Bip had arranged a conference with a Georgia plaintiff's attorney for after the services. I would have thought that he was motivated only by greed (I had never even heard him mention the woman's name until that afternoon) but he seemed to be having a very hard time with it. I thought that it may have brought back unpleasant memories of his own parents' deaths so I tried, albeit rather awkwardly, to be supportive.

"Let me know if there is anything I can do...for you or your family," I offered just as we made our final approach to the passenger drop-off area.

"She was it," he replied.

"She was what?"

"My family. She was the only one I had left."

"God. I'm sorry. I didn't realize..."

"Don't. It's not your fault, I never talk about them. You couldn't have known."

"Well I mean it. Let me know if you need anything."

"There is one thing," he replied as I pulled to a stop and put the Jeep in park.

"Sure, anything."

He reached into his shirt pocket and produced a claim ticket for a package that would be arriving at the bus terminal the following afternoon. He handed it to me. "Could you pick this up for me while I'm gone?"

"No problem."

"It's C.O.D. I'm sorry, I'm so mixed up I didn't think ahead. Can you just write a check and I'll reimburse you when I get back to town?"

"No problem," I repeated in a sincere voice, all-the-while biting my cheek. This was going to be a problem, not only because I was going to have to spend part of Friday evening picking the damned thing up, but mostly because of the C.O.D. part. My checking account was running low and Bip was the worst at repaying debts.

"It's pretty big, so you might want to take the back seat out of the Jeep before you go down there."

"What is it?" I asked, my voice less pleasant.

"Just equipment for the boat." Bip had a 24-foot sailboat. In college, when he had had time and money to burn, he had become an avid sailor, winning several regattas. After graduating from law school he started sailing a lot more and even entered some of the local races for sport. He was a predator on the water, doing whatever was necessary to win, including spending a small fortune on new and better gadgets and riggings for the boat.

"Another new sail?" I asked.

"Something like that. Look I have to go, I'm late. You'll get it tomorrow, right?"

"I'll be happy to. Don't worry about it. Just go." It killed me, saying those words.

"You're a real pal," he said, stepping out and slinging his bag over his shoulder.

I smiled.

Bip walked off, then turned and we both waved. I watched him go through the doors before I took off.

"What a pain in the ass," I mumbled as the last of the smile melted from my face. I bring the guy to the airport and at the last minute he's asking me to give up part of my Friday evening, to float him a loan, and to take the seat out of my Jeep so I can transport this obviously large, and probably very heavy, package back to our second-floor-without-an-elevator apartment. He was always doing shit like that to me. But what could I say? Someone had died. He was grieving and he was one of my best friends. What was I going to say, "No, pick up your own damned package."?

When I got back home Bets was in the bathtub, which I found stimulating. I tried to get something going with her, but she wasn't feeling well

– one of those "that time of the month" things – so I was forced to settle for a little T.V. I turned in early and found Bets already asleep.

Friday morning I drove the Jeep to work. It was sunny and the forecast called for a 20 percent chance of "mainly afternoon thundershowers." I took my chances and went with the top and doors off, with the back seat removed as well. I borrowed the District Attorney placard from Bip's BMW and parked across from my office in the "Law Enforcement Vehicle Zone." I had to drive downtown on Bip's account anyway, the least he and his employer the city could do was to allow me to park for free.

Flipper had not died, although he smelled as though he had. He was in his usual spot, and I panicked. I didn't have a dollar. He had been gone so long, and I had had a feeling in my gut that he would not be back. So much for my extra sensory perception.

I smelled him before I saw him, heard him before he saw me, and rushed back to the Jeep to search for change. I came up with a dollar and eight cents in dirty pennies, nickels, and quarters before heading back in his direction.

"Hello, Andy!" he shouted as soon as he spied me.

"Hey, Flipper" I answered once I got close enough not to have to shout. "Where you been?"

"I have been to the blubloblu," he answered.

I didn't want to know. I handed him the change. "Good to see you back," I lied as I headed for the door.

"You know, Andy," he began, "a man can measure his friends by the inconvenience they put themselves to in giving assistance at his request."

This confused me. I was not sure whether he was thanking me for the shoes, asking me to inconvenience myself to help him in his plight, or whether, in his usual clairvoyance, he was referring to the trouble that I was going through at Bip's request.

"That's right," I answered, still walking.

"I'll be seeing you later," he said as I swung open the door.

"Oh yea, I'm sure you will," I mumbled sarcastically to myself as I walked inside.

It was a fantastic morning. Everything just fell right into place for me. With three telephone calls I settled a case that had been lingering on my desk for three months. I had looked at that file cover every day and somehow I just felt that on that day it had finally ripened, the crop was ready for the pickers, and it turned out to be so. After dictating several demand letters and completing a petition for a 78-year-old man who had gone into the hospital to have his left leg amputated and woke up to find his right leg gone, I decided to take an early lunch. I had accomplished so much I felt as though I deserved a little break.

There was a noon Mass at the Jesuit Church on Baronne Street that I often tried to catch, when I had the time. On other days, when I left early for lunch, I would sometimes go by and say a few prayers and light a candle or two. This was definitely a two-candle day.

The heat and humidity had gone completely off the scales by the time I left the office. It was not a very long walk to the church, seven or eight blocks, and there were several air-conditioned buildings that I walked through along the route. Tony had filled me in on these, as well as the location of the church, when I had first begun working at the firm. He was a devout churchgoer and lunch eater and he knew all of the secret spots and passageways throughout the Central Business District. Even taking the route that Tony had developed, by the time I reached the church, greeted by the clanging of its bells, I was drenched with sweat.

The Jesuit Church is a truly magnificent structure, built in the Spanish Moorish style before the Civil War. Huge brass doors protect the dark, cool, and cavernous interior from man and elements lurking outside. Cast iron pews with wooden seats that once included doors opened only by those to whom the key had been issued lay in long rows before a gilded altar of gold and light. Above the altar, centered in a niche in the wall, a bright, white, marble statue of the Virgin stands, majestically overseeing and overshadowing all who enter. An upstairs section, with nearly half the capacity of the room below and now shut off from worshipers, is claimed to have been provided for the slaves of those attending during the pre-Civil War era. Icons and statues peer from every corner and crevice, staring somberly at all before them.

I grasped the heavy metal door and pulled, slowly at first, until momentum built so that its own weight carried it aside. Sliding past, into the coolness within, I entered the vestibule off to the right of the main entrance. It was dark inside and it took a moment for my eyes to adjust to the dim light and my ears to the quiet, such stark contrasts to that which lay beyond the massive doors.

An old woman in a tattered madras dress stood at the foot of the Mother Cabrini statuette, picking up, one by one, pennies and nickels left by the faithful paying their respects earlier in the day. Previous encounters had shown me that at least some of those making the offerings objected to the practice of the street people who made several passes daily to collect the pittance. I never really understood their reasoning – where did they intend the money to go? Surely Mother Cabrini was not going to descend from the heavens to pick it up. It seemed to me that instead she merely directed those poor souls to her statue where the money could be found. Mother

Cabrini, still caring for the poor.

The church's air conditioning unit was laboring particularly hard this day, battling to keep the heat and humidity beyond those mammoth doors. The good Jesuit fathers saw fit to keep it very cold in the church, perhaps to attract more followers, perhaps to keep them cool under those heavy robes. Whether intended or not, it served both purposes. Pushing lightly on one of the scarlet, padded swinging doors, I left the vestibule and entered the main hall of the church.

There were several people already in pews, all of them elderly women, and most with rosary beads in hand. I walked only as far as the last pew and knelt to rattle off a few of the prayers memorized in childhood. It did not take long, but after I had finished I sat for a moment and listened to the sweet noises echoing throughout the Antebellum structure with each pulling down of a kneeler or seating on a squeaky pew. I watched the reverent and obedient hard at prayer. Finally, I glanced up at Mary above, requested her blessing, and stood and walked away, head bowed, feeling quite insignificant.

All told I was in the church less than five minutes, but I figured that it was five minutes that most others had not even bothered to spend. That is how I was, in competition with everyone for everything, including church time.

On my way out of the church I touched the foot of the statue of Saint Peter. This was a ritual that I had performed and seen performed over and over again as the older parishioners made their way out of the church. The years and years of touching had caused Saint Peter's right foot to retain its shiny bronze color as the rest of his body had turned a dull green. Stranger yet, his left foot was clad in a bronze shoe while his shiny right foot had toes exposed, giving the impression, at least, that all of that touching had worn poor St. Peter's shoe right off of his foot. Who knows? The way things had been going lately, anything was possible.

As my hand slipped away from St. Peter's foot, I noticed a small pile of coins next to his heel. I considered leaving a little myself but decided against it, as I had to save it for Flipper. Then I went on to lunch and back to the office.

I wish I could say that the rest of the day was uneventful, but I cannot. In fact, and in retrospect, it was to turn out to be one of the most eventful days of my life. If I had known then what I know now, I would have gone straight from the church to my apartment, packed my bags, and headed back to my Mamma in the swamp.

Things had not been going extremely well for Keating & Fabacher. The firm had lost a couple of really big cases, which I was not involved in, thank you very much, and which had the corollary effect of our having lost a couple of really big clients. Then there had been the drop-off in litigation due to the collapse of the oil industry in Louisiana, which left few unscathed, and the entire area in a state of economic decline. We had already been forewarned not to expect our Christmas bonuses and there had been rumors of layoffs. Who would have ever thought that lawyers would have to worry about such things?

As a result of this economic crisis, our brave leaders thought it prudent to begin branching off into different areas of the law, accepting cases from clients who in the past would have been farmed out to other firms in town that did that particular kind of work. Tony and I had been assigned the area of Bankruptcy. We were to attend seminars and learn enough in as short a time as possible to begin handling cases of that variety. I was not very excited about the prospect of becoming a bankruptcy attorney, however, with the economy in the state that it was, we all felt that it should provide an abundant source of new clients, which in return equated to job security.

Tony had begun to jokingly refer to the two of us as the "Bankruptcy Section" of the firm, which was kind of nice, as it had a sort of bonding effect. We both felt that the writing was on the wall for poor ole J. Ryan, who had been assigned "Intellectual Properties." Somehow, in recessionary times, I just could not imagine a herd of inventors and novelists beating a pathway to the doors of Keating & Fabacher. It seemed obvious that if anyone had to go any time soon, it would be J. Ryan.

I was in Tony's office discussing a recent opinion of one of the local bankruptcy court judges when our secretary's voice broke frantically over the intercom.

"Mr. D'Ensina?"

"Yes, Margo," he answered.

"Is Andy still in there?"

"Yea, why?" he asked.

"Mr. Fabacher's been looking for him all over the place. He wants him in his office now."

I was on my way past Margo's desk before she had finished the sentence. "Thanks," I called to her as I strode down the hallway. I always made it a point never to keep anyone waiting, and especially not the man who signed my paycheck.

I passed J. Ryan in the hallway and sarcastically asked him how he was coming with the intellectual property.

"Intellectual property?" he asked with a smile. "You got the wrong guy," he continued, never slowing his pace.

There was something a little unsettling about the smirk on his face. And there was also something different about the way he smelled. Normally J. Ryan smelled as though he had poured an entire bottle of Polo cologne over his head in place of taking a shower. Now he smelled as though he had not even taken the shower.

I entered Mr. Fabacher's office without knocking, as instructed by his secretary, Lori. He was sitting at his desk and I could see the peak of someone's head rising above the high back of one of his client's chairs.

"Come on in, Andrew," he said. He never allowed himself the familiarity of calling anyone by any name other than their given name. There were no exceptions, not even for Jeremiah.

I walked toward Mr. Fabacher's desk, wondering who it was that I was about to meet.

"Andrew," he began, "I would like for you to meet… "

And then I knew. To say I was stunned would be an understatement. I was totally aghast. This was the last place that I would ever expect to have seen…

"…Mr. Christian Waterman."

I did not say anything at first. I did not move. I did not attempt to shake any hands. I don't think I took a breath and I am pretty certain that my heart stopped beating. What could he possibly be doing in Fabacher's office? Was he suing us? Had I done something? Was he trying to get a donation out of Fabacher and using my name? Whatever the reason it could not be good.

"Andrew!" Mr. Fabacher said rather sternly, indicating that I should shake Flipper's hand.

I tried to figure out whether I should tell him that this man was homeless, that he had webbed feet, that he was probably insane, that I hardly knew him. But I was speechless.

"We have met," Flipper spoke up.

"Yea," I responded uneasily, finally shaking Flipper's extended hand. "Kind of," I corrected.

"Oh, so that's it," Fabacher interjected.

"What?" I asked.

"That's why Mr. Waterman has requested that you be here," he explained.

"For what?" I asked.

"Well, to be a lawyer I suppose," he answered tersely.

"Are you all right, Mr. Jordan?" Flipper asked. He had actually bathed, shaved, combed his hair, and he was wearing a new, clean suit and the shark skin shoes that I had bought him.

"Yes," I stammered, "Fine. Thank you. And you?" I asked, in an effort to be civil.

"Good," he responded.

"Have a seat, Andrew," Mr. Fabacher instructed.

I took the client chair next to the one in which Flipper was seated, and looked nervously ahead toward Mr. Fabacher, wondering just how bad it was going to be.

"Andrew...," Mr. Fabacher began. He was a short man, balding, and with beady eyes. He had the "little man's" complex, some people call it "Napoleonic," and he wielded his authority like a battle ax, taking great pleasure in seeing others, especially men physically larger than himself (and most men were), squirm before him. "...Mr. Waterman is writing a book and has a rather unique story to tell. He would like for the firm of Keating & Fabacher to assist him in copyrighting his work as well as publicizing his story."

"Publicizing?" I asked.

"Yes," he responded, "helping him reach the public with his story, which involves a deformity..."

"Isn't that more of a job for an advertising agency?" I asked.

Obviously it was a stupid question...No, the question was not stupid, but presenting it in that form at that time to my employer was stupid.

"Do you have one in mind?" Fabacher asked, obviously angry.

"Well, I didn't mean...," I muttered, attempting to explain my way out of this mess.

"If you do, perhaps you could walk Mr. Waterman over there and they might want to pay you to do what I'm going to tell you to do."

"No, sir," I responded. "I mean yes, sir," I corrected, "what is it that you want me to do?"

"Mr. Waterman is handicapped. His feet are deformed, and he has explained to me that he would like our help in making his story known. Granted, this is not your typical go-down-to-the-courthouse-and-file-a-lawsuit case, but it could end up being just that. We need to research the issues as far as having Mr. Waterman declared handicapped, find out what that entitles him to and, if it is not sufficient, fight for his rights under the Constitution. As a result, we may end up going somewhat outside of the normal role of an attorney. We're on the cutting edge here, Andrew. This could open up a whole new field of law. Mr. Waterman thinks he has the right to have his story known and I, personally, tend to agree with him. If they won't let him on *The Angelique Brown Show*, we'll find out why, file a discrimination suit if necessary. There is a myriad of issues and opportunities here, Andrew, and it does not take much to envision them."

"Angelique Brown won't let him on?" I asked.

"I did not say that," Fabacher said smartly. "I said *if* they will not let him on."

"Do you want me to work with Jeremiah on this?"

"No, I do not want you to work with him on this," he responded, obviously trying to humiliate me further in front of his new client. "Why would you ask me that?"

"I just thought that since he was working intellectual property it would prevent us from doubling up..."

"He's not on intellectual property anymore...," he interrupted.

There was no need for him to finish his sentence. I knew what was coming. Suddenly it was all becoming clear, and I knew why J. Ryan had smiled at me in the hallway. My head began to spin, my ears grew hot, and I got really pissed.

"...*you* are now," he finished, ignoring my obvious dismay. "Jeremiah is going to take over bankruptcy. I have informed him that you will be switching with him."

My heart sank – I was doomed. One minute you're on top of the world and the next you're knocked to the bottom of the shit heap. Flipper had slapped me down with one of those huge, flappy feet of his. Why me? How had he gotten over on Fabacher? Had the old man lost his sense of smell? This man was homeless, he was wasting our time, and he was ruining my life.

Lori came in and handed a stapled bundle of documents to Mr. Fabacher. He studied them closely then addressed Flipper.

"This is the contract of employment," he explained. "It spells out our agreement and binds both of us to its terms."

Panicked, I knew I had to do something. I had to let Fabacher know what was going on, that Flipper was an insane homeless person who was not about to honor any contract. I just hoped it was not too late to reverse the deal with J. Ryan.

"Mr. Fabacher," I interrupted.

Fabacher stopped speaking and looked over to me with one of those you-had-better-have-a-good-reason-for-interrupting-me sneers on his face.

"Yes?"

"May I speak to you in private for just a moment?"

"What?" he asked with an incredulous look on his face.

"It will just take a second. There is something that I think you should know."

"As I was saying," he continued, turning his attention back to Flipper, "this will bind both parties. Now why don't you just review this and let me know whether you have any questions."

I breathed a sigh of relief, concluding that he was going to leave the office with me while Flipper looked over the contract. All was not lost.

"Is this a fair contract, Mr. Jordan?" Flipper asked me, holding the paperwork up in the air.

"Yes, of course," I replied. What else could I say?

"Where do I sign?" Flipper asked.

"Well, you really should look it over," Mr. Fabacher urged.

"I don't need to look it over. My attorney has just informed me that in his opinion it is fair. I trust him implicitly."

"That's very flattering," I interrupted, trying to buy time and a word with Fabacher, "but you really should look it over."

"Do your contracts intend to harm or cause injury to your clients?" he asked me.

"No, of course not," I answered.

"And this is your legal opinion?" he continued.

"Yes," I replied.

"Then I am satisfied," he said, reaching for Mr. Fabacher's fountain pen. He obviously knew what I was up to and did not want me alone with Fabacher.

"You do realize there will be a retainer?" I asked Flipper.

"Andrew!" Mr. Fabacher belted. "The financial aspect of our representation of Mr. Waterman is of no concern to you."

"Yes, I know," Flipper answered meekly. "I have already paid it. And, as I understand it, once the five thousand is expended you will let me know so that I can provide you with another such retainer which your firm will work against at the rate of one hundred twenty-five dollars per hour?"

"That is correct," Mr. Fabacher answered, smiling.

Where had Flipper gotten five thousand dollars?

"Will you walk me out, Andy?" Flipper asked.

I did not know how to respond. I had to talk to Fabacher before Flipper got out of the building, but he was really getting irritated with me. I felt as though one more slip-up could mean my job.

"I'll walk you out," Fabacher volunteered. "I am heading that way."

"May I speak with you for just a moment?" I asked Fabacher in desperation as we all stood.

"Later, later," he answered, "we can get together in the morning."

"Thank you very, very much," Flipper told Mr. Fabacher as he came around his desk and the two shook hands.

"Oh, no, thank you," Mr. Fabacher responded.

"And Andy will handle my case exclusively, yes?" he asked.

"Well, with a little guidance, yes. But he will be the main attorney on the file," Fabacher said, moving us all toward the doorway.

"I want his judgment," Flipper continued. "He is the only reason I have come here."

"Yes, I understand," Mr. Fabacher said through a strained smile, "he will handle it."

"Good," Flipper answered, shaking hands again.

We all walked to the elevator together, so I could not confront either of them. The doors opened and they both got on. With much irritation I bid them farewell and walked back toward my office.

Lori was working dutifully at filing her nails as I passed her desk. I stopped, turned around, and stood before her.

"Hey," she said.

"Hey," I responded.

We looked at each other for a second, then I spoke again.

"Did that guy really pay a retainer?" I asked.

"You should have seen it," she said, leaning forward and keeping her voice low, "I've never seen anything like it."

"What do you mean?"

"He came in here with a bag full of money and just plopped it on Mr. Fabacher's desk."

"A bag full?" I asked.

"A paper shopping bag. It was full almost to the top with money, small bills. Mr. Fabacher called me in and asked me to draw up a receipt and to have it deposited on the afternoon run."

"Did you count it?" I asked.

"Yes," she said, pursing her lips, shivering. "It was disgusting."

"What do you mean?"

"It was dirty. The bills were all crumpled up. I mean, they looked like somebody had dug them out of the trash."

"Did the money have a black film all over it?"

"Yea," she responded. "It even smelled bad. How did you know?"

"Lucky guess. How much was it?" I continued.

"Five thousand, to the dollar," she said.

"He really had five thousand dollars?" I was shocked.

"And not one bill bigger than a ten. It took me half the morning just to count it. I've washed my hands three times already and I still can't get that smell off." She shivered again.

"I don't understand it. Where could he have gotten that kind of money?" I mused out loud.

"Maybe he's one of these eccentric millionaires that lives in a big fallen down house and keeps all of his money in a mattress that they find one day buried under a ton of newspapers," Lori said, smiling.

"He lives on the street," I blurted out.

"How do you know?" she asked.

"I've seen him. Haven't you ever seen him sitting in front of the building in the morning?" I asked.

"No," she responded, "but I come in through the garage."

"Well he sits out there on a piece of cardboard and begs for money."

"Why would a millionaire beg for money?" she questioned.

"He's not a millionaire," I responded, not believing her naivete.

"How do you know he isn't?" she asked. "You think he collected five thousand dollars this morning? I'm telling you he got it out of a mattress, a dirty one. Mark my words."

"He doesn't have a mattress. He has a piece of cardboard, and he doesn't have a huge house," I retorted.

"How do you know? Have you ever followed him home?"

"No," I responded. Then I thought about it. She could be right. I had never followed him home. For all I knew he was a wealthy man acting like a street person. I had seen that in a cartoon getting dressed for work one morning. There was a rich old lady who dressed up like a street person then went around rewarding people that helped her. Maybe Flipper was such a person.

"You'll probably think this is really stupid," Lori continued, "but a cartoon the other morning had this old rich lady dressing up like a bag lady and this country guy gave her a ride somewhere and the next day she gave him a brand new car. He could be like that. Did you ever see that?"

"Lori, I'm a lawyer," I responded in as condescending a tone as I could muster. "Thanks, though," I said, resuming the walk to my office.

My office door had been closed and someone, someone who had handwriting just like Tony D'Ensina's, had taped a sign to my door which read, "Intellectual Property Department – Will Copyright for Food."

Not funny. I ripped the note up and slammed my door shut. I was irritated by the fact that I would not be able to talk to Fabacher about the Flipper fiasco until Monday. But then, perhaps it was all for the best, I thought. Lori had given me a good idea and this would give me a little more time to get all of my ducks in a row, so to speak, before I broke the news to Fabacher.

There was a note taped to my chair informing me that someone from the bus terminal had called to inform me that my package had arrived. I wondered how they had gotten my name but then reasoned that Bip must have called them from Atlanta to let them know I would be picking the package up. It was 3:30 in the afternoon, there were dark clouds forming outside of my window, and I had this package to pick up. The day was not going to get any better as far as I could see, and I needed a drink and a little lovemaking with Bets as soon as possible to get things back on track.

I told Margo I was leaving early and just left. Perhaps it was a dangerous maneuver, considering the precariousness of my new position, but I felt that my sanity depended upon it. If anyone asked, I'd just tell them that I went to the Tulane Law Library to check out some treatises on patents and copyrights. Still, I had to take a stab back at Tony and J. Ryan. On my way out I taped a new sign to my door: "Intellectual Properties Section – Happy Hour Today."

TEN

The bus depot is at the Union Passenger Terminal, which also services the railroads. The package pick-up is located around the back of the terminal, near to where the busses pull off of the nearby Interstate Highway. I parked the Jeep as close as possible, a few employees' cars distance, to the doorway and walked in just as a mighty clap of thunder burst overhead. There was no clerk in sight.

I rang the bell provided at the counter and waited several minutes before a man finally appeared wearing a grey uniform shirt, his name tag on the left front pocket, with the company logo stretched across the top of his right shirt pocket.

"What ya' need?" he asked, not very politely.

"I'm here to pick up a package for Bip Woodson," I explained,

"Got the ticket?" he asked.

"No, I didn't know there was one." I had forgotten it.

"There's always a ticket," he said smartly.

"Well I haven't got one."

He just stood there looking at me.

"Can't you look it up?" I asked.

"I could look in the register," he said matter-of-factly.

"Would you do that?" I tried to remain polite.

He turned and walked away without a word. Moments later he reappeared with a large ledger and began flipping through the pages, beginning with the classification "A."

"What you said that name was?" he finally asked.

"Woodson, Bip Woodson," I said, slowly and clearly.

He flipped to the "W's" and resumed his search.

"Wilson?" he asked, reading the first name he came to.

"Woodson," I replied,"W-o-o-d-s-o-n."

"And what you said his first name was, Burp?" He had to be fucking with me.

"It's Bip. Would you like me to find it?"

"Suit yourself," he replied, turning the ledger around to me. I began looking through the"W's," which were in no particular order. It did not take long to find Bip's package, but when I looked up the clerk had disappeared.

After about a minute of waiting I rang the bell again. He reappeared from behind a divider carrying a box marked "RUSTON PEACHES." The box was ripped on one corner and he had a peach in his mouth. He walked the box over to a table marked "Deliveries," put it down, took the peach out of his mouth and spoke.

"You an impatient mother, ain't you?" he said rudely.

"I found it," I answered with a smile.

"Lemme see," he responded, walking toward me. He took a bite out of the peach and a stream of juice ran down his chin and fell on his shirt. He put the peach back in his mouth, swung the ledger back around, and gave it a look.

After a moment he took the peach out of his mouth again, save the bite he chewed as he spoke.

"W-047," he said aloud, reading the number next to Bip's name. "W-047," he repeated, each time a new spray of peach juice emanating from his mouth, missing me but splattering the page. He left the book and walked back behind the partition.

"W-147?" he asked.

"Yes," I answered, knowing it was wrong, refusing to allow him to get the best of me.

He reappeared with a small package in his hand, about the size of a shoebox.

"Here it is," he said, placing it on the counter.

He took out a form from beneath the counter and began to write on it.

"Wait a minute," he said shortly. "This package for Cynthia Williams, I done got the wrong one."

I sighed. He had not been messing with me after all – he was just plain stupid.

"What that number again?" he said, looking down at the register.

"W-047," I said.

"You told me it was W-147," he responded.

"Sorry, I must have been confused."

"You must think I like walking around back here gettin' shit for you.

You think its funny?"

"It was a mistake," I assured him.

"Yea, a mistake. Where that number?" he said again, looking at the register.

"It's W-047, that's the right one," I insisted.

"I ain't listenin' to you no more," he said. "I'll be walkin' around back here all day if I do that."

"Woodson, Bip," he finally found it. "His name Bip?" he asked, "That a man or a female?"

"It's a nickname. He's a male," I answered. I just wanted the package and to get out of there.

"W-047," he said. "You was right after all."

"Will wonders never cease."

"What that supposed to mean?" he asked, not knowing whether to be offended or not.

"Nothing," I said, "it's just a saying."

He glared at me for a second, putting the last bit of peach, pit and all, in his mouth. Finally he turned and went to retrieve the package.

"Shit," he said, turning around as he reached the partition, "I done forgot the other one." He returned to the counter, picked up Cynthia William's package in one hand and spit the peach pit out in the other. Again he disappeared behind the partition.

He was gone for some time and I fully expected him to ask me what the number was again. This time I would make sure he got it right.

"Fuck, man!" he finally spoke, obviously wanting me to hear. "That's the biggest motherfucking package in the place," he said. He reappeared from behind the partition with nothing in his hand and the peach pit bulging behind his right cheek.

"I gotta get the damn dolly for this one," he mumbled, looking at me as though I were inconveniencing him by having him do his job.

He went to a small alcove on the other side of the room and retrieved a dolly. Walking as slowly as any human being possibly could, he once again made his way behind the partition. I could hear when the dolly stopped because it had a squeaky wheel and soon thereafter I heard a series of groans, grunts, and moans. Finally he wheeled the package out, bending slightly as he walked.

"Man, I done threw my back out gettin' your package," he told me.

Like I could give a shit. I just stood there silently, checkbook in hand, ready to do my business and get out of there. I was also dreading having to get the thing into the Jeep and hoped that he would at least be kind enough to let me use the dolly to bring it to where I had parked. I held no delusions of his helping me lift the thing into the Jeep.

"What's in this thing?" he asked sourly upon his arrival at the counter.

"I have no idea," I told him.

"Whatever it is it's a heavy sonofabitch," he complained, rubbing his back. "Here, you need to sign this," he said, as he threw me the shipping voucher.

I began to sign my name but he stopped me.

"Wait a minute," he said. "This C.O.D. and is only supposed to go to Mr. Woodson."

"He's out of town," I said, "so he asked me to pick it up for him."

"I could only release it to his signature," he said.

"You're kidding me."

"Serious as a heart attack."

"Can I sign his name?" I asked.

"Are you him?"

"You know I'm not," I said.

"I don't know nothin' 'bout that," he said. "A man wanna say he Mr. Woodson and sign his name so I don't have to carry that thing back to the back and I don't know whether he him or not."

I caught his drift. As best as I could, I forged Bip's signature on the voucher.

"That'll be nine hundred and seventy-two dollars," he said.

I laughed.

"Yea," I said. "How much?"

"Nine seventy-two."

"You're kidding."

"Man, I ain't kiddin. It say that right here," he pointed to the voucher that I had just signed, which stated that I swore the money had been paid. "You signed the damn thing, you gotta pay."

I could not believe it. Bip had inconvenienced me beyond what any normal friend could expect. Nine hundred and seventy-two dollars? It was bad enough I had to endure all that I had in picking the damned thing up.

"I'm not going to pay that," I insisted.

"You signed, you gotsta pay," he repeated. "It gonna be sent back tonight if you don't pay and they gonna wonder who signed the thing."

I reread what I had just signed. It was a sworn statement and I had forged Bip's name. I couldn't just leave it. They would send it back. I hated doing it. I mean I really, really hated doing it, but I wrote out the check and handed it to him.

He took the check and the voucher and wheeled the package around the counter.

"Here you go," he said.

"Thanks," I responded, putting a hand on the dolly.

"The dolly gotsta stay in here," he said with a slight grin.

"Come on," I pleaded, "I'm parked just right there."

"Company policy," he fired back,"it's in the manual."

"I'll give you two bucks if you let me borrow it for one second."

"Lose my job for two bucks, you got to be crazy," he said.

"You won't lose your job."

"Ten bucks."

"Five."

"I ain't helpin' you pick it up," he said.

"I know," I responded.

"But I will follow you out there to make sure you don't steal my dolly."

"I am not going to steal it."

"Gimme the five."

I handed him the five dollars and he turned the dolly over to me. He followed me to the door but decided not to follow me out after all when he saw that it had begun to rain.

"Great," I exclaimed. This was getting to be too much.

"I'm gonna need that dolly right back," he said, trying to rush me.

"I'm going."

"My supervisor gonna be comin' back any minute."

"All right," I said, opening the door. Bip was going to owe me, big time.

I wheeled the huge box out to the Jeep and with great effort lifted it inside. The box was getting very wet and probably would not hold in the rain, but I was beyond caring. I did not know what was inside and there were no real clues on the outside. Only the words "LA Undersea World" were printed in small letters on the shipping label just above Bip's name.

I leaned over and picked up the dolly, noticing for the first time a twinge of pain in my back. "Great," I mumbled, as I started wheeling it back, then stopped. Eyeing the clerk standing behind the glass door, with my five dollars in his pocket, eagerly awaiting my return, I had a revelation. He was dry and smug. I was soaked to the bone. I turned away and with all my might rolled the dolly down the driveway in the direction opposite the glass door. Grabbing my keys I ran and jumped into the front seat of my Jeep, threw it in reverse, and drove away, laughing, never even bothering to look back.

With water running across my face as the Jeep whirred through the storm, amid the lightning flashes and thunder claps, I was renewed. It had been a bad day, but now it was the weekend. Bip was gone and Bets and I had the house to ourselves. Things had begun looking up, actually, as I envisioned Bets and I in the throes of passion, just so long as my back held up.

ELEVEN

I TEND TO REMEMBER THINGS AS EVENTS rather than in an entire sequence. I remember the bus terminal incident well because it was such an inconvenience and a struggle. I know that the rain had let up by the time I got home and that I carried the package upstairs to the apartment, enlisting the help of Germaine, a local kid that did odd jobs around the neighborhood for a small price. I also remember that Bets and I did make love that evening, but it did not live up to my anticipation. I can't remember the details, only the disappointment.

I had told Bets that I had to go into the office to learn about "intellectual property" the next day. As I prepared to leave early that Saturday morning, she was still sleeping and I lifted the covers to get one last peak at her nude body. I guess you could say I had an above-average sex drive. At least it always seemed that way to me. She did not stir.

The morning was nice, the previous evening's storm having cleared the air and cooled the earth. I made an initial pass by my building, but Flipper was not there. Next I hit all the hot spots; the Methodist Mission, the Ozanam Inn, but he was nowhere to be found. I motored down each street in the French Quarter and went around Lee Circle and down to Lafayette Square. Two and a half hours later there was still no sign of him and the air was beginning to heat up. I drove back to the office, parking at a meter on Loyola Avenue.

The security guard made me sign in and I rode up the elevator alone. Our floor was deserted. Unlike a lot of firms, Keating & Fabacher did not burn either the midnight or the weekend oil unless there was a deadline that could not be met by working weekdays.

I walked down the dark hallway to my office, and noticed that the note I had left the previous afternoon was gone. Sitting in my chair, I read the two telephone messages that Margo had left for me: *4:00 – Bip – Called to remind you about something. Said not to leave a message* and *4:55 – Mark Jackson of The Angelique Brown Show – Please call 864-1290, ext. 349.*

The Angelique Brown Show? What was going on? I called the number but there was no answer. It would have to wait until Monday.

I spun around in my chair a couple of times, enjoying the cool air blowing down on me from the vent above. That is when I noticed a pile of books on my desk with a note taped to the one on top. *Thought you might like to have these. No need to thank me. J.*

"What an ass," I said as I picked up a book entitled *Copyrights and Patents*, and flipped through the pages. I stopped spinning, read one page, and fell asleep. I had closed my eyes for only a second and the next thing I remember the telephone was ringing.

"Hello," I answered drowsily, "Keating & Fabacher."

"Hey, Andy." It was Bets.

"Hey."

"Getting a lot done?"

"Oh yea," I said, flipping over the page I had read a few hours earlier.

"You getting hungry?"

"Uh," I stalled. I honestly did not know whether I was hungry or not. "A little bit."

"Want to come pick me up for lunch?"

"I can't, Baby," I said. I still had to see if I could find Flipper.

"You aren't going to eat?"

"I'll get something out of the machine," I said, referring to the vending machine down the hall.

"Potato chips and a candy bar for desert?"

"Mmmmmmm," I said, "The lunch of champions."

"Okay," she said, resigned to the fact that she would have to eat alone. "I'm gonna walk to the grill and get something."

"You're killing me," I responded, knowing that she was referring to the Camellia Grill around the corner from the apartment.

"If I bump into a cute guy on the way, it's your own fault," she teased me.

"Well I might just meet a babe on the way to the candy machine, share a pretzel with her."

"You'll *have* a pretzel if you do that. I don't want any diseases," she warned me.

"As if," I replied.

"I know how you men are."

"Boy, aren't we distrustful this morning."

"You mean afternoon."

"Yea," shit, afternoon? "afternoon."

"When are you coming back?" she asked.

"Before five," I answered, "we can go to dinner."

"Okay, I'll hold you to that."

"I promise," I responded.

"Bye."

"Bye," I said, hanging up the phone. We did not say "I love you" on the telephone. It just had never sounded right.

I closed the book on my lap and heaved it onto my desk. Sitting back in my chair, eyes closed, I contemplated life. Wondered where I was going. Where I had been. Where Flipper was. Suddenly my eyes opened wide.

Jumping up from my chair, I ran down the hall to Lori's desk. I opened a small box next to her paper clips and retrieved a key that opened her desk. Opening her top drawer, I took the key I found there and opened the file cabinet behind her chair. I searched the "W's" and found Christian Waterman's file.

Every new file opened in the office had a sheet stapled to the inside with client information, most important of which was the billing address. True to form, Christian Waterman's file had the sheet and the address – "Box 12, 762 St. Charles Avenue." Obviously an apartment building or condominium complex with different boxes out front. I rushed out of the office, thinking I would grab lunch after I checked out Flipper's pad, and pressed the "down" button on the elevator.

When the elevator arrived, the doors opened to reveal a beautiful brunette who looked somewhat familiar.

"Hey." My typical greeting. I stepped inside.

"Hey," she said, only much more loudly than I had.

She stood in the back left corner of the elevator and I took the back right. The doors closed and we began our descent.

"Working weekends now?" she asked.

I had been politely facing the doors, not looking at her, though I would have preferred to do so. The fact that she had spoken took me by surprise.

"Yea," I said, somewhat hesitantly. I turned to her smile.

We rode the rest of the way in silence.

"You too?" I asked, just as the elevator stopped.

"Me too, what?" she asked.

"Working weekends now?" I said.

"I usually do."

"Oh," I said, as the doors opened.

"But you wouldn't know that," she continued.

"Why do you say that?"

"Because you never do."

"How do you know?"

"Because I'm the one who is here every weekend."

"Maybe you just don't see me come in."

"Doubtful," she said, confidently. We had moved outside of the elevator and were standing in the lobby.

"Who do you work for?" I asked.

"Peniston," she replied.

"Peniston?" I asked.

"You don't even know who's in your building," she said, accusingly. "You've probably never even seen me before."

She did look very familiar. However, if I had seen her before chances are that I would have remembered, she was just that beautiful. About five and a half feet tall, her curly brown hair hung in locks past her shoulders. She was wearing jeans that were tight around what had to be a perfect butt which tapered up into an incredibly small waist. She wore a cotton T-shirt which hung loosely and teasingly upon round, obviously firm, and quite large, breasts.

"Not wearing that, I haven't," I flirted.

"What's that supposed to mean?"

"Nothing," I retreated temporarily, "only that what you're wearing looks great on you."

"Oh, and what you've seen me in before doesn't?" she trapped me.

"I didn't say that. You look very familiar. What's your name?"

"Carly," she responded.

"I'm Andy..." I said, extending my right hand.

"Jordan," she said.

"How did you know?" I asked, feeling really good. It was obvious that this wonderful creature had gone to the trouble of finding out my name. Me, the good looking, up-and-coming attorney. I was suddenly sure dozens of such women, that I had never seen before, knew my name.

"I guess I'm just more aware of my surroundings than you are," she said.

"No, really, how did you know?" I asked, cockily. Pushing her to admit that she had been interested enough to find out.

"I don't think I should tell you," she hesitated.

"You have to tell me now," I insisted. This was all very exciting, a huge ego boost.

"I was down here when you broke the door and I heard the security guard call out your name," she delivered the answer like a prize fighter delivering his knock-out blow. Somehow I was certain that she knew what I had been thinking – she had seen my conceit and had allowed me to expose it, setting me up before she delivered the final punch.

"Oh," I said, not a little embarrassed. "You saw that?"

"Yep," she said, beginning to laugh. "I was standing right here, looking over at the door and I saw you run in and SWING that door wide open, boy, and it just shattered!" She was laughing almost uncontrollably now, reliving the moment.

I smiled but I was dying inside. Then I remembered. I remembered who she was, where I had seen her before.

"You're the girl that let out that noise!" I said excitedly. Her laughing came to an abrupt halt.

"What noise?" she asked.

"That 'Baaaa Haaaa' sound," I said, beginning to laugh myself.

"I didn't make any 'Baaaa Haaaa' sound," she defended, no longer even smiling.

"Yes, you did," I continued, "just before you started laughing uncontrollably."

"It was hilarious," she said, beginning to laugh again.

"So was your laughing," I kept it up. Trying to save at least a little face, even if it was at her expense.

"Why did you open the door like that?"

"I was in a hurry."

"But you didn't have to SWING it open like that," she repeated, emphasizing the word and going through the motion of swinging the door open.

"Well, I think the door was defective. It shouldn't have exploded like that."

"I can tell you're a lawyer."

"And you're very pretty." The words just came out. I could not believe that I had said them.

She was obviously embarrassed and we shared a moment of silence as we both struggled with what to say next. She spoke first.

"Where are you going?"

"To lunch," I lied, the alternative being to tell her I was chasing my new client, Flipper, the Man from Atlantis, around town. "What about you?"

"The same," she answered, smiling. We began walking toward the door.

"Would you like to have lunch with me?" I asked. The words just seemed to come out all by themselves.

"Where are you going?"

"Why? You on a special diet?" I stalled for time, since I hadn't really considered eating. My mind was blank as to where I would go.

"No," she said, "I was just wondering where we were going."

"We?" I asked.

"Yes, we," she said. "You did really mean it when you asked me didn't you?"

"Sure," I said, reaching the door and opening it for her.

"Well lets go then."

"When do you need to be back?"

"Monday morning."

My heart took a little jump, or maybe it was my stomach. If Bets ever found out that I had gone to lunch with this beautiful woman after having turned her down, she would skin me alive, but I was not thinking about that at the moment. I would not say that I was captivated, but I was well on my way.

We loaded ourselves into the Jeep and I drove to the edge of the French Quarter, to a little hole in the wall. It's kind of a Mexican/Cuban/steak restaurant whose appearance is quite deceptive. If you didn't know any better you'd think they were serving up a new case of botulism on a daily basis, but the food is quite good and very, very cheap – and safe.

I felt bad as I watched Carly hop out of the Jeep, her back wet with sweat. She did not seem to mind, though, and I really liked that. Bets refused to ride in the Jeep on anything other than "crisp, cool days in Fall and Spring."

"It's really hot," I said, heading into the restaurant.

"Oh, but it feels great in the Jeep," she replied, her words going straight to my heart.

"You really think so?" I asked, fearing sarcasm.

"Yea," she said seriously, "Why? Don't you?"

"Sure, *I* do, but most other people don't."

"I love that. A Jeep, no top, no doors. It's very cool."

Now I was captivated.

Lunch was good. She had fajitas and I had the Cuban platter. We talked about a variety of things: where we were from, different people we both knew, things we liked to do. It seemed as though everything she said I could have been saying, as though we were together on some level, something I could not explain. It was truly refreshing.

I paid for lunch, we drove back to the building, and I dropped her off out front. Her back had gotten wet again, but she was all smiles. We said our goodbyes, me promising to break no more doors if she would keep that laugh away from me. I wanted to kiss her, but had to settle for watching her walk away. The way she looked in those jeans, Levi's could have made a fortune with a commercial. I knew then that she was going to become a distraction.

I sat, watching her until she disappeared into the building, then started the Jeep and drove by 762 St. Charles Avenue. Much to my dismay, it was no apartment or condominium complex at all. It was a copy center, one of those places with a room full of copying machines that you can use for a nickel or something. And over on one wall, toward the back of the store, was a row of boxes, mail boxes, available for rent.

TWELVE

FLIPPER WAS NOT IN HIS USUAL SPOT on Monday morning, which really disappointed me. I had dedicated a lot of time during the weekend to going over my cross-examination. Where had he gotten the money? How had this guy from The Angelique Brown Show gotten my number? What was he really up to? I went on to work without the answers.

As soon as the clock struck 9:00 a.m., I put the call in to Mark Jackson. It rang several times before someone finally answered. I asked for extension 349 and was put on hold, which meant that I had to listen to solicitations for guests for upcoming shows: "...in a parachute accident and lived to tell about it? If so, we would like to talk to you. Recording begins on September eleventh...Here in Louisiana we are blessed with a sportsman's paradise, but sometimes that paradise can turn vicious and deadly. Have you ever been involved in a sporting accident that has left you or a loved-one debilitated? If so, we would like to talk to you. Recording begins on September twelfth...Incest, it happens..."

"Hello," a voice interrupted.

"Hi," I responded, "Mr. Jackson?"

"Yes," he said.

"My name is Andrew Jordan, and I am returning your call from Friday."

"Oh, yea. Thanks for calling me back."

"What can I do for you?"

"I'm in charge of booking guests on Ms. Brown's show and someone told me that you represent the crown prince of a country, but they said they could not tell me which one."

He paused, but I did not respond. What was going on here?

"Are you there, Mr. Jordan?"

"May I ask who it was that you spoke to?"

"I'm sorry, but I can't answer that."

"Mr. Jackson," I said in a much more demanding tone, "I would like to know who has been telling you this."

"No, Mr. Jordan, you don't understand. They didn't say."

"So, someone just called you up out of the blue, and told you that I represent a crown prince?"

"That's right."

"And you actually called me based on that?"

"I call people for a lot less all the time," he responded.

"They told you I represented the crown prince of some unknown country?"

"Is it not true?"

"I'm sorry," I answered, "but I can't answer that."

"Look," he continued, "I understand the delicate position that you are in, but we are doing a show on 'Louisianians who would be King,' about people in the state with royal blood. We begin taping this Wednesday and the closest thing to royalty that I've been able to find is some quack from Des Allemands that has traced his family tree back to the Duke of Orleans."

"What does that have to do with my client?" I asked.

"So you do represent him," he responded joyfully.

"Yes, I do. But what does this have to do with him? My client is not from here."

"How long has he been here," Mr. Jackson asked.

"Not even a year."

"Well, Mr. Jordan, being a lawyer you should know that living here six months can change a domicile to Louisiana."

"Mr. Jackson," I replied, "I am aware that this may be the case in some instances, but not in this one."

"Is he wealthy? The reason I ask is that a lot of these titled people have no money and we would be willing to pay."

"Money does not seem to be a problem for this prince."

"Andy," he said as politely as he could, "if I don't find real royalty by tomorrow morning, Angelique wants to change the show to 'Louisianians who would be Mardi Gras Kings' and interview people that have been members of Mardi Gras krewes for generations without anyone in the family ever being selected king. We're trying to push this show regionally, and let me tell you, most people could give a rat's ass about who is and isn't Mardi Gras royalty."

"All I can do is ask my client," I said, ready to get rid of the guy.

"That's all I want," he said excitedly.

"I'll have to get back to you."

"Andy?"

"Yes?"

"While I've got you on the phone," he said a little hesitantly, "is this guy interesting?"

"You wouldn't believe it," I said, "straight out of the National Enquirer."

"Great," he said, "please let me know soon."

"I'll try to get with him today. By the way, how much *do* you pay?"

"Depends on how much we want them and how difficult they are. Basically just expenses. But you say your guy doesn't need that, right?"

"I'll have to let you know," I responded. "And Mark…"

"…Yea?" he asked

"This guy is a little eccentric. He doesn't look much like royalty."

"You should see the guy from Des Allemands."

"Gotcha," I said. We exchanged goodbyes and hung up. My hand was still on the receiver when Margo buzzed in over the intercom.

"Andy, Mr. Waterman is here and would like to see you."

"Send him in. Thanks Margo."

Flipper walked in, wearing the same suit that he had worn on Friday, and smelling as poorly as ever. With a huge grin on his face he marched over and sat in one of my client's chairs. I guess I should not have been surprised that he had shown up just when I really had to speak to him. That is just the way that things had been going.

"How are you today, Andy?" he asked in a very friendly tone.

"Great," I responded, "and you?"

"Never better," he said. "I feel like it's all going to work out."

"Flipper, where did you get five thousand dollars?" I asked, changing my mood from cordial to serious.

"From good people like yourself," he responded merrily.

"Five thousand dollars?"

"And much more, too," he said.

"You collected all of that from begging on the street?"

"Oh no," he responded, still smiling, "I sold my Mercedes, and rented out my flat in Paris."

"You can cut the sarcasm," I demanded, "I am serious and the status of this firm's relationship with you may well rest on your answer to this question. Now where did you get the money?"

"Andy," he said, more seriously now, "I am a poor man without a home, I depend on the kindness of others for my well being. You yourself have given me forty or fifty dollars since I met you and many are more generous than you. I have no expenses. I eat at the mission. I have little to spend the money on."

"Then why take it? Why do you take money from people when you have no use for it? You live like a parasite on society, getting your meals for free, living on the street, why take the money if not to better yourself, or at least to start supporting yourself?" I was really upset now.

"Andy," he began, frowning, "this is a great disappointment. What are you thinking about? You believe I take money for the sake of taking it? I have every intention of using it, and I have. Five thousand of it I paid to your employer. The contract I signed says I will need plenty more of it, too. I take the money because it is the standard by which your society judges a man. One's inner self, the love in his heart, and his capacity for good are of no consequence here where one with money is automatically adjudged of worth while one living like a 'parasite' on the street for lack of it is branded worthless and a failure. I have only one goal here, and you know what that is. I knew that one day money would be necessary and therefore I set out to get as much of it as possible for when the time came. And now, my friend, Andy, the time has come."

I had no response. Who was this guy? Everything that I had ever been taught, everything that I knew to be fact, went against believing his story. Yet there was something about him, it was so air tight. He was not lying to me. If he was not from Atlantis, I was convinced that he thought he was.

"How did *The Angelique Brown Show* hear about you?" I changed the subject.

"What do you mean?"

"I got a call from someone down at *The Angelique Brown Show* who schedules the taping segments and he said they're doing a show on royalty and they just happened to hear that I represent you."

"I don't know how they knew that," he insisted.

"I doubt that a little birdie just flew by and told him. And he called not two hours after you left here Friday. I find that a little suspicious."

"Andy, did you get me on the television?" he asked excitedly.

"I told him that I would have to talk to you first."

"Talk to me? Why? You know it is what I want."

"But I have these questions. And you are not..." I stopped myself.

"Not what?" he asked.

"I'm not sure you're ready," I responded, making it up as I went along.

"Andy, I am ready. I will be dead if I am not ready. We must do this. Call him back now."

"Wait just a minute," I insisted. "We've got to clear some things up first."

"Call him Andy. Do it now or I will ask Mr. Fabacher to do it."

"What?" I said, slightly intimidated. "Wait, Flipper, I represent you. You said it yourself. If you want me to call him then that is what I will do, and I have every intention of doing just that, but we need to discuss this first. I am your attorney. That is what attorneys do. We discuss things, weigh options, I give you advice. You have to let me do my job."

"Discuss then," he relented, "but hurry."

"The show is on Louisianians that would be royalty. Now how are we going to fit you in that?"

"You mean because I actually am royalty?"

"No. Because you are from Atlantis...you say you are from Atlantis. Not many people here believe in Atlantis."

"This is exactly why I must go on the television and tell them."

"Yes, but to get on television they want you to talk about something else. It is not a show about people that say they are from mythical places."

"It is no myth."

"Maybe not to you, but to about two hundred fifty million Americans it is. If I call this guy and tell him that the Crown Prince of Atlantis is my client and wants to be on the show, I'm liable to end up on the next episode about wacko attorneys. And they wouldn't let you near the studio."

"Yes," he said, "I see your point." He paused for a moment. "What do we do?"

"I don't know," I responded.

"Perhaps we should consult with Mr. Fabacher."

"No, I don't think so," I answered. Don't ask me why I said this. I mean, it would have been the perfect way to get rid of Flipper once and for all. *Excuse me, Mr. Fabacher, our new client would like a word with you. He wants to know how we get around the fact that he is heir apparent to the throne of Atlantis in getting him on the next Angelique Brown Show.* I guess the challenge had gotten to me, the excitement over the possibility of actually getting Flipper on *The Angelique Brown Show* to tell the whole world about Atlantis. There was little possibility that such an opportunity would again present itself in my practice. This would be a war story that I could tell for years to come. My competitive spirit had been aroused and had taken over.

"Maybe..." I began.

"Yes?" Flipper listened attentively.

"We don't necessarily have to tell him now. We can use it to build up the mystique. I could tell him you'll be there Wednesday for the show and we'll reveal your identity then."

"Will that work?" Flipper asked.

"Only one way to find out," I responded, picking up the telephone and re-dialing Mark Jackson's number. This time I was not placed on hold.

"Andy!" Jackson greeted me as though we were best friends.

"Hey Mark," I responded.

"Got some news?"

"As a matter of fact, my client is sitting here with me and he tells me that he is very interested in your offer."

"Super!" he said. "Let me get his demos."

"Excuse me?"

"His demographics. First, who is he?"

"What do you mean, 'who is he'?"

"What country? Your client, what country is he tied to?"

"I can't tell you that right now," I responded.

"We gotta know, Andy. We have to check him out. You would not believe the quacks that we get on this show. People will say anything to get on television. We get calls from Elvis twice a month," he chuckled.

"Well, he's not the crown prince of Graceland," I said.

"Well who then?"

"The Secret Service has instructed me that his identity cannot be revealed prior to his arrival at the studio. It would put him in too much danger."

"The Secret Service?" That had piqued his interest.

"Well, his country's Secret Service," I responded.

"This sounds great. I can't wait to tell Angelique. Look, can you at least give me a hint?"

"I don't know," I hesitated.

"Come on, East or West?" he probed.

"East or West what?" I stalled.

"An Eastern country or a Western country."

"Oh," I thought quickly, "East." Atlantis was in the Atlantic, right? And that was east of New Orleans.

"An Arab?" he asked excitedly.

"I've said too much already."

"I'll run it by Angelique. I don't know...We don't usually like doing this sort of thing. We have to check them out. Look, you're an attorney, can you vouch for the guy?"

Yikes! How to respond to this one? My credibility was on the line. I could not lie.

"Mark," I began, "all I can say is that this guy is real Angelique material. He will give you a show that will not soon be forgotten. He's big, very big."

"Good enough for me," he answered. "I'll just pass it by Angelique and will get back to you this afternoon. Will you be available?"

"Until five," I answered.

"Okay, talk to you before then," he said. "And Andy?"

"Yes?"

"Thanks a million, you don't know what this means to us."

"Sure," I replied, "Talk to you later."

"Okay." He hung up.

I sat with the receiver at my ear for a moment, thinking Flipper would not know that he had hung up, contemplating what I had just done. Too late to turn back now.

"All right, bye," I said into the silent telephone, then hung up.

"Good job, Andy," Flipper said, smiling broadly. "You did not even have to lie."

"Well, I did a good bit of stretching the truth," I responded.

"As any good lawyer would."

I smiled.

"You are saving my life," he added.

"Well you're not on yet. He has to sell it to Angelique. And then we still have to get you in front of the cameras and keep them from kicking you out once they find out who you are."

"Perhaps if we get them to your lake I could show them."

"Show them what?"

"A demonstration. I could go below for a while and then come back up."

"Underwater?" I asked.

"Sure," he said.

"For how long?"

"An hour, two, whatever they like."

"The show is only an hour long," I explained.

"Well, fifteen minutes then."

"We aren't going to get them out there," I said.

"It was only a suggestion."

"You can really do that? Stay under water that long?"

"Can a fish?" he asked earnestly.

"You are not a fish," I reminded him.

"You have never seen me in water."

"What would you do? Go under and just hang out a while? Sit on the bottom?"

"Or swim around, pop up here and there."

"Maybe we could tape it," I thought aloud.

"Tape it?" he asked.

"Yea, video. We could do a video tape."

"How would they know we did not tamper with it?"

"We'd have to prove that we could not have." I wondered whether he was trying to back out of getting into the water.

"How?" he asked.

"My friend Bip has a sail boat. We could film you going in the water and have him sailing around in the background. With him there it would be obvious that we did not cut the film because if we did the boat would be jumping around."

"Would that work?" he asked.

"I don't see why not. Would you do it?"

"Andy, I will do anything to help my cause."

"Today?"

"Right now if you like," he said. He was not backing out.

"No, after five." I said. "I'll call Bip and see if we can set it up. Be in front of the building at five and I'll have him pick us up." Since returning from his Great Aunt's funeral, Bip had been anxious and antsy. I was sure he wouldn't mind helping me out – it would give him something to do.

"Okay," he agreed. He stood and shook my hand.

"Good."

"I knew you would do it," he told me.

"We haven't done it yet," I replied.

"But we shall," he said with a wink, then he turned and walked away.

Once he had left I put the call in to Bip.

THIRTEEN

TRUE TO HIS WORD, MARK JACKSON CALLED ME BACK before the end of the day. He told me that "my client" had been okayed for the show. He tried to sound confidant but his voice betrayed him – he was nervous and I got the impression that he may have stuck his neck out based on my assurances.

After I hung up with Jackson I walked down the hall and brought Fabacher up to date on the matter, omitting any reference to Atlantis, of course. He seemed pleased that I had been able to facilitate a television appearance so soon. Being no fool, I took all of the credit and did not bother explaining how it had all just fallen into my lap.

I had given Bip very few details over the telephone, telling him only that we had a new client that Fabacher was really on my back about and that I needed to video tape him at the lake, which would require the use of Bip's boat and video camera. I cut him off after he had agreed to pick us up, before he had a chance to ask any of his usual one million questions. He pulled up in front of my office building at precisely 5:15.

I took the front seat and directed Flipper into the back. Somehow in the few hours since I had seen him last, Flipper's odor had gotten much worse. Bip's eyes locked on Flipper and then he shot a horrified look at me as we climbed in. I had betrayed him.

"Hey," I said as amiably as I could.

"Hey," he responded with the same look.

I knew the exact moment that Bip had got the first whiff of Flipper. His face had contorted as though he had just swallowed a mouthful of lemon juice. Flipper's was the kind of smell that ruined a car, its resale value declining further each minute that he sat inside. Bip immediately turned the air conditioner fan to "high" and opened the sunroof, then pulled away from the curb in a huff.

We had a long, mostly silent trip to the lake. Flipper looked out of the window, wide-eyed like a child on his first ride, intently watching everything we passed. Bip appeared to be holding his breath, the color of his face alternating between red to green; green when he breathed, red when he did not. The lake was a good thirty minute drive in rush hour traffic and my stomach was turning cartwheels by the time we got there. Bip drove as fast as possible, screeching to a halt and jumping out of the car as soon as we had reached the boat slips.

"Stay here a second," I told Flipper as I went to speak to Bip.

"Get him out of the car," Bip, red in the face, demanded as quietly as possible. "I'll never get that smell out of there."

"Look, I'm sorry," I explained. "I had no choice."

"Bullshit," he said, no longer attempting to whisper, "you could have loaded him in your Jeep."

"I didn't have time. He's gonna be taping an *Angelique Brown Show* segment the day after tomorrow."

"So?" he said, unfazed.

"I had to do this tonight and I didn't have time to go back and get the Jeep. Look, it's gonna get dark soon, can we just get it over with?"

"Get what over with?" he demanded.

"He says he's from Atlantis," I began to explain.

"Huh?" Bip said, as though he had not heard me correctly.

"He says he can stay under water for hours. Says he can breathe underwater."

"Right."

"Seriously."

"Cut the bullshit," Bip said, losing patience.

"I'm not bullshitting," I insisted. "He says he's from Atlantis."

"So he's crazy. Why are we here?"

"I'm not so sure," I said.

"You're not sure why we're here?"

"No, I'm not sure he's crazy."

"Have you lost your mind?"

"You haven't heard him, or really seen him," I said.

"I don't have to, Andy, because I am sane and as a sane person I know that Atlantis does not exist."

"I'm just gonna tape him. Did you bring the camera?"

"Tape him doing what?" Bip asked.

"Going underwater," I said.

"Andy, he can't breathe underwater. He's a bum, for Pete's sake!"

"Look," I replied, attempting to sound at least a little sane, "you know that he can't and I know that he can't, but he doesn't know it."

"What's your point?"

"He's got Fabacher all over my ass. He signed a contract with the firm and we're supposed to promote him."

"What?" he said, laughing.

"He's gonna write a book."

"Keating & Fabacher is representing a man that says he can breathe underwater? What do you mean promote him? You're all nuts." He couldn't believe it.

"Bip, my job is on the line," I said.

"Your ass is going to be on the line when the police pull his lifeless body out of the water and then they find out that you stood around and videotaped his drowning."

"Look," I offered, "we can tie a rope around him."

"You're totally fucking crazy. We'd both go to jail. Does Keating know what you're doing?"

I didn't answer.

"Mr. Keating? Does he know?"

Bip wasn't going to let up. "No," I said meekly.

Bip laughed a little more and gave me a look like he really thought that I may be crazy. We just stood there looking at one another.

"Bip," I made a final attempt, "can you just go out and sail around in a circle about twenty yards offshore?"

"Why?" he asked.

"'Cause I need a point of reference," I explained.

"For what?" he asked.

"So we can prove he isn't a fake." As soon as I had spoken the words I realized just how insane it all sounded. Of course he was a fake, there was no way he could breathe underwater. I had been, and apparently still was, a fool.

Bip did not know what to say. He just stood there, looking at me. Then something extraordinary happened.

"Andy!" Flipper called.

I turned toward the car. Flipper was not there.

"Andy," he called again. His voice was coming from behind me. Bip and I both turned to see.

Flipper stood on the deck of Bip's sailboat. He was completely naked, his genitalia hanging for all to see.

"Oh my God," Bip uttered.

"Flipper!" I yelled, "Get off of there, put your clothes on."

"What does he have on his feet?" Bip asked.

"Those *are* his feet," I answered.

"Get him off of my boat, Andy!"

"Come on," I called to Flipper, "we aren't going to do it here," I said.

Flipper just smiled. Then he waved and jumped, feet first, into the lake.

Bip and I were both horrified. We ran to the boat and looked over the side. There was no sign of him, not so much as a bubble.

"If he drowns they'll try us for murder!" Bip said frantically.

I ripped off my coat and tie, then my shirt, shoes, and pants. Clad only in my underwear, I dove into the murky water to search for Flipper. Bip undressed, only a little slower, and joined me. We alternated between diving under and treading water while calling Flipper's name. We checked all around the boat, between the slips, out into the lake.

There was a petroleum-based film on the water's surface that burned our noses and eyes as we swam past old shoes and bottles and a condom tied off at one end. Shell dredging in the lake had raked up so much muck from the bottom over the years that visibility under water was about half an inch, so we basically had to feel our way around, dreading success, which, of course, would mean making contact with his lifeless body. We kept going until we were near the point of exhaustion, in danger of drowning ourselves. Finally, our bodies failing us and in despair, we both climbed back onto the boat.

"You motherfucker," Bip cursed me between heaves of air. "You are going to ruin me because of some low-life, homeless, drowned, son-of-a-bitch like that."

"We need to get the fire department," I said.

"No, Andy, the coroner," Bip corrected me. "There is no saving him now. He's been under too long." Then, after a short pause, "Did anybody see us with him?"

I knew what he was getting at. "I'm gonna use your radio and call the cops," I told him. "Keep your eyes open for him."

"No," Bip said in a panic, "I'll radio, you keep looking." Bip stood and headed toward the cabin.

The slip was formed out of concrete, so there was nothing for Flipper to hide under or against. We had searched the sides of the slip and all around the boat. He had sunk like a rock and had not come back up. Still, I looked frantically around for signs of him. All the while, I was considering my fate. What would I tell the police? Fabacher? My mother? Bip was right, it could mean jail, ruination. I looked back and saw Bip just standing at the cabin door. I ran back toward him, furious.

"Bip, we have to call for help!"

He did not respond. He just stood there, paralyzed.

"Bip!" I screamed, "Snap out of it! The longer we wait the worse it is going to get."

I went up to him and began shaking him.

"Andy!"

It wasn't Bip.

I looked toward the bow, following Bip's eyes. Flipper was floating, lying on his back in the water, using his massive flippers to keep himself afloat. He wore a huge smile on his face which was, of course, the only thing he was wearing. He had been underwater for at least fifteen minutes.

Bip and I turned to one another in amazement.

"Get the camera," he said.

FOURTEEN

WE GOT HOME WELL AFTER DARK, the three of us. Bip had insisted on bringing Flipper back to our house. I suppose that after he had seen what Flipper was, he immediately realized his potential for profit. Bip saw himself as the next P.T. Barnum and he wanted a piece of the action.

"You know, *The Angelique Brown Show* doesn't pay," Bip told me as we climbed the steps to our apartment.

"What do you mean?" I asked.

"They don't pay you anything, not like some of those shows."

"What shows?"

"Any of the big ones."

"Like *The Tonight Show*?" I asked.

"No," he said, disgusted, "the ones like that new show, *Peepers.* They pay the big bucks."

"How do you know?" I asked, reaching the top of the stairs and beginning to unlock the door.

"I read about it. They paid that sex-slave woman a hundred and fifty grand for her story."

"Really?"

"Shit yea," he said, "even the tabloids pay big bucks."

"He's not interested in the money," I responded, opening the door and going inside.

"Great," Bip said, following, "we can talk about it later."

I held the door open for Flipper and then locked it behind him. He seemed awestruck by our home.

"I'm sorry," Flipper turned to me, "I need to defecate. I should have gone at the lake but I didn't realize. Could you tell me where?"

"Sure, follow me," I immediately spoke up then directed him to Bip's bathroom. I closed the door for him after he had gone in and held back my laugh until I returned to where Bip was.

"You motherfu..." he stopped as Bets came into the room. I was still laughing.

"What is that smell?" Bets asked.

I laughed all the harder.

"Andy's friend," Bip tattled.

"You're the one who invited him over," I said, still laughing.

"You could have shown him your bathroom," Bip said.

"Who?" Bets asked.

"A homeless guy," Bip explained.

"A streetperson?" Bets asked, suddenly frightened.

"He's a client," I said.

"You're representing streetpeople now?" she asked.

"Just one," I said seriously. "But he's not just a street person," I quickly added.

"What is he, then?" she asked.

"The Crown Prince of Atlantis," I answered, beginning another round of laughter.

"Ha Ha," she said.

"Don't say anything yet," Bip cautioned her.

"What do you mean?"

"He may just be who he says," Bip answered.

"Atlantis as in sliding into the sea Atlantis?" she asked.

"That's the one," I said.

"Right," she answered, thinking we were making fun of her.

"Wait until you see the tape," I said, "then decide."

"What tape?"

"The one we just made," I answered.

Bip set a curious look on his face, then walked toward the bathroom. "I thought he said he had to take a dump."

"He did," I laughed.

"He's got the bath running."

"And you're complaining?" I asked.

"Is that smell really a person?" Bets asked.

Both Bip and I shook our heads in the affirmative.

"Let him take the bath," she told Bip, "and show me the tape."

Just as we began to walk toward the den to play the tape, the bathroom door opened and we all turned and looked. Flipper, naked from the waist down and dripping wet, stood in the hallway looking at us.

"Do you have some more towels?" he asked.

We all stood there dazed for a moment. Why was he so wet?

"I made quite a mess," he continued.

"I'll get the towels," Bip said, jumping into action, concerned about his bathroom.

Flipper turned and went back into the bathroom as Bip retrieved several towels from the hall closet. He purposefully grabbed three of my towels, the big, soft fluffy kind, that I had purchased for mine and Bets' exclusive use, then hurried off to the bathroom.

"Uuuuhhhhhh!" we heard Bip exclaim loudly and with obvious disgust.

"I can only go while submerged," Flipper explained.

"Andyeeeeee!"

Bets and I hurried into the den to get the tape going.

FIFTEEN

AFTER THAT EVENING AT THAT LAKE, I was convinced that there was something very special about Flipper. Something in my conservative, Catholic upbringing was still resisting the notion that he could actually be from Atlantis, but I had come to believe in him as someone "not of this world." I was not sure where he was from, and even if he was from *there* he still could have been a little cuckoo. But I believed that he had been sent here, and to me, for a purpose. That made a lot of difference as to what I was to be willing to do to help him. I was still struggling, something like St. Peter sinking in the sea of Galilee, but he had me hooked on a far deeper level than I realized at the time.

The morning we did *The Angelique Brown Show* I had Flipper meet me at my office thirty minutes before taping was to begin. He was supposed to be on the set an hour earlier than that but I was taking no chances. I wanted them to have as little time as possible to talk to him before the shooting began.

Mark Jackson had already called me three times before Flipper arrived. I told him that my client was busy with matters of state and that Angelique would just have to wait. I tried to avoid answering any questions about whom my client actually was, but Jackson explained that it had reached the point where they could not let him on the show unless they had at least some background information on him.

"Well, who is he?" Jackson demanded.

"His name is Christian Waterman," I replied.

"Waterman? What kind of name is that?"

"A last name," I answered smartly.

"I mean what ethnic origin?"

"Got me."

"Cut the bullshit, Jordan. What country is he from?"

"Muldavi," I answered off the top of my head.

"Muldavi?" Jackson questioned.

"Yea, Muldavi," I said confidently.

"That's Middle Eastern, isn't it," he asked.

"Mark, you don't know where Muldavi is?"

"Well, yes, generally," he responded, "but I don't have a map right here. Can you at least give me some demographics?"

"What do you want?" I asked, prepared to make up whatever I had to.

"Like do they have oil? What is their main source of wealth? Who's the leader? That kinda stuff," he responded.

"It's a country of fishermen. Everybody there eats fish, lots of it, they are very plentiful," I answered.

"It's got a lot of water around it?" he asked.

"Yea, you could definitely say that."

"What about oil, they have to have oil, huh?"

"Yea, Mark, lots of oil. The king's name is Dog, Dog Waterman."

"Dog?" he asked.

"Yea, bark, bark. Dog," I answered.

"Like God backwards?"

I hadn't thought of that.

"They are a nation of extremely good swimmers and I would not be surprised if they begin dominating the Olympic swimming events."

"Like Kenya and cross country?"

"Exactly," I said.

"Well, what's he doing in New Orleans?"

"His father asked him to come."

"For what?"

"He's got a message to deliver to the U.S.…actually to the world…and he wants to use your show to do it," I said.

"Wait a minute, what are you talking about?"

"He has a diplomatic message to deliver to our country and he wants to begin with your show."

"What kind of message?" Jackson asked skeptically.

"A good one. It has to do with the environment," I responded.

"What's going on, Jordan?"

"Nothing's going on. You wanted royalty and you got royalty. Listen, you're getting an exclusive here, it's all going to start on your program. Angelique's going to break the story."

"What story?" he demanded.

"Look, Mark, it's getting late here, we barely have enough time to make it down there now. I have a tape that I'm bringing that explains it all."

"A tape?"

"We'll see you in a minute," I said, hanging up the phone before he had a chance to respond.

Flipper had showered and shaved and was wearing the same cheap suit that he had worn on the day he had met Fabacher. I had had it dry cleaned and pressed for him. We walked together, through downtown, and into the French Quarter, to where the studio was located. Along the way I tried to coach Flipper as best I could. I explained to him what I had told Mark Jackson and that they believed he was heir to the throne of Muldavi, a country that did not exist.

We entered the studio and were immediately taken to the set. There were five chairs, three of which were occupied by other supposed "royalty," which left one for Flipper and one for Angelique. A very nervous Mark Jackson met us and I handed him the tape.

"What is this?" he demanded.

"You won't believe it," I responded, "but you are going to need it."

"You're very late. Angelique is back there and she is fit to be tied. She cannot stand being made to wait. Are you guys ready?"

"Sure, which seat do you want him in?"

"Either one, y'all decide," Jackson answered. I thought the response very strange.

"Well which one does Angelique sit in?" I asked.

"Angelique doesn't sit, she stands, wanders in and out of the audience."

"Oh, so someone else is later than us," I said, more relaxed.

"No, you're the last two."

"Then why two chairs?" I asked.

"Angelique stands, you guys sit. Now get up there," he gave me a little shove.

"What?" I was confused.

"We're way behind. Get on stage so we can begin," he insisted.

"Me? Not me," I said in a low but forceful voice.

"Yes, both of you," he said.

"No, wait, I'm not part of this."

"You're on," he insisted.

"I can't," I said, "I'm an attorney, I can't just go on a show…"

"If you're not on, he's not on."

"What is this?" I demanded.

"Look," Jackson responded, looking me squarely in the eye, "I don't know what you two have going on, but I'm not going to be the fall guy. If your man is legit then you've got nothing to worry about and you'll get your ass up there. If he isn't then you won't and I don't have to worry about his turning this show into a huge fiasco. I wanted a pre-interview, you knew that, and I didn't get it and this is the only way to protect myself."

The show's theme music began playing in the studio.

"All right, here she comes," Jackson, snapping into action, yelled to the crew. "Roll tape!"

Flipper pulled at my arm, "Come on, Andy, we must go up."

"I can't," I said as Flipper dragged me toward the stage.

"It will be fine," he said, "it's the only way."

Suddenly the audience section was filled with light and Angelique appeared at the top of the grandstand. She flashed her trademark smile and then began her monologue about royal blood in Louisiana. Flipper sat next to the guy from Des Allemands and I sat in the last chair on the end.

After Angelique's monologue there was a commercial break and Angelique made her way down the grandstand. She was much shorter in person than she appeared on television. In fact, she was only about an inch this side of elfdom. She bounced down the grandstand, her little legs stretching between the steps, barely long enough to descend them without having to step twice on each one. She had black and grey wiry hair and as she neared I could see that her eyes were black, so black that you could not see where her pupils began and the rest of her eyes ended. One of her little hands grasped the microphone, her fingers not long enough to reach entirely around, as her other waved enthusiastically tovarious members of the audience.

I tried to call Jackson over but as soon as we made eye contact the bright lights were turned toward the stage and I was completely blinded. As I raised a hand toward the light it was suddenly shaded by the short, dark figure that had appeared on stage. Angelique.

I was a ball of nerves, physically shaking for the first fifteen minutes of the show. Luckily Angelique had begun introducing guests from the other end of the row which gave me a little time to calm down and to think of a safe way to explain my involvement in this whole mess. I had just stopped shaking when she started in on Muldavi.

The thought of running away suddenly occurred to me. However, the cameras had already gotten a couple of shots of my face and my disappearance would have caused quite a scene. Besides, I figured that if things started to turn bad and I stuck it out on stage, at least I would be in a position to provide a little damage control and to hopefully save the firm some embarrassment.

There was another commercial break, which should not have lasted very long since we were only taping the show, but Angelique was called away from the stage. In a short time Angelique reappeared, her smile no longer apparent, and her gaze fixed upon me.

"Are you ready, Mr. Jordan?" she asked.

Her question caught me by surprise. She was obviously upset. I opened my mouth to answer but the lights blinded me again before I had a chance to get a word out.

"Our next guest is a gentleman by the name of Christian Waterman, the Crown Prince of, let me see if I got this right, is it Muldavi, Mr. Waterman?"

Flipper just smiled.

"Mr. Waterman?" she repeated.

"Yes?" he responded.

"You are from Muldavi?"

"No, Ma'am."

"No?" she asked curtly.

"No, not Muldavi," he said.

"I'm sorry, then where is it that you are from?"

"Blub a blub a dub a blub blub," he answered. The audience broke into laughter.

"Excuse me?" she said.

"Blub a blub a dub a blub blub," he repeated, setting the audience off again. Angelique turned briefly to the crowd, forced a smile, then turned to me.

"Perhaps your attorney could answer the question for us. I would like to introduce Mr. Andrew Jordan of the New Orleans law firm of Keating & Fabacher. Is that correct, Mr. Jordan?"

"Uh, yes," I responded. I smiled nervously.

"Mr. Jordan, you and your firm represent Mr. Waterman, isn't that correct?"

"Yes, Angelique, it is."

"I understand from our program coordinator that you represented to him that you had a client who was the Crown Prince of the nation of Muldavi and that Mr. Waterman is he. Is that also correct?" She did not mince words. It had come down to this, admit to the fraud or lie and deny the whole thing.

"Well, Angelique," I began, having no idea of what I would say next. "Mr. Waterman came to our firm just last week and requested that we represent him in certain matters pertaining to his current situation. We, of course, accepted. Then I got a call from a Mr. Mark Jackson of your show who had heard of Mr. Waterman." I was rambling on, burning up air-time, avoiding the question.

"Is Mr. Waterman the Crown Prince of Muldavi?" she asked again.

I froze momentarily. I had to answer the question. I ran the options repeatedly through my head. Admit to fraud or lie? Admit to fraud or lie? Admit to fraud or lie?

"Muldavia," Flipper interrupted.

He caught Angelique off guard. She had me by the balls and knew it and Flipper hit her from behind. I was starting to really like the guy.

"Excuse me?" Angelique questioned him.

"Muldavia," Flipper repeated.

"Muldavia?" Angelique repeated. "Okay, so you are not from Muldavi, but from Muldavia?" she asked.

"That is correct," Flipper responded. "This is all new to Mr. Jordan and he obviously got the pronunciation wrong. The nation's name is Muldavia."

"Mr. Waterman," she turned on Flipper, "there is no nation named Muldavia."

"Not in your language," he replied.

This too caught Angelique off guard. Suddenly she realized that perhaps Flipper was from a legitimate country and had provided the name in his own tongue. She became more cautious.

"It's Muldavia in your language?" she asked, meekly.

"That is correct," Flipper responded.

"I am so sorry. Please, what does that translate to in English?"

Out of the frying pan and into the fire. I knew that the answer to the question would bring us right back to where we had just been. I had to get us out of there before my life and career were ruined.

"At..." Flipper began, but I interrupted him.

"I don't think you should answer any more questions, Mr. Waterman. It is obvious that this program is not going to treat you with the respect that you deserve."

"It is all right, Andy," Flipper responded.

"No, really, I must advise you," I continued, standing to leave, "don't say another word."

"The answer to your question, Miss," Flipper continued to Angelique, "is Atlantis."

I froze, shut up, sat down, and buried my face in my hands.

"Excuse me?" Angelique asked, her confidence renewed, her voice once again terse.

"Observe," Christian said.

All was silent. I removed a hand from my face in time to see Flipper pull his massive left foot out of his shoe.

"Oh my God!" the man from Des Allemands gasped.

The audience drew a collective breath.

"Oh, fuck," I said under my breath.

Angelique stood in amazement.

Christian followed with the other shoe then held both of his feet up to the cameras and waved them back and forth. Angelique walked over to examine them more closely.

"Angelique," a voice was heard over the loudspeaker. She stopped and turned around. "We're going to stop the tape. Please come to the control booth."

The audience was a-buzz with whispers, the cameras were all focused on Flipper's feet, which were visible on all of the studio monitors. Suddenly all the monitors went blank.

Forty-five minutes after she had been called away, Angelique returned. She apologized to the unhappy audience and to the rest of her guests and then explained that the taping was concluded for the day. She then asked Flipper and I to follow her to an office in the studio.

We left the set and followed her, as requested, entering a room with a long table and several chairs. Mark Jackson and two other men were already seated when we walked in.

"Mr. Jordan, Mr. Waterman." A tall, blond man, closest to the door, stood up and introduced himself. "I'm Bill Sommers, the station manager, and this is Leroy Nelson, the producer. I think you know everyone else."

"Yes. Hello." I responded.

"Please have a seat," Sommers said kindly.

After we were seated, Mr. Sommers continued. "Mr. Jordan, we have a slight problem here."

Although I sensed that he expected some sort of reply, I just sat and looked at him.

"Perhaps in this environment," Sommers finally continued, looking around the room, "you can level with us and tell us just what the fuck it is that you are trying to do."

"We're supposed to be on *The Angelique Brown Show*," I defended.

"This is a segment about persons with royal blood," Angelique interrupted, "and your client is here wearing flippers."

"My client is royalty," I answered.

"That's right," she continued, "Mr. Waterman just translated the word 'Muldavia' for us. Why don't you go ahead and tell us again just where that is now, Mr. Waterman."

"I'm speaking for Mr. Waterman and am advising him not to answer any further questions." I knew we were safe as long as they did not know whether Muldavia was a real place or not. Flipper's blurting out Atlantis could be explained away. I could go back to the office and find some place that could be Muldavia, perhaps some principality before one of the World Wars, anything to avoid the fraud.

"Andy," Flipper addressed me, "we must answer the question."

"Flipper," I answered, breaking into a sweat, "we don't owe them anything. In fact," I paused for effect, "I am considering taking legal action against the station for the way in which they have treated you and have insinuated from the very beginning that you were lying." I had them, if only he would keep his mouth shut.

"Flipper?" Angelique questioned, with a sarcastic grin.

"Mr. Jordan," Sommers spoke again, "if he is for real then what is this tape all about?"

The tape. I had forgotten about the tape.

"I'm sorry?" I asked, looking as Sommers lifted my tape in his left hand.

"This tape right here," he said.

"Oh. You mean Mr. Waterman's demonstration of his swimming ability?"

"I mean this piece of special effects that I am holding here. The one with the Crown Prince of Muldavia disappearing into Lake Pontchartrain while some sailboat circles in the background."

"Yes. What about it?" I had nothing else to say.

"Why did you give us this?" Sommers asked.

I had no response.

"Because Andy Jordan is a decent and smart man," Flipper answered. I made no attempt to keep him quiet, realizing that the situation could hardly get any worse.

"Do you want to explain that?" Mark Jackson requested.

"Because he knew that you would not believe me, that you would think that I was a crazy man whom he found living on the street and had brought onto your show under false pretenses so that he and his firm could make a little money."

So I was wrong. It could get worse.

"What does a tape with you submerging yourself have to do with us believing whether or not you are from Muldavia?" Jackson asked.

"Because Muldavia is really Atlantis," Flipper answered.

There would be no turning back now.

"I told you he said Atlantis!" Angelique exclaimed.

"Atlantis, the underwater land that your people for centuries have hypothecated about. We actually exist."

"Atlantis?" Sommers asked in disbelief, looking toward Mark Jackson. Jackson buried his head in his arms.

"Atlantis?" Sommers repeated, this time laughing a bit. "Mr. Jordan, were you aware of this when you attempted to get Mr. Waterman on this show?"

"Yes," I answered meekly.

"I think we have heard enough." Sommers ended. "You will be hearing from the station's attorneys." He stood up to leave.

"Bill..." Mr. Nelson spoke up.

Sommers stopped and looked toward Nelson.

"I just want to check something out," Nelson said.

Sommers sat down.

"Mr. Waterman," Nelson continued, "may I please see your feet?"

"For Christ's sake, Leroy!" Angelique exclaimed.

"Angelique, we all saw the tape," Nelson answered. "I just want to see this before I draw any conclusions."

Flipper took off his shoes and put his feet on the table. As Nelson examined them, Mark Jackson got out of his chair and came around to get a closer look.

"They're real," Nelson said after several minutes.

"What's that prove?" Angelique said. "It's a birth defect. Do you think he's from Atlantis?"

"I think he's got the biggest set of webbed feet that I or anyone else has ever seen and that he can either hold his breath for fifteen minutes or he can breathe underwater," Nelson responded.

"The tape's a fake, it's got to be," Angelique answered.

"Rodney took it apart. There is no splicing, no stopping. It hasn't been over-dubbed or altered in any way. This man disappeared into the lake and came out fifteen minutes later without any apparent ill effects to his health. Now I don't know where he's from, Atlanta or Atlantis, Muldavia or Mars, but this is big. This is news. And big news means big attention – national, Angelique, national attention. You want to take the show nationally and this might just be your opportunity."

"Are you insane, Leroy? Go national with 'Flipper - The Man From Atlantis'? They'd laugh us right out of the market," Angelique answered.

"Not the 'Man From Atlantis'. The 'Man-with-webbed-feet-who-can-hold-his-breath-for-a-damned-unbelievably-long-time," Jackson shot back.

"Bill," Angelique looked for support, "you can't go along with this. It's insanity."

"Leroy," Sommers began, "you think this would do it?"

"Hell, Bill, I don't know. But I do know that we ain't gonna get it with the Count D' Pontchartrain's oyster-fishing, eighteenth cousin twice removed from Bogalusa..."

"He's from Des Allemands and it's the Duke of Orleans," Angelique corrected him.

"I don't give a damn if he's the King of England," Leroy continued, "this is the most newsworthy human interest story that we've had around here for a long time. Everybody does all that other crap, fad diets, extra-marital affairs with their mother-in-law, bisexual twins. Nobody has this."

"It's risky," Sommers cautioned.

"We can control that," Nelson responded. "We can build slowly, see how it works itself out."

"Bill," Angelique pleaded.

"Might work," Sommers answered Nelson. "But my friend, you are going to be responsible. It's your baby, you'll have to stay on top of it, keep control."

"Absolutely," Nelson replied.

"All right then," Sommers said, standing from the table. "It's in your hands," he continued, heading for the door.

"Bill, wait," Angelique continued.

"You two work it out," he responded, opening the door.

"Bill," Angelique called.

He walked out and she got up and followed him, pausing to shoot a nasty look at Nelson, then slammed the door shut behind her.

"All right," Nelson said, turning to Flipper and me. "Let's talk."

SIXTEEN

THINGS REALLY BEGAN TO TAKE OFF AFTER *The Angelique Brown Show* incident. Apparently, all of those nightly gossip shows maintain spies across the nation whose duty it is to report any possible sleazy or interesting or sleazy and interesting news stories back to them. Their moles on *The Angelique Brown Show* wasted no time in telling them about Flipper and sending them bootleg copies of the tape we had made at the lake. By the time I got to my office the next morning I had messages waiting from three shows' executive producers. By midday, and following several telephone conversations with those executives and Bill Sommers, I had the pleasure of informing Mr. Sommers that my client was no longer interested in appearing on *The Angelique Brown Show* and that we had decided upon a show with more "national appeal." Flipper was going to air his story on *Peepers*, a new entry in the "sleaze T.V." market out of New York.

What I failed to mention to Sommers was that the show's executive producer, one James "Jimbo" McClean, had made me an offer that I could not refuse. The deal included a $150,000.00 purchase price for the exclusive rights to Flipper's story. Instead I told Sommers that we had been assured a much larger audience and that we would be treated with dignity, unlike our unfortunate experience with *The Angelique Brown Show*. When Sommers finally offered me $5,000.00, I was tempted to tell him what an insult that was and where he should shove it. Instead I politely declined, told him that it was not about money, and hung up the telephone.

When I told Flipper about the money he did not bat an eye. When I told him we were going to reach a national audience I thought he was going to cry. Whatever Christian Waterman was, he was not in this for the money. The same did not hold true, however, for Keating & Fabacher. When Fabacher found out about the $150,000.00, I thought he was going to cry as well. Almost immediately he wanted to up Flipper's retainer to $20,000.00. I explained to him that Christian Waterman did not have that kind of money and that *Peepers* would only pay 10 percent up front and the balance after the entire story had been shot. He finally relented, but insisted that he be kept up to date on all developments in the matter – so that he could bill accordingly for his time, no doubt.

Thanks to Flipper, "Intellectual Property" was no longer a backwater, dead-end position at Keating & Fabacher. Overnight Christian Waterman had become one of our larger and most important clients, and the firm stood to gain national recognition as his legal counsel. J. Ryan nearly stopped speaking to me altogether. I could understand that he was pissed. Just as it appeared he was going to be squeezed out of the firm, fate had reached down and rescued him, leaving my job in peril. Then, suddenly, and without even trying, I had succeeded in turning that situation completely around and had once again become the prototypical fair-haired boy of the office. Yep, good ole Flipper had put me back on top and this time I was there to stay.

The people at *Peepers* wanted to begin shooting the following week. Before that could happen, though, they insisted on having an in-depth interview with Flipper and on seeing a live demonstration of his underwater miracle. Their reporter, Amy Star, was flying down to New Orleans that evening and planned to begin the process first thing Saturday morning. There was an inordinate amount of work necessary to make sure that everything ran smoothly and by noon on Friday I had all of the details worked out – and I was exhausted.

At lunch time I bumped into Carly. She was getting on the elevator at the first floor as I was getting off. She gave me one of those big smiles that could melt a glacier and I gave her an excited, "Hey!" I tried to get her to miss the elevator and talk for a second but she wanted to ride up with the girlfriend that she was with. She gave me one of those you-had-your-chance-and-missed-it looks. It was strange, but my heart was pounding in my throat. I wasn't very hungry after that, thinking back to the weekend and the great time we had had at lunch.

I hadn't seen her again until just then, hadn't even bothered calling her. She had told me where she worked, Parsons or something like that, but I had not even tried to find it. The truth of the matter was that I had been feeling very guilty about having had such a great time with her, about having done that to Bets, especially now that we knew each other in the "family way" again. I had thought the lunch with Carly was just a fluke that I would get over, but now I was not so sure.

I decided to skip lunch and go back up to work. I found it hard to concentrate, so I started making phone calls, first to Bip and then to Bets.

Bip really surprised me in all of this. He and I were best friends, but Bip was somewhat of an elitist and I fully expected the bathtub incident to completely end any and all involvement that he was to have with Flipper. I had felt bad even mentioning his name after that. But as soon as I told Bip about *Peepers* coming down to do the story he offered the use of his boat and insisted that Flipper stay with us until the whole matter was concluded. I told him that the firm would spring for a hotel room but he said that my future was riding on Flipper and that if I let him out of my sight I should have my head examined. Of course, he did make one demand – that Flipper be allowed to use only my bathroom. I cringed, but agreed.

Flipper met me in front of my building at exactly 5:15 p.m. and Bip brought us home. Luckily Flipper had bathed (who knows where) and his odor was at a minimum. The drive was pleasant and though I don't remember what we talked about, I do recall that it was a surprisingly normal conversation.

After I had spoken to Bip earlier in the day, I had placed the call to Bets informing her that Flipper would be staying with us for a few days. She was a little less enthused than Bip had been.

"Andy, he stinks."

"Because he sleeps on the street."

"He's gross. You saw what he did to Bip's bathroom."

"I know," I replied, choosing not to reveal my deal with Bip at that particular moment.

"Where does he..." she hesitated "...go when he's on the street?"

"I asked him. He said fountains mostly. Swimming pools if he can find them, or even the river."

"That's just too weird. He's not normal."

"Look, he thinks he's like a fish, he doesn't know any other way. He says the water loosens his sphincter..."

She stopped me there. "Never mind! I'm sorry I asked."

"I know it's disgusting, but *Peepers* is paying him $150,000.00 to be on their show. I can't afford to let anything happen to him."

"150,000.00?" She asked, shocked.

"And I have a feeling that's just the beginning."

"That's not fair. What's he gonna do with that kind of money?"

"I don't think he really cares."

"Yea, right."

"Honestly. He just wants to make his point and scoot on out of town."

"And what about the money?"

"Well, I'm kind of hoping he might let me invest some of it for him."

Her end went silent.

"Hello," I prodded.

"What time are you going home?"

"As soon as I can get out of here."

"Great, I'll make dinner."

"Okay," I said, preparing to hang up.

"Andy?"

"Yea?" I responded. Her voice sounded a little strange, as though it were cracking.

"I love you."

The words took me by surprise.

"Me too," was all I could say.

"Hurry home."

"I will," I answered, smiling. Then I hung up.

We got home about the normal time, but found Bets already there. She greeted us all warmly, including Flipper, insisting that he "make himself right at home."

All of her resistance to him had dissipated and it didn't take a rocket scientist to figure out why. It was the money. It excited her and to be honest it affected me somewhat as well. Flipper was going to be swimming off to Atlantis soon and he would have no use for $150,000.00 less attorney's fees. If it were going to be wasted, I'd just as soon he leave it in the care of his new best friend.

Bets cooked chicken that night, which Flipper refused to eat, politely of course. He said he was only accustomed to eating sea creatures and did not want to develop an appetite for anything that he would not be able to eat in the future. There were no chickens in the ocean and he did not want to be craving any once he was back home. Instead, he consumed three cans of sardines from our "Hurricane Emergency Supplies" which we had packed away in the back of the pantry years earlier. He ate every last sardine then drank the juice when he was done.

After dinner we all sat around and talked long into the night. Flipper and Bets did nearly all of the talking, mostly about pollution and the environment and how humans were destroying it. Flipper told emotional stories of various citizens of Atlantis, many dear friends of his, who had met their untimely ends due, at least indirectly, to humans. One couple had happened upon a toxic dump site in the ocean and were horribly disfigured and suffered greatly before they both finally expired. Years earlier, with the advent of the steam engine, countless others had been struck in various parts of their bodies by ships' propellers and were disfigured or killed before the population finally learned that they could no longer swim alongside our seagoing vessels. This, he claimed, explained why there had been no sightings of mermaids since the era of the great sailing ships.

I am not certain how much of this Bip or Bets, or even I, believed. I was convinced that Flipper believed it and I don't think that any of us discounted him entirely. Ever since that evening at the lake, when Flipper disappeared beneath the water twice, Bip and I were not so certain anymore that Atlantis was a mythical place, that it did not actually exist, and that Flipper was not its messenger, bringing humans a warning about the way we live and the way it affects every living thing on our planet.

Bets ended the conversation by saying good night, but only after she had first planted her little seed. With Flipper in an emotional upheaval over the destruction being wrought by humans upon the innocents of his world she had said, "Wouldn't it be wonderful if there was an organization that did nothing but concern itself with the environment, with what we are doing to the environment, and funded projects to put a stop to it?" When I suggested that she look into GreenPeace or the Sierra Club she scolded me, informing me that, in her opinion, those groups had become too political and that what was needed was an organization answerable to no one, one that did not have to spend significant resources on management and fund raising, an organization headed by one woman whose sole concern was to rescue the planet, for only a woman could truly appreciate what was being done to "Mother Nature."

"Or at least to rescue Atlantis," Flipper added.

Bets just smiled and nodded in agreement, then she had bade us all a good night.

We made it through the night without hearing the water run in the bath tub, for which we were all thankful. The next morning we all rushed to get him out of the house before the "urge" hit him. We walked around the corner and had breakfast at La Madeleine French Bakery and Cafe, and then Flipper, Bets, Bip, and I all got into Bip's car and went downtown to meet Amy Star.

SEVENTEEN

SEPTEMBER HAD JUST BEGUN and the first cool snap of Autumn had hit Louisiana. An Arctic blast had finally pushed its way past Lake Pontchartrain and into the seething city below. Actually, by the time that great northern system had met with the heat wave that had held us in its grip for the previous three months, there was little "cool" left in the front. What it did accomplish, however, was to cause a dramatic drop in the humidity level, which made it feel much cooler and added crispness to the air. It was one of my favorite times of the year, when you know that fall is just around the corner for New Orleans – no more than another month or three away.

Flipper was a little congested that morning, continually heaving up mucus and spitting it out. I was worried that the change in weather might affect him, prevent him from making his scheduled departure.

"You feel all right?" I asked him on the ride over.

"Very much so," he replied, "never better."

"Does the water temperature affect you at all?" Bets wanted to know.

"No," he answered. "The salinity level does, though. That is the only thing that concerns me about this lake, freshwater intrusion."

"How salty does it have to be?" I jumped in with new concern.

"Enough to breathe."

"How much is that?"

"You just know it when you see it."

"You can tell by just looking at the water?" Bip asked.

"Certainly," Flipper said confidently.

"Wow," Bets said.

"Amazing," Bip added.

"I can tell by the color. If it is not right I would suffocate and die, much like a fish out of water."

"Or a saltwater fish in freshwater," I spoke up.

Bip and Bets looked at me as though I had said something stupid. It made perfect sense, so I smugly assumed they simply didn't know much about fish.

"Do you see fish under there?" Bets asked.

"Certainly. But I wouldn't eat these," Flipper answered.

"Why not?" I asked.

"Pollution. There is so much in that lake, and that concerns me as well. I could not survive more than a few days there. I don't know how the fish do."

"They say there are 'dead zones' out there," Bip said, "where nothing is living."

"If I swim through one, I am dead."

"You sure this is safe?" I questioned, genuinely concerned.

"I can swim around them. It is much like you driving over a bridge, you know the obstacle is there and you simply go over it or under it or around it. I am safe."

I felt much better.

We reached the the hotel and made our way to Amy Star's room just in time for our 10:00 a.m. meeting. The door to her suite was wide open, but we knocked anyway.

"Come on in, will ya?" Her voice was piercing, almost offensive.

We walked in and stood together, forming a small school in the suite's common room. Amy Star immediately burst into the room, her hands busily fixing an earring.

"Whoa! Didn't expect this many people," she said with a flash of teeth.

She looked exactly as she does on television, only slightly thinner. Her hair hung around her face and down her back in shiny brown and auburn locks and her eyes were an amazing shade of blue. Her manner, however, was much more boisterous than it appeared on the tube.

"I'm Andy Jordan. I spoke with Mr. McClean over the telephone," I said, extending my hand toward her.

She grabbed my hand and gave it a firm shake. "What's with the entourage, Jordan?"

"This..." I began to explain, but she cut me off.

"No, wait, let me guess," she said with a grin.

She walked up to Flipper and pointed to his chest, "This is the water guy, the webbed feet freak," she said.

"That is Mr. Waterman," I interjected, taking offense.

"Don't interrupt me, Jordy, I'm working here. My reporter's nose for the story you know. That's my talent, I know people. I'm what you call a people's reporter."

"Now let's see," she continued, walking over toward Bets, "You...No, you I'll save. This guy," she continued, stepping closer to Bip and shaking a finger, "this guy is your buddy, from school or something, sees me on television and jumps at the opportunity to meet me in person."

Bip sneered, shook his head no.

"Don't deny it babe, you know it's true, and your little girlfriend over here is too silly to know that when you are really putting it to her at night, you're actually thinking about me and puttin' it to me, ain't that right?"

"Wrong," Bip responded. "She's not even my girlfriend, she's his," he said, pointing toward me.

"Is she now?" Amy Star said with more than a note of skepticism, "I'd have figured him to have better taste than that."

"Ms. Star, I think we're getting a little personal here." I spoke up, attempting to salvage the situation. She was unbelievable. There was no cause to insult us like that.

"Look," she retorted, "you're the one that showed up to my interview with a fucking audience. They got any business in this story?"

"They are with me and yes, they do have a part in this," Flipper spoke up.

That he had spoken caught her off guard. "Good. It can talk," she rebounded, turning to Flipper. "Why are they here?"

"This gentleman has donated his services and his water craft to be used in the filming that you intend to do and this lovely young lady is the director of the trust fund which will be set up for the benefit of Atlantins and your people alike once I have departed..."

Bets weakened at the knees, but held herself up, a perky smile instantly replacing the scorn that she had worn for Ms. Star.

Flipper continued, informing us all, "...You will be writing your check to me in such a way that she can deposit it and we thought you might just want an opportunity to interview her toward that end as well. If you do not, they will be happy to go about their own business elsewhere."

"No, no," Ms. Star answered. "My apologies, Mr. Water-Man. I underestimated you. My apologies to you all as well," she turned toward Bip and Bets, "by all means, please stay."

I cannot say that Ms. Star was charming. In fact, she was loud and obnoxious, but she had this captivating quality about her. There was electricity in the air when she spoke and she had a way of making you tell her all about anything that she was interested in.

She interviewed us all separately, like sequestering the witnesses in a trial so that any liars will not have the benefit of hearing his or her cohorts' stories. Flipper's interview was the longest, she grilled Bets second, never even questioned Bip, and she saved me for last.

"You're kind of cute to be an attorney, aren't you?" she began. It was obvious that she was attempting to throw me off by distracting my attention away from the story. I had seen lawyers do it hundreds of times in deposition and at trial, cuddling up to the witness, gaining his confidence, distracting him from his story, just before they lowered the boom and left him disemboweled before the spectators. I was not falling for it.

"You must be from New York," I responded.

"Why say?" she asked.

"I don't know, your personality, your accent," I answered.

"What does a little Southern boy know about New York?"

"Wait," I answered, "No. You have roots in New York but your folks moved to Florida, and now you've returned to the City and have made it big."

"What gives? You been checking up on me?"

"No," I answered, "I went to Tulane. It's kind of the school M.O."

"You must be a pretty good attorney, getting me off track like that," she said.

"Two compliments in such a short period of time," I responded. "Do you treat all of your interviewees like this?" I was on a roll.

"Only the ones I want to fuck after we get finished," she answered.

I suddenly became light headed and felt a burning sensation in my ears. She had blind-sided me. I sat there speechless, staring into those big, blue pools of water, my mind totally disabled and devoid of any comeback.

She gave me a big smile, her eyes glistened, and she pointed an index finger at me. "Gotcha."

I smiled sheepishly.

"You were fucking with me, now get back boy, we got work to do."

"What do you want to know?" I asked, recovering.

"What are you doing later and is that milk-toast little girl really your girlfriend?" she continued.

"I thought..."

"I know, I'm bad. I'm just kidding," she smiled. "This is a pretty good story. Do you really believe this guy?"

"Off the record?" I said.

"Off the record?"

"I always wanted to say that," I explained.

She laughed.

"Look, it's far-fetched, I know, but this guy is different," I began.

"Tell me about it. I saw the feet," she said, rolling her eyes back in her head.

"I personally witnessed him disappearing into the lake for at least fifteen minutes."

"We've seen the tape," she answered, "but it doesn't really prove anything. Our tech says that the film was not cut but there could have been a tank under the water. Nobody can stay under that long."

"He did it once just before we shot the video, at another spot in the lake. There is no way he could have had two tanks at two spots in the lake."

"Why not?" she asked.

"He's homeless."

"So that makes him stupid?"

"No, I didn't mean that. He just doesn't have the resources. He didn't know where Bip's boat was and I am sure he doesn't have two air tanks that he keeps in a shopping basket on the street with him."

"He said he's living with you," she challenged.

"Temporarily, and not until after we shot that tape. There were no bubbles either. If he had had a tank, we would have seen the bubbles."

"It's not him I'm worried about, sweetie. As a lawyer, you could have set this whole thing up."

"Thanks a lot."

"Look, I hope it comes as no surprise to you that *nobody* trusts lawyers."

"They just don't know the right ones."

"Cut to the chase. This is all very suspect to me. I mean first of all, you and I and the rest of the sane world, small as that may be, and thank God because, were it not, who the hell would watch my program, know that there just is no Atlantis. Secondly this guy just shows up here and suddenly he has a lawyer and a television appearance and stands to make a bundle of money. And thirdly, he can only breathe in salt water? Come on."

"Hey," I answered, "most saltwater fish can only breathe in salt water. And he's definitely not in it for the money. He's giving it all away."

"Yea, so Miss Milk-toast was telling me. She's going to save the whales or something. Give me a break. That's a predictable scenario. I can see the follow-up story now – 'Trust fund director disappears with cash, Man from Atlantis no longer available for comment.' Probably vacationing together in Bermuda. Do you really believe in Atlantis, Andy?"

"No." I answered immediately, although I was no longer really certain. "Of course not, but this is no ordinary human either," I said.

"Why does it have to be in the lake, why can't we just ship in some Caribbean blue and put it in a big tank and let the whole world see him breathe underwater? There's your story. Is the water in the lake clear?"

"For about two inches, unless the sewerage gets in your way," I answered, only half-jokingly.

"You're kidding," she said.

"No, you can't see a thing."

"He says he has to test the salinity before he dives off and out of here, that the lake has differing salinity levels and therefore no one can pick an exact spot ahead of time. Sounds like a set-up to me."

"It is rather suspicious," I responded, considering it for the first time, but trying to appear confident.

"Damned right it is. Not exactly ideal circumstances, not to mention the fact that we only have a one-week window," she added.

"One week?"

"Yea, his 'year' is up next week. I like that part by the way, that's where the real human drama comes into this thing," she said.

"I knew he had a year, but I didn't know this was his last week."

"You're good. I think this might just work."

I was confused.

"You know," she continued, "it could just as easily backfire right in our faces."

"What do you mean?" I asked, totally in the dark.

"The scam. Look, we're gonna look this thing over. If it looks even slightly believable, we will do the story, but if it blows up it's you and the three musketeers out there that are left holding the bag," she explained.

"What do you mean?" I asked again.

"If this is not for real and it comes to light, that will probably be a better story than the first one. By the middle of the week this thing is going to be big, everybody is going to have heard about the 'Man from Atlantis,' and most people are going to be very skeptical. If you're scamming the public, you'll find yourself a main character in another of history's countless scandals. Either way, I've got a story."

I cringed. I had somehow gotten into this thing up to my neck without realizing it. Insanity.

After the interviews we dropped Flipper off downtown, on the street in front of the copy center, at his request. I was a little nervous about letting him out of my sight so close to "zero hour," but I had no choice. I could not hold him against his will and I certainly was not going to hang out on the street with him.

Bets and I took off to St. Francisville, Louisiana for the remainder of the weekend to relax in an Antebellum mansion that had been converted into a bed and breakfast. It was peaceful and beautiful. The grounds were covered with blooming flowers interspersed between moss-laden, hundred-year-old, live oaks and the place possessed a quiet that cannot be found in the city. It was exactly what I needed, and was the last such peace that I was to know for quite some time.

EIGHTEEN

BETS AND I GOT BACK TO NEW ORLEANS late Sunday night. Bip had left a note on the front door directing us to wake him when we came in, but we did not have to. He began calling my name as soon as I opened the door.

"Andy! Andy, come here. Hurry!" he yelled from his room.

I had heard this tone a thousand times before. This was something that really aggravated me about Bip. Anytime he saw something on the news that he thought was important he screamed for me to come witness. Nine times out of ten it was something that did not interest me in the least and it was never anything important enough to make me come running as he expected. I took my time at the door, in protest, and made my way to his room at my own speed. Bets went to our room.

"Where were you?" he asked with obvious disappointment as I crossed his threshold.

"We were in St. Francisville," I answered, knowing what he meant.

"No, just now. I was calling you to hurry up," he protested.

"I was getting my key out of the door."

"You missed it."

"What?" I asked, not really interested.

"It was on the news."

"What?" I repeated, impatiently.

"The Flipper thing. They had a report about it."

"What do you mean?" I asked, finally interested. "Why didn't you tell me that's what it was?"

"They were talking about the shooting," he began.

"Oh my God! Flipper got shot?" I asked, flustered.

"No, the shooting schedule, for the television show. Star has really been talking it up. They interviewed her about Flipper. Did you see the paper?"

"No. It was in there too?"

"Front page of the Metro Section, and it mentions you and Bets. The show must have issued a press release. Boy, I bet Angelique is really pissed now," he snickered as he fished the Metro Section out of the Sunday paper scattered across his bed and then handed it to me.

I scanned the article first, searching for the reference to my name, praying that Amy had not said anything that would embarrass the firm. I must have gone through it too fast because I did not see either my name or Bets'.

"I don't see it."

"Right there, 'Local man to appear on *Peepers*,'" he read.

"I mean the part about us," I clarified.

"Right there," he said, "'A local attorney' and farther down it says, 'his girlfriend.'"

It was in there all right. Amy Star had not used our names but she had indicated that a local attorney was handling all negotiations for Mr. Waterman and that the attorney's girlfriend was to head the trust fund which was to be created, "in the interest of preserving our habitat as it affects that of the colony of Atlantis," a direct quote from Bets if I ever heard one.

"At least she didn't give them any names or tell them what firm I was with," I stated, feeling much better about Amy Star.

"No, she saved that for television."

"You're kidding," I said, praying he was.

"I swear," he insisted. "She just said that she had had a meeting late in the week with 'Mr. Waterman and his attorney, Andrew Jordan of the Keating & Faubunk firm.'"

"Faubunk?"

"Yea, she fucked up his name," Bip said, laughing.

"I'm dead," I said, "he's going to crucify me."

"What, it's not your fault."

"Try telling Fabacher that. We are going to be the laughing stock of the city. And you know who's going to get the blame for that."

"It didn't sound that bad. What did you expect anyway? That your name wouldn't come out?"

"Sure I did, but now that it has, it's different. How could it not sound bad? It has to sound like we're representing a lunatic who is going to jump in the lake and supposedly never be seen again as he swims back to Atlantis."

"What sounds so bad about that?" Bip insisted. "We're lawyers. We get paid to represent lunatics. If you don't believe it, come down to the Criminal Courts Building."

"We all need to be locked up," I said.

"What you mean we, Paleface? Cages give me the willies."

I was scared – suddenly it was all just too real. The entire city now knew and I was to be on the hot seat, my reputation and future hanging in the balance. What if he was a scam artist? Of course he was, there couldn't really be an Atlantis. Still, the guy stayed under a hell of a long time, he had webbed feet. "You think it's possible?" I finally asked Bip.

"What?"

"That he is who he says he is."

"Man, you really do need a rubber room."

"How do you explain it then? You were there. How do you explain him staying under water?" I demanded.

"I can't, but then I don't have to. I just have to sit back like the rest of the world and wait to see where this whole thing ends up."

"You're a real pal."

"You got yourself into this one," he replied.

"I hope I can get myself back out."

With a half-smile he shrugged his shoulders. I shook my head and headed to my room, hoping I'd be able to fall asleep.

NINETEEN

I ARRIVED AT THE OFFICE BY 8:30 the next morning and was summoned to Mr. Fabacher's office by 8:35. When the call came from him, Margo announced, "A Mr. Faubunk would like to see you."

"Very funny," I replied, my stomach in knots.

Before firing me Mr. Fabacher ran through a list of clients, and specifically two old clients whom he had brought into the firm, that had telephoned him the previous evening, questioning the prudence of retaining, in matters of great import, a law firm that would not only represent a crazed street person capitalizing upon his birth defect and quirky identity crisis, but which would also be so involved as to have one of its own associates appear with him on the "sleaze T.V. circuit."

I tried to tell Fabacher that I had attempted to dissuade him for taking Flipper as a client, but he would not hear it. What was needed at this point, he explained, was for the firm to dump Mr. Waterman and to make a sacrificial offering to the public of a young attorney gone astray in his quest for success.

"How about J. Ryan," I suggested jokingly, just before heading off to clean out my desk.

That's when Mr. Keating came storming in.

"What is going on, Bill? Why have you two kept me in the dark on this news story thing?"

"I didn't even know about it," Fabacher weaseled out.

"My telephone hasn't stopped ringing," Keating continued.

I scanned the room for a rock to crawl under.

"Mine hasn't either," Fabacher chimed in angrily.

"We need to take some immediate action on this. These kinds of things need to be closely controlled."

"Already done," Fabacher beamed, motioning toward me.

"So this is your doing, Jordan?" Keating asked, finally turning his full attention to me.

"I suppose so," I said, not really certain as to how a sacrificial lamb was supposed to act.

"I don't think you can take this action on your own, Bill. We need to have a meeting of the partners," Keating went on.

"We don't need that for this, for Christ's sake, we're the only two senior partners," Fabacher protested.

"It is in our bylaws. No one can be made a partner without a partner's meeting. You know we have to vote."

I am not sure whether Fabacher or I was more confused. We were both struck silent.

"No offense, Jordan," Keating misread my silence. "It's all a matter of formality. Bill is right of course, we're the only two senior partners in the firm, but it has to be done by the book. I don't want you to get discouraged. We cannot afford to lose you now...I got a call from Hollywood this morning, first time that's ever happened to me. We're going to begin representing some pretty big names from there in local matters around here. And Bryan Whitney called. He has another book due out and he wants to talk to us about it. We're going to have to get Jordan an associate. You're the only person here that knows squat about intellectual property. Good job finding this kid, Bill."

"Uh, yea," Fabacher uttered, the worry apparent on his face.

I nodded. I knew nothing about intellectual property, but it was quite apparent that I had Fabacher over a barrel. He had just fired the hottest new lawyer in town, and Keating, the real power in the firm, wanted to make me a partner.

"Think you can handle it?" Keating asked.

"Well, Mr. Fabacher just told me he thought we could afford two new associates," I responded, smiling as Fabacher's face dropped. There was nothing he could say.

"Well, we'll start with one and see how that goes. You can do the interviewing," Keating assured me.

"Yes, sir," I responded, knowing I could hire the best recent law school graduate to fill me in on all the intricacies of intellectual property.

He turned to leave and I followed him out the door, having no desire to be alone with Fabacher, exhilarated by the fact that I would soon be his equal in the firm. As soon as the door closed Mr. Keating stopped and turned around, opened the door and put his head inside of Fabacher's office. I sped away.

"See you later, Faubunk," I heard him say and then he laughed uproariously.

I headed straight for my office, safe haven for one whose neck was so recently near the ax. "Yes!" I said aloud as soon as I was in. "Yes, yes, yes, yes!"

The rest of my day was totally consumed with Flipper's affairs. I received a memo from Fabacher, though unsigned, that directed me to prepare a press release for the firm, distancing us as much as possible from any direct involvement with Flipper. Keating wanted me to stay right on top of Flipper and Fabacher wanted distance. It was a narrow and precarious path to walk, but one thing was certain – I would have to take great care in making certain that Fabacher was spelled correctly in the release.

The task of drafting the trust agreement for Flipper's funds also fell to me. Fabacher directed me to name the firm as attorneys for the trust and to be certain that our services would be with compensation. Other than that, Flipper insisted that Bets be given the widest latitude possible in her decisions as to how the funds would be allocated. He said that it was the only way to ensure that she was free to make the right decisions for Atlantis.

I had met with Flipper in my office before lunch for the purpose of discussing the trust issues and to make certain that he was prepared for the "test shoot" scheduled for the following day.

"They are going to want you to go through the whole thing you know," I explained, "as though you were swimming back to Atlantis tomorrow."

"Thursday," he said.

"I know, but we have a test run tomorrow," I said.

"No problem. I'll disappear for a while and then I will be back."

"You sure that won't be a problem?" I prodded.

"A problem? No. Why do you ask?"

"Because if this thing doesn't work out it could totally ruin me."

"Why does what I do affect you so?"

"Because most people won't believe that you are from Atlantis. You are being paid a lot of money because you claim you are, and if they prove that you are not, then it looks like we were in this scam together. Lawyers cannot be caught in scams, it ruins them," I explained.

"And what do you believe, Andy Jordan?"

I just sat there, unwilling to answer.

"Andy, what do you believe?" he persisted.

"Flipper, sometimes I don't know what to believe. Sometimes I don't even know who I am, let alone who you are. I'm not sure about my job, about my girlfriend. I'm not even sure all the time whether my socks match my suit, and you want to know whether or not I believe that you are a member of some other species from a place beneath the ocean?"

He sat there, silent. Looking at me. Waiting for an answer.

"All right," I relented, "I'll tell you what I think. I think you have some kind of trick that you're playing here and that this vicious Yankee woman is going to expose it in front of the world and it is going to destroy me and everything that I have worked so hard to accomplish."

"That is not what you believe," he responded in a gruff tone.

I sat, dumbfounded, looking at him.

"If that were what you believed I would not even be here. That is what Andy Jordan the attorney insists he should believe, but that is not what he knows in his heart. Inside of you beats the heart of an Atlantin and inside that heart you know that what I speak is the truth. You speak only what common sense allows you to speak but not what is really in your heart. You know, you know, Andy Jordan. It is special now, now when you are the only one. None of the others believe it, not in their hearts, but by Thursday you will only be one of the multitude who believe and by then it will be too late. I will be gone."

He stood and walked over to the door.

"God, I hope you're right."

"Andy, ask only your heart. You have been thinking too long with your head. It is time for the truth."

He was right. I may have lost my mind, but he was right.

"How do you know? How did you know I would believe?"

"I've known since the first time I met you, and before."

"How?"

"Orange Beach."

A chill ran down my spine, my blood turned cold, and my mind clouded over. When I came out of it, Flipper was gone.

I sat in my office for a long while after that, doing nothing, trying not to think about anything, attempting to clear the fog that had gathered in my mind. I was scared. I was scared of failure, I was scared of being exposed as a fraud, I was scared of the possible criminal prosecution that could follow, and I was terrified that Flipper was right.

By the time I felt like moving it was 1:00 in the afternoon. I was hungry and I went for a shrimp po-boy. When the elevator doors opened, Carly was standing in the back talking to another woman.

"Carly," I found myself saying aloud as I walked on, staring at her, not even bothering to notice who else was around.

"It's going up," she said, smiling, turning away from her friend.

"Me too," I responded, my head suddenly unclouded.

"What floor?"

"Not sure," I answered, "do you know where Peniston is?"

"Never heard of it," she played along.

"I'll know when I get there."

The elevator stopped on the twenty-sixth floor and Carly and her friend got off. I followed them.

"Oh, is this the floor?" she asked.

"Must be."

"There's no Peniston on this floor."

"Oh, isn't there?" I responded smartly.

"Not that I know of." She and her friend giggled.

I followed them down the short corridor to where a receptionist's desk was situated. Large gold letters hanging on the wall behind her read *McShilston & Peterson*.

Carly told her friend that she would see her in a minute, then she pulled me aside.

"See, no Peniston," she said, smiling.

"Did I say Peniston? I meant Peterson. You must have misunderstood me."

"Oh," she exclaimed, "you looking for an architect?"

"I don't know, are you an architect?"

"No, I am a bookkeeper for an architect."

"Wow," I exclaimed, "just what I was looking for."

We both smiled.

"Why have you turned so cold toward me?" I asked awkwardly.

"What are you talking about? I haven't been cold to you," she defended.

"You haven't been like the first time we had lunch."

"You mean the only time we had lunch."

"Yea, that time," I said. "You were much warmer then."

"I haven't even seen you since then except that time in the elevator," she said. "And besides, it's not like you're ringing my phone off the hook."

"Hell, I've been calling some poor company named Peniston nonstop asking for you," I lied, "they're ready to prosecute me for harassing them. That's why I thought I should come up here personally."

"Nuh-uh," she said, not certain whether I was telling the truth or not.

"Honestly, how was I to know you lied to me?"

"I didn't lie," she snapped.

"You told me you worked for Peniston."

"I was just kidding. I thought for sure you'd know there was no such company in the building. All you have to do is look in the directory."

"Well, you have to forgive me then."

"No I don't," she persisted. "If you really wanted to you could have found out my telephone number."

"Not true," I said.

"Besides, I heard you have a girlfriend," she said.

"Who told you that?"

"Oh, a little bird."

"Who?"

"It's not a very big building. I know people that work in your office."

"Spies. Tell me who they are so I can have them fired," I teased.

"I'm not telling you who they are."

"We're not really close," I lied.

"Who, you and the spies?"

"Never mind," I said, beginning to lose my nerve.

"That's not what I heard. I heard you were living together and were going to be married."

"Total falsehood," I proclaimed, "We're not getting married yet."

"That's pretty sleazy," she said.

"What?"

"Living with her and trying to put the make on me. I certainly would not appreciate it if I were her."

"You are not her," I said.

"Damn right I'm not. If I were her, I'd leave you flat."

"Then we'd be free to date."

The response confused her.

"Can't a guy change his mind?" I asked.

"Sure," she said, "change it all you want, but why don't you do it on the 14th floor?"

"Hoooo, feisty," I said.

"Yep," she responded, "That's me, feisty girl."

"All right," I continued, beginning to leave. "See you around?"

"I'm sure you will. Small building, remember?"

"Like an elephant," I said, heading off toward the elevators.

When I got back to my office, Tony and J. Ryan immediately followed me inside.

"Look, guys, I'm sorry, but I'm really busy."

"Mr. Hoity-toity Intellectual Property is too busy for his old friends," J. Ryan ribbed me.

"You better watch what you say," Tony jokingly warned him, "he's liable to be your boss soon."

"I'm sorry," I said, realizing I was being rude. "This shit is driving me crazy."

"You sure that's the only thing driving you crazy?" Tony asked.

"What is that supposed to mean?" I asked, knowing that the two of them were up to something.

"Who's the new babe?" J. Ryan came right out with it.

"What new babe?" I asked, as though I did not know who they were talking about.

"Carly," Tony said in an exaggerated voice.

"Carly who?" I continued playing dumb.

"Carly of the elevator. Scrumptious Carly of the twenty-sixth floor. You know exactly who," J. Ryan said.

"We passed you getting off the elevator," Tony explained, "and you were so enthralled with her you didn't even acknowledge us."

"I was not enthralled."

They both laughed.

"I'm serious. I just met her. There's nothing going on."

"Yea, right," J. Ryan said doubtfully.

"I have a serious girlfriend."

"So?" J. Ryan continued.

"I know that means nothing to you, but it does to me."

"Are you telling me that you wouldn't consider dumping Bets for any other woman?"

"No, I wouldn't," I insisted, trying to convince myself.

"And you don't have any interest in this Carly girl?" Tony asked, sounding disappointed at missing out on some juicy gossip.

"No more than strictly as a friend," I lied again.

"Good," J. Ryan said.

"What do you mean, 'good'?" I asked.

"Nothing, just good. Good means good."

"Okay, then. What else?"

"Nothing, that was it," Tony answered. "I guess we'll let you get back to work."

"It's only until after this week. I have so much to get ready," I explained, feeling guilty about rushing them out of my office.

"Sure," J. Ryan said, a big smile planted on his face.

"Maybe we can all do lunch together next week," I suggested.

"Sounds great," Tony said as the two of them walked out of my office.

"We can invite your 'friend', Carly," J. Ryan jabbed one last time as he left.

I forced a smile, then put my head down and got back to work.

TWENTY

TIME PASSED QUICKLY and the day of the big test-shoot was upon us. Bets couldn't get out of work, but the rest of us arrived at the designated spot on the lake at 6:30 Tuesday morning. Bip dropped off Flipper and me, then went on to get his boat.

The shore of Lake Pontchartrain is covered in grass and over the years has been built up into a two-tiered levee. The first tier begins at the lake with a system of cement steps, called the "seawall," running the length of the shore. The area above the steps is a grass-covered park and the steps themselves descend approximately four feet from this built-up area into the lake. Across a street, past the park area, is a much more dramatic levee, suddenly rising an additional eight or more feet higher than the lower level. Amy Star had her cameras and crew positioned about midway along the seawall. They were busy at work and she was with her makeup team when we arrived.

Among the crew at Ms. Star's disposal were two frogmen, one equipped with an underwater camera. I could tell that their presence bothered Flipper.

"I don't want them too close, Andy," he said.

"Who?" I asked.

"The divers. The carbon dioxide expelled from their tanks depletes the oxygen in the water," he explained.

"Okay," I agreed. "Is the oxygen going to be sufficient here?" I asked.

"I must check," he said, heading toward the water.

Amy Star was sitting on one of those director-type chairs having her make-up applied. I walked over to speak with her.

"Good morning," I said.

"Yea," she responded, "we'll see."

"Weather's perfect," I continued, referring to the low humidity level.

"How's he feeling this morning?"

"Fine," I responded, "he's checking out the oxygen level in this section of the lake."

Ms. Star clutched the hand of her make-up artist and moved it away from her face. She gazed over toward the lake where Flipper's head was still visible above the top step of the seawall.

"How's he gonna do that?"

"He does it by sight," I said.

"Hey, Brian!" she called to a young man standing nearby. He turned toward us. "Get a camera on him. I want you to get everything he does." The young man nodded, snatched up his nearby video camera, and trotted over to where Flipper was.

"He says the carbon dioxide from the frogmen's tanks will deplete the oxygen in the water," I informed her.

"They're liquid oxygen with carbon filters."

"So?" I asked.

"They don't make any bubbles. It's state-of-the-art for underwater photography."

"I'm sorry?"

"Those are not your ordinary tanks. They recycle the air. They filter out the carbon dioxide so there won't be a problem."

"Oh, liquid oxygen, sure," I said. Boy, did I feel stupid.

Ms. Star's make-up artist continued her work and I walked back toward Flipper. He was ascending the seawall, Bryan and his camera in hot pursuit.

"How is it?" I asked as I neared.

"Pretty good right now," he answered, "I don't know how it will be once it starts heating up. Lots of salt water in there. The freshwater is lighter and floats to the top."

I had never considered the concept of water floating on water before.

"She says the tanks are bubbleless," I told him. "They don't emit any carbon dioxide."

"Are you certain?"

"That's what she says."

"This would be a good day for swimming to Atlantis, Andy."

"What?"

"The water is right, the tide is right, the weather is good too. I could make it today," he explained.

"Not today," I said. "If you do it today, the whole deal is off. We...You won't get the publicity."

"You mean you won't get the money. If I disappear today I am certain

I would get the publicity," he said.

"But your message..."

"Don't worry," he interrupted, "it won't be today."

We walked along the seawall, away from where all the action was taking place, then sat on the steps while the crew made their final preparations. One of the frogmen descended the steps near us and plunged into the dark waters. He disappeared immediately under a shroud of white bubbles and green water. The bubbles quickly disappeared, however, and he was gone.

Flipper and I sat for a long while waiting for the frogman to resurface. There was no sign of him, no trail of bubbles to show that he was still breathing. About five minutes later his confederate walked up to the water's edge and, seeing no evidence of his friend, turned to us.

"Have you seen him?" he asked.

"Not since he jumped in," I answered. "Those tanks are really..." The second frogman was gone before I could finish.

A clamor rose behind us and we turned to see what it was. The second frogman, assisted by two of the crew, was hurrying to put on his tank and regulator. Even Brian turned his attention from Flipper and began filming the event as it unfolded.

I stepped up and hurried over toward the commotion.

"What's wrong?" I asked.

I heard the second diver telling someone near him that the other frogman was only supposed to be under for a moment. Something had to be wrong. He finished dressing.

With flippers and mask on, and aided by a man on either side, the second frogman made his awkward journey to the lake. We all followed, hearts pounding, Brian recording the entire event. The pace was slow initially, but sped up as the two men helping the diver lifted him off the ground and carried him at a jogger's pace toward the water.

Suddenly, the quick pace turned to a dead halt. Everyone stopped. Those in front with the diver gasped, then let out various expressions of surprise and joy. I made my way to the front, needing to know what was happening.

As I stepped from behind one of the men in front, I witnessed a sight that truly, in retrospect, changed my life. Before my eyes, climbing the seawall, dripping wet, was a naked Christian Waterman, webbed feet and all, and I do mean all, and there, on his side, leaning on him for support, was the diver who had disappeared into the lake.

"There is a wicked...pull down...there," the frogman gasped. "It pulled...my legs...under the steps...I couldn't move."

We all surrounded them, Flipper and the frogman, as they made it up the last step.

"Are you all right, Tom?" someone asked.

"He saved me," he responded. "I could not get loose. I was getting...water in my mask, I thought I was...dead and all of a sudden something pulled me to the surface."

Everyone stared at Flipper. Staring not at his nakedness, nor at his feet, we all took a good look at the Crown Prince of Atlantis.

Amy Star came running up, make-up finally in tact. She had gone into her trailer and had missed the whole event.

"Did you get it Brian? Did you get it?" she asked as she approached.

I knew Brian had not gotten the shot. He had been interested in the second diver, the one who would have performed the rescue. How was he to know that Flipper would jump in, become the hero?

"I think so," he obviously lied.

"Great!" she said, "What a great sideline, 'The Man from Atlantis rescues one of our own frogmen.' We couldn't have planned it any better."

"There was a lot of running around," Brian added. "I'm not sure it's going to be good quality."

"Okay," Amy took over, "Let's run through it. You," she said to Tom, "you think you can get back in the water?"

The rescued diver looked up at her as though she were crazy. At that moment she may have been.

"You couldn't pay me enough money to get back in there, lady," he answered. "I wouldn't be around to spend it."

"Pick up your check," she responded, "you're off the set. What about you?" she asked the other diver.

"Fuck that. Where's my check?" he responded.

"No, fuck you, you coward. You didn't get wet, you don't get a check."

"Oh, yea?" he said threateningly.

"Yea!"

"We'll see what the union has to say about this."

"Fuck your union," she replied.

Both of the divers stormed toward their trailer to gather their belongings.

"Brian, it will just have to do," she told the nervous cameraman.

I watched Brian's face shrink. There would be hell to pay.

The rescue, it turned out, really had a profound effect upon the crew. Flipper, with no equipment at all, not to mention clothes, had saved one of them. He had been able to accomplish what a skilled diver with underwater gear could not. Whether anyone else was convinced at that point that Flipper was truly who he claimed to be, I don't know, but he had managed to gain the respect of everyone there. They liked him, they respected him, and they were on our side now.

Bip finally arrived with his sailboat and forty minutes after the near drowning, we were ready to begin filming. The frogmen were gone, but Flipper was ready and unafraid.

With careful maneuvering, Bip pulled up to the seawall and dropped anchors in both the front and rear of the boat, and Brian and I climbed aboard. Bip's boat, *The Great White*, was an all white sailboat with an inboard motor and a cabin that slept two. There was a chrome railing, nine inches off the deck, that ran the length of the boat save the front-right bow area, where an earlier accident had caused some minor damage which Bip never seemed to get around to repairing.

I hoisted the bow anchor and Bip pulled on the one astern.

"Shit!" he exclaimed.

"What?" I asked.

"That was a brand new anchor," he said, holding the frayed end of the rope in his hand. "It must have gotten pulled under the seawall."

Using the boat's motor, Bip hurried away from shore and put out into the lake. When we had gotten approximately 100 yards offshore, he addressed Brian.

"How's this?" he asked.

Brian nodded and Bip killed the motor.

"Andy," Bip told me, motioning toward the mast, "help me with this and I'll show you what you picked up for me."

"Picked up?" I asked.

"Yea, at the bus station."

"Oh," I said, remembering. "What was it?"

"My new mainsail," he answered, beginning to turn the crank to raise the sail.

"That was a sail?"

"Yea," he answered. Then he addressed Brian, "This way I'll be able to maneuver around for you without all that engine noise."

"Great," Brian responded as he readied his camera.

"Sure seemed heavy for a sail," I said.

"What?" Bip asked.

"The package," I continued, "those suckers are heavy."

"There were two sails actually, this and a spinnaker, and some cleats and ropes."

"That explains it," I said.

The sail was raised. It was totally white except for a small, red, two-headed eagle in the top corner.

"What do you think?" he asked.

"Beautiful. What's the other one look like?"

"The spinnaker?"

"Yea."

"The same, only it has a huge bird on it, running the whole length."

"You want to put it up?" I asked.

"I didn't bring it," he replied, "we couldn't use it right now anyway."

"Why not?"

"They're ready!" Brian called, receiving the signal over his radio headset. "You think you can bring us in just a little closer?"

"Sure," Bip said. Bip had learned to sail before he had learned to ride a bike. He was extremely good at it and savored any opportunity to prove it.

Brian began filming as Bip maneuvered the boat closer to shore. I looked out and witnessed Flipper, naked again, dive into the water.

"Are y'all going to show that on television?" Bip asked.

"What?" Brian answered, distracted.

"The nudity?"

"We'll fuzz it out," Brian said quickly. "Sorry guys, but we need to keep it down so I can hear the radio."

Bip and I looked at each other and smiled.

"Holy shit!" Brian yelled.

We both turned toward his voice.

Brian was filming right next to the boat, down toward the water. We looked. It was Flipper. In what seemed less than sixty seconds he had somehow managed to swim the nearly one hundred yards against the current of the dark brackish waters to where we were waiting offshore. I gasped, not believing my eyes, watching him, his head out of the water, smiling for the camera. Suddenly, he gave a little wave then put his head into a wave, exposing his back, then buttocks, legs, then webbed feet as they gracefully disappeared into the depths.

"He's already out here," Brian said excitedly over the radio. "Where'd he go?" he asked Bip and me.

We did not know. He had disappeared as quickly as he had come. We all searched the horizon, but Flipper had vanished.

We waited and waited. Fifteen minutes, then twenty. Finally Amy gave Brian a message that he relayed to me.

"Amy says for you to go ahead and call him up."

"Huh?" I asked.

"We're not getting any shots. She says to go ahead and tell him to come back up."

"Oh, you mean stick my head under water and tell him to come on up?"

I asked sarcastically. Bip and I laughed.

"Just get him up."

"I can't do that. I can't..."

"Where?" Brian said into his headset. "Oh, I got him," he said, turning his camera toward the bow of the ship.

"Aye, Andy!" Flipper called to me from the water.

"Hey!" I responded, excitedly.

"What else should I do?"

"Swim around a bit and then go on back in," I said.

"Amy wants him to the shore for an interview," Brian said, receiving the message from his headset.

"Okay," Flipper answered me.

"Wait. Flipper, go back to shore now," I said, relaying the message.

"Okay," he said again, disappearing below the water.

In less than a minute he was climbing up the seawall. We could see someone in the crew drape a robe over him as three cameramen and Amy Star converged upon him.

"Bring me to shore," I told Bip.

"Aye, aye, sir," he said sarcastically.

"Please," I added.

"Okay," he said, "but we need to take the sails down."

By the time we had taken down the jib and mainsail and motored to the bank, Amy Star had finished her interview. Everyone seemed pleased, and several members of the crew were talking to Flipper, slapping him on the back, having their pictures taken with him. I jumped ashore and hurried to where they were.

"How did it go?" I asked Flipper.

"You tell me, Andy."

"Oh, the swimming?" I responded. "That was fantastic, totally amazing."

"Yes?" he said.

"Yes," I answered, showing that I no longer doubted him and was no longer worried about the possibility of being ruined by him.

"How was the interview?" I asked.

"Good," he said.

"What did you say?"

"She asked where I had learned to swim like that and I told her that every child in Atlantis learns to swim like children on earth learn to run. Then she asked me how long I was able to hold my breath and I answered only a few minutes. Then she asked how it was that I could then remain under the water for so long and I told her that it was because I was not holding my breath, and they all laughed. Then she asked what would happen on Thursday, and I said that first the world would be made aware, and then I would return to my people forever. And she told me, 'I can't wait', to which I responded, 'Neither can I.'"

After we had spoken a little longer Flipper went to Amy Star's trailer to get dressed. Amy came out and walked over to me.

"I owe you guys an apology," she said.

"For not believing?" I asked.

"I don't know how you do it. To tell the truth, I don't even really want to know. I like the idea that just maybe it is all somehow true, kind of like finding out all of a sudden that there really is a Santa Claus living at the North Pole. You guys have a real sellable story here, it's really gonna work. We satellited the video to New York and they're going to use a five minute segment tonight as a teaser for Thursday. If we could just hold it over another week we'd probably set a ratings record."

"It's already in New York?" I asked, stunned.

"I know, I know, that wasn't part of the deal. Look, McClean is willing to come up with another seventy-five thousand. If you can convince Flipper to stay another week, we could probably offer about half a million," she said.

"You're kidding," I responded.

"Did you see what he did?" she asked. "I've witnessed a hell of a lot in this job but that really takes the cake. The man can breathe under water and swim as fast as a shark."

"Porpoise," I corrected.

"Why, are they faster?"

"No, just that sharks are their enemies and porpoises their friends."

"Andy, Andy," she repeated.

"What?"

"Porpoises are their friends? Do you really believe this stuff or are you just selling me a bill of goods here?"

"I had no idea he could swim like that," I insisted.

"Tell me no more. As far as we are concerned we have the one and only man ever known to ascend from the depths of the ocean to live in our world and *Peepers* is going to show the world his return to the sea."

I nodded.

"What about the extra week?" she asked. "Any possibilities there?"

"He'd be dead," I answered.

"Not much of a story in that, is there?"

"Nope."

"Okay. I want to talk to you about something else," she said.

"What?"

"I have a friend in New York that is tied into a major toy manufacturer. I took the liberty of calling him just now and told him about this guy. If this thing goes over like I think it will, he wants to put out a 'Man from Atlantis' toy modeled after Christian. He might even be able to work a Saturday morning cartoon deal, and that's major dollars."

"Great," I responded, "how do we do this?"

"I gave him your number. He'll get in touch with you. He was really excited about it so I wouldn't doubt that he's called your office already. I also know another guy who sets up deals for movies of the week. I really think he'll be interested. If you want, I'll have him call you too."

"Sure," I said greedily, overcome by the dollar signs.

"One thing though."

"What?"

"If anyone asks, I never hooked you up with these people. My cut comes out of their end, but I can't let the network know."

"Okay, sure," I said.

"Okay then," she responded, "Thursday. I'll see you then."

"Nothing tomorrow?"

"I've got to be in Milwaukee tonight. There is some dope there who supposedly has the world's largest collection of beer cans of which the collector has actually consumed the alcohol. See what I mean? If people will watch crap like that, what do you think they're going to do with your guy? Batten down the hatches, Bub, hope you're ready for the celebrity."

"Me? Celebrity?"

"You've never seen how this works before. Things won't be the same."

"I think I can handle it."

"That's what they all say," she said, smiling. We shook hands and then she turned and walked toward a waiting limousine. She was off to Milwaukee and I was on top of the world.

I made it back to the office just before noon. Margo handed me a pile of messages.

"The phone has been ringing off the hook all morning," she said. "Every kook that gets the paper has called."

"Great," I responded. "Any serious calls?"

"Loads of reporters, about twenty people who claim to be old friends of yours, and even calls from out of town, two from New York, one from Chicago, and a video game company in Osaka, Japan. Talk shows, and get this, some guy from *The Tonight Show* called saying they were trying to fill a five minute spot next Wednesday and wanted to know if you would be available!"

"Can't, he'll be gone next Wednesday."

"Who?" she asked.

"Flipper. He's swimming away in two days."

"The Atlantis guy?"

"Yea."

"They didn't say anything about him. They wanted you."

I was dumbfounded. Me? They wanted me for *The Tonight Show*? My God, I'd be famous. Think of the money!

"Is he real?" I barely heard her.

"What?" I asked, shaking my head slightly to clear it.

"The Atlantis guy, is he really from there? There's not really any such place, is there?"

"Do you think it's possible?" I asked.

"I doubt it. But I guess it could be. It was in the paper and all."

"Just watch tonight and on Thursday night and make up your own mind," I said, walking into my office to begin returning calls. I thought about the things that Amy Star had said. If Margo, a reasonably intelligent young woman, could believe it was possible that Atlantis existed, even before seeing the evidence, then by the time it was all over with, there were sure to be believers everywhere.

At 1:00 Keating, Fabacher, and I all had a conference to discuss the situation as it was developing. I brought them up to date on the day's events, the program scheduling, and the toy, cartoon, and movie possibilities. They brought me up to date on the notoriety, mostly good, that the firm had been receiving and their fears as to the hell there would be to pay if this whole thing did not work out. I confided that I too had been quite nervous as to the possible outcome but that the morning's filming had convinced me that there was absolutely nothing to worry about.

"Had you been there, you would have no reservations at all," I assured them.

"I'm happy to see that you are so confident," Mr. Keating said. "I suppose it would be too late to disassociate from it now anyway."

"Yes, sir," I chimed in. "From what I understand there is going to be approximately five minutes of coverage tonight on *Peepers*. I'm certain that if you watch you'll feel much better about all of this."

"I'll have Lori tape it," Fabacher said. "We can all watch it in the morning."

"Fine," Keating answered.

"Yes, sir" I responded.

"Okay then," Mr. Keating said, signaling that the meeting was over and I could leave.

"Yes, sir," I repeated, heading for the door.

"Oh, Jordan," Mr. Fabacher called after me.

I stopped, turned toward him.

"I am having a little client gathering tomorrow night at my residence," he said. "I would like it to be sort of a send off for our friend, Mr. Waterman. Do you think you could have him there?"

"I'm pretty sure," I said.

"See that he is," Fabacher replied.

"What time?"

"Anytime between six and six-thirty."

"Yes, sir."

"I'm inviting all of the attorneys in the firm and their wives or girlfriends," he added.

"Thank you," I responded.

"Well that's just fine," Keating interrupted in a disapproving voice.

"What's that?" Fabacher asked, concerned.

"Inviting wives and girlfriends."

"Would you rather it be stag?" Fabacher asked.

"No," Mr. Keating answered. "I just wish you would make it one or the other. Now I don't know which one to bring."

Keating roared with laughter at his own joke, Fabacher faked a chuckle, and I gave Mr. Keating a nervous smile, preferring not to be let in on such confidences. I made my way out of Fabacher's office, feeling quite uncomfortable.

"What an asshole," I thought of Fabacher. One minute he wants to disassociate himself completely from Flipper and me, and the next he's throwing him a bon voyage party.

It didn't bother me for very long though. I had much to do and time was rapidly evaporating.

TWENTY-ONE

TUESDAY NIGHT WE SAT QUIETLY AT HOME, with the telephones unplugged, watching the evening broadcast of *Peepers.* There was the usual fare of movie stars caught cheating on their spouses and the story of a "troubled" young woman who had attempted to set her sleeping grandparents on fire. As the show lumbered on toward the final five minutes of its one-half hour time slot, there was absolutely no mention of our story. Then, with barely four-and-a-half minutes left, the anchorman made the announcement:

"When we come back, we have something truly shocking to show you. It is beyond the realm of anything ever seen on this or any other television program. Correspondent Amy Star is in New Orleans with a special report concerning a full one-half hour broadcast that we will be airing from the shores of Lake Pontchartrain on Thursday. I saw the video that she and her crew shot this morning and can tell you that you really do not want to miss this one. It's a miracle in Sin City and it's all coming up next on *Peepers*!"

Then they broke for a commercial.

"They aren't going to have time to show anything," I complained.

"They don't want to show too much," Bets replied.

"Where's Flipper?" Bip asked, suddenly missing him.

"He wanted to spend the night downtown," I said.

"WHAT?" Bip and Bets said in unison.

"You let him?" Bets said in disbelief.

"I don't own him," I protested. "What was I supposed to do, kidnap him?"

"Andy, if anything happens to him we have nothing," Bets said.

"If someone recognizes him, you might never see him again," Bip added.

"I couldn't talk him into it," I said, really worried now. "He promised to stay here tomorrow night and to come to Fabacher's party."

"You mean the party that everyone but me is invited to," Bip sulked.

"Sorry, Buddy," I responded. "It was beyond my control."

"No matter," he replied. "I wouldn't have gone anyway."

"Yea. Right." I responded.

"It's true, I won't even be here."

"Where are you going?" Bets asked.

"Tomorrow afternoon is the New Orleans-Biloxi Regatta," he said, "I'll be on the water."

"You're not going to be at the taping?" I asked.

"I've been registered for this for eight months. It's why I got the new sails."

"I know, but you won't see Flipper," I said. "You won't even be able to tell him goodbye. You're never going to see him again."

"Sure," Bip answered, "just tell him to look for *The Great White* as he swims through the Gulf to Atlantis."

Bets laughed.

"Tell him to stick his head up and tell me bye. Maybe he can even help me out in the race," Bip continued, "give me a little push."

"You are unbelievable," I said. "You won't ever see him again."

"I'm the defending Champ," Bip insisted. "I have to be there to defend my title. This was planned long before he decided it was his last chance to swim off to the underworld. Besides, I think I've seen enough of him to last a lifetime."

"You just aren't interested because you don't have any financial stake in the outcome," Bets observed.

"Which is exactly why you two *are* interested," Bip responded.

I intended to deny his allegation, but could not find the correct words to properly express my denial before the show had returned to the air...

"And now, in New Orleans, here's Amy Star with this breaking story. Amy?"

The picture switched from the studio in New York to Amy Star standing at the Lakefront earlier that morning.

"Thanks Jeff. I am standing here on the shores of Lake Pontchartrain in the Lakefront area of New Orleans, Louisiana. As impossible as it may sound, there is a man here claiming to be none other than Christian Waterman, son of King Dog Waterman of the Court of Atlantis. No, this is not some Mardi Gras parade, we're talking the real McCoy here, Atlantis, the – until now – mythical undersea world."

It was going well. There was a stiff breeze blowing Amy's hair around and her voice had a real urgency to it, almost like a reporter giving the details on some shocking or tragic occurrence.

"At approximately 9:30 a.m. Central Time, my crew and I witnessed an incredible feat – no pun intended," she smiled as though the thought had just occurred to her, "...and you'll see why I say that in just a moment. We don't have much time so we are going to roll some of the tape right now and I'll just keep talking throughout."

Suddenly the picture switched to Flipper, standing on the seawall, his naked backside obscured by a fuzzy blue dot. It focused for a moment on his big, webbed feet and then drew back again as he dove into the water. Almost immediately, he appeared hundreds of feet offshore, near Bip's sailboat, waving from the surface of the water. "The film was not cut here folks. He actually swam out to the waiting boat in the length of time that you saw," Amy continued. "Then, without any warning at all, he disappeared into the depths of the lake and remained submerged in excess of fifteen minutes."

"There y'all are!" Bets screamed. Bip's and my shoes were visible as Flipper submerged again and a timer appeared on the screen.

"Of course we won't be able to remain on long enough to show the length of time that he remained beneath the brine, but I can tell you that it was in excess of twenty minutes. We have a shot of him resurfacing..."

There was an obvious jump in the filming sequence and the timer went from eighteen seconds to twenty-one minutes and thirty-nine seconds. Suddenly Flipper's head popped out of the water.

"This is the most incredible thing that this reporter has ever witnessed," Amy Star went on. "The waters this morning were so rough that our own diver nearly drowned due to the undertow, and this man, this Man from Atlantis, actually jumped in and rescued our diver who had been dragged into a cavity beneath this sea wall."

Of course there was no footage of the rescue. I wondered what kind of hell Brian had been made to endure for that. There was a shot, however, of a naked, yet blue-fuzzballed, Flipper walking the frogman up the steps of the seawall.

"We've got the whole story, why he's here and why he has to depart Thursday or face the consequence of death. We will record the exit from this world of the Man from Atlantis, and you can see it all right here on *Peepers*."

With that Amy's picture disappeared and our television screen was transported back to the studio in New York.

"Don't miss that, Thursday, exclusively on *Peepers*," the anchorman said, as the music faded in and the credits began to roll across the screen.

"I cannot believe he isn't here," Bets repeated.

"He was fine on his own for eleven months, one more night on the street won't kill him," I pointed out.

"If I had not seen what happened this morning with my own eyes I might be afraid that he was trying to get a day's head start getting out of town with the dough," Bip said.

"Bets has all the money," I countered.

"You better keep an eye on her tonight," Bip teased, "she might be running off with Mr. Atlantis."

"It's a lot of money, Bip, but it's not *that* much money," Bets responded. "It's not enough for me to have kids with webbed feet and a house with toilets big enough to accommodate Orca."

"I don't know..." Bip said.

"Know," Bets replied.

I did not sleep well that night. I was not worried about Flipper skipping town or Bets running off with the money, but something inside just kept reminding me of what a mess my life would become if anything happened to Flipper before Thursday got here.

Bets got up to go to the bathroom twice during the night. Either she had never gotten up in the night before, or I had never noticed. I didn't let her know that I was awake.

TWENTY-TWO

I HAD MARGO SCREEN ALL OF MY CALLS on Wednesday. This Flipper thing had begun to take on a life of its own and I was awed by the amount of interest that had already been generated. Reporters from as far away as Australia were calling me and several local civic organizations, including the Aquarium of the Americas, wanted to know whether Flipper would be available for fund raisers. A representative from the Mardi Gras Krewe of Atlantins also called to discuss the possible ramifications of our having violated their registration of the tradename for exclusive use in the State of Louisiana. And the book, movie, play, and television offers began pouring in.

These were the people I got to talk to, and for each of them there must have been at least ten "kooks" wanting to talk to me that Margo had to deal with. One was a man who insisted that the world would come to an end if Flipper was not allowed to return to the ocean on Thursday, a woman from Mississippi called saying that Flipper was her long-lost son that she had had upon her husband's return from some freak occurrence at sea, and three different Lord Dog Waterman's called wanting to speak to their "boy." After Margo told me about all of these people I called up my contact at the New Orleans Police Department and had extra security assigned to the filming on Thursday.

There was no way that I could possibly give my attention to so many details in the day remaining before Flipper's departure, so I tried to concentrate on the larger opportunities and those that would no longer be available once Flipper had swum off into history. However, one thing was for certain. If I had only met Christian Waterman a month earlier, he would have left millions more dollars behind for the salvation of Atlantis.

By 10:00 a.m. on Wednesday I had a faxed copy of a contract on the

"Water Man Doll," which included an option for the rights to any cartoon that may be developed, and had begun negotiations on a Movie-of-the-Week deal. The toy contract was contingent upon Flipper's swimming away before he could be proven a fraud, but the Movie-of-the-Week people were not so particular. They wanted the deal whether Flipper really was from Atlantis or not. In fact, I kind of got the impression that they would have preferred that the whole thing ultimately be uncovered as a huge fraud. The scandal angle seems to appeal to more evening network television viewers than does the fantasy angle. Non-sexual fantasy, that is.

According to the trust agreement, Flipper was totally withdrawn from the negotiations process. He had completely signed over all of his rights to the trust, making Bets the individual responsible for selling those rights for the benefit of the trust. I figured this would make things a lot simpler anyway. Flipper could not be expected to negotiate on an even keel with humans who had been doing it for centuries, and certainly Bets would be willing to defer to my judgment when it came to making such deals. Unfortunately, and as I should have expected, I had once again terribly underestimated the little redhead from Kansas.

"I don't want any royalties for any toys or cartoons," Bets insisted. "I know kids and they are not going to like a doll that has big flappy feet."

"The experts seem to differ in opinion, my dear," I tried to persuade her.

"Well they're not convincing me," she said. "Ten thousand up front and a 30 percent royalty?" she said in disgust.

"Do you know what 30 percent of the Ninja Turtles is worth?" I asked. "It was my idea to get the big royalty and less up front," I continued. "Between what the network is paying us and the other rights we have to sell, you'll have plenty to work with. This will be a long-term income provider. The potential is enormous."

"Long term?" she mocked. "Do you know what long term is to a child? About fifteen seconds. As soon as that man throws his naked ass into the lake and disappears there won't be a kid around who could even tell you his name. Do you know how many 'Water Mans' there must be for every 'Ninja Turtle' that makes it? I want cash up front, Andy. I'm not accepting anything less. If the damned royalty is worth that much then they should be thrilled to come up with a quarter of a million to keep it."

"They'll probably jump at it," I said, "and tomorrow will be too late to change your mind."

"I'm not going to change my mind," she replied nastily.

"You..."

"Just do it!" she interrupted. It was a vicious response, unlike any I had seen her display before.

"Okay," I said, in an equally bitter tone.

The change in Bets had begun gradually, but had picked up momentum the closer we got to Flipper's departure. It was a side of her that I truly had no idea ever existed. They say that money does strange things to people and suddenly we were talking a hell of a lot of money. She had become blinded by it, totally obsessed, and though she had always had a sternness about her, it had suddenly turned to just plain old meanness.

As I predicted, the toy and cartoon people were eager to accept Bets offer, except that they insisted that the payment under the contract not be due until one month after Flipper's departure. After forty minutes of negotiations I had that time down to two weeks.

I worked through lunch and was glad that I had when Flipper showed up at twelve thirty. It was a great relief seeing him standing there, but more than that I found myself feeling very melancholy. It was like seeing an old friend just before he's about to be sent off forever.

"Andy," he said, standing in my doorway, "you look very busy."

"You don't know the half of it," I replied, smiling.

"Busy is good."

"Busy is very good," I affirmed. "And it's all because of you."

"I thought so."

"Where have you been?"

"Telling people goodbye," he answered.

I hadn't really considered that, that he would have other friends, whom he had met on the street, to bade farewell.

"Where did you sleep?"

"With friends."

"I guess you can meet a lot of people in twelve months," I said.

He walked into my office and sat himself in one of my client chairs.

"You can meet all kinds of people," he said.

I could sense that something was bothering him. "Something happen last night?" I asked.

"Nothing bad," he responded. "Why?"

"You just seem a little distracted," I said diplomatically.

"The largest shark in the ocean is the most gentle. They are all unpredictable. One minute they will allow you to stroke their bellies and the next they will devour you."

"I don't follow," I said nicely. Actually, I expected him to come back with one of his "Bluh blub blu blub"s. What he was saying was not making any sense to me. He was foreign and I was somewhat relieved by all this. I had become a little too involved with Flipper. I had begun to like him and now I was reminded that perhaps he was a little insane and that my life would be much more normal once he was gone.

"I know you don't," he replied, a little angrily. He stood up.

"Don't get upset," I pleaded.

"Sometimes you must first listen to the sound of the ocean before you can hear the roar of the wave."

I was definitely confused. "You and I speak different languages," I replied.

He turned to leave, stopping at the door, looking as though he were near tears.

"You are a good man," he said, "a porpoise amongst the sharks."

"Are you going to be downstairs this evening?" I asked, needing to know before he disappeared.

"I will be there," he said with a frown. "I will be waiting."

"Great," I replied, relieved.

He simply shook his head and walked out.

I got back to work, not once stopping to consider any of what he had said. Only long afterward would I attempt to make any sense of it all.

Time really flew by that afternoon. I did not leave my office to so much as go to the bathroom or to grab a cup of coffee. By the day's end I had laid the foundation for over eight hundred and fifty thousand dollars worth of deals related to Flipper and his departure to Atlantis. From Hollywood to the local snowball concession at the following day's event, I wheeled and dealed until near sunset, amassing as much cash up front as possible. Margo handled all of the other one million details: police protection, crowd control, barricades, permits, passes for school children from selected districts, invitations for the Mayor and City Council. Even the Governor indicated that he might attend, but canceled out, opting for a trip to Las Vegas. All in all, it was probably the busiest day in both mine and Margo's lives and by 5:00 it was really only half over. The gathering at Mr. Fabacher's house may have been referred to as a party, but for all of us from Keating & Fabacher, it was work. The partners were going to get as much mileage as possible out of all of this attention being thrust upon us, and it was up to us to make certain that it was taken advantage of and presented in the most favorable light.

TWENTY-THREE

BETS HAD TAKEN BIP TO THE MARINA that morning then taken his car on to work. We were supposed to use it to go to the party that evening, but it had died on her a block away from home and she had to get Germaine and two of his brothers to push it in front of the house for her. The Jeep was the only other alternative and Bets informed me that I would have to affix the top and doors so that the wind would not "muss up" her hair. I was really getting tired of taking orders from her.

Bets adorned her newest, bibbed, maw-maw dress for the party and rolled her hair up it into a giant, tight, bun. I hated it, her entire "conservative" look. Her hair and head looked like a round turret mounted upon a Moorish Mosque, and the bib on her dress made her tits completely disappear. I like long, flowing hair, and she knew it. I was certain that she had put it up that way only to annoy me, and she could at least wear a dress that showed she had a butt and breasts. Still, I was intelligent enough to hold my tongue and, painfully, told her that she looked nice.

Seeing to it that Flipper had a bath and was dressed in the new suit that Bets had purchased for him made us quite late for the party. During the entire drive over Bets was ordering me to slow down, complaining that the wind was messing up her hair. I had refused to put the top and doors on the Jeep and, despite her complaints, did not slow down one bit. I put it all off on our being late and drove as fast as possible, hoping that the increased wind velocity might knock that ridiculous thing off of her head.

The Fabacher home was on Audubon Place, an exclusive neighborhood just off of St. Charles Avenue. There is a guard posted at the street entrance twenty-four hours a day to keep all undesirables out (undesirables being anyone who does not live there or who is not invited there for a specific purpose). Tonight we were desirables.

Driving almost to the end of the street, I pulled up to one of several valets standing in front of the Fabacher mansion. I left the engine running and hopped out, walking around to assist Bets out of the passenger seat. Once she was unloaded, hair still in place (unfortunately), I lifted the seat to let Flipper out of the back.

"Hey, that's him," one of the valets cried.

Flipper stepped out of the Jeep and was immediately surrounded by the five valets on duty.

"You're the fish guy, aren't you?" one asked.

"He's not a fish," a second chimed in.

"He has flippers and breathes underwater," the first defended.

"Yes, I am he," Flipper responded.

"Wow," a third young man gasped, "he's the dude."

I took Flipper by the arm and began leading him away, momentarily forgetting about Bets.

"Ahemmm!" she coughed loudly. I turned around and grimaced.

"Sorry," I said.

"What is wrong with you tonight," she asked as I went back and collected her.

"It's been a rough day and I have a feeling that this isn't going to be any picnic. I'm really nervous."

"Well I'm not. Why don't you just let me do the talking."

The power and greed had really gone to her head. I slipped my arm under hers and the valets walked the three of us to the door.

"Is someone going to park that?" I asked them, motioning toward my Jeep.

"Yea, dude," one responded.

We made it to the door which was opened by a servant dressed in tails, and were immediately greeted by Lori, Fabacher's secretary.

"Where have you guys been?" Lori asked impatiently.

"We had to get ready," I said.

"Well Mr. Fabacher is spazzing out. He sent Tony and some others out looking for you. He wants you to join him right away."

"Okay," I answered, "Is something wrong?"

Lori took my arm and began pulling me through the crowd. I made sure that Flipper followed. "Wrong?" Lori asked rhetorically, turning toward me only long enough to speak the word as she hurried us toward our destination. "You were supposed to be here," she said, turning her head again toward me to speak, then back into the crowd. "Everybody's been asking where he is," she said, repeating her head routine. "Even the Mayor is here."

As we neared Mr. Fabacher, I could see that he was standing in a group that included the Mayor, several City Council Members, Mr. Keating, and two of the firm's biggest clients. Just as we arrived he turned toward us and I could see both relief and anger on his face, not at all unlike a mother who has just found her lost child in a crowd.

"Well," I heard him address his distinguished crowd, "here he is now."

The "he" no doubt was Flipper, but I felt compelled to speak anyway.

"I'm sorry we are so late," I told them, "we ran into a little trouble getting ready."

"Mr. Mayor, Councilpersons, Jim, Dan," Fabacher began, totally disregarding me and the fact that I had spoken, "I would like you all to meet Mr. Christian Waterman."

"Evening, Sirs," Flipper greeted them, every bit as loudly as he had greeted passers-by on the street. For a moment I feared he may resort to old habits and request change for a po-boy.

The Mayor laughed nervously, extended his hand for a shake.

Flipper took his hand and shook it, but refused to let it go, just as he had done with me on the street that day.

"Good grip," the Mayor said, laughing nervously again, looking to those standing around him.

"Imagine this," Flipper said, "Me, in this fine home, surrounded by all of these fine people and fine things, shaking the hand of the Mayor."

"Yes," the Mayor responded. He turned, red-faced, toward Fabacher and grinned, his hand still held captive by Flipper's.

"How many times I have imagined it," Flipper continued.

"Really?" the Mayor asked, flattered, though nervous that he was being held against his will.

"Yes," Flipper responded.

"Well, I've looked forward to meeting you as well," the Mayor returned the compliment.

"Since when?"

"What?" the Mayor asked, shocked.

I glanced over at Fabacher. He was frozen, sensing that the entire affair could blow up in his face at that very moment.

"How long is it now that you have looked forward to meeting me?" Flipper asked.

"Oh. Ever since I heard of you," the Mayor replied. "You are quite an amazing individual."

"Last time I saw you, you weren't so anxious to know me," Flipper continued.

Now I was beginning to get nervous. I considered whether I could do anything to change the subject of conversation, but it was already too late.

"Oh?" the Mayor questioned nervously as he made obvious attempts to free his hand.

"Yes," Flipper continued, "I was in a cardboard box, freezing my tail bone off down in front of the Pontalba Apartments. You came out and told your driver to radio the police 'and have this eyesore removed.'"

"I didn't know you had a place in the Pontalbas," Mr. Fabacher said with some enthusiasm, shamelessly attempting to divert attention and to change the subject, but sounding foolish in the process.

"He doesn't," Flipper responded, releasing the Mayor's hand.

"Gentlemen, Ladies," the Mayor began in tactful anger, "I am sorry but I have another engagement that I must attend. If you will excuse me." He walked away without saying another word.

My stomach was turning over as I saw my career flash before my eyes.

"Well," one of the firm's client's said after the Mayor was out of earshot, "I guess now we know where 'Hizzonnor' has been keeping 'hizzgirl-friend'."

The others began to laugh. Even Fabacher joined in when he saw that the water was safe.

"He's a lame duck," one of the Councilwomen added. "He's on his way out. I can't believe he just tucked tail and ran like that."

"What an arrogant son-of-a-bitch," the other client said.

"You are a very unusual man, Mr. Waterman," the second Councilwoman spoke up.

"And you haven't even seen my feet yet." Flipper charmed them and they all laughed.

He was a hit. At least with everyone other than the Mayor, whom, it was now apparent, was so unpopular that being disliked by him was actually a positive in many circles.

I did not speak to Flipper again for the remainder of the party. Fabacher and Keating monopolized his time, keeping him close by and showing him off to everyone like he was a prize pony or something. This was all fine with me. There was plenty of expensive food and drink and I decided to enjoy myself.

Bets and I went to the bar, and she ordered a cranberry juice with a lemon wedge. I requested a bourbon and 7-up. She frowned at me.

"You have a really big day tomorrow," she scolded.

"Yea?" I responded.

"You aren't going to want to get up in the morning if you drink that. Why don't you tell him to hold the bourbon?"

"It's one drink, for Pete's sake," I complained. She was really starting to get on my nerves. Everything was going great and here was Bets, once again, raining on my parade.

"Okay, but don't blame me in the morning."

"What makes you think I would blame you?"

"I'm just saying," she continued in her motherly tone, "I don't want to hear any complaints in the morning."

"Could you make that bourbon a double?" I asked the bartender, just to piss her off.

That really did the job. She took her drink from the bartender and stormed off into the crowd. I waited for my drink then set off in the opposite direction.

I had not walked very far when Tony D'Ensina surprised me, grabbing my arm from somewhere in the crowd.

"So there you are," he said.

"Oh, hey, Tony," I responded, stopping to talk to him.

"We were out looking for you."

"Yea, I know. Sorry."

"No problem, it was kind of nice to get away from all of these social wannabe's for a while. You know, why is it that when common people get elected to office they automatically think that it raises them to the highest of social levels? You ever see Jimmy Stewart try to do that in *Mr. Smith Goes to Washington*? They're elected at a certain social level and that is the level they should govern from. Like England with the House of Lords and the House of Commons. America could learn a lot from Britain about social status."

I had already tuned him out.

"I went by your house, it's still there," he finished, probably sensing that I was becoming bored with his dissertation.

"Glad to know it," I responded.

"There's a friend of yours here," he said teasingly.

"There are a lot of my friends here," I replied.

"Yea, but this one will surprise you."

Just as he said the words I caught sight of her and my heart skipped a beat. On the opposite side of the room, dressed in a short black dress that fit perfectly over her shapely body, Carly stood with drink in hand, chattering away with someone I could not see.

"How did she get here?" I asked.

"You ever see *Guess Who's Coming to Dinner*?"

"With Sidney what's his name?"

"Yea, the white daughter brings him home to meet Mom and Dad," Tony explained.

"She's here with Bobby?" I asked, referring to Bobby Coleman, a law clerk and the only Black employee at Keating & Fabacher.

"No," Tony replied with a laugh. "What I meant was guess. He's not Black, although he is the black sheep of the firm."

"Oh, no," I said just as someone between us moved to reveal J. Ryan as the culprit. "J. Ryan?" I asked.

"I didn't tell you," Tony said.

"That slimy asshole."

"Now, now," Tony said gleefully, loving the controversy, "it's not like you're dating her or anything. You have a serious girlfriend, remember?"

"Yea," I said, "but I told him about her. He knows I'm interested."

"You told us both that you weren't. Except as a friend, I think you said."

"Bullshit, Tony, he knew. I don't care what I said, he knew that I liked her and he did this just to get a dig in on me. That guy really knows how to crawl up under my skin."

"I don't know anything," Tony said, distancing himself from the controversy as usual.

"Yes you do. If you didn't, you wouldn't have told me she was here like you did. You bankruptcy guys just take up for one another."

At that Tony let out a howl, and once I realized what I had said, I laughed as well.

"This firm is turning into a regular *Peyton Place*," Tony commented once he had stopped laughing.

"The point is, J. Ryan knew I was interested in her. He should have left her alone."

"She's something else," Tony continued prodding me, "smart, sweet, and gorgeous."

That was it. Without another word I headed across the room to J. Ryan and Carly. I was going to speak to them, although I had absolutely no idea as to what I was going to say.

"Andy!" J. Ryan greeted me excitedly as I approached.

"What? No kiss on the cheek?" I responded sarcastically.

"Not in public," he joked back.

"I see that the 'J' in your name stands for Judas. I always wondered."

"Judas was a Jew, wasn't he?" J. Ryan replied.

"Well, well, imagine seeing you here," I said, turning my attention to Carly. My heart was pounding. The more I saw her, the more I was drawn to her.

"It's a pretty small world, isn't it?" she said with a huge smile.

"But I'd hate to have to paint it!" J. Ryan joked. Nobody laughed.

"I didn't know you and J. Ryan knew one another," I continued.

"Sure," J. Ryan piped in, making certain he was not excluded from the conversation, "we go way back. Our mother's were best friends. We used to take baths together."

Carly smiled again.

"Now, now, Jeremiah, it's more like back to Tuesday afternoon isn't it?" I corrected him.

"About that," Carly responded. Then to J. Ryan, "So, it's Jeremiah?"

"Cute, Andrew," J. Ryan responded.

"I love that name," Carly continued. "I almost named my son Jeremiah."

J. Ryan smiled broadly. My heart stopped – she had a son?

"You have a son?" I asked, with a deliberate smile, attempting to make it sound like no big deal.

"Yea. I ended up naming him Taylor."

"Much better choice. How old is he?" I asked.

"Three-and-a-half."

"So, is there a Mister Carly?" J. Ryan chimed in.

"Huh?" she asked, confused.

I decided to help her out. "I think what J. Ryan is asking, in his normal, tactless manner, is whether or not you are married."

"Oh. No, I'm not."

"Divorced?" J. Ryan pressed.

"No."

"Widowed?" he continued.

"J. Ryan!" I protested.

"No," Carly replied.

"Ahhhh haaaaa. Well what's left then?" He was relentless.

"I got pregnant and refused to marry the bum," Carly volunteered. "It's the smartest thing I've ever done."

"No reason to compound the problem." I don't know why I said that. I think I had heard it somewhere before and it just came out.

"You have any pictures?" J. Ryan asked. I wished I had thought to ask that. J. Ryan was never distracted by the possibility that he might hurt someone else's feelings or cause them to feel awkward and, subsequently, he was much more relaxed and a lot less reserved in conversation than I was. In many ways this worked to his benefit. Almost immediately he could speak to anyone as though they had been friends for years. He said whatever came to him while I weighed the possible effects of anything I might say before uttering the first word.

"Of course," Carly said, reaching into her purse. She produced a picture of an absolutely adorable dark haired, dark eyed little boy sitting atop a slide in his Sunday best.

"Hum," was all that J. Ryan had to say before passing the photograph on to me.

"He's beautiful," I said. "He looks a lot like you."

"No, he doesn't," she immediately disagreed, "he looks exactly like his father."

"No, he doesn't."

"How do you know?" she asked. "You don't even know what his father looks like."

"Yea, but this child looks like you."

"Well, I don't think so."

"She's right," J. Ryan chimed in, "he looks just like me."

"Baaaa-haaaa," Carly laughed, though she muffled it somewhat.

"Ha!" I said, laughing, "there's that laugh again."

She frowned at me.

"I'm just kidding, I think it's cute," I said.

"No, you don't. Otherwise you wouldn't always be making fun of it."

"Come on, give me a break," I pleaded. I had really been enjoying our conversation.

"Hey, Bets!" J. Ryan belted out all of a sudden, his eyes focused somewhere behind me.

I could not tell whether it was a ploy of his or whether she was really behind me. Cautiously, I turned, smiling.

"Hey, Bets," I said. She was directly behind me sipping her juice, dressed in her boob camouflage with hair still piled high. I know that sounds terrible, but with Carly standing next to her in that tight, black dress, Bets looked like some kind of pitiful, waify, adolescent playing dress-up. I was embarrassed.

"Hi," she replied, sourly.

"Ready for another drink?"

"I think we should go."

"Bets, we can't. I have to wait for Flipper."

"I have to work tomorrow and I am really drained," she explained. "Can you just run me home and come back?"

"I'll take you," J. Ryan volunteered, surprisingly.

"Thank you," she told him.

"No, I'll bring you," I said, looking suspiciously at J. Ryan.

"Never mind. I can take a cab if it's too much of an inconvenience. You're obviously very busy."

"Don't be ridiculous," I insisted, "it's only five minutes away." I was actually excited at the prospect of Bets leaving early. That meant a whole evening of not having to worry about how much I drank, or to whom I spoke.

We left with no fanfare and I tipped the valet a dollar to retrieve the Jeep. The ride home was silent. It was obvious that things between us had changed, but not a word was spoken of it.

"Thanks, Sweetie," she said as I pulled up in front of the house. She gave me a little kiss before hopping out of the Jeep.

"I'll walk you up," I said.

"No, you need to get back."

"It will only take... "

"Don't worry about it," she insisted, "have fun. I'll keep the bed warm."

"Okay," I replied, surprised that she had not put up a fuss about my going out again without her. I actually began to feel a little guilty, undeserving of the trust that she had in me.

Bets walked up the stairs and I waited until she was safely inside. I had pulled in behind Bip's car, which was parked directly in front of the steps, and had to back away before I could leave. With much anticipation I sped back to the Fabacher home.

When I arrived at the party for the second time, I realized that other than J. Ryan and Carly, no one else had even noticed that I had gone. The senior partners were still parading Flipper around and everyone's attention was upon him.

I located J. Ryan and Carly in the same spot where I had left them less than fifteen minutes earlier. Tony D'Ensina had joined them and I walked over.

"There he is again," J. Ryan announced as I approached.

"Hey Andy," Tony said.

"He's like a bad cold," J. Ryan continued. "Can't shake the guy."

"Very funny," I responded.

"We were just talking about the Regatta," Tony said.

"New Orleans-Biloxi?" I asked.

"Yea, they had the television on in the other room and a news report interrupted to announce that one of the boats had disappeared."

"What?" I said, shocked. "Did they say which one?"

"No, they haven't said yet."

"Bip's out there."

"I thought he probably was," Tony replied.

"Yea, they started this morning. Did they say what happened?"

"No, only that one of the boats had failed to make the afternoon checkpoint and that they were out looking for it."

"Who's Bip?" Carly asked.

"Andy's roommate," J. Ryan responded.

"Oh, how awful," she said.

"I'm sure it's not him," I assured her, "he's a great sailor. He's all right."

"Are you going to the shooting tomorrow?" Tony asked Carly, moving on to another subject.

"I think so," she responded. "J. Ryan asked me to go with him. I have to see if I can get off of work. I want to bring Taylor."

"J. Ryan won't be there," Tony said.

"Yea, right," J. Ryan responded.

"We have to do that Americana Steamship petition."

"We'll get it done," J. Ryan insisted.

"Yea, tomorrow. It prescribes Friday."

"I'll go in tonight and work on it," J. Ryan suggested.

"Tonight when?" Tony asked.

"Right now," he said. "This is an historic event. We can't miss it."

"You're going to do it tonight?" Tony asked.

"Do you mind?" he asked Carly. "If we leave now, I can go tomorrow."

"I'll bring you home if you want to stay," I blurted out to Carly, my heart speeding out of control.

"Huh?" J. Ryan said.

"Sure it's no problem?" Carly asked.

"None at all," I said.

"You want to stay?" J. Ryan asked her.

"Do you mind?"

"No, of course not," he lied. "I guess I'll just pick you up tomorrow then."

"Great, as soon as I clear it with work."

"Where's it going to be out there?" J. Ryan asked me.

"The great departure, you mean?"

"Yea, where is he going to jump in?"

"The same place he did yesterday. Just take the road out to the Lakefront and you can't miss it."

"Okay," J. Ryan said. "I'll see you tomorrow," he told Carly, attempting to kiss her on the lips. As she turned her head and smiled at me, his kiss landed on her cheek.

Tony began humming a tune that I guessed was the theme to *Peyton Place*, which only he would have recognized anyway.

J. Ryan shook Tony's hand, then grabbed my shoulder and squeezed it hard. Then he was gone.

"That's one of my favorite movies," Carly told Tony.

"What?" he asked.

"*Peyton Place.*"

"You know that? What did I say about this woman?" Tony said to me.

"You were right," I replied.

"What?" Carly asked.

"Even better than I originally suspected," Tony added.

"What?" Carly insisted.

"He was just paying you a few compliments earlier," I said.

"Y'all want drinks?" Tony asked.

"Sure," I said. "What are you having?" I asked Carly.

"Scotch and water."

"Two," I told Tony, hoping I'd like scotch.

"Coming right up." Tony excused himself and headed over to the bar.

"So that's your fiancee?" Carly asked once Tony had gone.

"Huh?"

"With the uh…" she said, cupping her hands together and putting them on top of her head to simulate Bets' hairdo.

"Oh, Bets?" I said.

"I don't know, we weren't introduced, but J. Ryan said y'all are getting married soon."

"What?" I protested. "No, he's full of shit."

"She's not your girlfriend?"

"Well, yea, well kind of," I responded.

"Isn't that like being kind of pregnant?"

"Well, we used to be a lot closer than we are now. We're really on the way out now," I explained. "Fiancee? No, we aren't getting married, that's for sure."

"Oh, I guess I was misinformed."

"Quite."

"She lives with you though?" Carly continued.

That damned J. Ryan had told her everything.

"Well…" I hesitated.

"Kind of?" Carly joked.

"Yea," I said, smiling. "It's temporary, very temporary."

"So when is all of this going to happen?"

"What?"

"When is she moving out?"

"My aren't we curious about Andy's personal life," I accused her, wondering what she was getting at.

"You didn't answer the question," she persisted.

"I know. I don't know..."

"I don't think you two are right for one another."

"That's a pretty bold assessment, considering you just saw her for the first time."

"It's obvious. Why do you go out with that woman?"

"We've been going out for four years."

"So?" she asked

"So, that's a long time."

"Are you in love with her?"

"What? Yes, I love her," I said, beginning to think that this woman was a bit too pushy.

"That wasn't the question. I asked whether you were *in* love with her, not whether you loved her. Or do you not think there is a difference?"

"Well sure...there's a difference." I was on shaky ground.

"Well, are you in love with her?" she insisted.

"What do you mean? I told you I love her."

"You love your mother, you can love your best friend, but to be in love with someone is totally different. You can love a woman that dresses like your grandmother and puts her hair up in a little ball on top of her head and who henpecks you over how many drinks you have when you go out. She can have a lot of great qualities that you admire and want to be around, but that doesn't mean that every time you see her your heart jumps and you want to touch her or make love to her, have your kids with her and spend the rest of your life with her. You can't marry someone just because you love them."

"We're not getting married..."

"I can't believe I'm saying this to you," she said, suddenly losing her nerve.

"No, it's good, it's true. It's good to know."

"No, you don't understand," she explained. "I'm not like this. I don't usually talk to people like this or let them know what I'm feeling."

"Could have fooled me."

"I don't. I'm serious."

I could see that she was.

"Okay, I understand," I said.

"No, you don't. You see, everything I just said, that's how I feel when I see you. I can't believe I'm telling you this, but that is exactly how I feel about you and I am scared to death that you'll never give me the chance to find out if you and I were meant to be together." She turned her head away from me in embarrassment.

I was shocked. I did not realize it before she said it, but her words were exactly what I had wanted to hear. They explained exactly how I felt about her, what my heart had been expressing every time it thumped out of my chest just because I saw her. I was in love with her, but until that moment I had not known it. Just as I was about to reply, Tony walked up with our drinks.

"Here you go," he said, handing Carly hers first.

"Thank you," she told him, taking the drink but with her eyes now fixed on me.

He handed me a drink and I spoke up.

"I think I'm in love with you."

The words surprised him. "It's only a drink, Andy, it's not a proposal. God, is this guy easy."

Carly flashed a big smile, laughed at Tony's joke. I did too.

"I saw Martin Fletcher over there," with extreme social grace, Tony made up an excuse to leave us alone. "I need to go talk to him. Look, if I don't see you guys again before the party is over, I'll see you tomorrow at the lake."

"Great," I said.

Carly smiled.

Tony walked off.

"What about your girlfriend?"

"I love her. I told you that. I'm not going to lie to you. We've been together for four years and we've been through a lot together. I always thought, somewhere in the back of my mind, that we would get married some day. But I have to tell you, there is something that I feel for you that I don't feel for Bets. In my heart I know that she and I aren't right for each other, but in my head I'm not convinced that you and I are. We hardly know each other. I found out tonight that you have a son and you know practically nothing about me."

"Except that I'm in love with you."

"But do you love me?"

She started to answer, then stopped herself. After a moment she spoke, "I guess I can't know that yet."

"Exactly. It takes time. I don't know about Bets, but I owe her something. Oh God, I don't know exactly what I am saying. This is a really confusing time for me. So much is going on right now..."

"I know," she said understandingly.

"I need a little time. I need to get tomorrow out of the way and I need to clear things up with Bets. I don't want to lose you in the meantime. I know that sounds selfish, but I owe her that."

"Okay," she said.

"I have all this other baggage to take care of right now," I continued.

She nodded in agreement.

"Look, this is almost over. We'll grab Flipper and I'll take you home as soon as it's done."

"He's with you?" she asked.

"Yea, is that okay?"

"Yes. I would really like to meet him."

"No problem. Come with me," I said, taking her arm momentarily to get her moving. It was the first time that we had touched and she was soft, and warm, and instantly familiar.

We walked around the house looking for Flipper. He was no longer with either Fabacher or Keating and I finally asked Lori if she knew where he had gone.

"He excused himself to go to the bathroom."

"Which bathroom?" I asked.

"I told him he could use the one upstairs."

"Oh my God!" I responded. "Lori, does it have a bathtub?"

"You should see it. It's practically a small swimming pool with jets built in all around it," she explained, her eyes lighting up.

"Oh, shit!" I said, bolting toward the stairs. Carly and Lori followed.

I bounded up the stairs and toward where I thought the master bedroom would be. My instincts were correct and I could hear water running behind a closed door. Never even considering the possibility that it may be Ms. Fabacher retiring early to her nightly bath, I rushed in and threw the door open.

I was too late.

Backing out as fast as I could, I held my breath and slammed the door shut behind me.

Carly and Lori came into the room.

"Did you find him?" Carly asked.

"I'll tell you later," I answered, trying to hurry them out of there.

Promising a complete explanation, I succeeded in convincing them to go back downstairs. I then promptly returned to the bathroom and instructed Flipper to clean off, dry off, get dressed, and report downstairs immediately. I held my breath for as long as I could, but had to breathe again before I could get out of the room. The smell was nauseating, as though he had been dining on raw fish, and I felt as though I would vomit.

Returning downstairs, making certain I was not seen, like a spy in a late night movie, I found Carly and Lori talking.

"Lori," I said in a panic.

"What?" she asked, she and Carly both moving closer to me to find out what had happened.

"Does anyone else know that he went up there?"

"I don't think so. Why?"

"Yea, what's going on?" Carly asked.

"He has a nasty habit of confusing the bathtub with the toilet," I explained.

"Oh, no," Carly said. I could see she was struggling to keep one of her "Baaaa Haaaa"s in.

"Eeeewwww!" Lori exclaimed in obvious disgust. "He was taking a bath in the toilet?"

"No, it's the other way around."

She thought about it for a moment, then gasped.

"Oh my God!" she said. "In the bathtub?"

"Bingo," I responded.

"What are we going to do?"

"Nothing. We can do nothing."

"He'll fire me," she said. "I better go clean it up."

"You don't want to do that," I warned her.

"He'll kill me."

"Not if he doesn't know that you know."

"But I told Mr. Waterman to go up there."

"But nobody else knows that," Carly said, laughing now.

"He probably won't even know who messed it up," I added, "unless he comes in and catches you cleaning it."

Flipper descended the stairs, unnoticed by the crowd in the next room. He walked over to me wearing a smug little grin on his face.

"Perhaps we should leave," he suggested.

"Capital idea," Carly responded.

"Let's say our goodbyes," I added.

After making the excuse that swimming to Atlantis required much energy and lots of rest, we bade our farewells and practically ran out of the house.

"Flipper this is Carly, Carly, Flipper," I said as we all walked quickly down the sidewalk toward the waiting valets. They obviously had seen us coming because one had already been dispatched to retrieve the Jeep before we got there and in less than thirty seconds we were on our way.

Carly lived on Moss Street, along Bayou St. John in the Mid-City area of New Orleans, about a twenty minute ride from my apartment Uptown. She gave me directions and talked with Flipper the whole way to her house. I just sat and listened, admiring her and the way her brain worked (not to mention the way it was packaged).

They were still talking after we had reached her house and I had turned off the engine. Suddenly Flipper asked me an amazing question.

"Andy," he said.

"Yea."

"Andy, have you ever been in love before?"

"What?" I didn't want to answer.

"Have you two been talking?" Carly asked me.

"Us two? You mean you two," I accused her back.

"We haven't been talking about that," she insisted.

"Why do you ask me that?" I put it to Flipper.

"It was just a question that came to me."

"I think you should answer him," Carly prodded.

"Actually I was just thinking about that," I finally admitted.

"That is probably why I asked."

"Do you read minds?" Carly wanted to know.

"Perhaps," Flipper responded. "It is similar to the way we communicate under the sea."

"I think I have," I said, wanting it to be known, "at least once before."

"When?" Carly asked, very interested.

"A girl in college. Someone that I was infatuated with for a very long time before finding out that she was interested in me too."

"Ah. But infatuation and love are not the same thing," Flipper said.

"Yea, but they aren't far apart. After I got to know her the excitement never left. I think that's being in love."

"So where is your love?" Flipper asked.

"That one? Her fiancee flew down to find out why she had stopped answering his letters and returning his telephone calls. Then she stopped answering my letters and returning my telephone calls. He moved right back into the picture and I got moved right out."

"That's terrible," Carly said.

"I wrote her a letter and later found out that he had read it. I was pretty stupid back then, I still had a lot of growing up to do."

"He read your letter?" she asked.

"Yea. She told me that, the last time I talked to her. It was really embarrassing, I bore my soul to her in that letter and this guy reads it. I was so stupid...I compared her to a ship."

"A ship?" Carly said, surprised.

"Yea, a ship," I said soberly. "I told her that when she came into a room she was like a great ship. Everybody turned to see her, awed by her, and she parted the crowds before her like the water off the bow."

"Baaaa-haaaa," Carly had tried to contain it, but could not. "I'm sorry," she said, between gasps of laughter, "you compared her to a ship?" she laughed again. "That's the funniest thing I have ever heard."

Initially I was offended by her insensitivity, but soon joined in her laughter. It was ludicrous. "No wonder she dumped me," I added, "I compared her to a fucking ship."

When we had finally stopped laughing, Flipper, who had remained silent, spoke up. "But a ship can be beautiful," he said.

"Baaaa-haaaa," Carly began again, and I joined in. It was contagious.

"I have to go before I pee all over myself," Carly said as she got out of her seat.

"I'll walk you to the door," I responded, jumping out of the Jeep and meeting her on the other side. She fumbled for her key as we walked up the sidewalk and when she had found it, she placed it in my hand. I unlocked the door and pushed it open.

"Thanks for the ride," she said.

"Carly..." I began.

"If you are going to compare me to a boat stop right there," she said jokingly.

I smiled, laughed.

"I am very attracted to you. I just need a little time to sort it all out."

"Haven't we been through all of this?" she asked, cutting me off.

"Yea. I'm just afraid you'll move on before I have a chance to figure it all out."

"Andy, I'm not going to just sit around and wait for you to make up your mind. To be honest I don't think the chances of another guy like you showing up anytime soon to sweep me off my feet are too great, but until you make your decision I can't just wait around on you. I'm not like that."

"You're right..." I said, seriously.

"I know. I am right."

"Yep, the chances of someone even nearly as good as me showing up are impossible," I joked, laughing.

She laughed too, then suddenly put her lips on mine. We kissed long and deeply. I could feel the chemical reactions going off between our bodies. It felt like love. It was not fair to Bets, but continuing to live the lie with her would not be either. I saw that now.

I pulled away from her, grinned, "Boy, is J. Ryan going to be upset."

We both said goodnight and I saw her inside.

When I returned to the Jeep, Flipper was sitting in the front seat.

"Let's go somewhere so we can talk," he suggested.

"Bets is sleeping back home and Bip is gone. We can go back there."

"Let's not disturb her."

I drove to Cooter Brown's, a pool bar near my house known for oysters-on-the-half-shell and import beers. Being a Wednesday night it was not crowded and we had no trouble sitting in one of the two booth-seats there. I ordered a Xingu beer and Flipper ordered two dozen oysters.

"Andy," Flipper began, "after tomorrow I won't see you again."

"I know," I answered sadly.

"I wanted to thank you properly for everything and I am not really sure how to do that."

"No need, you already have," I assured him. "You've made me famous."

"That is not necessarily good. Sometimes famous becomes infamous."

"Well yea, but I'm not going to be infamous."

"Listen to me, Andy," he said with urgency, leaning across the table. "Never let them change you. Of the entire time that I was living on those streets like a dog, you are the only true human being that I met. I know you were not thrilled about my friendship, just as I know that you cared. Droves of people walked past me every day, most not bothering to even look at me, ignoring me even when I called out to them. Others gave me money to clear their own consciences or to make them feel good about themselves, but most of them would not look at me either, and if they did it was either in disgust or in thanksgiving that they were not me. Only one person would buy me shoes and actually walk me over to get a pair, and then let me choose the ones I wanted. You let me choose. You did not thrust your charity upon me like a yoke for me to wear. You could have gone and chosen a cheap pair of shoes and dropped them off at my feet as you passed by one morning, but instead you decided to treat me with a little dignity. You treated me like a human being, because that is what you are."

"I wish that were true," I responded, knowing it was not.

"It is true," he insisted.

"No. I despised you. Actually, I feared you. I thought you had some kind of control over my life. I feared that if I did not please you, then my life would be fucked up until I treated you differently."

He looked at me, smiling.

"Those shoes," I continued, "I didn't want to buy you those expensive shoes. I wanted you to get the cheap ones, the ones that would probably have been worn out in a week. I felt I had to go with you and like you trapped me into buying the shoes that you wanted because I was so weak. I'm no hero, I'm just a superstitious putz."

"It is a shame that you cannot see yourself for what you really are," Flipper interjected. "You do not treat yourself fairly. Do you think it is second nature for anyone in your position to do what you did, to help a lowly, smelly, homeless creature like me? I don't doubt that there might have been other forces at work inside of you, but had you not had the compassion inside, none of it would ever have come to be."

"Can I ask you something?"

"Certainly," he responded.

"When I first met you, I could hardly understand a word that you were saying. Your English was not very good and you would go off and start speaking gobilty-gook. Now you speak so damned eloquently. Why is that?"

"I was a very sick creature when you met me, Andy. I had lost all hope and was resolved to dying. This is what you have given me, I have become myself, returned to what I once was. Oh, how I wish you could come with me to my world. Oh, how I would love to show you the beauty and wonders that abound there. We are loving, caring, sophisticated creatures, we Atlantins, and I wish I could show you that."

"I wish you could too," I said. I was absolutely serious. I wanted to see it, experience it first hand. "Can you tell me where it is, and what it's like?"

He began to speak longingly of the family and home he had left behind. He told me first of his father, the guiding force in his life and in the lives of all of his subjects. His mother, the most beautiful female in all of Atlantis – what a gentle and unselfish woman she was. And of his younger brothers and sisters, ten in all. He described the sea and its creatures, many of which I had never before heard of and which he professed had not yet been discovered by man. He could not tell me how to get there. It was more a state of being than a place, you either knew Atlantis or you did not, he explained. He talked for nearly two hours and I sat, listening, taking it all in, finishing my beer, then ordering another.

A month earlier I would have thought he was crazy and myself insane for sitting there, listening to him. But I believed him. He spoke with such conviction as to leave absolutely no doubt as to his true citizenship of Atlantis. I sat in awe, wondering what I had done to deserve the honor of being a participant in this miracle.

After he had finished speaking of the place to which he was to return to the following day, and had devoured a third dozen oysters, Flipper sat back in his seat, closed his eyes and drew a deep breath. I sat there, watching him, imprinting the image of his face upon my brain so that in years to come I could relate this night and describe him with some degree of accuracy to those of my grandchildren interested in hearing the story retold for the thousandth time.

"It is truly paradise," he continued, his eyes still closed. "Not like here."

"There are a lot of beautiful places here," I contested.

"I'm not talking about scenery, Andy, I'm talking about love. About a place where that feeling that you now have for Carly, that excites you from your head to your toes and fills your mind with the most wonderful feelings, you have for everyone and everything – always. A state of eternal joy and goodwill for all."

"There must be some sadness," I insisted.

"Only from the outside, never from within."

"Don't your people die? You don't feel bad about that?"

"Death is but a rebirth for us, usually to a happier place with our Heavenly Father, sometimes to your world, but if so, always back to Atlantis."

"You make earth sound like hell."

"Isn't it?"

"It's not that bad," I defended, though not very convincingly.

"It is a place where brother puts himself ahead of brother, you covet your neighbors' daughters and possessions, you destroy yourselves for the sake of that which you call progress but which is exactly the opposite. Do you believe in God?"

The question distracted me. "Of course," I replied. "Do y'all?"

"Surely. Did He not create all creatures in heaven and on earth?"

"Yea, I just didn't think you would know about Him."

"When He returns, will your people forget their worldly distractions and heed Him?"

"I have no idea. I personally intend to."

"I hope He gives you time. And, for your sakes, that He returns as a wealthy, strong, white, heterosexual male because if He is any less, most of you will have a hard time accepting and facing Him. You would not stoop to acknowledge anything less."

I did not respond. The vision disturbed me, frightened me. It was too much to think about. Then my response came to me.

"But I've acknowledged you."

He stared seriously into my eyes, then his face broke into a smile. "So you have, my brother. So you have." Then his eyes flared.

"Andy," he said, "you are a porpoise amongst the sharks and you face them alone. Never lose faith in your brethren."

"Okay," I said, not understanding what the hell he was talking about. It's how he was. He'd be perfectly normal one moment and then speak pure nonsense the next.

"Carly, she is truly a porpoise. Your souls swim together. I believe she is a gift sent to you by my father for your service to his son. Accept this. Tomorrow my message will be heard by all, my vow fulfilled, and in this you have been pivotal."

I just nodded along with him. It sounded good but I wasn't really buying that Carly was sent to me from Atlantis. I saw it as a "thank you" and I accepted it at that. The beers were beginning to take effect, it was late, and it was time to go.

We left the bar and drove back to my apartment. Bip's car looked like it had been moved up, so I parked directly in front of the stairway and crawled out behind Flipper, then ascended the steps with him. Once inside, I directed him to Bip's bed and I went to mine.

Bets was fast asleep, laying on her side of the bed. I crawled in quietly, without touching her, onto my side and immediately fell into sleep.

TWENTY-FOUR

I AWOKE TO THE TELEPHONE'S RINGING at nine o'clock on Thursday morning. Bets was not in bed, and I groped, half asleep, for the phone.

"Andy?" It was Bets, and she was obviously upset.

"Yea. Bets?" I said, wondering where she was and why she had not woken me before she left.

"God Andy, it's awful," she said, crying.

She must have found out about Carly.

"What?" I stalled, fearing her answer.

"Did you see the paper?"

"No, I'm still in bed," I was relieved. Obviously it was some lesser tragedy.

"They think Bip's dead," she cried.

"What?" I asked, sitting up, now fully awake.

"His boat never showed up and they haven't been able to find any sight of him. They think he went down," she continued, crying harder.

"Where are you?"

"I'm at work."

"Let me get the paper and call you back. I'm sure he's all right. He's a great sailor," I assured her.

"I don't know."

"I'll call you back," I repeated.

I jumped out of bed and ran to the front door. The paper was on the porch and I opened it, my hands trembling. In the bottom left-hand corner of the front page the headline read *LOCAL ATTORNEY MISSING AT SEA*, and in smaller letters *Officials Fear the Worst*. The article was brief, mentioning Bip's name and *The Great White* and reporting that he had failed to make the afternoon checkpoint in the regatta. The Coast Guard was not dispatched until nearly three hours after the last boat had cleared the checkpoint, and they had been unable to spot him before nightfall. No radio transmissions had been received and they planned to continue the search at first light. I went back inside and called Bets.

"It doesn't say here that they think he's dead," I began.

"It says they fear the worst. Worst means dead."

"No it doesn't. Not necessarily."

"Well what's worse than death, then?"

"They could barely have begun looking for him. He wasn't missing until the afternoon checkpoint, and they didn't begin looking until three hours after that. There is no way they searched very long before dark. I'm sure he's out there floating around somewhere."

"Why wouldn't he have radioed if he were okay?" she insisted.

"His radio is obviously broken. He would have radioed if he were sinking, wouldn't he? He probably just got off course," I tried to reassure us both.

"Bip?" she said incredulously. "Bip was raised on the water. He won this thing last year. He would not get off course."

She was right. "Look, let's not get too upset until we hear something," I pleaded.

"I can't believe you. He's your best friend and he's lost at sea and you could give a rat's ass."

"That is not true, I'm worried sick. But it doesn't do us any good to presume he's dead when we don't know. I'm sure they will find him today."

"You aren't going to do anything?"

"What can I do?" I asked. "Rent a helicopter?"

"You can use your influence to get him found."

I laughed. I couldn't help it.

"My influence? What influence? I don't have any influence. Influence with whom?"

"You're a lawyer, aren't you?"

"Yea, me and about ten thousand other people in this town. And most of them don't have any influence either."

"If you were any kind of lawyer, you would."

"What's that supposed to mean?"

"Nothing," she responded.

"Don't take it out on me. I didn't do anything. I know you are upset but..."

"Yea, I'm upset."

"Well I am too."

"Why are you upset?" she asked.

"What? Come on, my best friend is lost at sea, remember?"

"That isn't the only reason I am upset," she continued. "Didn't you even wonder why I wasn't there when you woke up this morning?"

"I thought you were just letting me sleep in."

"Where were you last night?" she asked accusingly.

"At the party," I responded innocently.

"With who?"

"With Flipper and about a hundred other people. You were there, for Pete's sake."

"And after that?"

"Flipper and I went out for beer and oysters and a talk," I answered, conveniently skipping the part where I had my tongue in Carly's mouth.

"And before that?"

"Before what? What are you getting at?" She knew. But how?

"You know damned well. You were with HER, weren't you?"

"Who?" I asked innocently, knowing that we both knew the answer.

"That girl that J. Ryan was with, dressed like a bimbo."

"She wasn't dressed like a bimbo," I defended Carly.

"Oh, I guess you like the way she was dressed. You must hate what I wear."

"I don't hate what you wear," I lied.

"You must if you like what she was wearing. That tight, black dress that showed every curve of her tight little ass."

"Well yours is just as nice and tight if you'd ever just let anyone see it," I blurted out the truth.

"I am not like that. You've known it since we first me. Where did you go?"

"I told you."

"Where did you go with her?"

"I brought her home, that's all. Flipper was there to chaperon."

"Did Flipper kiss her goodnight too?"

"What were you doing, watching us?" I asked, not really believing that she had.

"You kissed her, didn't you?"

Then it hit me. Bip's car – it wasn't in front of the steps when we got home the night before, but I hadn't thought anything about it. She had gone somewhere after I had dropped her off. She must have suspected it and followed me. I had a sinking feeling in my stomach. The game was up.

"We need to have a talk," I told her in as soft, and sweet, a voice as possible.

"Bullshit!" she yelled, crying all the more. "We don't need to talk about anything. I trusted you."

"Bets," I pleaded, "you don't understand."

"You're damned right I don't," she said angrily, "I gave you everything, EVERYTHING," she stressed, "and this is how you repay me. I should have known."

"Bets, listen."

"You probably gave me AIDS!" she screamed.

"I don't have AIDS."

"How do you know? Do you give them all blood tests?"

"Who all? There aren't any 'all,' it's just her."

"Don't even talk to me," she said. "I am going to pick my things up while you are at the taping. I'll leave the key in the mailbox."

I knew she was in pain, but I was rather happy to hear that she was moving out. It had to end. I knew it, and she would as well, in time. She was leaving, moving back to her apartment. We could end this thing. I could talk to her later, explain why it had to end, why it was the best thing for both of us.

"Okay," I responded calmly.

"Okaaaaay?" she asked in disbelief.

Women, how can you ever understand them? She says she's leaving, moving out, I tell her okay and she gets pissed. Had I fought it and pleaded with her to stay she would have gotten equally as pissed for my trying to talk her out of it.

"Whatever you say," I told her.

"Whatever I say?" she repeated.

"Yea, whatever you say."

"I say you never be an adulterous son-of-a-bitch and keep your hands off other women when you're supposed to be with me. But it's too late for that. You can't take this back, you've ruined *my* life, and God, I hope you didn't give me any diseases. 'Whatever I say?' I say you make it all never have happened." She was speaking in quick, angry sentences that barely made any sense.

"How do you suggest that I do that?" I asked.

"I will let you know!" she said, slamming the telephone down in my ear.

I hung up the phone and walked into Bip's room. Flipper was asleep in his bed with the covers pulled over his head. For an instant I thought it was Bip. I suddenly experienced overwhelming angst. Bets was right. Bip would not have strayed off course. Something was very, very wrong, and I had the awful feeling, deep within me, that he wouldn't be back.

TWENTY-FIVE

FLIPPER AND I ARRIVED ON THE TELEVISION SET at the Lakefront just before our noon deadline. There were already droves of people lining the perimeter and the first school bus had just pulled up to deposit its load of children. Everything looked different with all the people, the barricades, the set. It was a much bigger ordeal than I had expected. I had grossly underestimated the interest that the story had generated.

The crowds pointed and yelled as I drove Flipper by in the open Jeep. Some of them even cheered. It was very exciting, exhilarating, yet Flipper seemed totally withdrawn from it all. He just sat there stoically in the passenger seat as I drove through the police checkpoints and up to the set.

The sight of the lake brought my worries about Bip back to me.

We were met on the set by Amy's assistant, Tommy, who directed us both to makeup. Flipper objected to having any makeup applied to his skin, claiming that it would only add to the lake's pollution once he dove in. He did allow them to comb his hair and to apply a few dabs of water-based makeup under his eyes. Flipper also objected to the Speedo swimsuit that Tommy insisted he wear underneath his clothing.

"I will not be able to swim with that monstrosity around my waist."

"Look, this is in front of a live audience. There will be women and small children out there. This is not our doing. Your attorney brought in the crowd and the cops. The law says you have to cover your body."

"You wanted the people to deliver your message to," I said, defending my part in this. "He's right. It's illegal to go out there in the buff."

"It will destroy my rhythm, cause friction, I could sink with it on."

"You only have to jump in with it. You can rip it off as soon as you get in the water, and out of eyesight of Sister Martha Mary's third grade religion class," I suggested, trying to reach a middle ground.

Flipper finally relented and, under protest, went into the adjoining bathroom to put the thing on. With that done, the only thing left to do was sit around in the makeup trailer waiting for the one o'clock filming to begin.

While we were waiting, Amy Star came in.

"Hey guys," she said in a perky tone. "Andy, is that our Bip missing in that Regatta thing?"

"Yea," I responded glumly, nodding my head.

"That's very interesting. I think we might try to get an angle on that."

"What's this?" Flipper asked.

"Bip," Amy answered before I could speak. "You know Bip. He took his sailboat out for that race and disappeared. Maybe your people got him. Some trade."

Flipper looked concerned. "Why didn't you tell me this?" he asked me, hurt.

"I didn't want you to have to worry about it."

"Andy, you disappoint me."

I did not respond, only lowered my head.

"Look, I gotta run through this schedule," Amy continued as though Bip's disappearance was of no real consequence. "I'll start with a brief narration of the salient facts surrounding the story, then we'll pan over to Mr. Waterman and get his interview, then you'll be allowed five minutes for your statement concerning Atlantis and the effects wrought upon it by humans, etcetera, etcetera. Then we'll have the big send-off and a final interview with you, Andy, wrapping it up with a brief closing statement by yours truly. But you won't care about any of that," she told Flipper, "because by then you'll be kicking your way on home." She winked.

Flipper grinned and winked back at her.

"Oh!" Amy exclaimed as though she had just been hit with a revelation. "Where is little Ms. Milk-toast? Was she on the boat to?"

"No," I replied. "She couldn't make it."

"Couldn't or wouldn't?"

"It's really none of your business," I answered. She had offended me with her belittling of Bip's situation and making fun of mine.

"My, my, we can see who didn't get laid last night," she snapped back. "Down boy," she said, heading toward the door.

I really felt like getting into it with her, teaching her a little about Southern gentleness, but it just wasn't worth it. There were more important matters on my mind.

After Amy left, I sat quietly with Flipper, worrying about Bip, and about the interview I would have to give after Flipper's departure, and trying not to think about Flipper's leaving.

"Andy," Flipper spoke just before one o'clock.

"Yea?" I asked.

"Don't worry about Bip," he said. "Once I'm in the water, I will find him. The seagulls report that he is probably all right."

"Yea," I answered glumly, envisioning him finding Bip's grey, half-eaten body on the ocean floor somewhere.

"And you have done the right thing with Bets," he continued.

"Who told you that? A sea turtle?" I asked.

He did not respond.

We sat quietly for a moment. Then Tommy came in to bring us out.

"You guys ready?"

"Guess so," I said.

"Yes," Flipper responded.

"Well then let's get to it," he said, motioning.

"Is Brian here?" I asked, curious.

"No, Brian isn't with us anymore."

Flipper and I got up to leave.

"I'm sorry I snapped at you like that," I told him.

"The human heart does not handle sadness very well," he told me, "and you have much in yours today. I understand."

"Thanks. I want you to know, I'm really going to miss you."

"And I you," he responded. "But know this – when I reach Atlantis on this day, your name will be known in my father's house and there will be a place for you, my porpoise friend."

I smiled at him then turned toward Tommy standing at the door with a confused look on his face. We walked out, and onto the set. As we did, a cheer arose from the crowd. It was amazing. Surrounding the stage, fifty feet away on all sides and behind police barricades, were stadium seats, filled to capacity with ecstatic children and adults. A camera man directed his attention into the crowd and another cheer arose, children waving, pushing, trying to get on television. It was a magnificent sight, and I was proud to have played a part in it all.

We walked to the two chairs in front of the lights on the stage and took our seats.

Flipper leaned over to whisper something in my ear.

"I really got that son-of-a-bitch Faubunk last night, didn't I?" he said naughtily.

I tried to keep from laughing, but couldn't. He had done it one purpose. If any of you saw *Peepers* that night and were wondering why I was laughing when the show began, now you know. It relaxed me. I think he knew that it would.

I was still laughing when Amy Star appeared on stage and another cheer arose from the crowd. She joined us, waited for the noise to subside, and then began.

She started off by introducing herself and announced that this was a special one-half hour, live segment of *Peepers*, devoted entirely to the phenomena that we were all about to witness. Then she introduced Flipper and me.

Next she spoke for about ten minutes, relating the story and showing clips from the earlier shooting and from the video which Bip and I had shot in anticipation of *The Angelique Brown Show.* She ended with the announcement that she would be right back to speak personally with "the man claiming to be from Atlantis."

During the commercial break I really began to get nervous. I had never been on television before and the pressure really started building inside of me. Flipper, on the other hand, sat calmly in his seat, never breaking a sweat, as though he was a veteran of the television talk show circuit.

"We're back!" Amy said as the red lights lit up on the three cameras before us.

"And now I would once again like to introduce you to the man who has caused all of this commotion, Mr. Christian Waterman, the Man from Atlantis."

The crowd cheered and all three cameras zoomed in on Flipper.

"Call me Flipper, please," Flipper said into his microphone. "All my friends do and I have found that all humans are my friends."

"Well, thank you," Amy said.

"No, Amy, I would like to thank you. I would like to thank all of you wonderful people who have come out here today and I would especially like to thank my good friend, the man to whom I owe my life..."

My heart was pounding and my head spinning. There was no way that I was going to be capable of uttering a single syllable.

"...Mr. Andy Jordan," he finished.

The cameras turned to me. I smiled. I kept smiling, nervously. The muscles in my face responsible for making me smile were aching, twitching under the strain of forcing that smile to remain on my face.

"Thank you, Fl..." I finally began to say, just as the cameras turned from me to Amy Star, who interrupted.

"Now, Mr. Waterman...I mean, Flipper," she corrected herself, "all America today is waiting to hear the answer to a single question. Is there really an Atlantis?"

"Most certainly," Flipper answered without hesitation, "it is where I was born."

"And Atlantis is populated with others like you?" she continued.

"Over ten thousand," he responded, "much like myself, though we may take many physical forms."

"Now you can live either above or below the water?"

"Only for short periods of time, above. You see, we are water people. We take oxygen from the sea. We also have lungs like you that we can utilize for short periods of time, when necessary."

"But you have been here for nearly a year. Is that a short period of time to you?"

"Oh, not at all," Flipper replied. "However, by the sacrifices of the people of my world, my capacity was increased in order to allow me one Atlantin year's time in which to complete the purpose of my being here."

"And that is really why we are here today, isn't it?" she asked rhetorically.

He nodded in agreement.

"You have been charged with a great duty?"

"Yes, I have. My father, Lord Dog Waterman, Ruler of Atlantis and the seven seas, has requested my presence in your world. I was given but a single year's time in which to deliver his word to your people and then I must return to Atlantis forever. Failure to deliver his message would mean my damnation to your world which would consume me now that my year is ending."

"Well then, by all means, please deliver your message," Amy insisted, moving out of the sight of the cameras.

Flipper stood, looked directly into a camera, then began.

"Good people of the Earth's lands, I, Christian Waterman, eldest son of his Excellency, Lord Dog Waterman, Ruler of the oceans, Purveyor of all that he swims, sends you greetings and wishes for peace and harmony. Our worlds, linked unmistakably and inseparably, are dependant upon one another. Your carelessness and contempt for this, our planet, threatens us, your brethren of the sea. Petroleum products from your great vessels, wastes from your factories, byproducts of your wealth, even the used condoms from your toilets, are all poisoning us."

Immediately after Flipper had said this there was a great commotion in the crowd off to our left. We did not know what had happened, but a later news report stated that one of the nuns in the crowd had nearly fainted when Flipper mentioned condoms in front of her class. None of this bothered Flipper, who continued as though nothing had happened.

"Our people are ill, our children unhealthy, our friends, the fishes of the sea, are dying. You must put an end to it. Each of you who hears this word must consciously make an effort to allow this no more, to end what exists, to prevent that which may otherwise occur and to inform others of this message. The death of Atlantis can mean but one thing: the death of the seas, the death of this world, ours and yours. This is our request, this is our warning, now is your final opportunity."

Flipper paused momentarily and turned to me. I smiled at him, then he gave me a wink and turned back to the camera.

"That was my father's message, but in my year I have learned much. Foremost of which is that my time here has been wasted. You, my friends, do not listen, you speak. You do not conserve, you use. You do not care, you achieve 'success.' You are blind and thus cannot see that you are all from the same Maker, placed in a bad situation to prevail together, rather than feed upon one another. You are porpoises, yet behave as sharks. Only in self control and selflessness can you survive. Listen, I beg you, for all of our sakes. If you can care about a people that until now you believed were but myth, then how easy it should be to care about those you have seen every day of your lives. All it takes to fulfill my father's message is to heed mine. Stop putting yourselves first and begin worrying about your fellow man and woman. If you do, I promise that you will be happier for it, and so shall we."

With that Flipper ripped his shirt from his body. Screams once again arose from the audience. He smiled, held his hands high in the air and the crowd roared.

Flipper then plopped down onto the stage and quickly removed his shoes. He held his huge, flappy feet up for the cameras and a gasp arose from the audience.

The air around us was charged with excitement, my hair stood on end and my flesh tingled. All eyes were upon the great Atlantin. Whipped into a frenzy, we were consumed by the moment. Flipper was in total control.

Suddenly he stood, then leaped from the stage and ran toward the lake. People were crying, begging him not to go, screaming as loud as they could. Worried policemen grabbed their batons, threatening any who attempted to cross the barricades.

"My God, he's going to do it!" Amy Star uttered ecstatically into her microphone.

Unimpeded by officer or barricade, I jumped from my seat and followed Flipper to the water's edge, Amy and her cameramen following close behind.

Flipper stopped atop the cement seawall and pulled off his pants. He turned and smiled at me, looking totally ridiculous in that little Speedo.

"Go ahead," I yelled to him, knowing he'd do it anyway.

"Sorry, Amy," he yelled to her as he peeled off the swimsuit. Wild screams and the shrill of children's laughter rose above the sustained roar of the crowd.

"Are you getting this? Are you getting this?" Amy yelled to her cameramen, obviously no longer concerned about the legality of his nudity. It was total mayhem.

Flipper gave one final wave to us all before slowly turning away. Then he bent his knees ever-so-slightly and, with one great push, heaved himself off the top step and out, over the water. It was a magnificent leap into the air culminating in a totally splash-free entry into the water.

With his departure, as though on cue, the crowd noise fell. Just then a church choir that Amy had positioned to one side of the stage opened up in a beautiful harmony, sounding as though an army of angels had descended from the heavens to placate the masses upon Flipper's departure. Tears bubbled in my eyes, then rolled down my cheeks in a moment that I shall never forget.

Suddenly, excited screams from the audience drowned out the choir. I looked in their direction, and followed their pointing fingertips. About seventy-five yards offshore Flipper reappeared, his body seemingly half-way out of the water, facing the shore. He was waving, motioning his right arm in a giant semicircle from one side of his body to the other, and was saying something. The cameras were recording the action as Amy and her crew began trying to quiet the crowd. They stopped the choir abruptly and the crowd soon followed.

An eerie silence fell over the Lakefront, an impossible silence. Ten thousand ecstatic people, at least a quarter of them school-aged children, stood in utter silence, straining to hear the words that Flipper was calling out. Like a distant bell over the water, the ringing of his voice echoed, louder and louder, until, finally, his words were clear. Soft, distant, but clear.

Out of the silence, across the water, came his words. "Andy. Do not despair, I will leave you a sign. They will listen." The tears coming faster now, I strained to hear him, tried to make sense of what he said.

Just as suddenly as he had appeared, and to much fanfare, Flipper plunged his head beneath the water, his huge feet automatically springing into the air, hanging there for a second, then sleekly disappearing beneath the waves.

The crowd went crazy and the choir struck up their hymn anew. The hum of chatter filled the air, nearly drowning out the beautiful sounds of the choir, everyone speculating where Flipper would surface next. We searched for a long time, scanning the lake, responding with excitement to several false sightings, looking for Flipper's next appearance. It never came.

He was gone.

Although the cameras recorded several shots of my weeping face, time did not allow for my interview. Forty-five minutes after it had all begun, the cameras were turned off and the crowd started to disperse.

"You done, good, Kiddo," Amy told me, hugging my neck.

"So did you," I replied.

"Well get ready, because it all changes after today. Maybe we'll come back and do a follow-up, in a couple of years."

"It'll cost you," I said, before telling her goodbye. And that was it. It was suddenly all over.

Flipper's departure had saddened me more than I had anticipated. I felt a great loss. It was then that the full weight of anxiety involved with Bip's disappearance finally hit me. There was nothing I could do to bring Flipper back, but I had to do something about Bip. Bets had been right about that.

I walked quickly toward my Jeep, ignoring calls from the departing spectators who would have picked my brain for information about the now-famous Man from Atlantis, tuned them all out. I did not hear Carly until she grabbed my shirt.

"Hey!" I said, stopping, happy to see her.

"Hi," she smiled, equally excited.

She was beautiful, absolutely radiant. The heaviness lifted from my heart and nearly disappeared altogether.

"Where are you off to in such a hurry? I was calling you and you just kept on going." Then she let go of my shirt.

"Oh, I'm sorry. I was trying to get out of here without having to talk to any of these people. I forgot you were going to be here."

"Thanks a lot."

"I'm sorry," I said, feeling awful, "you don't know how great it is to see you." I stepped in to give her a kiss and only then noticed the little boy at her side.

"Is this Taylor?" I asked, knowing that it was from his picture.

"Yes," she said excitedly. "Tell Mr. Andy hello."

"Hi," he said. He was adorable. I don't care what she thought, he looked exactly like his mother.

"Hey," I responded, "did you like the show?"

"Where did the flipper man go?" he asked.

"He swam back home."

"I saw you," he said, indicating that he had seen me on the stage.

"He's the flipper man's friend," Carly said.

"Yep," I affirmed. "Could y'all see?" I asked Carly.

"Yea, J. Ryan got us a great spot."

"Where is he?"

"He went back to the office," she explained. "We came in separate cars. I have to bring Taylor back to daycare."

"Can you take the rest of the day?" I asked.

"What?"

"Take off the rest of the day, spend it with me."

"Yea, I could call in to work."

"Would you?"

"What about you?"

"They don't expect me in until Monday," I answered.

"What about all those things you have to think about?"

"Well, one of them is at my house right now packing her things to take home."

"Really?" she exclaimed, her eyes lighting up.

"Yea, it all just kind of fell right into place. I think she followed us last night."

"Oh God. Is she stalking you?"

"No," I laughed. "As it works out, it's good that she did. Now it's all out in the open."

"Is she all right?" Carly asked, her concern surprising me.

"Not really, but she will be."

"She must hate my guts."

"I don't think either of us will ever make her top ten friends list."

"Oh well," she responded, smiling.

"Yea, oh well," I repeated. "So what do you say, can you? I really want to be with you."

"Is something the matter?" she asked, sensing my worry.

"Bip, my roommate. He was sailing in the New Orleans-Biloxi Regatta yesterday and he dis . . ."

"So it was your friend's boat?" Carly interrupted.

"Is my friend, yes," I corrected her.

"I'm sorry, I didn't mean 'was' like he is no longer…oh, that's awful. Have you heard anything else?"

"No, just what was in the paper. I was going to run over to the Coast Guard Station and see if they had heard anything." The Coast Guard maintained a station on the lake, not far from where we were.

"We'll come with you. I can use the phone there," she said.

"You want to come in the Jeep?"

"You want to ride in Mr. Andy's Jeep?" she asked Taylor.

"No top, no doors," he responded. Carly laughed. "I was telling him about your Jeep," she explained.

She was telling him about me. How exciting, I thought.

"Well come on," I said.

I picked Taylor up and put him in the back seat, securing him with the seat belt. Carly climbed in on the passenger's side. We drove the short distance over to the Coast Guard Station and I went inside.

The officer on duty was a short, stocky, bearded man with curly red hair. He looked friendly enough, like a little leprechaun, but he operated strictly by the book.

"I'm sorry sir, we are not allowed to divulge any information to non-family member civilians," he informed me.

"But he's my roommate. He has no family, just me."

"I am sorry sir, but 'roommate' does not qualify as family. However, if you would be kind enough to provide us with your name, address, and telephone number, we may want to get back to you with pertinent questions, should the need arise."

I felt like telling him to shove his pertinent questions up his ass, but resisted the urge on the off-chance that I might be able to be of some help to Bip. I gave him my home and office telephone numbers and addresses.

"Thank you sir," he said.

"Just please find him," I replied.

"It's not uncommon, you know," he told me just as I turned to go, "for a sailing vessel to disappear in the Gulf of Mexico for days or even a week before finally being spotted. Barring a hurricane, the occupants are almost always found alive."

"Thanks," I told him, feeling guilty for having been short with him earlier.

"Don't worry too much. We usually find them and they are usually all right."

I gave him a smile and a nod of my head, then went back outside feeling much better than when I had gone in. I found Carly and Taylor standing at the water's edge.

"What did he say?" she asked.

"Nothing new yet, but he said it's not uncommon for a sailboat to be missing even a week, and that the people on board are usually fine. Unless there's a hurricane."

"Well, that sounds good."

"Yea, I feel a lot better. Bip's been in sailboats since he was a kid. He knows the water, so I'm sure he's okay."

"I'm sure he is," she agreed.

"Where's the flipper man?" Taylor asked, gazing out at the lake.

"He's gone," I said.

"When's he coming back?"

"He's not."

"Didn't he like it here?" he asked innocently.

"I don't think he did."

"I think he'll come back," Taylor said, looking out over the lake.

I looked at Carly and we both smiled. "Did you call your office?"

"Sure did," she said, pointing to the pay phone on the wall of the building. "I told them I would see them in the morning." With that she took my hand and squeezed it. I held hers tightly.

We spent the rest of the day at the Audubon Zoo and the Children's Museum. Carly and I had beers at the Zoo and Taylor had a snowball that turned his lips, teeth, tongue, and who knows what else, blue. It was wonderful.

We were the last to leave the Zoo and drove the short distance from there to my apartment. I was somewhat hesitant about doing this, not certain that Bets would be gone, but I had no choice. Just to be safe I left them outside and ran in to get some cash that I had laying around. I could tell that she had been there and she had pretty much taken everything that was hers – along with a few items that were not.

I returned to Carly and Taylor in the Jeep and we drove to a little seafood restaurant on the Lakefront for dinner. I wouldn't say that I was drawn there, but with Flipper and Bip both in the water that evening, it just seemed the appropriate place to be.

After dinner we took a short stroll along the lake's shore. I carried Taylor and he fell asleep in my arms. He was such a great kid, full of spunk. He kept saying "Andy this," and "Andy that," acting as though he had known me forever.

"He really likes you," Carly said.

"It's very mutual," I told her.

"He doesn't usually get that close to people so quickly."

"Me either," I said, looking into her eyes. She leaned into me and we kissed.

We ended up at their car and Taylor woke as I put him in his seat and buckled him in.

"Goodbye, Andy."

"Goodbye, Taylor. I'll see you soon."

"Okay," he said with a big smile as he rubbed his tired eyes.

I walked around to the driver's side to talk to Carly. "What are y'all doing this weekend?" I asked her hopefully.

"I'm going to my Mom's in Covington," she said. It was a small town, just on the other side of the lake.

"The whole weekend?" I asked, more than a little disappointed.

"From right after work tomorrow until Monday morning. I usually just drive right into work from there. Do you want to come?" she asked politely.

"Are you serious?"

"Sure, she wants to meet you," she said.

"You told her about me already?"

"Yes. Didn't you tell your family about me?" she teased.

"I haven't even talked to my Mom since I've known your name," I confessed with a giggle.

"Well, do you want to come?"

"I'd love to, but I can't this weekend. I've got a lot of things to take care of and I need to be around in case they need me for Bip," I explained.

"I know," she said sympathetically. "I really wish you could come, or I could stay."

"Can I have the number?"

She gave me her mother's telephone number and a final little kiss before driving off. I went back to my empty house all alone. Exhausted after the tiring week I had had, I stumbled to my bed, dropped fully clothed upon it, and fell into unconsciousness.

TWENTY-SIX

I AWOKE THE NEXT MORNING, sensing someone standing over my bed.

Bip! I thought, turning over, opening my eyes.

It was Bets. She was gathering the few things that she had somehow managed to leave behind.

"Good," she said, "you're awake."

"Good morning," I tried to be polite.

"You can help me carry this suitcase out," she ordered, motioning to one of my large suitcases that she had placed in the middle of my bedroom.

"That's my suitcase," I said childishly.

"Fine. You want your fucking suitcase?" She began opening it.

"Never mind," I quickly responded, envisioning her throwing things around the room, causing a scene. She was pissed, it was obvious, and I really couldn't blame her. She could have the damned thing.

"No, no. Take it," she insisted. "I give you the best years of my life and you can't even let me borrow a simple suitcase."

"You can have the suitcase," I said, hopping out of bed. "I'm sorry, I wasn't thinking. It's no big deal." I grabbed the suitcase by the handle.

"It's like overnight you don't trust me anymore. One night you're drooling on me as you screw my brains out and the next you kick me out without so much as a suitcase."

"I didn't kick you out," I defended, "it was your idea to pack up and leave."

"You want me to stay?" she asked sarcastically.

Aye, yie, yie – no, I didn't want her to stay. "I think you have already made that decision," I said.

"No, you did!" she responded angrily. "That's the point."

With that, on the verge of tears, she stormed out of the room. She had succeeded in making me feel like shit. I picked up the suitcase and followed. It was heavy, very heavy. I wondered what she might have put inside, but was not about to stop and search through it now. Whatever it was, she could have it. Good riddance. Fair trade.

"Bets, I'm sorry."

"Fuck you," she responded, heading for the front door.

"Look, here's your suitcase. I'll bring it down for you."

She turned to me, so quickly in fact that I nearly ran her over. "Why, Andy?"

"What?" I stalled.

"Why her and not me?"

"Bets, you have to see it. We're just not right for each other."

"Bullshit, Andy. That's crap. Is she better in bed? Is that it?"

"No."

"She's not? You're leaving me for someone..."

"No. I don't even know how she is in bed."

"Yeah, right."

"I swear."

"Oh, so is that your deal? Is that what you do? She's your new project?" she asked bitterly. "Just tell her you won't marry her unless she screws you, that one works. And when she does and you get tired of her just move on to some new objective."

"That's not fair, Bets."

"Oh? I'm not being fair? I just want to know, Andy. Have you been doing us both at the same time?"

"Bets! No. Honestly..."

"Because if I catch some kind of disease from that tramp, I'm gonna kill you."

"You won't," I assured her. She was obsessed with this disease thing.

"I better not."

We stared at one another for a moment, then I spoke.

"Bets, it just happened. I'm sorry, really sorry. You are a wonderful person. It's just like a light went on and I could see that you and me just aren't meant to be."

She just looked at me for a minute, then she laughed. She laughed! Granted, it wasn't much of a laugh, but still, I expected anger, frustration, even tears, but not laughter. This was new territory for her, laughing at her own tragedy.

"That was funny?" I finally asked.

"You're so pathetic," she said, turning to the door. "You're not worth it. I hope you're happy with your new, ready-made family."

I knew she didn't mean the good wishes, but all-in-all, she was taking it pretty well. I followed her out of the house, down the stairs, and to the street.

"Did you call a cab?" I asked, knowing she didn't own a car.

"I drove," she answered smartly.

"Whose car?"

"Mine."

"Yours? You bought a car? Where?"

"Right here," she said, standing at the trunk of a brand new, red Mercedes convertible. She pushed a button on her key chain and the trunk opened.

"What bank did you rob?" I asked, shocked.

"It's not really mine. I lied," she answered.

"Oh. Have a boyfriend I don't know about?"

"You think you're the only one who can play around? I can do a lot better than you."

"You really had a boyfriend?" I asked, beginning to get pissed. At least I waited until the end, but she…

"What if I did? What if I was screwing around on you the whole time? You have the nerve to get upset about it?"

"I wasn't screwing around on you," I defended.

"You live in a fantasy world, Andy. And no, I'm not like you. I don't have a boyfriend. The car belongs to my new employer."

"You got a new job? Doing what?"

"You of all people should know. You set the whole thing up."

"What?" I demanded, suspiciously.

"The Trust of Atlantis."

"WHAT?" I responded, furious, dropping the suitcase in the street.

"Hey asshole! My stuff is in there!" she yelled.

"Like I give a fuck? You bought *this* with the Trust's money?"

"Yes," she responded in an I-did-it-and-what-are-you-going-to-do-about-it tone.

"Bets, are you crazy?"

"What do you mean, crazy? Crazy for trusting you maybe."

"Have you ever heard of fiduciary duty?" I explained. "Do you know what happens to trustees that breach their fiduciary duties?"

"Who do I owe that duty to, Mr. Attorney?"

"To the trust."

"And who runs the trust?"

"That doesn't matter. It isn't your money in the trust."

"Whose is it?"

"Flipper's."

"So I owe this fiduciary duty to Flipper?"

"Yes. Of course," I responded, hoping that she finally understood.

"Fine. Then answer me this, barrister," she began with a nasty grin on her face. "What happens in the case where you owe a fiduciary duty to some freak that jumps into a lake claiming he's swimming off to Atlantis?"

"I can't believe this," I said in shock.

"What, Andy? Do you really think that big asshole was from Atlantis? Do you actually believe that he swam off to be with his father lord dog whatever the hell he is? You need help." She was laughing at me.

Suddenly I was angry at myself for apologizing to her. I wanted to tell her how low she was for having used Flipper, and me. How she had never cared about anything but the money, never believed in him, and only lied so that she could get control of the trust. That I was thrilled that I had not married her, that I had found Carly in time.

"You bitch!" was all I could manage to say.

"Nice, Andrew," she taunted me, laughing, reaching for the suitcase.

"You stole that money!" I accused her. "It was all just a big con to you, wasn't it?"

"You're a lunatic," she brushed me off and grabbed the bag, straining to lift it.

"It was all a scam to you, wasn't it? You buttered yourself right up to Flipper, talked about all that ecology bullshit, how you wanted to save Atlantis, just so you could get your hands on the money. You knew he'd be gone and that you'd have complete control, and as soon as he jumped into the water you could spend to your little heart's content. I don't care what you call it, Bets, it's stealing. Pure and simple, it's stealing and that's all it is. I'm not letting you get away with it."

"I didn't steal anything," she answered angrily. "As trustee of the fund, as the person who is going to be negotiating with Exxon and Dow and Governors and Legislators, I felt it appropriate that I not drive up in a tiny, clunkity, rust bucket and expect to be taken seriously by them. How far do you think I would get? They would laugh me off. But when I drive up in this, with my new wardrobe, they..."

"Wardrobe?" I interrupted.

"Yes," she explained, "it's one in the same. Those people need to see that I have influence and that I have money and that I am not afraid of spending it to see that what I want done gets done."

I suppose what she had said did make some sense, although I think she was merely using it to justify spending the money on herself. She could have settled for a Lincoln, or a Cutlass, even.

With great effort she heaved the suitcase into the trunk and slammed it shut. I stood there, mouth agape, helpless, as she walked around and climbed into the driver's seat.

"By the way," she began as she grabbed the door to close it. I walked nearer.

"There is an earth summit in Belize on Tuesday and there is a certain someone that I would like to take with me," she continued.

"You're telling me this?"

"It is not personal. He is very important to the conference. He will give the Trust of Atlantis immediate credibility."

"Who is he?" I demanded.

"I can't say right now," she responded curtly.

"So what do you want from me?"

"I need you to purchase the tickets, and as the Trust's attorney of course, you can bill us."

"Forget it."

"What? You aren't going to advise the trust? Maybe I should give ole Bill a call," she answered, referring to Mr. Fabacher.

"That isn't a legal function. You can buy your owned damned tickets. I am not going to aid in your stealing this money."

"I can't do it myself because no one can know that he is coming with me. If anyone does, the whole effect will be spoiled. You are in the perfect position to help out the trust. Buy the tickets in our names, mine and yours, so that no one knows. Then they will think he is you, my attorney."

"Who will think that?" I asked.

"Whoever might be curious enough to try and find out," she said. "This is big corporate stuff. I'm going for their jugulars. There's lots of espionage and intrigue in big business, or didn't you know?" she asked condescendingly.

"Don't talk to me like that."

"Fine, I'll just talk to Bill. If you can't handle the big time, I'm sure J. Ryan..."

"I'll get the damned tickets," I interrupted her.

"Good. When?" she demanded. I hated her.

"First thing Monday," I said.

"Today, Andy," she insisted.

"I'm not going in today."

"Have Margo do it. Call her. It's important. Besides, it will probably cost the Trust less money the sooner you get it done."

I nodded my assent, not wanting to say another word to her.

"I kind of like this new relationship we have here," she chided as she put on a brand new pair of Vaurnet sunglasses and started the car. The engine roared at first, then settled into a steady hum. Part of me was jealous and wanted that damned new car.

"Oh," she said, putting the car into gear.

"Something else?" I asked through clinched teeth.

"Hear any more about Bip?"

I shook my head in the negative.

"Let me know if you hear anything," she said.

"You look like you're really worried about him," I responded sarcastically.

"Under this cool exterior lies a woman in ruins," she answered dramatically. "It's killing me, and so are you," she said. She dropped her foot on the accelerator and lifted the other off of the clutch. The engine raced, the tires squealed, and she was gone.

As she drove off I hoped that at least some small part of her was sincere in her work for the Trust of Atlantis. She was right as far as her fiduciary duty was concerned. She had absolute authority over the money, and if she decided to go on a spending spree only Flipper had standing to question her actions. And Flipper was gone. However, the fund did owe the firm almost twenty thousand dollars and I was going to make certain that it was paid first thing Monday morning, before Bets had time to buy any more cars or clothes.

As soon as I got upstairs, I called Margo and asked her to fax the firm's bill to the Fund for immediate payment and order the airline tickets in mine and Bets' names as Bets had requested. Of course, I didn't know the fax number, so I told her just to call information, look it up, do whatever, just get the damn bill over there.

"With those two requests it sounds like you and the old lady are fixing to run off with the rest of the loot," Margo kidded.

"Not quite," I answered. I did give it a little thought though. All that money. It could go a long way in Central America – we could have matching Mercedes. But the thought of having to spend it with Bets soured the vision. I went back to my room and back to sleep, not waking again until Saturday morning.

The weekend was uneventful. I disconnected the telephone and spent a good deal of time on Saturday reading all of the coverage on Flipper in the past two editions of the newspaper. Most of it was positive and nice. There were interviews with several people who had witnessed his departure, and many who said that it had touched or changed their lives. There were articles concerning politicians' renewed interest in cleaning up the lake, youngsters talking about forming clubs to work on environmental projects, and even a group who claimed that Flipper had actually been some sort of prophet in anticipation of the Second Coming.

And then there was a picture that some reporter had snapped of Carly, Taylor, and me after Flipper had taken off. I cut it out. I really missed them, calling to speak with them twice daily at her Mom's house across the lake.

At one point I almost drove over there to meet Carly's Mom, but, to be totally honest, I was scared. I guess it is something that I should have gotten over in high school, but I never did. I was more nervous about meeting Carly's mother than I was about anything that had happened recently in my life.

There was no new word on Bip. I called the Coast Guard station at least eight times that weekend. I was really missing him too, and it worried me sick that he could be out there, injured, or worse, and that they could not find him. I was helpless to do anything, but did find some solace in Flipper's assurance that he was all right. I looked forward to Monday – Carly would be back and work would help take my mind off of Bip.

TWENTY-SEVEN

I HAVE COME TO BELIEVE THAT IN ONE REGARD, there are three types of people in this world: the lucky, the unlucky, and the other. The lucky, they are the ones with the Midas touch, they win the lotteries – some more than once – they inherit money from relatives they never even knew they had, and they are successful in everything they attempt. These people are balanced out by the unlucky, those who no matter what they do will never have enough money to pay off all their bills, who do not have enough fingers to count the number of family members that have died tragic and useless deaths, and who will never even meet that one special person that was made just for them. And then there are the rest of us, the masses, we balance ourselves out. I am the type of person that if I ever won the lottery, the next day I would accidentally run over some poor slob and lose all of my winnings to him and his family. I will probably never starve, but I suspect that I will never know what it feels like to live in the lap of luxury either. It is just the way that it has always been.

That being the case, I should have realized that there would be hell to pay for the little slice of heaven that I had experienced in falling in love with Carly and in knowing and helping Flipper.

By the time I awoke on Monday there was still no sign of Bip and the morning news anchor announced that the Coast Guard was calling off its search. I felt miserable about it. My best friend had disappeared. He could have been dying at that very moment, and there was absolutely nothing I could think to do to help him. I felt useless. It was a time in my life that otherwise should have been filled with joy and excitement; I had met the woman of my dreams and I had accomplished the impossible by showing the world a man from Atlantis and having the world believe it. Not only that, but in the process I had made a lot of money for the firm, which was paying dividends in my career path. I dare to say that I had become somewhat famous in my own right.

Getting ready for work that morning, I suddenly thought to talk to Mr. Keating about Bip. He had political connections around the state, and even in Washington. Perhaps he could have the search continued, maybe even get the Navy involved.

The possibilities excited me so much that I rushed to get out of the house and even drove into the office. I figured that I had earned the privilege anyway and thought I might just drive in all week long.

When I walked past the receptionist in the office, I heard her announce my arrival over the office intercom system. By the time I had passed through the door behind her and into the working section of the firm, several employees, mostly non-attorneys, had gathered and actually gave me a little cheer. Each of them took turns congratulating me, patting me on the back, shaking my hand.

"I saw you on television," one said.

"That was incredible," someone else commented.

"Congratulations."

"Were you nervous? Way to go."

"You looked great."

"How did it feel?"

I smiled and thanked each of them, shook their hands. My face red, my ears burning, I finally made it through the gauntlet and to my office. Margo followed me in and shut the door.

"Just one question," she said, excitedly.

"What?" I asked, still smiling.

"Is he for real?"

"Who?" I asked, knowing the answer.

"Waterman," she responded.

"Haven't we had this discussion?" I asked. "What do you think?"

"He seemed real to me. My Mom swears he's real and my Dad thinks you're both flakes."

"I might be," I laughed, "but I tend to agree with your mother."

"So he's never coming back?"

"Don't think so. He said he wasn't."

"Too bad," she said, disappointed.

"I don't know that I could take any more of the excitement if he did."

"Well, you better get ready for this then," she told me, pulling a small slip of yellow paper from behind her back.

"What is that?" I asked suspiciously.

"It's Friday's deposit into the trust."

"We got checks already?"

"Already?" she asked, incredulously, "Friday we received eight of them by Federal Express."

"From who?"

"From the T.V. people, the movie people – the Hollywood movie people and the T.V. movie people – the book people, the underwater gear people, the toy and cartoon people..."

"Toy and cartoon people?" I interrupted.

"Yea, they sent a huge check."

"They weren't supposed to send it for two weeks," I countered.

"Yea, but they called and asked Mr. Fabacher if they could send it now because they wanted to begin production immediately and they wanted to make sure that we couldn't back out."

"You're kidding!"

"No, people are really going crazy over this. Haven't you seen the paper?"

"Yea, but I never thought it would get this big. I mean it's all pretty incredible."

"It's nine hundred sixty-two thousand five hundred dollars incredible," she responded.

"What?" I said, my jaw going slack. "Bring that over here."

I looked at the slip of paper. *$962,503.21.* I could not believe it.

"My God," I said.

"Mr. Keating and Mr. Fabacher are going crazy. They want to know what kind of deal we have with the Trust of Atlantis."

"Oh, that's right," I said, my memory jogged. "Have we gotten the check from Bets?"

"No. But she called and said she would be dropping it off when she came by to get the tickets."

"When is she coming?"

"She said around 3:30."

"When does the plane leave?"

"Tomorrow at 10:00 a.m."

"Make sure the firm gets reimbursed for the tickets too," I reminded her.

"I know. I've already told her how much they were."

"Good job. Thanks for taking care of all of that for me."

"No problem," she responded. "I like it. It makes me feel a little bit famous myself."

I smiled.

"Oh, yea," I remembered. "Could you check and see when I can get in to see Mr. Keating?"

"Sure, I'll do it right now."

"Thanks," I said, watching her head off toward her desk.

After Margo had gone, I called Carly and we talked for over an hour about my concern for Bip, and about her weekend at her Mother's, and about how much we had missed one another. I finally had to get off of the telephone when Margo came in and told me that Mr. Keating was ready to see me.

You would have thought that I was Tom Keating's best friend when I walked into his office.

"Come on in, Andy," he said with a big smile and a wave of the hand. He directed me to one of his client's chairs and even offered me one of his imported cigars.

"No thanks," I said, "I don't smoke."

"Neither do I, but it doesn't stop me," he responded with a chuckle.

I laughed nervously.

"Well this is quite a little feat that you have pulled off here," he continued, closing the cigar box on his desk.

"What do you mean?"

"This television thing. The phones haven't stopped ringing. We've had to hire a new girl to help answer them, and we are going to hire two more attorneys for our intellectual property section, which, of course, you will head up."

"Mr. Keating..."

"Andy," he interrupted, "from here on out it's Tom to you. Our senior partners are like family. We are on a first name basis. It's friendlier, you know, and it sets us apart from the underlings."

"Senior partners?" I asked.

"Yes, we've decided you should skip right over the junior partners. You've got a lot on your plate, you know," Keating explained. What he meant was that if I decided to leave the firm, its newfound prosperity would walk right out of the door with me.

"I don't know what to say," I responded.

"Now I know you are not a partner yet, but that is only a matter of time. The next partner's meeting is Wednesday. Have to do it by the book you know, and then it will be official. You can go ahead and start calling me Tom. The meeting is really only a formality."

"All right – Tom," I said, uncomfortably.

"Good," he responded. "Now, I hope it's not a problem, but until it's official you won't be able to move into your new office either."

"New office?" I asked.

"Yes. The back corner."

"But that's Tony's office."

"Not after Wednesday, it isn't. We want the senior partners in the corners. It is more demonstrative of our status. I know it's going to be a little awkward, seeing as D'Ensina has been your superior up until now, but I assure you that he will understand. He'll just have to get used to calling you Mr. Jordan."

"Right," I chuckled.

"No. I'm dead serious about this, Andy. We have to maintain a certain order around here and that order is that the partners are the troop leaders. We must be regarded with some degree of respect or the entire system will fail."

I couldn't believe it. Just couldn't imagine Tony having to call me "Mr." anything. He was going to hate me. He'd probably quit. I couldn't stand to do it to him.

"When is Tony going to be told?" I asked.

"The announcement should be made Thursday," Mr. Keating – Tom – replied.

"Shouldn't we give him some warning?" I asked.

"Wouldn't be in the correct order of things. He can find out with the rest of the firm on Thursday."

Bullshit. I'd have to tell him myself.

"That is enough about everyone else. I know there was something that you wanted to talk to me about, but I wanted you to know just how pleased we are with you. You handled yourself with the utmost professionalism and it has meant an awful lot to this firm. I wanted to be the first to thank and to congratulate you."

"Well, thank you," I said.

"Tom," he insisted.

"Tom."

"Good then. We are going to be very busy around here. We need a good troop leader. Sure you'll be up to the task?"

"Yes, sir. I am certain that I will be," I responded, doubting the truth of it.

"All right. Well, what was it that you wanted to see me about?"

"Well, Mr.... Tom," I corrected myself.

"Yes?" he prodded, smiling.

"I was wondering if maybe you could help me with something."

"What is it?" he asked, raising an eyebrow.

"A very good friend of mine, my roommate in fact, Bip, Theodore Woodson, is missing."

"The sailor?"

"Yes."

"That was your roommate? Why, I had no idea. I've been reading about him, but I had no idea that he was your roommate. It is a very small world, isn't it?"

"Yes, sir," I replied. "I was wondering..."

"But I sure would hate to have to paint it," he laughed.

"Excuse me?" It was obvious that J. Ryan had been brown-nosing the old man.

"The world. It's a small world but I would hate to have to paint it. It's a joke. Haven't you ever heard it before?" He looked at me as though *I* were the moron.

"Yes, sir," I replied, forcing a small laugh.

"I thought you must have."

"What I wanted to ask was," I forged ahead, "...well, you see, I read this morning that the Coast Guard had called off the search."

"Yes, a pity. He was with the District Attorney's office, wasn't he?"

"Yes, sir. But what I was wondering...could you possibly talk to someone to get them to try a little longer."

"Try what?"

"The search, get them to keep looking a little longer," I explained.

"But he's dead," Keating replied matter-of-factly, as though Bip were anyone, just another name in the obituary.

"They don't know that. They haven't found any sign of him yet."

"Yes, but the paper said he was dead. As a matter of fact, I saw where the District Attorney has scheduled a memorial service for him in the morning."

"They can't know that he's dead if they haven't found him," I argued.

"They looked for days. No sign of him, right? Nobody can live out there for that length of time without being seen. He's got to be dead or they would have found something by now. You know, I was in the Navy, back in '42. We didn't have half the stuff they have today, but I can tell you if they haven't found him by now, he is in another place."

I looked at him hard. He was probably right, but he had been my one chance to do something and he wasn't coming through.

"Look," he continued, obviously seeing the disappointment on my face, "those people know what they are doing. If they've called the search off it's because they have searched every possible place and just haven't found him. That boat is sunk, it has to be. There's just no other explanation."

I grew a little dizzy. Until that moment I had not really believed that Bip was dead. It was just too unreal. But now I could see. Tom Keating was right. Each day the chance of Bip being found at all, let alone being found alive, grew more and more slim. He wasn't coming back.

"Well, thank you," I said meekly, picking myself up out of his chair.

"You are very welcome, Andy," he responded with a smile as I left.

Outside his office, I drew a deep breath and headed straight for Tony's, passing by Lori's desk along the way.

"Congratulations," she whispered to me as I neared.

"For what?" I asked, knowing she must mean the success of the send-off on Thursday.

"The promotion," she continued under her breath.

I was surprised. No one was supposed to know until after the partners' meeting. So much for Tom Keating's "correct order of things."

"Thanks," I said nervously, wondering how many other people knew.

"He hasn't said anything yet," she continued as I turned to leave.

"Who?" I asked.

"Bill – Mr. Fabacher," she quickly corrected herself. There had been a rumor going around the office for some time that she and Mr. Fabacher were much more than just boss and secretary.

"About what?" I asked, thinking she was talking about my partnership.

"The bathtub," she said incredulously, as though I should have known.

"Oh!" I remarked with a chuckle, recalling the scene. "I wonder if he suspects anyone."

"He's acting as though it never happened. He hasn't said a word about it to anybody."

"Keep your fingers crossed," I told her as I began walking away. "And keep me informed."

"Okay," she replied.

The door to Tony's corner office was closed, and I entered without knocking as I always had. He had been sitting behind his desk reading the latest issue of *Town & Country* Magazine, but in one smooth motion he sat up straight and scooped the magazine onto his lap.

"Hey," he greeted me, smiling, then immediately looked back down at a file on his desk as though he had been working on it before I came in.

"Hi," I replied.

He closed the file and sat back.

"Mr. BMOF in my office, to what do I owe the pleasure?"

"B-M-O-F?" I inquired.

"Firm. Big Man On Firm. I guess technically it should be BMIF, Big Man In Firm," he corrected.

"Very funny," I said. "Is that in some movie?"

"Nope. Just a little originality I thought I would share with you. Congratulations." He seemed sincere enough.

"For what?" I played dumb, just in case.

"Haven't they told you?" he seemed surprised. "You're going to be made a senior partner Wednesday. I guess you'll be my boss."

"Right," I said, acting as though I did not believe the announcement and was just hearing of it for the first time.

"Seriously," he insisted, "they are voting on it Wednesday. I can't believe you don't know."

"I don't think so."

"You'll see. And too, I wanted to tell you, when you get them to redo this office, you should have them put in new carpet and put a phone jack in on the other side of the room so your desk can face the windows."

"What are you talking about?"

"You do know they'll move you in here," Tony answered calmly.

"They wouldn't take your office." I acted repulsed.

"I'm sure they will. They can't have a senior partner down the hallway and a lowly junior partner like myself in luxury up here."

I was relieved that he had heard and that he had even figured out the office move.

"I hope they don't do that," I said innocently.

"Don't worry about it. Between you and me, I've already started looking around."

"Looking around?" I asked, feeling a pain in the pit of my stomach.

"Yea, I've been here for nine years and am no closer to making senior partner than you or J. Ryan were two weeks ago. In fact, now that you have moved ahead of me it will probably be another nine years before I make it."

"That's not true," I insisted, trying to make him feel better.

"Look, I don't blame you. You're a fine attorney and I'm sure you'll do well. You just got the lucky break this time. But I'll tell you one thing. You guys will miss me when I'm gone."

I agreed with him.

"You know," he continued, "you may not believe this, but I always thought this might happen. From the very first week you were here I could see that you fit in perfectly. You were just what they needed. Someone with a clear head who could get the work done. All you needed to do was to find a way to pull in some substantial business, and shit, you've done that. You really should consider going out on your own. You could do very well and you wouldn't have to worry about sharing it with those two ego maniacs."

"I wouldn't know where to start."

"Well, you could go in with an old veteran that did." He looked down at his file as soon as he had finished the sentence, seemingly embarrassed at having made the suggestion.

"I don't know, Tony. That's a huge step," I answered, having no intention of striking it out on my own when I was about to be made one of only three senior partners in an established firm.

"You're probably right," he relented. I detected disappointment in his voice, injury in my rejection.

"I mean maybe after a little while..." I tried to better the situation.

"Yea," he replied stoically.

"...You know, after I'm a little more established."

"Sure," he said quickly, then changed the subject. "Well, what else is up?"

"Not much."

"I really need to get to work on this file," he lied. "Could you pull the door closed for me?" he asked, pointing.

"Sure," I said. "Want to do lunch this week?"

"Maybe," he replied, trying to look engrossed in his open file.

"Okay," I said.

He did not respond. I left his office and closed the door behind me.

Carly had to work through lunch, so I had a sandwich at my desk. Tom Keating's secretary brought me a stack of twenty-two resumes of attorneys who had applied for the two positions that the firm had advertised in the weekend paper. Most had been faxed over from offices where these attorneys were obviously unhappy. A few had even been hand-delivered. She told me that the firm was also going to hire two full time secretaries and another law clerk, and that I was to make these personnel decisions as well. This was to be given priority over everything else so that we could begin turning out work and billing our new clients. After looking them over, I had Margo schedule fourteen of them for interviews.

It was nearly three in the afternoon before I had an opportunity to take a break. I put in a call to Jim Miller, an assistant district attorney who had been Bip's closest friend at work. He was obviously upset when he answered the phone.

"Jim?" I asked.

"Yea. Hey Andy, how are you doing?" he replied in almost a whisper.

"Okay, I guess."

"I know. We're trying to hang in there too. Have you heard anything else?"

"No," I responded. "Just that they called off the search."

"I think he's gone, Man," Jim responded, sounding as though he were about to cry.

"I can't give up yet," I responded. "He knows the water too well."

"I hope you're right," he told me, but I could tell he believed I was not.

"Oh, I saw you on television, by the way."

"Oh yea?"

"I guess you're in the big time now. Movie star."

"I wouldn't go that far."

"Are you coming in the morning?" he asked, referring to the memorial service.

"I just heard about it," I responded.

"You're kidding."

"No. Seemed like one of you guys could have told me about it."

"I guess we all just assumed that Bets would have told you since she was the one who organized the whole thing."

"What?" I said, surprised. "Bets organized it?"

"Yea. She was in here Friday and again this morning."

"That bitch," I said.

"You guys have a fight?"

"Yea, we split up."

"Well there you have it. That's why you didn't know."

"Yea, but she could have at least told me," I said. "She's not even going to be there."

"What?"

"No. She's flying out tomorrow morning."

"That's strange."

"Not after the way she's been acting. It's par for the course."

"Well look, I've really got to run," he told me. "It's been nice talking to you."

"You too, Jim. I'll see you in the morning."

"Great, Andy," he said, then we both hung up.

I immediately buzzed my secretary.

"Margo?"

"Yes?"

"Let me know when Bets comes in to get those tickets. I need to talk to her."

"Too late. She just left."

"What? When?" I asked.

"Five minutes ago."

"Did she drop off the check?"

"Yep," she said merrily. "Mr. Fabacher is having Marc bring it right over to the bank. Rent is due tomorrow."

"Did she say where she was going?" I asked.

"No. She seemed real happy though. She said to tell you that she loves you and would see you in the morning."

"What?"

Margo did not respond.

"She said she'd see me in the morning?"

"Yea, that was it."

"Were those tickets refundable?"

"Totally. First class, too."

"Okay," I said. "Thanks."

I reasoned that Bets must have been planning to postpone her trip until after the service. Once she had her hands on the tickets, she could easily exchange them for another flight. However, she was acting very peculiarly. Perhaps the breakup had affected her more deeply than I had initially thought, or maybe she was in over her head with all that trust money. Whichever, I was going to have to keep a closer eye on her. I was just thankful that the check was in hand and on the way to the bank, because with it rode my future with the firm.

That evening I had Carly and Taylor over for dinner. I cooked gumbo and Coke-and-Ketchup chicken. I wanted to show her what a complete man I was. I burned the chicken, but she ate it anyway. Taylor had peanut butter and jelly.

After dinner Taylor and I played on the floor for a long time, and Carly sat on the couch just watching us. I could tell that her feelings for me were growing stronger by the moment. I finally put in the *Beauty and the Beast* video tape that we had rented and Taylor fell asleep before it was half over. Carly and I sat up talking about one another, asking questions, finding out just how much we really had in common. Before we knew it, it was three in the morning. Time had literally flown by.

After I had carried Taylor to the guest room, Carly and I kissed deeply and romantically. She and Taylor slept over that night. They slept together. I slept alone.

TWENTY-EIGHT

CARLY LEFT THE HOUSE AROUND FIVE IN THE MORNING so that she would have time to get ready for work and to get Taylor ready for daycare. I got up with them, and she and I had coffee while Taylor ate cereal. Before she left Carly told me that she was certain that there was something between us that was "not of this world." It reminded me of the things that Flipper had said. Who knows, maybe we were once a couple of porpoises playing in the ocean. When you got right down to it, all of that mumbo-jumbo stuff really did not matter much to me. What was important was that we had met, had made the connection, and that we both knew that we wanted to be together for a very long time to come.

"Sorry you had to get up so early," I apologized as they headed out the door. "I promise to make it up to you."

"You already have," she answered, giving me a big kiss.

After that it was useless trying to get back to sleep so I began jotting down some notes about Flipper, how we had met, all that had happened. I thought it might come in handy if *The Tonight Show* thing ever materialized or if I ever decided to write my memoirs. Bets had sold the rights to Flipper's story, but I still had the rights to my own.

I was in the office by 8:30 so that I could at least make an appearance before I had to leave for Bip's service, which was scheduled for 9:00. I went into my office and called Carly. They told me she was busy so I told them not to leave a message, I would call her back later. As soon as I hung up, my phone rang.

"Hello," I said.

There was no answer. Only silence, then a dial tone.

I called the receptionist and asked who had called and she said she did not know. It was a man, but he had not given his name.

I hung up the telephone, stood up, and grabbed my jacket. It was 8:40. I walked out of my office and past Margo's desk. She was talking to someone on the telephone.

"I'll be at the District Attorney's office," I whispered to her. She motioned for me to stay.

I stopped, listening to her side of the conversation.

"Are you sure?" she said. "Can you check it again?" There were a few moments of silence and I was growing impatient, as I was about to be late for my best friend's funeral service. "I can't believe it," she said, hanging up the telephone without saying thank you or goodbye.

She looked up at me. "Let's go in your office," she told me with some urgency.

"Margo, I'm late. Can't this wait?"

"No!" she insisted, springing up from her desk.

I followed behind her. As soon as I was inside, she closed the door.

"What's wrong?"

"The check to the firm bounced."

"What check? Bets' check?" I asked, my heart beginning to pound.

"That was my friend Diana at the bank. She said she got the check just before they closed yesterday and she was going to run it through for me. When she tried, it came back NSF."

"That's a mistake," I insisted. "There's nearly a million dollars in that account."

"Andy," she said gravely, "the account was closed. All of the money was wired out."

"To where?"

"She wasn't supposed to tell me, but she did anyway. Switzerland."

"Oh, shit!"

"What are we going to do? Mr. Fabacher wrote out a bunch of checks yesterday. They are going to be bouncing all over town."

"Don't tell anyone," I told her harshly. "I'll take care of it. I have to get out to the airport."

"But, Andy," she said, as I moved toward the door.

"Don't tell anyone!" I demanded. Then I noticed the frightened look in her eyes.

"Look," I tried to calm down and explain. "I don't know what's going on, but it has to be Bets. I'll go out to the airport, get her back here, and we can straighten the whole thing out."

"Andy, I know you have a ticket for that flight," Margo said, like some kind of junior sleuth. I resented the accusation.

"No," I insisted, "Bets was bringing someone else, she just wanted it in my name..." I stopped, realizing how suspicious it all sounded.

"Andy," Margo said softly.

"Margo, it's not what you think. Believe me. We've been together for a long time. You know me better than that. You know I would never do anything like that."

"I purchased those tickets," she said, worriedly. "I made the deposits, took care of the account. What if they think I was in on it?"

"In on what? There is nothing to be 'in' on," I insisted. "I am going to get Bets before she gets on that plane – that's it – and we will get it resolved. But I have to go get her. If that airplane takes off with her on board, it'll be too late. It'll destroy me."

"When will you be back?" she asked anxiously.

"A couple of hours at the most. I will call you just as soon as I find her. Now I have to go."

Margo looked very worried, the stress evident in her contorted face, in her glazed-over eyes. She just stood there, frozen before me, so I grabbed her by the shoulders and moved her aside, against the wall. I could hear her sobbing behind me, but I had to go.

I rushed out of the door and down the hallway. Tony was walking the opposite direction.

"Hey, where's the fire?" he asked.

"I'm late," is all I said. Seeing him, I had the picture of George Bailey in my head, rushing about town after Uncle Billy loses the money, his wonderful life suddenly rendered hopeless by one, single twist of fate. It was exactly how I felt as I ran for the elevator.

I tried to remain calm, but I was actually much nearer a state of total panic. I prayed to God that Bets had moved the money in order to invest it, or to make sure it was as safe as possible by placing it in a Swiss Bank. I tried to convince myself.

Still, something in the back of my mind kept feeding my fear, telling me that I was being naive. If this were a plot to hurt me for the break-up, she had really gotten me good. I knew that if I did not catch her before she got on that plane, I would be destroyed. Scandal and financial ruin were my future.

I drove out of the Central Business District and got on the Interstate Highway at Poydras Street. Half a mile later traffic was at a near standstill. An accident or something up ahead had it backed up, bumper to bumper. My angst increased exponentially as the minutes dragged on, until I finally reached the point of total hysteria. My life as I knew it was totally dependent upon my arriving at the airport on time and there I sat stuck, helpless, doomed.

I am not certain exactly when it happened, but the panic finally wrested control of my body away from my mind and from that point forward I functioned as a mad man. It began with the constant blaring of my horn, which was quickly joined by the wild flailing of my left arm outside of the driver's side window. I accentuated this gesture with a loud stream of obscenities pouring forth from my vocal chords upon anyone unfortunate enough to make eye contact with me. I was quickly let through traffic, across three lanes, and onto the shoulder, where I proceeded to drive in excess of ninety miles per hour. The Jeep was rumbling, its engine straining, emitting an odor of burnt rubber, but, temporarily insane, I kept the accelerator pinned to the floor. It's all a blur from that point on; the cars blurring by, the sound of my horn joined by theirs, the sight of the pickup truck that pulled out in front of me to commit a little shoulder driving of its own.

I was right on him!

Slamming on my brakes, I headed for the median. My Jeep was an older model, notorious for flipping over. Suddenly my worries over Bets, my reputation, and possible arrest were gone, giving way to the more primal emotions of the fright and horror you experience just before succumbing to a painful death. The Jeep was out of my control. Guided by some greater force, it slid through the grass and mud, made soft by a recent rain. I think that rain saved my life. The mud helped to slow me down. I left a beautiful set of ruts behind me, extending about the length of a football field, as I skidded straight up the center of the median, like a giant toboggan whizzing uncontrollably down a mountainside. I strained to keep the wheels straight. Miraculously, I did not flip.

As soon as I had slowed enough to regain control of the vehicle, I immediately pressed the accelerator to the floor and headed toward the opposite lane of traffic. At first all four of my tires spun in place, making a "whirring" sound in the grass and mud, but then the four wheel drive clawed the ground and I fish-tailed around and found myself heading toward the Bonnabel exit in an east-bound direction. The Interstate was no good, so I had to try an alternate route. I sped through the suburban streets, praying that I would make it there before take-off.

I did not reach the airport service road until almost 10:00 a.m. The traffic and the longer route had delayed my arrival by over half an hour. I scanned the runway, looking for airplanes taking off, my only hope being that Bets' plane had been delayed. It had to be late. Something just had to go right for me after all that I had been through.

I did not have time to park in the garage so I drove directly up the ramp to the area designated for cars dropping off passengers. It is a no parking area, but I pulled into the first available bay and, with the engine still running, hopped out and sprinted toward the door, ignoring the shrill report of the Airport Security guard's whistle.

"You can't leave your vehicle there!" he shouted.

I ran in, acting as though I had not heard him, resigning myself to having to pay the fine and towing charge.

Moisant Field is small and somewhat isolated from the world. No one goes through New Orleans. You either get here or you get out, that's it. The terminal is compact, easy to reach, and is extremely easy to get around once inside. This, I thought, was to be my saving grace, the configuration that would allow me to accomplish my goal at the completion of my Herculean effort.

Bets was flying Lacsa Airlines to Belize, and when I reached the ticket counter there was a long line. I breathed a sigh of relief. Lacsa was a small operation and did not have that many daily flights, certainly not two around ten in the morning. It was the sign that I had been looking for, some assurance that her flight had been delayed.

I slowed to a fast walk, my heart still pounding, but feeling a little more at ease. I searched the crowd for Bets, but she was not there. I walked up to the ticket counter, past all of the passengers waiting in line, moving my head from side to side to let all those behind me know that I was not cutting in line, but was merely attempting to locate the departure screen. Lacsa had none.

A passenger was leaving the counter just as I walked up and I caught the clerk's eye.

"Excuse me," I said.

"Yes?"

"This is the flight to Belize, right?"

"No, I'm sorry, sir, that flight left at ten," she responded with a smile.

"Was it on time?"

"Yes sir." She motioned for the next passenger in line to step up.

"Could you tell me if a Betsy Davenport was onboard?" I continued.

"I'm sorry sir, but we aren't allowed to give out that information," she politely replied, reaching behind me for the papers of the passenger standing there.

"But this is an emergency."

"Sir," she said more sternly, her smile turning to a frown.

I did not move aside. I didn't care. "I have to know whether she was on that flight!"

"Sir, you will have to wait your turn in line."

"It is a matter of life and death!" I pleaded.

"Excuse me just one moment please, Ma'am." She smiled to the little woman behind me, then shot me a look that could kill before walking over to where her supervisor was standing.

I turned around and smiled at the tiny, old lady standing there. The sharp slope of her nose gave away her Central American Indian heritage. Her skin was dark, dry, and wrinkled, and she had a mole just below the left corner of her mouth from which several long, bristly, black hairs had taken root. She did not return my friendly gesture.

I turned back around as the clerk reappeared with a young looking man.

"May I help you over here, sir?" he asked, motioning me toward the side.

I nodded my head and moved over, allowing the woman behind me to step up to the counter. As soon as I was face to face with the man I began to speak, but before I could get the question out, he asked me whether I was Andy Jordan.

"Yes, I am," I responded, conceitedly reasoning that he must have recognized me from my recent television appearances.

"She left something for you," he said.

"Who?" I asked, dumbfounded.

"Ms. Davenport. Excuse me, I will be right back." He walked through a door behind the counter and reappeared almost instantly with a piece of luggage. I immediately recognized it as my own. It was the suitcase that Bets had loaded into her Mercedes on Friday.

"Here you are, sir," he said, "but I have to ask you to sign for it."

"She gave you this?" I asked, confused.

"Yes, sir," he said, pulling out a small slip of paper and a pen.

"Did she say anything?"

"She waited for you until just before the plane was to depart. She said she thought you may have been held up in traffic, so she left your bag and had me reissue your ticket for tomorrow morning's flight," he explained.

"For me?" I asked. "Are you sure she said it was for me?"

"Mr. Andy Jordan," he answered, then moved the piece of paper toward me and handed me the pen. "Sign right here please." I signed the piece of paper, then grabbed the ticket and my suitcase. It was heavy. I prayed that she had packed it with a million dollar bills, but somehow I knew that she had not. I decided to get it out of the airport before finding out for sure.

I turned around to head back to the Jeep but was immediately confronted by two Airport Security guards. One grabbing my arm, the other my bag.

"Going somewhere, Mr. Jordan?" the one holding my arm asked.

"I know, I know," I said. "Look, I'm going to move it right now. If there is a fine I'll pay it. I was just in a real big hurry..."

"You might not want to say anything before you speak to your attorney," the other advised me.

"I am an attorney," I scolded him.

They were both silent. One pulled out a pair of handcuffs.

"For a parking violation?" I questioned, finally beginning to realize there was something more to all of this.

The guard with my bag took his walkie-talkie from his belt and spoke into it.

"Inform the Jefferson Parish Sheriff's Department and N.O.P.D. that we have the suspect in custody," he said.

"Suspect? What do you mean, 'suspect'?"

"Are you waiving your right to an attorney?" he asked as his partner slapped the cuffs around my wrists. The cold steel sobered me up quickly. I shut my trap.

I was taken back to New Orleans, booked into Central Lockup on South White Street, and charged with theft, embezzlement, and fraud. I told them that they could ask me questions but that they weren't getting any answers until I had my lawyer present. I thought I was being smart, making a sharp legal maneuver, allowing them to tell me their side of the case through their inquiries. The questioning went on throughout much of the night and I was finally lured in to responding.

"Where is Ms. Davenport?"

"I don't know. That's why I went to the airport. To find her."

"What happened to the money?"

"You'll have to ask the Trustee that one. It's probably invested and you've made a false arrest here. You should speak to the department's attorney. I could sue for a lot of money."

"If it's invested, then why were you in such a hurry to get to the airport this morning?"

I dummied up on that one.

"Where is Christian Waterman?"

That was easy. "A million people saw him jump into Lake Pontchartrain. Don't you guys have a T.V. around this place?"

"What do you know about the disappearance of Assistant District Attorney Woodson?"

That one really hurt. It also scared me because it was obvious that they were attempting to connect Bip's disappearance with me, and Bets stealing the money.

I, of course, denied everything. I could do this because I was innocent. I had done absolutely nothing wrong, but try convincing a police interrogator of that at 3:00 a.m.

"If you had nothing to do with it, then where were you going with that suitcase?"

"Nowhere," I answered, "the guy at the Lacsa counter handed it to me. I didn't bring it there."

"Do you deny that it is your suitcase?"

"No. It's mine, but I didn't bring it there. Betsy Davenport did."

"And I guess you have no idea how one of your suitcases just happened to be at the airport ticket counter. And I guess you don't know how that ticket to Belize, with your name on it, got to be there either. Do you know why it was that you were screaming through traffic and running to the ticket counter to pick these things up before the plane took off?"

"I want my lawyer now," I said, realizing that I was getting nowhere, and just how bleak the facts were beginning to look.

For a man, innocent or guilty, to hire an attorney to prove his innocence in a court of law, and to hold a reasonable expectation of acquittal, he must possess and be willing to part with a small fortune. Good legal help does not come cheap and great legal help costs more than most new homes. Despite this fact, and contrary to popular belief, not all lawyers are filthy rich. And we don't eat our young. In my case the former was particularly true. I had about three thousand dollars in two bank accounts, and I owed Visa and American Express nearly twice that amount.

I had no one to turn to for money. The firm was sure to disown me, and I did not have much family. I was an only child, born late in the lives of my parents, after they had given up all hope of having children, a miracle baby. My father had died years earlier. He left Mom the house, but she had little else. I could not ask her to put a mortgage on the only piece of security that she had in the world so that I could afford a lawyer. Besides, my mother and I had grown apart over the years. I had become a big city attorney. I no longer had time to drive out to see her. Hell, I barely found the time to call her once a month. I had more important things to do. I had become an important man. I had become an arrogant asshole.

Because it was so late, they put me in a cell separated from the rest of the prisoners, and one in which I did not have a roommate. I sat there, on my bunk, for hours, thinking about who I might get to defend me in this matter for under three thousand dollars. I came up blank. My bail setting was scheduled for the next evening. It would have to be the public defender. I despaired.

The next morning I used my telephone call to try and reach Carly. I had to explain to her what had happened before she read the police accounts in the morning newspaper. I had no idea as to what I would tell her, but I had to hear her voice. The greater part of my despair was the realization that I could end up losing her over this terrible mistake.

The receptionist at Carly's office asked who was calling.

"Andy Jordan," I replied.

The inflection of her voice immediately perked up. You'd have thought I had said "John Dillinger."

"*Andrew* Jordan?" she asked, as though it may have been some other Jordan.

"Yes," I replied.

"Aren't you in jail?"

"Just do your fucking job and put me through to Carly," I snapped. I regretted it as soon as I had done it. My brutality could only serve to reaffirm my guilt in her mind and I was certain that everyone who worked there and who walked into that office for the next month would hear about it.

There was a long, silent pause, lasting several minutes, then a sharp "click" which was followed by a dial tone. I hung up. Either I had really pissed off the receptionist and she had not put me through, or Carly did not want to speak to me. I could not bear to call again to find out. I quickly dialed my office, knowing that Tony would be in the weekly partner's meeting.

"Jeremiah St. Rock Hayes," I said to the receptionist at Keating & Fabacher, disguising my voice.

"Who's calling, please?"

"Mark Sampson," I replied.

She put me through.

"Good morning, Mark!" J. Ryan answered, as though he and Sampson were old buddies.

"Knock it off, you asshole," I said. "It's me."

"Andy?" he asked, surprised.

"Isn't it more believable than Sampson?"

"Boy," he said, "I heard. You were in the paper. It's all over the news. Did you guys really get the loot?"

"You're a real pal, you know that? I had nothing to do with it. It was all Bets. She set me up big-time."

"The paper says they nabbed you at the airport making your getaway. It said they pulled you off of a plane to Belize."

"Hell, no!" I said. "I wasn't anywhere near any airplane. I was trying to get Bets before she left the country. Didn't Margo tell you guys?"

"Margo?" he questioned, surprised. "She's the one who ratted you out."

"Margo?" I asked, refusing to believe it.

"Hell, man, she was down the hall before the elevator doors closed behind you. She went straight to Fabacher and told him you and Bets stole all the money from the trust and were heading off to Central America to retire. She said you made her buy the tickets and all so that she'd go to jail instead of you."

I couldn't believe it at first, but I guess I really can't blame her. She was afraid that she would be implicated. But, still, I was disappointed that she had not had a little more faith in me after all of the years that we had worked together.

"She's practically a hero around here since they caught you."

"They think I did it?" I asked.

"Loyalty is fleeting, my man, especially when there's three million dollars involved."

"Only a million," I corrected.

"You sly devil."

"J. Ryan."

"Hell, I'd do five to ten for that much money."

"I'm fixing to do more than that for nothing," I insisted. "I'm innocent."

"Whatever."

"I swear it, J. Ryan."

"You're not kidding?"

"No. That's what I've been trying to tell you."

"Oh, man. That sucks." It had finally sunk in. "What are you going to do?"

"I'm gonna fight it," I said. "That's all I can do."

"You should get Joel Ondrejko. He's kick-ass down there. They would probably plead you out to half the minimum as soon as they saw you got him."

"I can't afford him," I said.

"Yea, right," J. Ryan replied sarcastically.

"Fuck you," I said seriously. "I had nothing to do with it. I don't have any of the money. In fact, I'm about broke."

"Oooh, Public Defender. Gnarly man."

"Can you think of anyone who could help me out? Think about it. Maybe somebody good that needs the publicity?"

"Nobody around here," he said. "I'd probably get fired if they knew I was talking to you now."

"You can't think of anyone?"

"No, but I'll ask Tony. He knows a lot more people that work for free than I do. Look, I'll come down there and see you. They'll let me in with my Bar card."

"You would do that?"

"I'm not as big an asshole as you think I am."

"Thanks," I responded, "I would really appreciate it. It's pretty damned scary, you know?"

"I'll try to make it before the weekend, and two pieces of advice – don't bend over for the soap and don't sleep on your stomach," he teased.

"Don't worry," I said.

"I better go man, don't want to get caught. You know."

"J. Ryan?"

"Yea?"

"Have you seen Carly?" I asked, hoping.

"No. Not since the other night."

"If you do, would you tell her this is all bullshit?" I asked.

"Sure," he replied, sincerely.

"And that I've been trying to call her?"

"Okay, man," he said, rushing. "I really gotta go now. I'll get with Tony and I'll come see you," he finished and immediately hung up the phone.

"Goodbye," I said, the dial tone buzzing in my ear.

After I got off the telephone, it was time for showers. This is a communal activity in prison, one in which all of the participants are made to undress, step into a huge, locker-room type shower, and then pick up fresh clothing as each exits through a door on the opposite side. To be sure, I think I set the prison record in the shower event. Upon being exposed, my little white ass sprinted from one end of the shower to the other, feeling the full blast of water for all of two seconds before exiting on the opposite side to collect my towel. A column of hardened criminals, and possibly hardened innocent people like myself, followed behind, laughing and pointing.

That day I also lost the luxury of my private cell. I was placed in a cell with two fellow inmates, both career confidence men with no known violent tendencies. I found out early that being an attorney in jail does have its perks. The guards were very careful to make certain that I was treated properly. I was seen as a potential troublemaker, one who could stir up lots of publicity and potential litigation for the prison director to have to deal with. If I was not treated properly, or so the reasoning went, there would be an endless stream of lawsuits filed by me, on my own behalf and on behalf of countless other prisoners who may feel that their civil rights were being ignored. Although I knew absolutely nothing about Constitutional Law, having made a "D" in the course in law school, I was happy to let the guards think it was my forte. I had visions of homosexual rape and I was prepared to do just about anything to avoid that happening.

When I was taken away for court that evening, my two cell mates bade me farewell.

"I think I'll be back," I told them.

"Doubtful," one said.

"What do you mean?"

"They don't want you here," the other replied.

"They'll give you recognizance," the first added, indicating that they believed I would be let out without having to post bond.

I am somewhat ashamed to admit that my two cell mates knew vastly more of the workings of the criminal justice system than I did. After reviewing the matter and the evidence, and the absence of Bets from the country, and taking into account that I was still a member of the Bar, the Magistrate Judge set my bail at twelve thousand dollars. I invested half of my life's savings in a twelve hundred-dollar surety bond, the prospect of spending the night at home worth every penny of it.

By the time I was released it was nearly two in the morning. I opened the door, walked outside, and was suddenly drenched in a flood of light arriving just ahead of the chatter of reporters jostling for position and calling out my name.

"Mr. Jordan! Mr. Jordan!...Andy!...Were you involved? Where is Ms. Davenport?...Mr. Jordan! Was it all a hoax from the beginning..."

Blinded, I pushed through them, shielding my face from their cameras like a criminal, trying to break free.

"...What was Keating & Fabacher's involvement in this?...Did they know? ...Where is Christian Waterman? Was he in on it?"

Then one went too far. He got right in my face, refused to let me pass, and belted out the wrong words. "What was Carly Devillier's part in all of this?"

I felt like an animal, caged, enraged, my back to the wall, and this asshole is trying to pull Carly into it? I lost control, lashed out, and caught the skinny little asshole square in the jaw with my fist, sending him reeling to the pavement in a splash of blood and spit.

"You leave her out of this! It's not right!" I screamed. With that the others gave way and I burst through their roar and the sea of light, making a break for Tulane Avenue. A cab was passing and I threw myself in front of it, bringing it to a screeching halt. I just jumped in, not even bothering to notice whether or not anyone else was inside, and gave the driver my address.

I cried in the back of that cab, all the way to Fern Street. I cried for losing Carly, as I knew I would. I cried for allowing my life to get so screwed up, for being such a trusting dolt. I cried for the shame of my downfall, and for the suffering that it would cause my mother. And I cried for Bip, for his disappearance, and my resulting isolation. I had no money on me, and I must have looked pretty pitiful, because when I came back out of the apartment to pay the driver he had taken off, comped me the ride.

I tried all night to reach Carly, but she never picked up, and her answering machine was turned off. I also tried her mother's home several times, but kept getting a busy signal there. Those reporters must have been hounding her. It was torture not being able to speak to her, to at least try to explain some of it to her, to apologize for what I was putting her through.

The crying had stopped by the time I got home. Instead, I replaced it with despair, contemplating the possibility of spending serious time in jail. I felt trapped, the walls closing in on me. I had to get out of the house. Although it was late, I knew where I had to go. It was the only logical place. I was drawn there, to the lake.

There was a full moon that night, it's reflection stretching across the lake from the horizon to where I stood on the shore. A stiff, salty breeze blew in my face, refreshing me, calming me. It was then, for the first time since his disappearance, that Flipper came to me.

At first I thought it was the moon and my mind playing tricks on me. He was in the water, waving to me those few moments before he disappeared beneath the waves, as real as any of the times I had been with him previously. Then he went under. Only this time, I was with him.

His transformation was like nothing else I have ever experienced. He did not swim away, as I thought he had, but rather allowed himself to sink to the lake bottom, next to a couple of air tanks and an underwater propulsion sled. He was smiling and the water around him was as clear as glass. Beautiful fishes of every shape, size, and color appeared, flapping their fins as though floating on air, propelling themselves toward him, drawn to the spot, as I had been.

To him the water was no impediment. He made use of neither the tanks nor the sled, breathing and moving about as easily as one upon the shore. Then it began.

I noticed it first in his eyes, spreading quickly to his teeth, then hair, and then the rest of his human form. It was a light and then it was not, originating from within him and from without. There is no way for me to relate, in earthly terms, this glow which steadily enveloped him, transforming him, beautifully, into a being for which my entire human experience offers no comparison that would allow me to even remotely describe the magnificence I witnessed. Somewhere, within the recesses of the all powerful mind lies the complete explanation, the detailed description, but the faculties of human correspondence remain so relatively crude as to make the mortal relaying of the salient details abjectly impossible.

This, I saw. And then he was gone.

I was alone, in the brine where he had left me. Gone too, were the beautiful fishes that had surrounded him, suddenly replaced by sharks: huge, grey, cold-eyed man-eaters, intent on devouring my flesh.

I was jolted awake as I avoided the predators and found myself in the grass, beside my Jeep, naked and soaking wet. I stood and turned toward the still waters. The sun was just beginning to come up and the lake had taken on a surreal, brilliant, neonish aqua-marine glow. I was captivated by its beauty and rarity. A slight breeze blew past me and it was then that I first realized my nakedness. I hurried to dress, making certain that no one had seen me.

TWENTY-NINE

IT WAS THURSDAY MORNING, daybreak, and I sat behind the wheel of my Jeep, trying to convince myself that I was not going mad. I had somehow lost consciousness and memory, replaced by a hallucination, I reasoned, although it had been neither drug nor alcohol induced. Nonetheless, despite my situation, I felt a great calm within my soul. Gone was my despair, at least for the moment.

I drove along the Lakefront, toward home, keeping an eye on the lake and its shrimping fleet hard at work. Then I passed a bevy of police cars and vans and a gathering crowd, congregating near the place where Flipper had left us, but I dared not stop to see what was going on.

I made it home, showered, shaved, then put on my newest suit to go into the office. I actually considered leaving the country. I could drive back home to Hackberry, tucked away in the swamps of Southwest Louisiana. I knew people there who could get me out by boat, people I had grown up with. The ties down there are never broken, no matter how long you have been gone. When you return you are treated the same as if you had never left.

The telephone rang.

"Hello!" I said, longing for Carly's voice at the other end.

"Andy?"

"Yea," I said, recognizing my friend's voice. "Hey, Arlie, how you doing?"

Arlie Mouton was an English teacher at Tulane. He was originally from Jennings, Louisiana, about thirty minutes north of Hackberry as the crow flies, and we had met while I was in law school. As is common for people from our part of the country, we had known a lot of the same people long before we had ever met.

"I'm glad I caught you," he said, with a slight Cajun accent. "I thought you might be in jail already."

"I got out last night."

"I read all that bullshit. That little Yankee bitch really put it on you, didn't she?"

A tear welled up in my eye. It was such a comfort to know that despite all that had been published, and all that had been said by the media to the contrary, there were people, such as Arlie, who knew without question that I had done no wrong.

"She sure did, man," I replied.

"What are you gonna do?"

"I don't know. She really did a good job. It looks like we were in it together."

"You better not trust a New Orleans jury to figure out that you weren't."

"I don't see that I have any choice."

"You might," he responded in a low voice.

"What do you mean?"

"I know some people back home that might be able to help."

"I thought about that," I said, "but I think I better take my chances."

"Life is a long time."

"It wouldn't be life," I corrected, smiling, amused by his ignorance of the legal system. "I don't have any kind of a record and thieves don't get life," I explained. "The worst I'm probably looking at is probation. And bankruptcy and disbarment," I added.

"For murder?"

"I'm not being accused of murder."

"The morning news said they had charged you with his murder."

"Who's? Bip's?" I asked, recalling the insinuation during my interrogation.

"No, the Atlantis guy. They found something in the lake."

The news shocked me and I did not respond.

"You knew that, didn't you?" he asked.

I said nothing. My brain was numb. I couldn't get it to think.

"Andy?" he said.

"Flipper? He's dead?" I asked in a whisper.

"What?" Arlie asked, unable to understand me.

"They found Flipper?" My heart sank.

"Not yet, I don't think. They just said some guy was shrimping in the lake and he pulled the stuff up right by where you guys were when he left."

"What stuff?"

"Some kind of air tanks and one of those...I don't know what ya' call 'em...like on those underwater shows..."

"An underwater scooter?" I blurted out, recalling my dream, chilled by the realism.

"Yea..." Arlie replied, his voice dropping off, reconsidering my innocence, "...you knew about that?"

"No. Look...you wouldn't believe me. Is that all they found?"

"What else is there?" He inquired, in an almost interrogating tone.

"Like a body?"

"Not yet, but they say it is only a matter of time. They're sure he's dead because of the poison."

"What are you talking about? What poison?" I asked, immediately recalling the freshwater spots and dead zones that Flipper had said were so dangerous. He must have swam into one.

"He was murdered."

"I don't understand," I replied, begging for an explanation.

"There was poison in one of his tanks. Somebody had put poison gas in it."

"You have to be kidding," I said.

"It was on the news," he insisted. "They traced it all back to you. They said you posed as Bip, and signed for some of the equipment yourself, at the bus station."

As though someone had finally hit the light switch, that is when it all became very real to me. That is when I began to get really scared. The only time that I had been to the bus station in recent memory was to pick up Bip's package for him, and now he was gone. My world was shaken. Could Bip have been involved with Bets' scheme? Were they capable of murder? My life was beginning to look like one of those stupid plots you see on a late night movie, something unbelievable. Only it was real, and it was happening to *me*. I hadn't done anything wrong, but somehow I had been made the idiot patsy. How was I to extricate myself with Bip gone?

"There weren't any tanks," I finally mumbled.

"I don't know. That's what I heard."

"What a fucking nightmare! Flipper is dead?" I could not believe it.

"Andy, listen, I know this guy in Lafayette, Stevie Broussard. He flies down to Columbia once a week," Arlie began.

"Let me call you back," I said abruptly.

"Okay," Arlie responded. "But if you want me to arrange it with Stevie, we don't have much time."

"All right," I said.

I hung up the telephone and sat on the kitchen floor. My knees just kind of collapsed beneath me actually. I could not pick myself up. I could not even begin to conceive what was happening. Flipper was dead. The air tanks and the underwater scooter from my dream were real? How had this happened? Bets was gone, the money was gone, Bip was probably dead. How could Bets have done all of this? Was Bip involved? Flipper? All I really knew was that I looked like a fraud, possibly a murderer. I looked involved. I was involved – up to my ass.

THIRTY

ALTHOUGH I PROBABLY SHOULD HAVE, I did not call Arlie back. In future days I would regret not having done so. After all, his suggestion made a lot more sense than the course that I ultimately did take. I mean, how bad could Columbia be?

I knew that the police must be searching for me and anticipated their arrival at my door any moment. I had to do something, and finally managed to regain control and lifted myself from the floor. After that I was unstoppable. I tore out of my apartment, not even delaying long enough to lock the door. I ran down to the Jeep, determined to get to the office before the police did, not knowing exactly what I would do, but planning to think it all through on the way over.

I drove the speed limit, tried not to attract any attention. The top and doors were off of the Jeep and I felt naked, exposed. People knew who I was, they knew the police were looking for me. I expected to be pulled over at any moment.

The deck was stacked against me. Bets had taken all of the high cards and there was no way that I could win. When I reached the office, I pulled into the garage. I was much less noticeable coming in the back way, and was not seen getting on the elevator. It took me to Carly's floor.

I walked off the elevator and saw that the receptionist was busy reading a magazine and speaking to someone on the telephone through the headset she was wearing. She did not see me until I was almost upon her. When she finally did look up, she gasped for air and told whomever it was that she was speaking to that she would have to call them back. Then she just stared at me without saying a word.

"Hi," I said.

She remained mute.

"Is Carly here, please?" I asked politely.

"No," she said timidly, "she took a vacation."

"Vacation?" I doubted

"Yea," she muttered.

"Where to?"

"Uh, sir," she responded, "I'm really not allowed to tell you."

"Could you at least tell her that I came by?"

"Okay," she answered abruptly.

"My name is Andy."

"I know."

"Thank you," I said, turning and walking away.

I waited a moment for the elevator. After it had arrived and I had stepped on, I heard the receptionist's voice, speaking to someone on the headset.

"You won't believe who just walked out of here," she said. The elevator door closed. I rode down to the fourteenth floor and went to my office.

My own receptionist was every bit as surprised to see me as Carly's had been.

"Hey, Emily," I said.

"Good morning, Mr. Jordan," she tried to say pleasantly.

I walked around to the door behind her.

"I don't know if you can go in there," she said as I reached for the door knob.

"Why not?"

"I don't know. They just told me to keep it locked."

"Are you letting anybody through?"

"Why, yes, sir," she said.

"Just not suspected thieves and murderers today?" I joked.

"Yes, sir," she answered, seriously.

Just then the door swung open and one of the women from the bookkeeping department came strutting through. I grabbed the door and walked inside before either of them could say another word.

"Liz!" I heard her scold the young woman as I went inside.

I walked down the hallway, past a gauntlet of surprised expressions. These were the same faces that only a few days earlier had been joyfully congratulating me, telling me what a wonderful person and attorney I was. Now they had turned hostile and scared, wearing their betrayal upon them.

As I walked past Margo, she turned away and began sobbing bitterly. I am not sure whether it was out of shame or sorrow, but I did not stop to find out. She, more than any of them, had betrayed me. I stormed into my office, slammed the door behind me, and began gathering the possessions dear to me.

There was a box of old textbooks in one corner of the office which I emptied onto the floor. I carried the box to my desk and took the things I wanted: the fountain pen my father had given me upon graduation from law school, and only a week before his death; a picture of my mother and myself at the Bar swearing in ceremony; my law school diploma and license hanging on the wall behind my desk; and the clock radio that Bip had given me for Christmas one year and that I kept next to my desk. The box was full.

I should have gone then, but instead I placed my possessions on my desk and sat back in my chair for the last time. I looked around my office, wanting to memorize every detail. I had worked so hard for all of it, for what I had believed so important, allowing it to blind me to so many other things. In a flash it was all taken away. Like everyone else, I had my faults, but none of them, I pitied myself, had warranted this.

My door flew open. Tony stepped into my office and sealed the rest of them behind it.

"What are you doing here?" he asked.

"I had to get my things," I said.

"They are calling the police."

"So what else is new?"

"Do you have an attorney yet?"

"You volunteering?" I joked.

"Yea, and I thought I'd gouge out my left eye while I was at it. I'm not kidding, you don't have much time. Do you have a lawyer?"

"Tony," I answered, "I could barely afford to get out of that hell hole. I hardly have a quarter to flip in the air."

"That's what I thought. Look, I might know someone who can help you," he announced.

"Really?" I asked, surprised.

"My cousin. I might be able to convince him to do it for the publicity, and if he gets you off, some money down the road."

"Are you serious?"

"Yes, I'll call him this afternoon. But you have to do something for me. You have to get the hell outta Dodge."

"What movie is that from?" I joked, but he was not in the mood. "All right," I relented, taking my box in hand. "Thanks, Tony. You don't know what this means to me."

"I'd probably still do it if I thought you were guilty, but I know you're not," he explained. "I also know all about that little stunt you pulled the other day in my office, trying to let me down easy when they were going to take away my office. You're a terrible liar."

"You're a real pal," I said, not knowing what other words to use. Of all of them, when it had come to the difficult part, he had truly remained a friend.

Down deep he was a nice person, and it was a quality over which neither he nor his breeding had any control.

"Now you need to get the hell out of here. It's not going to look good if they arrest you here."

"Okay," I said, standing, grabbing his shoulder. "Thanks."

"Don't mention it," he replied, as I let go of his arm and walked toward the door. "I'll have him get in touch with you, or I will," he assured me.

"You surprise me," I said, opening the door. He only smiled.

I turned and found myself face to face with two of the building's security guards. They flinched, threatened by the vicious murderer before them. Both Fabacher and Keating stood behind them, at a safer distance. I just had to laugh.

"Tom. Bill. My partners. Came to see me off? What a wonderful surprise," I taunted them.

"Hold him until the police get here," Fabacher snapped.

The guards reached out to grab me, but I retreated into my office, behind my desk. "I'll just wait in here," I said.

They followed me in.

"Wow, this is like a *Wall Street* flashback," Tony commented under his breath.

"Mr. D'Ensina," Keating addressed Tony.

"Yes, sir?" Tony responded, snapping to attention.

"Could I see you for a moment, please?"

"Yes, sir," Tony obeyed, walking past me and out of the room. He, Keating, and Fabacher all disappeared down the hallway. I went and sat in my chair again, this time with the two guards in front of me.

"You guys don't carry guns?" I asked with a crazed look in my eye as I simultaneously began opening one of my desk drawers. I pulled slowly and deliberately, staring them down all the while.

They shook their heads "no" in reply, watching nervously as I reached into the drawer.

"You should. This is a real dangerous city, you know," I continued, pulling gum from the drawer. I pulled it out fast, thrust it in my hand toward them.

"Want some?" I asked loudly as they both jumped and scanned the room for cover.

They didn't want any. I took a piece out and put it in my mouth, enjoying the flavor as we sat in silent anticipation of the arrival of representatives of the New Orleans Police Department.

THIRTY-ONE

MY SECOND EXPERIENCE IN JAIL was much less pleasant than my initial incarceration had been. This time I was there as a murder suspect and, attorney or not, I was placed in the maximum security wing.

My new cellmates were of the violent variety, two fellow murder suspects, known as Lil' Boy and Second Line. Lil' Boy lived up to his nickname. He stood only about five feet tall and could not have weighed more than ninety-eight pounds soaking wet with his fully loaded .44 magnum revolver in his belt. He had been a hit man for one of the local drug lords. His "piece" and nasty disposition had made him a giant on the street, but in jail he was nothing but a stupid, skinny, little punk with a very bad attitude. Consequently, he was not handling prison very well. I gathered from later conversations with other inmates that he had initially been put in a cell with three much larger and equally violent members of a rival drug syndicate who had taken turns owning him each night. After a week of that hell, they finally transferred him out of there and into the cell with Second Line, who had no more than ten or fifteen pounds on Lil' Boy. The two had become friends.

Though I must do so here, I don't like discussing the time I spent behind bars. I suppose it is somewhat like my late father's refusal to discuss his experiences in the Pacific during World War II. The food was miserable, the company deplorable, the boredom lethal. The first night that I was in, Lil' Boy and Second Line sat on Lil' Boy's cot rolling dice.

"We seeing who gets you first," Lil' Boy finally said to me.

Before the last syllable had cleared his lips I was off of my bunk and on top of the two of them. I am no bruiser myself, but I was fighting for something that I hold very dear – my ass.

My first move was to hit Lil' Boy with a fist from behind. I succeeded in disabling him but it felt as though I had broken a couple of knuckles on his skull. Undeterred, I jumped on top of Second Line, pounding him with each of my fists in rapid succession. As soon as I had taken the fight out of him, I turned back on Lil' Boy, who had gotten up, and beat him mercilessly until he finally crumbled on the floor and begged me to stop.

"So who wants to fuck me first now?" I asked, still in a rage.

"Nobody," Lil' Boy answered. "I was just jokin' anyhow."

"You got any more jokes?"

Lil' Boy shook his head "no."

I felt good. I had established my dominance. There would be no question now as to who was king of our little jungle.

"Dat's all right," Second Line said, picking himself up off the floor, his nose bleeding, and his left eye swollen half shut. "I'm jest gonna kill you in your sleep."

This announcement really disturbed me. I would not be able to turn my back on either of these guys now, having no doubt that he meant what he said.

"Then I'll just have to kill you first," I said, lunging at him, gripping him around the throat.

"He don't like killin' him in his sleep jokes neither, Second," Lil' Boy joked, wanting no part of me as I strangled his friend into unconsciousness.

It took Second Line about ten minutes to wake up. I worried that he might lapse into a coma or even die, but I didn't regret what I had done. Early on in my practice I had represented an ex-convict who had sued one of the state facilities for an injury he had received while incarcerated. In one of the discussions I had with him, he told me that the first thing he did when he was put in a new cell was to make it clear that he would kill anyone who posed any threat to him. He explained that until it was understood that he was totally committed to carrying out his threat, he would be in constant danger. At the time I never thought I would have any use for the advice. It just goes to show how quickly your situation in life can change.

Second Line began to stir.

"Shit!" I exclaimed, "you ain't dead yet?" I climbed on top of Second Line's chest and placed my hands around his throat.

"Guard!" Lil' Boy called.

"Shut up, Lil' Boy," I screamed, "or I swear you'll be next."

"This mother fucker crazy," Lil' Boy yelled.

Second Line's eyes began to bulge.

"He gonna leave you alone," Lil' Boy pleaded for his friend's life.

"Is that true?" I asked Second Line.

He seemed to nod in approval. I released his throat and stood up.

Prison is not like the school playground where you fight with someone one day and somehow that makes you best of friends the next. Second Line and Lil' Boy never became my friends, and I never really trusted them, nor did I ever have a good night's sleep knowing they were locked in with me. But in the short time that I was their cellmate, they never again directed any kind of threatening gesture toward me.

Tony came to visit me my second day in jail, and J. Ryan was with him. We met in a small room, sitting across a table from one another, with a guard watching at the door.

"Did you get to talk to your cousin?" I asked.

"Yea," Tony responded, "but he can't do it. He has three other murder cases going right now, and two of those are pro-bono."

"Well thanks anyway," I said, attempting to hide my great disappointment. "I guess I'll take my chances with the Public Defender's office."

"Maybe you won't have to," Tony replied.

"You have another idea?" I asked, hoping.

"Well, J. Ryan does," Tony answered.

"How about if I take it?" J. Ryan spoke up.

I was floored. How could he take my case? The firm could not possibly allow it.

"The firm's not going to..." I began

"I got laid off," he interrupted.

"They laid you off?" I asked.

"Two attorneys and three staff," Tony interjected.

"What's the deal?" I asked.

"We lost more than half of our clients," Tony explained. "All the banks and all but one insurance company."

"You're kidding," I said, shocked. "Because of me?"

"Our very own Typhoid Mary," J. Ryan quipped.

"Boy, they must really hate me down there," I said.

"That's putting it mildly."

"We've nicknamed you 'Torpedo Jordan.' One blow and you've sunk the whole ship," Tony added.

"I'm really sorry, J. Ryan," I said, feeling awful.

"Hell, it's probably for the best anyway. Those guys are a bunch of assholes."

"Present company excluded," I said.

Tony smiled.

"J. Ryan told me he was going to open his own practice," Tony explained, "and I told him what he needed was to make a name for himself. I told him he should volunteer to represent you."

"And you would do it?" I asked J. Ryan.

"I've never done any criminal work before," he cautioned me, "but I figure this way you and I could work together, and maybe do a pretty decent job."

"You know I can't pay you anything," I said.

"Well," J. Ryan began, "I figure that I'll get my money's worth, especially if I get you off. At the very worst no one would expect me to win anyway, and I should get in the paper and on television pretty much on a daily basis."

"You can't buy that kind of advertising," Tony said, as though to imply that J. Ryan's fee had been paid in that instant.

"That's true. Plus, deep down, I'm really a nice guy," J. Ryan added with a smirk.

"Well, what do you think?" Tony asked.

"I'll understand if you want the P.D.'s office," J. Ryan said. "At least you'd get someone who's done a lot of criminal work."

"Yea, pleading people out and trying to keep up with a caseload of a hundred and fifty clients," I said. "If you're willing to do it, I'd really appreciate it."

"You've got it," J. Ryan stated confidently.

"We can do it together," I said.

"Well then, I better get out of here and let you discuss this with your client," Tony interjected, standing to leave.

"Tony," I said, "Thank you. You really took care of me. I won't forget it."

"Yea, thanks," J. Ryan added.

"Don't worry about it. Keep me posted on how it's going," Tony said, "and I'll let you know how things go at the office. Boy, is Fabacher going to blow a fuse on this one."

We all smiled in anticipation of that happening, and Tony turned and walked out.

"We better get started," J. Ryan suggested. "Why don't you fill me in on all that you know?"

I started from the very beginning, explaining the whole thing to J. Ryan, giving him every detail, relating each to things that were going on in the office at the various times so that he would have a frame of reference as to when everything had occurred. We talked for two-and-a-half hours, and at some points it felt almost like I was free again, almost as though we were sitting back in my office with J. Ryan's feet propped up on my desk, my Ray Bans on his nose. I almost began to feel as though I were a real person again.

After I had finished giving it all to J. Ryan, he said he was going to go to the District Attorney's office the next day to see just what they had on me. He told me that my bail setting on the murder charge had been scheduled for the following afternoon, and that he had already made arrangements to be there.

"Kind of cocky, huh?" I asked. "You were that sure I would say yes?"

"I pretty much knew that you could not afford to say no, even if you wanted to."

"I really appreciate this," I told him sincerely.

"It's a good deal for both of us. You know me. I wouldn't be doing it if there wasn't something in it for me."

Somehow I doubted that. A week previous I would have believed him, but it seems that people have a way of surprising you. Somewhere along the way, despite all of our differences, J. Ryan and I had become friends. It was not, however, until that very moment that I really knew it.

J. Ryan got up to leave.

"I'll see you tomorrow then?" I asked.

"Wouldn't miss it," he said.

"If you have time, come by every day," I continued. "It's nice to get out for a while."

"Okay," J. Ryan said kindly.

"And if you see Carly, tell her I said hi, and that I have been trying..." I stopped, thought a minute. "Never mind," I said, "don't tell her anything." I realized that she was no longer mine. I did not deserve her in here, and it was obvious that she had not attempted to contact me. I couldn't blame her. In fact, she could have made it much worse by denying me openly. At least this way I could make up my own reasons for having lost her. I had nothing left to offer Carly, not as long as I was this shell of a man, not as long as I was in jail.

J. Ryan did not come by the jail to see me the following day, so I did not see again him until my bail setting, which had been set for 4:00 in the afternoon. The guards brought me into an empty courtroom around 3:50, and J. Ryan showed up at 4:00 on the dot, after the two assistant district attorneys and everyone else had already been seated.

"Where have you been?" I asked.

"At the D.A.'s office, all day," he answered.

"What did you find out?"

"It's not good..."

"All rise!" the bailiff called out, before J. Ryan could fully respond.

We all stood up as the magistrate entered, not sitting again until he had instructed us to do so. We were the only matter on the docket. They actually had a special session set up just for me. My case would be receiving a lot of attention, as I was becoming notorious. Following the usual formalities, one of the prosecuting attorneys, a woman, stood to address the court.

"Ms. Loretta Robinson for the State, Your Honor. We are before the Court this afternoon for bail setting and determination of counsel for Mr. Andrew Jordan."

"What is Mr. Jordan charged with?" the magistrate asked.

"Well, Your Honor," she began, "there are several theft charges outstanding for which a bond was set in the amount of twelve thousand dollars. Since that time, Your Honor, the defendant has also been arrested for the murders of Mr. Harold Boier and Mr. Theodore Woodson, who, Your Honor knows, was a member of our staff..."

My ears began ringing. The entire weight of the situation had finally come to bear fully upon my mind. I knew they suspected me in Flipper's disappearance, but now they were charging me with Bip's murder, and who the hell was Harold Boier? I had never even heard the name before.

There was no telling who Bets had killed to frame me. Perhaps this was only the tip of the iceberg. In my true pessimistic form, I began imagining them finding ice lockers filled with bodies, digging up bones for years to come, transporting me across country to pin yet another unsolved murder on me, a never-ending nightmare. I tuned out everything around me. Panic had set in. A double murder? I could be charged with a capital crime. The death penalty had suddenly become a possibility.

By the time I returned to my senses, J. Ryan had risen and was speaking.

"...we believe that five million dollars bond is rather extreme under the circumstances, Your Honor. Mr. Jordan has been an exemplary member of the Bar, he is well established in the area, and he practically turned himself in. He is not a risk to run, Judge."

"Not a flight risk?" Ms. Robinson stood, interrupting. "Not two minutes after he was released from custody last time, he punched out a reporter. Your Honor, this is a violent man charged with a capital crime. Let us not forget that he was initially apprehended in the airport, with a suitcase and a ticket in his hands. The defendant is also suspected of stealing nearly a million dollars. We do not want him thinking that he can post bail with those ill-gotten gains. What's more, Your Honor, Mr. Woodson was a law enforcement official and an officer of this court..."

"Whose body has never been found," J. Ryan interrupted. "Your Honor, the State's entire case is purely circumstantial. They have no bodies. I don't see how they can even hope to prove that either of these so-called victims is dead, let alone that my client murdered them."

J. Ryan was good, I have to give him that.

"Is this true, Ms. Robinson?" the magistrate asked.

"Your Honor, we haven't recovered the bodies, yet, but we do have substantial evidence," she explained. "The Sheriff's Office is dragging the lake and has divers in the water. I am certain that it is only a matter of time. And even if they don't find a body, the other evidence is so overwhelming..."

"So the victims could both still be alive?" the magistrate interrupted.

"Highly improbable, Your Honor."

"But all the same, they could walk in this court room tomorrow, correct?" he asked.

"No more than Elvis could, in my opinion, Judge."

"All right, I've heard enough," the magistrate said.

J. Ryan was smiling. He had won the first round.

"I am not going to take the State's recommendation of five million dollars bond. Under the circumstances, I find it appropriate to set the bond at five hundred thousand dollars for each murder count."

Some victory, I thought to myself. J. Ryan had gotten my bail cut down all right, but it was still in the stratosphere. There was no way that I could come up with that amount of money, so I resigned myself to the fact that I would have to remain in jail for the duration.

We all stood again as the Judge exited the courtroom. I turned to J. Ryan.

"They're charging me with Bip's death?" I asked.

"Incredible, isn't it," he said. "It's a regular witch hunt over at the D.A.'s office. I've been there all day. They're gathering wood and stacking it in the lobby so they can burn you at the stake when this is all over."

"Who the hell is Harold Boier?"

"Get ready for this," J. Ryan said. "That's your boy, Flipper. His real name is Harold Boier. He's from somewhere down in Mississippi, and he was born with that birth defect, the feet. He's just a loser. Get this though, six years ago he qualified for the Olympics in swimming but then they said his feet were an unfair advantage and he just dropped out of college and out of life. He started drifting around, living on the street. He's been arrested several times by the New Orleans cops for vagrancy."

"Can we talk about this later?" I asked J. Ryan, beginning to feel quite ill. I needed time to absorb it all, to accept it before I could begin trying to deal with it. I was humiliated and discouraged. I had been such a fool. I had believed in Flipper and in Atlantis, only to find out that he was just a bumpkin from the sticks – just like me, only with screwed up feet.

The guard led me back to my cell where I stayed for two days. In those two days, I ate part of one meal and slept a total of five or six hours. I could not come to grips with the fact that Flipper had been a total fake and had played me so easily. They had Dixie-cupped me, used me, and thrown me away. I thought about it all, viewed it from every angle, and finally came to accept what had happened. In those two days I had metamorphosed, come out from the safety of my cocoon, and saw my world for the fraud that it had actually been.

I was ready to see my attorney, participate in my defense. J. Ryan came down to the jail wearing blue jeans and a cotton pullover shirt.

"Looks like business is booming!" I kidded him.

"I don't have time for business. I've got one case and it takes up all of my time," he responded seriously. He was so focused that it took me by surprise.

"This is all that you're doing?" I asked.

"And I don't have enough time to do this," he said. "I've been in the library learning all about criminal procedure, and when I'm not there I'm over at the police station or the D.A.'s office, or back at Keating & Fabacher."

"What? What are you doing back there? That's a conflict," I told him, alarmed by his announcement.

"Chill out, man. Only to go through the boxes of documents that I subpoenaed there."

"You're kidding," I relaxed and laughed. "They must hate that!"

"They have me in this little office with the air conditioning turned off, and only one light that works. Tony calls it 'the dungeon.' I am not allowed access to anywhere else but the one room. I even have to go to the next floor to take a leak," he explained. "But I love it. I'm their worst nightmare. They cringe every time I walk through the door, worrying about what I might find to tie them in with all of this. I do a little bit at a time so that I have to keep making appearances there, just to rub it in their faces a little harder."

"That's great," I said, laughing again.

"I've got to admit that I am enjoying it."

"But how are you feeding yourself?"

"Hell, they're still paying me my severance, three months worth. I pick up a check Friday as a matter of fact. And I have some stowed away," he explained.

"I feel bad taking up all of your time."

"Hey, that's the deal. I'm happy with it. We do have a problem though."

"What's that?"

"It's a capital case, so you could get the death penalty."

"You just figuring that out?" I asked, concerned.

"Not that. Of course not. The problem is that I've only been out of law school for three years. If the Court appoints someone to represent you in a capital case, they have to have at least five years under their belt."

"But you weren't appointed," I said.

"Yea, but when you're not appointed the Court can appoint someone else to help you who has been out for that length of time," J. Ryan explained.

"We don't need anybody else," I insisted, worried that an outside attorney would be a hindrance rather than a help.

"Tell it to the judge. He says we do. But I've got an idea."

"What?"

"I think I know an older attorney who would help me out, but I can't tell you who until I've talked it over with him."

"When can you do that?" I asked.

"Right now. I just needed to know that I have your 'okay' on it."

"Do it," I charged him. Then I asked how my case was coming.

"All right, I guess. The Sheriff still hasn't found anything," he said, distracted. I could tell that there was something bigger on his mind that he was not telling me.

"What is it?" I insisted.

"What?"

"I can tell there's something bothering you. What's up?"

"I don't really know how to ask you this..." he hesitated, then dove right into it. "They say some weird things have been going on over in the lake."

"What kind of things?" I asked, eerily curious.

"Well yesterday one of the sheriff's divers was attacked by a twenty foot Mako. They don't even have those in the Gulf."

"Did he kill him?"

"Took a big chunk out of his leg."

"No, the shark. Did they kill it?"

"I don't think so. But that isn't all."

"What else?"

"Andy, it's like the whole world is down there. The lake is crammed with boats from everywhere. The lake shrimpers have been filling up their boats in like an hour, crabs are walking onto the bank in droves, people are scooping them up with nets. It's like all the sea life in the gulf is being sucked into that one place. The water is clearer than anyone can ever remember it being, *ever*. They're catching trout and bass off the piers. Jesus, usually you're lucky if you catch an old tire out there."

I shuddered as he spoke. I had spent the past two days denying that which I knew in my heart to be true, retreating from my situation into the lie that Flipper had been a hoax. Somehow he had known, known how I would react, how I would doubt him. And he had sent his sign.

"And you should see the Lakefront," he continued. "There are people living there, like a little city holding vigil. It looks like Jazz Fest down there. They wait for the Sheriff's boats to come in at night, and cheer when they haven't found him. It's like they all want him to be real, like the Second Coming or something. It's really starting to freak a lot of people out."

"The lake is clear, you say?" I questioned, growing excited by the news.

"You can see all the way to the bottom, except in the places where the schools of fish are too thick to see through."

"Does anybody know why?"

"Hell no. Some say it started with an influx of algae eaters that began the clean up and drew smaller fish that drew in larger ones, others say it's a change in the salinity level that made all of the sediment drop out of the water and sink to the bottom. Others say it's a miracle but those people can't figure *you* out. It's the end of the world and you are either Prophet or Pilate. Nobody knows what to believe."

When he said that I knew what he was getting at. What he had hesitated in asking me. So I answered.

"He's the real thing, J. Ryan," I declared, fully believing it myself, vowing never to doubt him again. "It's like suddenly my head has become as clear as the lake has, and I can see. I don't know how to explain him yet, J. Ryan, but I can tell you one thing. They aren't going to come up with a body."

J. Ryan nodded in appreciation. I had answered his question, given him at least some basis upon which to believe the unbelievable, as those at the lake had done on their own. Suddenly, the world had become a much different place and I was standing in the middle of it all, yet to be declared as hero or adjudicated as villain.

J. Ryan left and did not return until the following day. The older attorney whom J. Ryan had been talking about was Tony. He went over to Keating & Fabacher as soon as he left me, but Tony had to meet with him in front of the building as J. Ryan was not allowed in his office. Ten minutes later Tony had gone back inside and tendered his resignation. The once-proud firm was on the way down. The scandal had dealt it a death blow and it was breathing its last. Fabacher had already informed Tony that he would be the next attorney to be let go, so he decided to jump ship before the ship sunk and pulled him under with it. He even managed to take a few clients with him.

In the local newspaper that day, the headline of the Metro section read *YOUNG DISTRICT ATTORNEY DECLARED HERO – Foul Play Suspected After his Discovery of Murder Plot.* The article, which described

Bip in glowing terms, hypothesized that he had happened upon the conspiracy of murder and theft wrought by his sinister roommate and roommate's girlfriend. Bip, the article theorized, had been silenced before he could expose the perpetrators and their murderous plot.

Knowing that he had participated in my downfall, but still of the opinion that, for the most part anyway, Bip had been but another victim of Bets, I did not mind his receiving a little recognition. In spite of it all, Bip had been my best friend. We had been through a lot together, lived together for six years, been as close as brothers. That people would actually believe that I had murdered him weighed heavily on my mind. It was but a cruel and unjust byproduct of Bets', and possibly his own, greed.

A related article in the paper announced that the Sheriff's Department had called off the search for Flipper's body. Two more deputies had had close calls with sharks, and they concluded that any dead flesh in the lake had certainly been consumed by the swarms of carnivorous creatures that had inhabited it of late.

It became apparent to me that my fate had already pretty much been sealed. Without Bip or Flipper to testify against Bets, my only hope was to create as much doubt as possible. Jail was really beginning to take its toll on me. I was miserable, made even more so by the realization of the wonderful place to which Flipper must have fled. I wanted to be there too. I still had not figured out how he could be the Crown Prince of Atlantis and be born in Mississippi. I finally just left it alone, reasoning that it was a mystery whose time to be solved had not yet arrived.

I instructed my attorneys that I wanted as little delay as possible. Many defendants try to string out the process, delay the inevitable result of conviction, and being sent to the state penitentiary at Angola, Louisiana. I wanted it over with. If I was going to be convicted, I wanted the death penalty. I preferred death to life in jail hell. Although they did not agree with it, Tony and J. Ryan honored my request and had us put on the docket in record time. Barely three months after my arrest on the murder charges, the trial was set to begin.

THIRTY-TWO

J. RYAN AND TONY HAD DONE SUCH A COMPLETE JOB of preparing for the trial that we all knew how hopeless it was, though none of us once admitted it aloud. The evidence was just overwhelming. Every fact made it appear as though Bets and I had conspired to use Flipper to fool the public and to make a fortune, and then killed him so that we could run off to Belize together with the money. I had no witnesses, no one who could stand up and refute anything that was going to be said about me. I had nothing to show that I had not been involved. And to make things even worse, the very people who had been cheated and lied to in this scam were the same people who were going to pass judgment on me. They were the public, my peers, the jury.

Loretta Robinson's opening statement lasted fifty-six minutes. I timed it. She explained to the jury what each of the counts against me were, and what she would have to do in order to prove each one. Then she went through her scenario of exactly what she thought had occurred:

"Each of these counts, each of these crimes, involves a single motive – greed. Andrew Jordan was not a poor man. He earned a good living. He obviously liked to spend money, and in order to spend money you have to get money. This is a man who wanted the finer things in life. He had worked hard to put himself through law school, hoping that this would be the avenue to wealth and fortune, the good life. But, ladies and gentlemen, when he got out he discovered one of the harsher realities of this life. Nothing is just given to you. Only by hard work and sweat of the brow do the riches of life finally come. Mr. Jordan was not making that fortune, and four years after he had graduated from law school, making a good salary as far as the average person is concerned, but still with hardly a penny to his name, he saw an opportunity for easy riches. He saw a shortcut and he lunged at it.

"I would like to remind you that we are speaking of a very intelligent man here, a man with two degrees, and a man with a mind so creative that, at least for a while, he was able to fool thousands, perhaps hundreds of thousands of people, into believing that a simple man off the street, a poor, down-on-his-luck, homeless man, was some kind of prince from an underwater kingdom. What's really amazing is that he foresaw that he could turn this charade into a million dollar enterprise. And that is exactly what he did. He fooled a lot of people and it compensated him nicely – for a while.

"Well I tell you, ladies and gentlemen of the jury," she continued, raising her voice for effect, "his days of fooling the public are over! He has been found out! Once you have seen the evidence, there will be only one possible conclusion that you can come to. That he is guilty on all counts.

"Mr. Jordan is smart, yes, he certainly is. But he is also guilty. It is true that Mr. Jordan was not alone. He was aided by his longtime companion, Betsy Davenport, who has gotten away with the money and, seemingly, murder. Do not be distracted and do not be fooled, ladies and gentlemen. Ms. Davenport's day of reckoning is coming, but that is an entirely different matter. You are here today to adjudge the guilt or innocence of just one man, and that is Mr. Andrew Caleb Jordan. He stands alone before you today, and it is your duty to determine his individual guilt or innocence in all that has transpired.

"The State of Louisiana is going to prove, and the facts will show, that Mr. Jordan, from the beginning, knew exactly what was going on. You will see, and we shall show, that Mr. Jordan made initial contact with Mr. Boier, that he purchased the underwater equipment necessary to carry off his fraudulent caper under Mr. Woodson's name, that he arranged to have large sums of money delivered to the control of his girlfriend and accomplice, and that he had planned it so that just as the walls came tumbling down around the entire scheme, he and Ms. Davenport would be safely whisked out of the country with the million dollars that their fraudulent scheme had produced. The State of Louisiana will also show, and you will see, that Mr. Jordan conspired in and carried out the murders of two innocent people, Mr. Harold Boier and Assistant District Attorney Theodore Wilhelm Woodson...," here she paused, for effect, wiping the corners of her eyes with a tissue, "...we all knew him as 'Bip,'" she continued with as much emotion as she could muster. "It is difficult to say which of these two deaths are most detestable, that of a poor, helpless, homeless man, taken advantage of, used for his deformity and then disposed of like so much garbage, or that of the young, brave, civil servant who befriended the defendant and whom the defendant coldly and ruthlessly murdered when it was feared that he may expose the plot before the getaway could be made.

"Ladies and Gentlemen, I implore you, listen to the evidence, keep in mind the genius criminal intellect that we are dealing with, and come back with guilty verdicts on all counts. Thank you." She lowered her head, closed her eyes, and stood silently before the jury as though in meditation. Then, dramatically, she lifted her head, made eye contact with each juror in turn, then pivoted and sashayed back to her seat.

"Jesus," J. Ryan whispered to me in awe, "normally you have to pay to see a performance like that!"

"Yea, well I'm fixing to pay with my life if Tony doesn't win them over right now," I quipped nervously.

Tony stood up to address the jury. His opening argument lasting all of five minutes:

"Ladies and Gentlemen of the jury," he began, "the only trickery that you are going to see in this trial is more of what you have just witnessed. An overzealous District Attorney, with nothing more than circumstantial evidence, attempting to make an innocent man out to be the most cruel, cold, and calculated murdering fiend of the twentieth century. Watch closely, because right before your eyes, during the course of this trial, the district attorney is going to pull several rabbits out of her hat.

"First," Tony continued, pretending to pull a rabbit out of a hat as he spoke, "she is going to tell you how Andrew Jordan represented Mr. Boier, how he lived with Ms. Davenport, how his actions made it easy for her to escape the country with a million dollars. Then she is going to want you to jump from that set of facts all the way over to convicting Mr. Jordan on charges of fraud and murder. You heard her. She would like for you to forget that the real perpetrator behind all of this is gone, out of the country. The real murderer here is Ms. Betsy Davenport. She left the country, with the money, and left poor Andrew Jordan holding the bag. He is a victim, not a criminal.

"The State's case is merely an optical illusion. The real criminal is not here, so they nab the person closest to her and, using their mirrors, try and make it look like he is the one who did all of these terrible, horrible, things. Andy Jordan could have left the country on that morning with Ms. Davenport if he had so chosen. But he did not.

"Why not? Because he is innocent, because he had no idea that anything had happened, because he had nothing to do with it other than he himself being a victim of the plot hatched by Betsy Davenport.

"Next, Ms. Robinson is going to tell you that Mr. Boier died on the bottom of Lake Pontchartrain and that – watch very closely ladies and gentlemen, here comes the next rabbit – Andy killed him. Never mind that they haven't found a body, and that there is no way to physically connect

Andy to his death other than his having done his roommate a favor by picking up a package for him. Never mind any of the facts, Ladies and Gentlemen. That is how magic works.

"And, finally, dear jurors, the magical District Attorney is going to pull the biggest rabbit of all out of her bag-o'-tricks. You are going to learn that one day Bip Woodson decided to sail off to Biloxi and that he was never heard from or seen again. Bip could be anywhere. Maybe he went off to Jamaica, or better yet, Belize, or maybe his boat sank, or he could be in the belly of a shark. For all we know he sailed into the Bermuda Triangle and was taken up into a spaceship. Perhaps he's cruising the galaxy right now, who knows? But what the State of Louisiana is going to tell you is that although no one really knows for sure whether he is dead or not, Andy Jordan slaughtered him, HIS BEST FRIEND. That Andy somehow killed him while he was hundreds of miles away in the middle of the Gulf of Mexico.

"As you consider the evidence presented, keep foremost in your mind the words, 'beyond a reasonable doubt.' The state must prove each charge to you beyond a reasonable doubt. And if you watch this magic show very carefully, you will certainly have many doubts about the guilt of Mr. Andy Jordan. He is charged with the murder of two people who, in all likelihood, are not even dead! If you do not believe that they are dead, then you cannot and must not convict Andrew Jordan of these crimes!

"If you want a culprit in all of this, look to Belize, look to Betsy Davenport and her million dollar getaway fund. If you want a victim, look right over here. Look to Andy Jordan."

With his own bit of drama concluded, Tony took his seat next to me. I patted him on the back. It had been a job well done.

Loretta Robinson rose to present the State's case.

Her first witnesses were the investigating police officers, an accountant, Mark Jackson of *The Angelique Brown Show*, and a second lieutenant in the Coast Guard. They testified collectively about my involvement with Boier and Bets, the money that was made in the deal, and the deaths and/or disappearances of Bip and Harold Boier. Most of what they said was absolutely true, and was consistent with what I have written here. Tony and J. Ryan could not do much to discredit anything that any of them had said, and their cross examinations were brief and unremarkable.

Fabacher took the stand against me next in order to explain to the jury how I had clearly hoodwinked the firm, how I had had Flipper go in there and request that only I be allowed to handle his case, how I had demanded and been given total control over the matter, and how I had cheated the firm out of its $20,000.00 fee. He described me as a loose cannon on the deck of the USS Keating, and how once this thing had grown too big, the firm's partners were helpless to do anything but sit back and hope that it all turned out for the best. He was sickening, and I was ashamed for having worked for a man so devoid of character.

Tony did not even cross-examine Fabacher, though the personal temptation to attack and humiliate him must have been nearly irresistible. He thought it in my best interest to avoid the confrontation and to get my old boss out from in front of the jury as quickly as possible.

The next set of witnesses were representatives from the toy, book, and movie companies with whom I had dealt prior to Flipper's final farewell. Each of them testified as to my absolute insistence that all monies be paid up front and immediately. They said I was holding a fire sale of all of the rights to Flipper's story and image, and that I had practically given the rights away for a fraction of their royalty values in exchange for cash deals up front. This was unheard of in the industry, and people were rushing to get a piece of the action before I gave it all away. The only conclusion that could be drawn from this line of testimony was that I was a cash hungry fiend who was planning to skip the country with the dough at the very earliest opportunity.

The State's next witness was a Mr. Harold Green. I recognized him as soon as he limped past me on his way to be sworn in.

"Mr. Green," Ms. Robinson began, "where are you employed?"

"By the bus station," he replied.

"And in what capacity?"

"What?"

"What do you do for the bus station?"

"I work for 'em," he responded, "in the package department. At least I did before I went on medical leave of absence."

"So you're a package and shipping clerk?"

"That's what I said."

"And how long have you been employed by the bus station in that capacity?"

"What?"

"How long have you worked there?"

"Six and a half months, about," he answered.

"And during your six and a half months of employment with the bus station, did you ever have the occasion to see or meet the defendant in this matter, Mr. Andrew Jordan?"

"I don't understan' the question," he replied rudely.

"Have you ever seen that man over there?" she asked, pointing to me.

"Him? Yea," he said.

"Let the record reflect that the witness has identified the defendant,

Andrew Jordan."

"What?" he said.

"Mr. Green, could you please explain to the jury how it was that you came to see Mr. Jordan?"

"He come to pick up a package."

"When was this?"

"I don't know," he responded.

"Let me show you this," she said, walking back over to her table. Her assistant handed her a piece of yellow paper which she brought over to Tony for his approval, and then brought to the witness. "Do you recognize this document?"

"You mean this piece of paper?"

"Yes," she responded, obviously beginning to grow irritated.

"Yea."

"Could you tell us what it is?"

"It's a C.O.D. receipt that we use at the station."

"And what does that receipt show? What information does it have on it?"

"It say that Mr. Theodore Wooden..."

"Woodson?" she interrupted.

"Yea, Woodson, picked up a package and give me a check for nine hundred seventy-two bucks."

"And who was the package from?"

"Lah Undersea World," he responded.

"L.A.?" she asked.

"Huh?"

"Isn't it L.A. Undersea World?"

"I didn't know you wanted me to spell it," he responded.

"Mr. Green, what does this receipt have to do with the defendant?"

"Well that Mr. Wooden right there," he said, pointing at me.

"Let the record reflect that he is pointing at the defendant. Mr. Green, are you saying that the defendant is Mr. Woodson?"

"Dat's what he tole me," he responded.

"Would you please explain to the Court exactly what happened on the date that this receipt was signed by the defendant."

"Well, it were a really rainy day, cats and dogs, and we wasn't very busy. And then all of a sudden like, right before goin' home time, that man come in and start ringing the bell on my desk. So I went runnin' on out and he give me a ticket for this package. No, no, he didn't have no ticket, so I axed him his name and he say it were Theo Wooden. I remember now cause I had to look it up and go get his package an all. An' then I went and got it, and I remember because it were so heavy dat dat's da day I hurt my back and when I filed my comp claim and didn't get to go back to work again."

"So the defendant was the last person that you served before you were injured?"

"Dat's right. Oh, dat there was a heavy package," he said.

"And you've been on a medical leave ever since?"

"Yea, my doctor say my disces is bulgin'," he responded.

Ms. Robinson went back to her desk and, after all the formalities, returned with my canceled check.

"Is this the check that the defendant gave you?"

"Yea, shore is," he said, just glancing at it.

"And it's in the amount of nine hundred and seventy-two dollars?"

"Yea, dat's a partial C.O.D."

"What's a partial C.O.D.?"

"Dat mean dat part of the thing already been paid for, like a deposit or somethin', and the nine hundred money is just the balance left after dat," he explained.

"So the value of the package from L.A. Undersea World that the defendant, who told you that his name was Theodore Woodson, picked up was worth at least nine hundred and seventy-two dollars?"

"Probably at least twice dat," he responded.

"Objection! Your Honor," Tony stood up. "That answer is unresponsive and purely speculative."

"Sustained," the judge immediately responded. "The jury will disregard that portion of the defendant's testimony."

"I have no further questions, Your Honor," Ms. Robinson said, heading to her seat.

Tony stood up and approached Mr. Green.

"Mr. Green," he began, "do you like peaches?"

"Objection, Your Honor," Ms. Robinson stood immediately. "How could that be at all relevant?"

"Your Honor, it goes to the events of that day and how well the witness truly remembers them, and possibly to his own credibility," Tony immediately fired back.

"I'll allow the question for now," the judge replied.

"So do you like peaches, Mr. Green?"

"They alright."

"Do you remember eating a peach on the day that the defendant walked into the package center?" Tony asked.

"No, not dat I recall."

"So you could have been eating a peach?"

"No, I was not."

Tony walked over to the table and J. Ryan handed him two sheets of paper.

"Mr. Green, could you please tell us what these two pieces of paper are."

Green looked them over, then frowned.

"So I forgot. I was eatin' a peach dat day," he grumbled.

"What was that?" Tony followed up.

"I said I ate da damn peach!"

"Mr. Green!" the judge interjected, "I will not have that kind of language spoken in my courtroom. One more word like that and I will hold you in contempt and you will be spending a couple of nights in the back!"

I glanced over at Ms. Robinson. Her confident smirk had eroded into a nervous smile. She strained to keep the worried look off of her face as Tony dissected Mr. Green's testimony with surgical precision.

"What I asked you Mr. Green, was to identify those pieces of paper for me," Tony repeated.

"Your Honor," Ms. Robinson stood up, "they are no longer relevant. Mr. Green has admitted eating the peach, which is not even relevant in the first place."

"Answer the question, Mr. Green," the judge barked, making it obvious that Green was not going to get any breaks from the court.

"Dis one is a customer complaint and the other one is a accident report form," Green explained.

"This first one, the complaint, it's from a Mr. Clint Williamson, is it not?"

"Dat's what it say."

"And Mr. Williamson's mother in Ruston, Louisiana, sent him a whole case of Ruston Red Peaches, and when it got to New Orleans, the box had been torn open and two of those peaches had mysteriously disappeared, hadn't they?"

"Yes, sur," Green replied.

"But this second piece of paper explains that their disappearance was not so mysterious, doesn't it?"

"You tell me," Green said.

"Well, doesn't this say that after you hurt your back they found a peach pit in the back so they thought you might have slipped on it. But you stated you had not, because you had been eating the peach at the time that you were hurt?"

"Yea, dat's right, I done tole you I was eatin' the peach."

"And where had you gotten the peach from, Mr. Green?"

"Your Honor..." Ms. Robinson interrupted.

"Overruled."

"Where had you gotten the peach from?"

"From dat Mr. Williamson's box," Green replied sheepishly.

"Now you had forgotten all about that when I first asked you the question, hadn't you?" It was brilliant. Green either had to admit to a flawed memory or to having lied on the stand.

"Yea, so what?"

"What else have you forgotten about that day?"

"Probably alot," he responded, "but I remember dat mu…" he stopped himself, "da defendant over there."

"And why is that?"

"Because he was a wrong dude. I knew there was somethin' bad about him the minute I laid eyes on him. When he leff, I let him use my dolly to carry his big ole heavy package out in the rain wit, and don't you know instead of bringin' it back he jus threw it out into the middle of the drive, wit me watchin' him do it."

"And that made you mad, didn't it?" Tony asked.

"You right it did," Green responded.

"Mad enough to have pounded him if you had had the chance," Tony continued.

"If my back hadn't been hurtin' I would have gone out in dat rain and done it, you right I would have."

"Mad enough to want to see him go to jail, or worse…"

"Objection!," Ms. Robinson yelled.

"Mr. D'Ensina," the judge said calmly, "I think you've made your point. You've taken it about as far as I am going to allow you. Move on to something else."

"Yes, Your Honor," Tony responded.

"Mr. Green," Tony continued, "isn't it true that the defendant gave you a check written in the name of Andrew Jordan?"

"Yea," Green said.

"And you watched him write it out and sign it?"

"Yea."

"And isn't it true that he told you he was there to pick up a package that Bip Woodson had ordered, and that he never actually told you that his name was Bip Woodson."

"I guess it's possible. It's been a long time now, several months," Mr. Green responded.

I smiled and breathed a small sigh of relief.

"And Mr. Green, you don't know what was in that package that injured your back, do you?"

"No."

"You just know that it was heavy."

"Shore was," Green replied.

"Thank you Mr. Green. I have no further questions, Your Honor," Tony said. He walked back and sat next to me. I gave him a nudge of approval with my elbow.

The prosecution's next witness was a dive master who testified concerning the equipment found in the shrimper's net. The tanks were exactly like the ones that the *Peepers* divers had used which produce no bubbles. He testified that one of the tanks was nearly empty and that the other was filled with a mixture of oxygen and poisonous gas. The tanks had been attached to an underwater self-propulsion unit, like one of those little underwater scooters that Jacques Cousteau's men are always using. He theorized that on the date of the filming Flipper had descended to the bottom of the lake and located the scooter. The dive master testified that there must have been enough oxygen in the first tank for him to catch his breath and to move quickly offshore on the scooter for his resurfacing.

At that point the prosecutor played a copy of the tape that had been taken by the film crew that day. It was very surreal watching it, with Flipper lunging into the water, then resurfacing, calling my name.

The diving expert continued, theorizing that after Flipper had gone back under he had strapped himself onto the propulsion unit and begun to move, but it was then that he must have realized that the oxygen in the first tank was spent. At that point, the dive master testified, he apparently switched tanks, went a little farther, then fell to the bottom, unconscious. The weight of the tanks and scooter would have kept them there for eternity, had it not been for the shrimper's trawl that brought them back to the surface.

The dive master next testified that both the tanks and the propulsion unit had markings and serial numbers that matched the equipment sold by L.A. Undersea World to Bip, or me pretending to be Bip.

"Mr. Harkrider," Ms. Robinson continued. "Mr. Boier's body was never recovered. Would you, in your opinion, find that inconsistent with your theory that he died that day on the bottom of the lake?"

"Not at all," Harkrider replied, like a trained seal. "Lake Pontchartrain is a mixture of fresh and sea water opening into the Gulf of Mexico. It is a carnivorous jungle down there, especially as of late. I understand a disproportionate amount of sea life has been spotted there, including two of nature's greatest scavengers, sharks and crabs."

Several members of the jury cringed, probably crab-eaters concerned that they may have dined upon crustaceans that had devoured Flipper's corpse.

"His remains also could have been carried out to sea by the Lake's strong currents," Harkrider continued, "or may even have become embedded in the very soft mud bottom. They say the mud is as deep as the water in some spots. In the fifties or sixties an entire passenger jet went down in the lake and neither it nor anyone aboard has ever been seen again."

"Perhaps they ended up in Atlantis," Ms. Robinson quipped to the delight of the audience but the ire of the judge.

"Objection!" Tony yelled.

"Sustained," the Judge immediately responded. "Ms. Robinson, you know better than that. This is a court of law. Such behavior in the future will not be tolerated."

"Yes, Your Honor," Robinson replied with a smirk on her face that made me hate her. "I have no further questions."

Tony cross-examined the dive instructor about his depiction of the events of that day, and forced him to admit that he had no first-hand knowledge of exactly what Flipper had done. He had merely taken the evidence, both the tape and the equipment, and, in his expert opinion, theorized the events as they must have occurred. One interesting bit of cross-examination came when Tony questioned the witness concerning several blotches of red paint that were found on both of the tanks after their discovery in the lake.

"Now Mr. Harkrider," Tony asked, "what would the significance be, if any, of these red paint marks on each tank."

"There is no significance that I know of," he answered.

"These are brand new tanks though, are they not?"

"They were at the time."

"There is nothing related to diving that would account for these markings then?"

"No sir," he responded. Then added, "It looks to me, by the way they are made, that it was just the result of some carelessness on somebody's part. Looks like they had painted something and then laid the tanks on it before it was dry."

"Thank you Mr. Harkrider. I have no further questions, Your Honor."

"One re-direct, Judge," Ms. Robinson said, standing.

"Mr. Harkrider, couldn't it be that perhaps someone painted the tanks red to mark them as the tanks they wanted to use as a means of poisoning..."

"Objection. Calls for speculation on the part of the witness," Tony said.

"Sustained," the judge answered. But it was too late. The jury had already heard.

"I withdraw the question," Ms. Robinson said, sitting back in her seat with a smile.

Mr. Harkrider was the final witness of the day. Court broke at 5:30 p.m., and I was escorted back to my cell.

That evening I called home to Hackberry for only the second time since my arrest. I had asked my mother not to attend the trial. It would have been too expensive for her and I just did not want to put her through it. As a compromise she made me promise to call her with updates. I told her that I thought it had all gone very well, that the D. A. did not have a very strong case, and that I would see her by New Years. By the time I hung up, there was much less worry in her voice. I knew then that if there was to be bad news on future nights, I would be incapable of bringing myself to tell her.

THIRTY-THREE

CARLY AND TAYLOR WERE AT HER MOTHER'S HOME that evening, trying to escape the publicity by heading out of the city to the quieter, less densely populated northern shore of Lake Pontchartrain. They walked, holding hands, into a stiff, salt-filled breeze, a huge, orange sun fading into the half of the lake behind them. As they walked, she explained to her young son why he could never see me again.

"Some people can be bad and you just don't know it," she told him. "It isn't always easy to know just who is good and who is bad."

"Is Mr. Andy bad?" he asked.

"Yes," she said bluntly, "he is. And I had no way of knowing it."

"Why is he bad?"

"I don't know, sweetie. I wish I did."

"Look, Mommy!" Taylor suddenly exclaimed.

"What?" she said, exhibiting her big, beautiful smile.

"Look, in the water!" he was so excited.

"What sweetie?" she asked, growing excited herself. "I can't see anything."

"It's the Water Man, he's here, he's here!" he was shouting now, jumping up and down.

Suddenly, Carly's smile turned to horror and she grabbed Taylor and held him close. Out of nowhere, just ahead on the shore, lay the bloated, decaying body of Harold Boier, identifiable only by his large, rotting feet.

She turned away in disgust, shielding the boy's eyes from the sight, then turned to look again. His body was gone, replaced by that of the dead, fly-infested porpoise that I had set adrift on Orange Beach. She stared at it, dazed and confused, then watched in amazement as a beautiful light appeared from within, then enveloped it, carrying it to the lake, plunging it beneath the waters. Suddenly the entire lake was illuminated, dazzling, cleansed.

I awoke in a cold sweat.

Since Flipper's departure I no longer dreamed as I had before. My unconscious visualizations had become much more clear, vividly detailed, and frightening. It were as though there was a projector rolling and my mind was the screen. They were virtual reality, played in the forefront of my brain. I was there, just as I had been at the lake. My dreams had become less frequent and all were of this caliber. Either I had such dreams or none at all. There was no in between. Either the projector was turned on, or it was shut completely off.

Morning had broken, and it was time to dress for trial.

J. Ryan walked in to the courtroom and immediately handed me a full-page article about my trial and all that had been going on at the Lakefront. The police had finally forced everyone away from the south shore and barricaded the entrances, fearing that the situation would get out of hand.

Three of the temporary residents there, who had been sharing a tent with four or five others, had begun stirring up the crowd after claiming that "The Atlantin" swam up to them in the lake during a midnight dip. They said that they recognized him from the television, although now he was sporting a glow, "like he had gotten too close to a nuclear accident, man." They claimed that he had announced that he wanted everyone to know that he was real and that I was innocent. They further related that he had said that he cleaned up Lake Pontchartrain as a gift to the city that had once accepted him, and that if "earth people" did not begin believing that he was real and that I was innocent, it would all be reversed.

It excited me until I got to the part of the article explaining how these individuals and their communal tentmates had all subsequently been arrested by the New Orleans Police Department for possession and distribution of LSD, which was used as the "official explanation" for their putting an end to the vigil. I finished the article just as the Judge took his seat at the bench.

The prosecution began the day with the shrimper who had found the underwater gear in the lake. According to his testimony, he had gotten an early start that morning and was doing well before his trawl got caught on something.

"I was afraid it might be an ol' wreck," he said in a thick Cajun accent. "You know dare's ships and planes down dare dat nobody's ever found. I taut dat I mighta caught me one."

"What did you do?" Ms. Robinson asked.

"Whale, it was a good ways back behind da boat so I couldn't see what it was and I jus about cut da rope whan it finely start to come on. So I jus pulled it on in and foun all dat stuff in it."

"The tanks and the underwater propulsion unit?" Ms. Robinson prodded.

"Yes, Ma'am, I guess dat's what you call it. It was a big load on my wench, but she pulled it on in an all," he said proudly.

"And that's when you called the police?"

"Yes, Ma'am. Dat's whan I went in and radioed da Coast Guard. I knew nobody wold jes leave dat expensive equipment layin' aroun' like dat. Either it had fell off somebody's boat or somebody was down there."

"Thank you, Mr. Boudreaux. Your witness, counselor," she addressed Tony.

"The defense has no questions of this witness, Your Honor," Tony responded.

"The witness is excused," the judge said.

Next came a chemist, a so-called poisonous substance expert, and his evaluation, which was nothing new to anyone. The gas in the tank was carbon monoxide. Breathing carbon monoxide in great quantities would put someone to sleep in moments, to death in minutes.

Tony had few questions for him, but he did ask him whether he had determined a cause of death for Mr. Woodson. This question met with strenuous objection from the defense and was withdrawn. "I just couldn't resist," Tony whispered as he took his seat.

The prosecution's final set of witnesses were the most damning to my cause.

Jorge Martinez was first. He was the young man behind the Lacsa counter that Bets had spoken to and left my suitcase with prior to her leaving the country. Some of his testimony, related to what Bets had told him, was excluded as hearsay after objection by Tony. Other parts were allowed as supposed admissions of guilt. The jury was allowed to hear that Bets had left the suitcase with him, with specific instructions to give it to me, along with a reissued ticket for the following day's flight. He also testified extensively as to all that had transpired after my arrival at the counter, including the fact that I had recognized the bag as my own and had accepted it, along with the ticket, signing the voucher as he had requested.

Following Mr. Martinez was officer Frank Reich of the New Orleans Police Department. He was the man who had opened my bag and had documented everything inside. It was all laid out in the court room and the prosecution went through it item by item. As he described each one, Ms. Robinson took the particular object, each one already pre-packed in a clear plastic bag and marked for identification, and passed them along to the jury members for their inspection.

"Item No. 1 is a .38 caliber handgun, recently fired with four bullets in the carousel. The weapon is registered to Mr. Theodore Woodson."

"Item No. 2 is Mr. Theodore Woodson's driver's license."

"Item No. 3 is a bloody shirt, size 28, with what appears to be a bullet hole in the chest area."

Bip wore a size 28, I wore size 35. Bets had conveniently left me with the murder weapon and the shirt Bip must have been wearing when he was shot.

"Item No. 4 is another pair of underwear, Fruit of the Loom, Size 34. There is a significant tear just below the crotch area."

So I was too lazy to buy new underwear. Only a mother could ever foresee that it may one day be passed around the hands of twelve people who, in a day or two, were going to decide whether I should live or die. With everything else that I had to worry about, I was still relieved that my mother had not been in the courtroom to see that torn pair of drawers.

"Item No. 5, a polyester dinner jacket, powder blue with darker blue striping."

I swear it was not mine. It was my size but it was not mine. It must have been Bets' idea of some kind of joke. She had probably purchased it at the Salvation Army or some thrift store and put it in there. I had not worn anything like that since the seventies, and then only because my mother had very little fashion sense.

"Item No. 6 is a pair of swimming trunks."

"Item No. 7 is Mr. Jordan's passport."

"Items 8 through 27 are ribbed condoms. In a variety of colors, I would like to add."

This was, no doubt, for Carly's benefit. Bets had thought of everything. Actually, I was grateful that she had not had the time, or the forethought, to locate some with "extra small" printed on the package.

It all seemed so ludicrous to me, and I hoped to the jury as well. I mean, who would be so stupid as to pack a getaway bag with a victim's bloody shirt, a murder weapon, and a year's supply of condoms? Perhaps ole Bets wasn't as clever as she thought she was.

After the jury had finished fondling all of my personal items, the prosecution called its next to last witness. Of all those called, she would prove to be the most damaging to my cause. In the end it was her testimony that I could not overcome. She was so believable, as she should have been, because she was telling the truth.

"Would you please state your full name for the record," Ms. Robinson instructed.

"Margo...I mean, Margerie Angela Ricalde."

"And Ms. Ricalde, by whom are you employed?"

"I'm a legal secretary at Keating & Fabacher," she replied.

"And did you occupy this position in August of this year?"

"Yes Ma'am," she answered, "only now I work for a different attorney."

"Who were you working for at that time?"

"Well, I was working for three attorneys."

"And who were they?" Ms. Robinson insisted.

"Well, Mr. D'Ensina, Mr. Hayes, and Mr. Jordan."

"You mean all three of the gentlemen sitting at the defendant's table?"

"Yes, Ma'am."

It looked like a conspiracy.

Tony, J. Ryan, and I all wore nervous grins.

"Ms. Ricalde, were you working for Mr. Jordan after Mr. Harold Boier, a-k-a Christian Waterman, dove into Lake Pontchartrain on national television."

"Yes, Ma'am, I was."

"Was there anything that occurred at that time which maybe made you a little suspicious of the activities that Mr. Jordan was carrying on?"

"Yes, Ma'am," Margo nervously replied.

"Could you please explain this to the court."

"Well, the day after that had all happened, Andy – I mean, Mr. Jordan – had taken the day off. The telephone did not stop ringing all day long, people wanting to talk to him, wanting interviews, and to make deals with the Trust of Atlantis. And the mail was coming in in bunches too, with all kinds of checks. The Trust received nearly a million dollars on that Friday alone, some of it Federal Expressed."

"Was this unusual?" Ms. Robinson asked.

"Yes!" Margo exclaimed. "We never got that kind of money through the firm. It made me really nervous. I was in charge of seeing that it all got into the account that Ms. Davenport controlled."

"Ms. Davenport?" Ms. Robinson queried.

"Yes, Ma'am. It was set up that way. Supposedly, Mr. Waterman – uh, Mr. Boier – had wanted Ms. Davenport to have complete control of the money. Mr. Jordan drew up the documents and had me set up the bank account in that way."

"And Ms. Davenport was Mr. Jordan's girlfriend?"

"I think they were engaged," Margo said, "at least that's what she told me once."

"Objection!" Tony barked.

Margo jolted and glanced briefly at our table.

"Sustained."

"You say that Ms. Davenport was Mr. Jordan's girlfriend?" Ms.

Robinson reiterated.

"Yes, Ma'am, for about four years."

"Okay, you can go on," Ms. Robinson instructed.

"Well, all this money was coming in and I was seeing to it that it went into Ms. Davenport's account. And then Mr. Jordan called me that morning and he didn't seem to be concerned with any of the business or anything. He was very brief, and just told me to make airplane reservations for he and Ms. Davenport to Belize for the following Tuesday morning. I thought it was a little strange..."

"Why?" Ms. Robinson probed.

"Because he had never asked me to make plane reservations before, and certainly not for him and his girlfriend, and now they were leaving the country, and all of this money was coming in. It all just kind of gave me the creeps."

"Did you tell anyone about your suspicions at that point?"

"Just my husband."

"But not anyone at Keating & Fabacher?"

"No, Ma'am."

"Go on."

"Well, I went ahead and made the reservations like he had asked me to and had the tickets sent to the office. Then I just tried to forget about it all for the weekend," Margo said.

"Okay," Ms. Robinson prodded, "so what happened after the weekend?"

"Well, on Monday everything seemed to be okay. Mr. Jordan was a little concerned about Mr. Woodson, his missing roommate, but not quite as much as I would have..."

"Objection."

"Sustained."

"Sorry," Margo said.

"It's all right, just go on," Ms. Robinson instructed.

"Well everything seemed okay on Monday. Ms. Davenport came by and dropped off a check from the Trust of Atlantis for the firm's fee and she said to tell Mr. Jordan that she would meet him in..."

"That's hearsay, Your Honor," Tony said, standing.

"Sustained. Ms. Robinson, perhaps you could direct this witness's testimony in a more concise manner."

"Why don't we move on to the events of Tuesday morning, Ms. Ricalde," Ms. Robinson suggested.

"Tuesday is when it all came to a head. I got to the office a little bit early because I had a lot of Mr. D'Ensina's work to catch up on. Around 8:30 a friend of mine at the bank called to tell me that the check that Ms. Davenport had written had been returned NSF. And not only that, the entire account had been closed and the money wired to an account in Switzerland."

"What did you do when you found out this information?" Ms. Robinson asked.

"Mr. Jordan was standing right there, getting ready to leave, when I was talking to her. So as soon as I hung up I got him to go into his office and then I told him."

"How did he respond?"

"Like a crazy person," Margo answered, her eyes beginning to water up. "He grabbed my shoulders and pinned me against the wall of his office. He kept telling me that it wasn't true and that he was going to go to the airport and get Ms. Davenport and the whole thing would be straightened out."

"What did you do?" Ms. Robinson asked.

"There was nothing I could do. I was getting scared. He had never acted like that before. Then he told me, twice, not to tell anyone about it. He kind of threatened me. Then he said he had to go to the airport and he ran out of the office." Margo was crying now.

"What did you do then?" Ms. Robinson asked as tenderly as she could fake.

"I started crying. I thought he must be running out to the airport because the plane would be taking off soon and he was going to take it and leave with the money and I would be the only one left. And I hadn't done anything wrong, but it sure looked like I had." Margo stopped a moment to dry her eyes.

"Take your time, it's all right," Ms. Robinson said in a sweet little tone that made me want to puke.

"I was so scared!" Margo insisted. "I didn't know what to do. Finally I just ran down the hall to Mr. Fabacher's office and told him about the bounced check, and the missing money, and that Mr. Jordan had gone running off to the airport. And I told him that he had made me buy him and Ms. Davenport those tickets to Central America."

"What did Mr. Fabacher do?"

"He called the police and the airport security and told them to keep him off that airplane."

"Ms. Ricalde, how long did you work for Mr. Jordan?"

"The whole time he was at the firm. I started about a month before he did," Margo said.

"And did you like Mr. Jordan?"

"He was the best boss I've ever had, and we were friends." Her tears came faster now.

"It's hard to sit here and say all these things about him, isn't it?"

"Yes, Ma'am."

"And the only reason you are saying them is because they are true, aren't' they?"

"Yes, Ma'am, every word."

"Thank you. I have no further questions," Ms. Robinson said, returning to her seat.

There was not much for Tony to work with. Margo was a good witness. She had just told the truth.

"Ms. Ricalde – Margo," Tony began, "it wasn't normal for Andy to be dealing with hundreds of thousands of dollars, was it?"

"No, sir."

"You were both new at that, weren't you?"

"Yes, sir."

"And it was very unusual for him to treat you like he did on that Tuesday morning, wasn't it?"

"Yes, sir."

"He was otherwise very friendly, wasn't he?"

"Yes, he was."

"Now on that morning, was there not a service that was supposed to be held at the District Attorney's office for Bip Woodson?"

"Yes, sir, there was supposed to be."

"Loretta, did y'all have that?" Tony asked, turning to Ms. Robinson.

"Your Honor!" Ms. Robinson complained.

"Never mind," Tony said.

He turned back toward Margo.

"Hadn't Mr. Jordan told you that he was going to attend that service?"

"Yes, sir," Margo replied.

"And until you told Mr. Jordan that the money was missing, he was his normal, rational, friendly self, was he not?"

"I guess so. He was trying to rush out just before I told him, though. He said he was going to the service, but he could have really been going to the airport."

"But he wasn't 'crazy' at that point, correct?"

"No, sir – I mean, yes, sir. He wasn't crazy at that point, not until after."

"Margo, what time was that airplane scheduled to take off?"

"Ten in the morning."

"And what time did you tell Andy about the bank account?"

"About a quarter of nine."

"So, just before a quarter of nine he was fine, acting normally, and then, just after a quarter of nine, when you told him about the missing money, he turns as you said, 'crazy', and runs out of the office, correct?"

"Yes," Margo said, interested.

"Now, the airport is a good forty-five minutes from downtown, isn't it?"

"If traffic is good, I guess."

"That wouldn't have given him much time to get to the airport and onto an international flight, would it?"

"No, not too much."

"If Andy had planned to be on that airplane, don't you think he would have been rushing and acting crazy before you told him about the money?"

"Objection. That calls for speculation!" Ms. Robinson said.

"I withdraw the question, Your Honor," Tony said politely, turning toward me and returning to his seat with a smile. The jury had heard what he had intended.

Margo was excused. She walked past me, with a tear in her eye and gave me a look that told me she was sorry. My eyes bubbled up, and in that instant I forgave her. I could never trust her again, but still I forgave her. She smiled back.

Ms. Robinson called a DNA expert as her last witness who identified the blood on Evidence Item #3 as Bip's, tying the bloody shirt in my suitcase inextricably with Bip. After his testimony, she announced to the court that the prosecution had concluded its case. It was already 4:30 in the afternoon, and the judge decided to declare a recess so that we could begin presenting our case in the morning.

After court that evening, Tony, J. Ryan, and I sat around discussing what the prosecution had presented and weighing the pros and cons of my taking the stand the next morning. I finally told both of them that I thought my testimony would be mostly self-serving, and that it would not carry much weight with the jury. I also told them that, in my opinion, they had done an excellent job in discrediting the key prosecution witnesses. If the prosecution had failed to make its case, my testimony would not be necessary and may only serve to resurrect some doubts in the jury's mind concerning my character. There were too many questions that I just could not answer, and that would make me look like I was hiding something. Tony agreed and thought it best that I not open myself to attack, but J. Ryan strenuously argued that the jury needed to meet me, to know who I was and to be able to relate the person to the being that they would be passing judgment on.

Tony and I outvoted J. Ryan. Perhaps this is where a $250.00 an hour defense attorney would have made the difference, but, right or wrong, we were going to go into court on the following morning and tell the judge and jury that we had no case to present. Relying on our belief that the prosecution had failed to carry its burden of proof, we were going to place the matter in the hands of the jury.

That night, I dreamed again. It took up right where the last one had left off, with me in the lake, but with the sharks gone.

I was in the water, being carried along by some undetectable force, my life sustained by an unknown presence. In the distance, ever visible, beckoned the bright glow familiar to me now as Flipper. The glow grew nearer at frightening speed, either it or I was fast approaching. Suddenly it was here and I there, upon the golden streets of the City of Atlantis.

A grey porpoise appeared, suspended before me, moving forward, and I followed as I knew that I should. I moved through the corridors of an ancient city, flanked on all sides by glowing pedestrians, their form more spiritual than human, at once familiar and foreign, friendly and aloof.

I followed my guide, past columns and temples, either Greek or Roman, corresponding to my lack of education as to the difference, knowing that their existence in that form was but a function of my preconceptions, for the benefit of my comprehension, and that in actuality they were but a facade built of my own imagination. I knew then, as I do now, that Atlantis, in all its splendor, was not so much a physical place as it was a state of mind within some varying plane of existence.

Suddenly, and inexplicably, as otherwise occurs only in dreamstate, I was within a wondrous palace before a throne occupied by a being so magnificent that my memory had not the capacity to hold its description other than to know that I had witnessed the spectacle. In a chair to its right, my guide, instantaneously transforming from porpoise to Christian, took his seat. He, I cannot describe either. I can only say that he was more energy than form, and that to merely gaze upon him brought such joy as to make his form irrelevant. I knew that I was seeing him as he really was, his earthbound webbed feet having been every bit as much a product of my learned and preconceived consciousness as feathered wings upon Heaven's angels.

I awoke with his father's words still in my head. "Kill your sharks and make his words truth."

I had no idea what they meant. Perhaps that I should testify, but it was already too late for that.

To deny that I considered the possibility that I was going insane, losing my mind, would be but testament to my insanity. I did harbor such fear, but never allowed it to take a foothold in my consciousness. Instead I chose faith over feeblemindedness, adjudging it to be the better portion.

THIRTY-FOUR

IT TOOK THE JURY EXACTLY FORTY-EIGHT MINUTES to return with verdicts of guilty on all counts. I stood there, stunned, listening to the words as the judge read them, unwilling to accept them. Next we began the death penalty phase, the part of the proceeding where the jury decides whether the convicted is to live or die.

This time, after the prosecution had made its case for putting me to death, I did take the stand. I told the jury that life in prison was no option. I would prefer to die, and would like for the sentence to be carried out as quickly as possible.

My announcement caused quite a stir in the courtroom, which the judge quickly hushed. The jury went out for a few minutes, then returned and granted me my wish. I was remanded to the custody of the officials of the state penitentiary at Angola, to be held in the death row section thereof until such time as my death sentence could be carried out by lethal injection.

Tony cried at the sentencing. I hugged both he and J. Ryan afterward and commended them for the great job they had done. Tony told me that they would appeal on the basis that I had received inadequate assistance of counsel. I smiled, begged him not to, and told him that I could not stand prison for that long. J. Ryan just stood motionless. Although he had known how hopeless my situation was, I think that he somehow expected to win, as though his hard work and determination were enough to get me off. I was taken away.

THIRTY-FIVE

ALTHOUGH I WAIVED ALL APPEALS and made no attempt whatsoever to have my conviction overturned, I sat on death row for nearly three months' time. Though far from likable, I found it preferable to the Orleans Parish Prison. I had my own cell and a lot of free time on my hands. I did a lot of thinking, and a lot of writing, and I became good friends with my guard, Walter Jackson. Walter was a career prison guard. His father had been a guard at Angola for twenty-eight years before his death, and Walter had been there for sixteen years before I arrived. I found it ironic that Walter, this gentle giant born and raised there, had lived practically his entire life at Angola, as though it were a life sentence imposed by his birthright. There were paroled murderers and rapists walking the streets of New Orleans who had spent less time within the prison walls than Walter had.

In the entire three months that I was there, I watched exactly one television program. Walter had come to me one morning and handed me his tiny television. Although it was strictly forbidden, he knew that I would be interested in what was on. It was an edition of *The Angelique Brown Show* entitled "People who were not fooled by Andy Jordan." Among the guests were the Mayor of New Orleans and a woman from Ville Platte, Louisiana who had refused to allow her son to attend the send-off at the lake with the rest of his class for religious reasons, although it had caused much grief at home. Angelique was also proud to count herself in that number, going so far as to say that at one point she had personally seen to it that we were not carried on *The Angelique Brown Show*, which resulted in our being picked up by *Peepers.*

The Mayor's account was most distasteful as he recounted the incident at Fabacher's party. Only in his version he recognized Flipper immediately as a fraud and exposed him to the party. He said that no one believed him and that he was forced to leave as he could not remain in the company of so many sheep being led to the slaughter by a homeless nobody and the unscrupulous genius of Andy Jordan. That was the point where I turned it off and gave the damned thing back to Walter. I thanked him, but asked him never to loan it to me again.

Tony and J. Ryan came to visit me a few days before the execution was scheduled to take place. It certainly was good to see them. They told me that they had attempted to see me on several previous occasions, but that visitation to the death row section was so restricted, even for attorneys, they had been unable to make it before then. We talked for a very long while. They told me about everything going on and about how well their practice was doing. Apparently I was not the only person who appreciated the great job they had done in my defense.

Before they left, J. Ryan handed me an 8 x 10 photograph taken of Flipper and me at the lake just before he dove in and swam away. It was not a very good picture of us. It was out of focus, as though it had been taken with one of those instant cameras that had focused on the lake rather than on Flipper and me, but I appreciated getting it. He said that it had been sent to him anonymously, but we both suspected that it had been Carly. Perhaps it was only my personal fantasy that she had cared to send it, but I kept the photograph next to my bed and stared at it for hours at a time during the few days remaining before my death.

That night Walter asked, as was his duty, what my last meal was to be. I thought back to Bip and Bets, and how on the trip to Destin we had played a little game, asking one another what our last meal would be if we ever had to make that decision. I, at least, never for a moment suspected that one day one of us might have to actually do it. I racked my brain, but could not remember what my answer had been. I was thus forced to start from scratch.

I first tried to think of something exotic to tell Walter, then something impossible, "pastry from Paris, postpone the execution until it can be delivered," but I knew that was unrealistic.

"Why don't we give them something to write about?" I finally suggested.

"Now you're talkin'," he responded.

"I want to start with a shrimp cocktail and a seaweed salad. Then seafood gumbo and sushi rolls. And for the main course I want a shark steak, grilled, with some kind of sauce."

Walter smiled and took it all down. "Sure you want to do this?" he asked.

"What the hell," I said. "And a Snickers bar for dessert."

"What the hell," he repeated, laughing.

I felt better. After that I prayed, then enjoyed a very restful night's sleep.

The following morning Amy Star and one of her cameramen came to my cell. My own mother could not get in to see me before the final day, but then my mother did not have the power to broadcast an expose' on the Department of Correction's penitentiary system if she were refused an audience. All other visits had to be held in a special room with a glass partition between the prisoner and the visitor, but Amy and her cameraman were allowed face-to-face contact. They had a pass to shoot film footage there. Amy asked to interview me, but initially I declined.

"Look, off the record," she began, "you and I both know who the real culprit in this whole thing was. Admit it baby, she played you like a cheap piano and left you to the sacrificial fire."

"I guess we underestimated Ms. Milk-toast, didn't we?" I added.

"Well, she didn't do it alone," Amy Star said. "I'm sure her accomplice helped her out with a lot of the thinking."

"Her accomplice?"

"Yea, the one she killed and put on you."

"You mean Bip?" I asked.

"Let me tell you about your buddy Bip. We've been doing a lot of research here trying to dig up some dirt on you guys. By the way, we haven't found any on you or Ms. Davenport yet. Is there anything you would like to share with me?"

Before I could answer, she continued speaking.

"Boy, prison sure hasn't done you any harm, has it. You look pretty damn good in that orange jumpsuit."

"I bet you say that to all the death row inmates you interview," I answered.

"Only the ones I want to..."

"I know, I know," I said. "Tell me about Bip."

"Old Teddy Woodson? Let's see," she said, flipping through her note pad. "Here he is, Theodore Woodson, born October 2, 1957, in Madison, Wisconsin."

"Wrong guy," I interrupted. "Bip was 33 and he was born in Providence, Rhode Island."

"Andy," Amy smirked, "you ever wonder why it is that all the rest of us innocent people are here on the outside and you are locked up on death row? Why don't you just listen and learn something? Your friend would have been 37 last October and I doubt he's ever even been to Rhode Island. He was raised in a well-to-do family. His grandfather had made a lot of money during the depression and the family was sort of just existing off of that wealth."

"Okay, that's right," I said, "then his parents got divorced."

"They got murdered," she corrected.

"Oh, yea, he did mention something one time about one killing the other or something."

"They were found dead together in their bed. The pictures are brutal. Somebody used a claw hammer on them. Ole' Bip was the cop's number one suspect, but they could never prove anything, so he walked away with just over a million dollars. He was spending it like a maniac up in Wisconsin, and they were keeping a pretty close eye on him, but then one day he just disappeared. He finally turned up in New Orleans, attending law school, and living with you."

"Are you sure about this?" I asked, stunned.

"Positive, it all checks out. We are certain that he was in on this thing at least at some point before his disappearance. I guess Bets just got a little greedy and wanted the whole thing for herself. Kind of humorous in a way, the con-man out-conned by little Ms. Milk-toast."

Suddenly I knew. I knew who my sharks were. They had been there all along. Bip and Bets. And I knew what must be done. They had to be exposed. Flipper's memory and the message that he had delivered had to be given another chance to take root in the public's mind. I knew that there were those, who like me, still believed, the ones who had camped out at the Lakefront for so long. There must have been plenty more. Amy Star's being there was no accident – she was the only one who could help me pull it off.

"I have something to show you," I said, getting up from my bunk. I walked over to the wall where I had taped up the picture that J. Ryan had given me and pulled it down. I brought it over and handed it to her.

Amy studied the photograph for a moment, then looked up at me.

"This was taken at the filming. Just before he jumped in. Right?"

"That's right," I agreed. "I haven't been able to stop looking at it."

"Someone has a bad focus. Is this some kind of human interest angle?" she asked.

"Are you familiar with my trial?"

"Yea, we got a transcript. We were over in Orleans Parish last week taking footage of the equipment that Boier had used underwater."

"Did you see the red paint on the tanks?" I asked.

"Yea, I think I noticed that," she responded, probably lying.

"Look to the left of my head. What do you see?"

"The lake and a couple of boats."

"See the red one?"

"Yea, the red sailboat," she responded.

"That's Bip's boat," I declared.

"What?" she said, shocked. "Are you sure?"

"I wasn't until just now," I said, "it all fits. The color on the boat is the same as on the tanks. They must have painted it when Bip was supposed to have been sailing to Biloxi. I noticed it last night – the railing on the front looks like it's missing where Bip's was, only Bip's boat was white, and the picture is kind of far away and a little blurry, so I wasn't sure."

"Bip's alive then?" Amy exclaimed.

"Sure looks that way to me," I said.

"Who took this?"

"I don't know," I answered.

"We have to bring this out, Andy!" she said excitedly. "You just saved yourself a trip to the gas chamber."

"Lethal injection," I corrected her.

"Same difference," she said, coldly.

"I don't think so."

"They'll have to give you a new trial. This is new evidence. We can have this blown up. We probably have footage of it. I mean, we can probably get a shot of Bip on the boat! This is wonderful!"

"Amy, you can have the picture and you can have the interview, but only on the condition that none of this comes out before my execution is carried out."

"Are you crazy?" she asked me. "We're talking about your life."

"And boy what a life," I said, waiving my arm around my cell. "This only clears me in Bip's murder. It does not clear me of any of the other charges. I would have to spend a lifetime here, or even worse, over there," I said, pointing to the other part of the prison. "I could not take that. It would be condemning me to a life of hell. I would rather take my chances in the next life."

"But we can't withhold this," she said, "what would people think if it came out that we could have saved your life?"

"It won't come out. We can do the interview and I can leave the picture along with a written statement to be opened after my death. You could do one of those mystery-revealed type broadcasts with it, build up the suspense. That way, after I am gone, the truth comes to light. I am cleared of involvement in Bip's murder, don't have to spend the rest of my life in jail, and you get a great story."

"I don't know about the ethics involved," she seemed genuinely concerned, although her eyes sparkled at the thought of the ratings.

"Ethics? Amy, get real. You work for *Peepers.*"

"I resent that," she replied, appearing offended. "Do you treat all reporters like that?"

"Only the ones I want to make famous after my death."

"Any other demands?" she asked, grinning ruefully.

"Yea, two," I replied. "First, a hundred thousand for the exclusive."

"No disrespect, Andy, but there is no way I could get it before...you know...and after that you won't be in a position to spend it."

"It's for my mother. She doesn't have anything. No security at all. It's not much, but it will help her out a lot."

"I may be able to do a little better than that."

"Thanks," I replied sincerely.

"What's the other thing?"

"I want you to end the broadcast as a tribute to Flipper. I want you to replay the message he delivered just before he left."

We both smiled. We had a deal.

THIRTY-SIX

AMY AND I TAPED MY FINAL SEGMENT about an hour later. It began with her interviewing me, asking difficult questions: how I felt and about the people that I was leaving behind, how I felt about my impending death, that sort of thing. Then we moved on to the topic of Atlantis.

I had decided ahead of time to hold nothing back. If the world was to believe me insane, then so be it. The intended result was too important to risk screwing it up. The whole country was going to learn about Atlantis from possibly the only human ever to have experienced it. So what if they thought I was crazy. I would be dead.

I began with my meeting Christian and my relationship with Bip and Bets, and then the dreams I had been having. I related them to the camera as I have here. Amy and the cameraman were spell-bound, hanging on my every word. I finished with the lines that came to me, as I knew they would, for in reality they were not mine at all, but those of a much higher force.

"No one has been killed. My old friends Bip and Bets will live to tell you this, and you then will know that what I have said is true. I want you to know that I hold no animosity toward anyone, least of all the ever-embattled public, forever cast in doubt and pessimism by irresponsible press and politicians."

"When this does come to pass, and it appears now that I will not be here to witness it myself, I want the world to reconsider what has occurred here, the miracle that has taken place. You once allowed yourselves to believe in it, your minds to escape into the fantastic realm of its possibilities, and we were all better for it. Don't let that go. Don't let the sharks of this world take that away from you. If nothing else, Flipper's brief visit here has shown us that this can be a much better place if we would all just try to be ourselves, what our parents have raised us to be, if we would only start trying to take care of one another rather than just worrying about how much we can do for ourselves. The message is the right one, regardless of whatever opinion you may have of the messenger. I learned it too late and implore each of you to believe it, not for me, but for yourselves and for those to come after you. Before it is too late."

After I had finished we all sat in silence for a while, until I caught Amy wiping a tear from her eye.

"You can't let your subjects get to you," I told her, smiling.

"I usually don't."

"Then I'm honored," I beamed.

She chuckled.

"Listen," I continued. "Would you do me one more favor?"

"What's that, Kiddo?" she responded, attempting to be as chipper as possible.

"Could you be there? Where I can see you?"

She looked shocked, burdened by the words. "I have a pass, but I wasn't planning on using it." Tears welled in her eyes.

"Amy, baby," I said, growing emotional myself, "you better look out. You're losing those killer reporter instincts."

"You want me there?" she asked directly, straightening up, wiping her eyes dry.

"I'd like to have at least one friendly face to look at."

"You got it."

It was the last thing either of us said to one another. We both smiled, then she left.

THIRTY-SEVEN

THE NIGHT BEFORE MY SCHEDULED EXECUTION a thunderstorm knocked out power in half of the prison. It was strange to have a storm of that intensity during the winter, and it ushered in a cold front that made the following day the coldest of the year. It was to be my last day in prison, my last day on earth, yet I was excited. I was going to see my mother, and finally this whole nightmare would be taken to its inevitable conclusion.

The priest was the first to arrive and he remained there throughout the day. Other visitors followed.

My mom was ushered in just before lunchtime. It was bittersweet, seeing her. I had missed her so much, but still, it was without a doubt the most difficult thing I had ever had to do. And it would be even harder on her.

My heart leapt as that sweet little lady was escorted in to see me. Because she was immediate family and this was my last day, we were allowed in the same room. I hurried over to her, held her tightly, and immediately began to weep.

"Oh, Baby," she whispered in a quivering voice. "I promised myself I wouldn't let you see me cry but I can't do that if you're gonna cry too."

"It's all right, Mama," I answered, burying my head in her shoulder, feeling her warmth, taking in her familiar smell – the smell of home. It was like going back, like being a child again when no problem of mine was too great for my parents to remedy.

We remained that way for a long time, and I was at peace. Finally, after I had regained control over my emotions, I gathered the strength to pull away. We both smiled, then sat next to one another at a small table in the room.

"Andy," she finally said in her soft voice.

"How are you, Mom?" What a stupid question.

"I guess I've been better," she responded. "How have you been?"

"Ah, I'm fine, Mama," I stared at her. It was so very good to see her.

"I wish I had gone to the trial now," she lamented.

"Don't, Mom."

"This is the first time that I've seen you since last summer, except for the newspapers and television," she explained.

"I know, I missed you. How are your roses?" She had a beautiful rose garden on the side of our home.

"All eaten up by bugs," she said, smiling.

"Yea, I bet," I responded sarcastically, knowing she was exaggerating.

"Mabel Doucet found out she has cancer in her lungs," she announced suddenly. Mabel had been Mom's next door neighbor for forty years and had probably smoked two packs of cigarettes every day for the last thirty-five of them.

"Not too surprising," I said.

"It's really going around now."

"Mom, it's not like the flu, you don't just catch it."

"I don't know, seems like people do."

"I think its all the chemical and oil and gas industry down there. And her smoking," I offered.

"I think it must be in the water."

Our conversation was struggling.

"You know, Andy, I don't know what's going on," she began. "This world just ain't right no more. Things have just gone all haywire."

"I know, Mama."

"Look at ole Mabel, and look at you. It's just not right."

"You're right."

"You didn't kill no one and here you are and they're fixin' to..." she took a deep breath and tried to hold back tears.

"I didn't kill anyone, Mom. The jury just couldn't see that," I explained.

"I know, baby," she said softly, still not crying.

"It's okay, Mom. I am finally going to a Judge that knows what the truth is. I'm going to be fine. Don't worry about me. I'll be a lot better off than you will be. You need to take care of yourself."

"One thing you never expect in life," she said, a tear finally rolling down her cheek, "is to outlive your own children. You bring a little baby into this world," she looked up at me with swollen eyes, "ah, you were such a beautiful baby boy. And good too. I told your daddy, 'This one's going to be something special.' When the doctor told us we couldn't have no more, we accepted it as God's will and thought it must by why you were so perfect."

She stopped and stared at me.

"Mom," I pleaded, on the verge of breaking down again, but she ignored me.

"I always just knew you were gonna be there to bury me when I went to your father, maybe you'd have a couple of little grandchildren by then for me to know that you wouldn't be all alone. And now," she said, sobbing softly, "it's me who's gonna be alone. I have to bury you and I just don't know how to do that."

I was crying. I had no words to console her. I was so angry at Bets and at Bip for the pain they were causing her.

"I get so sad when I think about you, Baby," she told me.

"Mom, don't," I said, "it's easy for me. You have the hard part."

"I know it ain't, Baby. Havin' death loom over you like a cloud, knowin' the hour of your death, I know it's not easy. And I can't believe they've done this to you. I would change places with you right now if they let me. Why not take this old woman and leave the young man who can do some good in this old world? It's just not right, it's not supposed to be this way, it's just not supposed to be. What am I gonna do? What am I gonna do without my Andy?"

We both sat there and stared at one another, crying and exchanging "I love you"s until the guard came and told Mama it was time to leave.

She kissed me on the cheek and we embraced again. "Do you want me to stay tonight?" she asked, referring to my execution.

"Oh, Mama, you go on home," I cried, knowing that she would be unable to bear my execution but would endure it for me if her presence could lessen my own suffering.

"I'm gonna go home now, Andy," she told me, pulling away. I held on to her hand for as long as I could.

"Okay, Mama," I said, relieved that she was not going to stay for the execution. "I love you."

She smiled and picked up her purse. There was a safety pin holding one of the straps to the body of the purse, and for the first time I noticed that she had worn a new dress to come to see me. It was full of colorful flowers, and I am certain that she had sewn it herself for this very meeting. How she must have fretted over the decision, knowing she needed a new dress, picking out the material that would be just right, wondering whether I would like it. And I didn't notice until it was too late, I did not have the chance to tell her how pretty it was, to let her know I appreciated the trouble she had gone through to see me, for her last visit to see her condemned son. Once she turned to go, she never looked back, and I was glad. I was glad because, as I sat there, watching her, seeing how little she had, remembering all of the sacrifices that she had made so that I could become some kind of "successful big-city lawyer," and now realizing how much she would have to struggle as she grew older without me, the tears streamed endlessly down my face. I was ashamed. I had strayed from the goodness she had instilled in me and now she was having to pay for it.

As soon as Mama was gone, I stood and walked with Walter to my cell. He said nothing, and I was grateful for that.

I slept through lunch and did not awaken until nearly three in the afternoon. Walter was standing at my feet when I opened my eyes.

"Sorry to disturb you, Andy."

"It's all right," I said, "what's wrong?"

"Nothin's really wrong," I was relieved. "But there's some people here that would like to see you if you want to."

"Who?" I asked.

"It's a Mrs. Boier and her son. It's that Mr. Harold's mother and brother. The judge told them they could attend the execution and that they could see you, if you would agree to it," Walter explained.

I was really not up for this. The visit with my mother had worn me out. I was prepared to sleep until the time had come.

"No, Walter, I can't" I said.

"I'll tell them," he replied, turning.

Walter walked back out of my cell and turned down the hallway. I pictured my mother. Then I thought about Mrs. Boier, to have lost a son without notice, with no one to explain to her what had happened. The questions she must have. I felt that I owed it to Flipper's Mom to at least speak to her before it was too late and I was no longer available.

"Walter, wait!" I called after him.

He reappeared.

"I'll talk to them," I said.

"You sure?"

"Yea. At the very worse, if they are hostile, I can just walk out of the room."

After a brief absence, Walter came back and escorted me to the interview room. On the opposite side of the two-inch thick, bulletproof glass sat a very large woman wearing a faded dress that looked as though it had been last year's curtains. Standing next to her was a gaunt young man with a scruffy face who bore no resemblance to Flipper whatsoever. I walked in and sat down.

"Thank you for seein' us sur," the woman said in a heavy Mississippi accent.

"You're welcome, Ms. Boier," I replied.

"How have you been, son?" she asked kindly.

"Fine, Ma'am," I responded, confused by her kindness. "I'm really sorry about your son."

"Well thank you. Mr. Jordan, do you know why my son had to die?"

"To tell the truth, Ms. Boier, I think it was for the same reason that I have to die. Greed. Somebody else's greed."

"You didn't kill him, did you?" she asked.

"No, Ma'am, I did not," I said, surprised that she had asked.

"I know."

"You do?"

"Yes. Emma Gibbs told me," she responded.

"I'm sorry," I said, "but who is Emma Gibbs?"

"The little Gibbs girl, from down in the Delta. She was born with the veil over her eyes," she explained.

"The veil over her eyes?"

"Yes sur, she just come out that way. Those people can talk with the ones that have passed you know," she told me calmly. I glanced over at her son. He stood stone-faced at her side.

"Dead people?"

"Yes, sur," she responded.

"Does she still have the veil?" I asked, not understanding.

"Heavens no!," she exclaimed, almost laughing, "it's just a small layer of skin, the doctor cuts it right off."

"Ah," I said, confused.

"She spoke to Harold the other night," she told me matter-of-factly.

"Your Harold?"

"Yes, sur, come to her in a dream he did. Told her that you wasn't the one who had him killed. Said you was just the patsy, a porpoise amongst the sharks," she said, cracking a smile. "That Harold always could turn a phrase."

"He said I was a porpoise amongst the sharks?" I asked, a shiver running down my spine.

"That's what she said. Said it was them other two, the girl and the lawyer friend, they are the ones what took my boy."

I was shocked. How could she possibly have known all of this? I had heard of various superstitions, Ouija boards, people communicating with the dead, but I had never experienced it first hand before.

"Harold was that way too, you know," she continued, "he was strange from the start. He knew a lot of things just because he knew 'em, that's all.

Never could really explain it."

"He was queer, Mama," the other son finally spoke. She ignored him.

"I'd have thought he'd of seen those other two comin', though," she concluded.

"So..." I hesitated. Then, risking being crude, asked what I had to know. "You really are his mother, then?" If she were, I was insane, and Atlantis just a myth.

"Yes, sur. Why do you ask me that?"

"I'm sorry," I said, suddenly shaken.

"Did he tell you something different?" she continued, prodding.

"He said he was from Atlantis."

"Georgia?" she asked, confused.

"No, Ma'am, never mind."

She stared at me, hesitating, as though contemplating whether or not she should reveal to me what was on her mind, or whether she should leave. Then she began.

"Christian was my youngest. Born after his Daddy left us."

"He died?" I asked.

She seemed embarrassed and I regretted asking the question.

"Yes," she finally responded. "He was a fisherman, you see, he'd be gone for months at the time when the fish was runnin'. Then one time he just didn't come back. They said he fell off the boat, but I'm more likely to believe that it wasn't no accident."

"You mean he was killed?"

"No," she said immediately, seeing that I had gotten the wrong idea. "He was jest different. The last time he come to us he was different, said he had seen somethin' that there wasn't no explainin'. He couldn't wait to get back on the water after that and he was so happy that I jest knew he wouldn't be comin' back. I had Christian nine months to the day that he left."

"Did he say what he had seen?" I asked.

She shook her head. "After that I knew the baby was either sent to me from good or evil, so I named him Christian and hoped that that's the one it was. Oh, he wasn't no normal boy, and I don't just mean his feet. He was as hard-headed as they come, insistin' on doin' things his way. But he was mighty sweet too. He was nice to everybody, never hurt no one, liked touchin' folks and animals."

I glanced over to her son, who had raised an eyebrow at that revelation.

"He told me that he was only here for a year," I said, wondering whether she had an explanation.

"Oh, time never did mean much to my Christian. He was always sayin' how a year here was like two weeks where he was from – like he was from another planet or something," she smiled.

"How old was he?"

"We lost him on his twenty-fourth birthday." With that she began to weep softly and I just let her cry. There was nothing for me to say to lessen her grief.

"Come on boy," she said finally to her son as she struggled to get her weight out of the chair. "Sorry to be takin' up your time on this, your last day and all. I really appreciate your kindness in seein' me. I jest had to hear it from your own mouth and all. We won't be stayin' for the execution now." She smiled and turned away. I sat, watching her.

Suddenly she swung back around. "Good luck to ya, now, and I'll keep your pore Mamma in my prayers darlin'."

I smiled and said thank you. She turned around and they left. Walter walked me back to my cell.

I did the math after that. One year here being two weeks there, two years equaling roughly a month. Twenty-four years, Flipper's earthly age, equaling one year there – the one year he told me had. I had chills running down my spine as the numbers unfolded before me. Everybody would like to see an alien, or an angel (if it were friendly of course), but once it happens your entire view of the world is skewed, everything viewed from a vantage point unknown to those untouched, making you insane to an ignorant world.

I did not want to be an outcast in my world, an abducted earthling to those who had not seen what I had seen. For such a long time I had divided my time between denying that Flipper could have happened and contemplating how astonishing the world was after he had. I finally reached the unavoidable conclusion that made my own transformation complete and had sealed my fate forever. I was comfortable with my situation. I had been presented a miraculous gift, and I had come to terms with it.

Before dinner I said three full decades of the rosary with the Father and he heard my confession. He said a Mass for me, and I received communion. I appreciated the Mass and sacraments as I had appreciated none before, perhaps because I was so near to my own judgment, my own meeting with my Savior.

THIRTY-EIGHT

THE SHARK STEAK WAS ACTUALLY VERY GOOD. After eating, I returned to my cell and asked the priest to leave me alone until eight thirty, when I planned to say another three rosaries. I closed my eyes and tried to relax.

My mind kept wandering back to my mother's visit. Her realizing the agony that I was feeling subconsciously, because, although death may be preferable under the circumstances, there is no way to approach it without at least some degree of fear and anxiety. Her words had reminded me of the story of the Cyclops, or at least a version that I had seen on television once. It was said that the Cyclops had given up one of its eyes in exchange for knowing the date, time, and method of its own death. This ability, which the Cyclops had paid so dearly for, ended up being a curse rather than the great gift that it had anticipated. Great depression followed the poor creature, who, from that day forward, lived in anticipation of an end over which it had no control, each day having only its death to look forward to. Its life had become finite, and although it had always been finite, without the knowledge of its end, life had seemed nearly infinite. Likewise, the burden of knowing the hour and method of my death was beginning to weigh heavily upon my own mind.

I had been lying there for about twenty minutes when Walter walked into my cell.

"Nobody else," I said. "I wasn't this busy when I was a lawyer."

"Mr. J. Ryan called," Walter said.

"Shit!" I exclaimed, sitting up in my bunk. "He didn't get a stay order, did he?"

"No, not that," he responded.

"Good," I said, more relaxed.

"He said he had been in the judge's chambers for three hours this afternoon trying to get you one last visitor," Walter explained.

"Another reporter?"

"No. He said you'd want this one. He said if you wouldn't see her to tell you that he was gonna ask her out, and he knows you wouldn't want that to happen to her."

My heart stopped. It had to be Carly.

"Is she here?" I asked, at the same moment thrilled and terrified.

"She's waitin' in the room, but they'll only let her have five minutes," he said.

I jumped out of bed and ran down the hallway. Walter followed me as fast as he could, searching through his keys to find the one that unlocked the interview room. I had so much to tell her, so much to explain. At that moment I could have kissed J. Ryan.

I stopped at the door and anxiously awaited its opening. As soon as Walter had done so, I rushed inside, then froze when I saw her. She looked up as soon as I came in.

She was even more beautiful than I had remembered. She sat on the other side of that glass like an angel who had descended from heaven to be with me in my final hour. I was completely overwhelmed, captivated by her. Somehow I floated over to my chair and found myself sitting face-to-face with her.

"Hi," she said softly, her eyes welling up with tears.

"Hey," I responded, feeling my eyes dampen.

"How have you been?" she asked, looking away, trying not to cry.

"Oh," I said, "I've been better."

"How are your appeals going?"

"I don't have any," I said.

"But this is just the first time...I mean tonight..."

"It's gonna happen tonight," I said.

"But don't they always give you a few stays or whatever? Isn't J. Ryan going to get a judge to try to stop it, or the governor?"

"No," I said.

"Why not?"

"Carly," I explained, "I told him not to. There's no point."

"What do you mean?" she said. "They'll kill you."

"There's no new evidence. Bets did too good of a job. There's just no way to prove that I wasn't involved."

"But they could still catch her," she said.

"Yea, when she's fifty or sixty, maybe. Carly, I couldn't take it in here that long, I couldn't spend my life in here."

"I'm so sorry," she whispered.

"It isn't your fault. You don't have anything to be sorry about."

"Andy," she said, crying now, "I am so sorry."

She broke down and began to sob uncontrollably.

"Hey, hey," I said, trying to console her, to make her feel better.

"Oh, God," she said between sobs, finally turning to look at me.

"Carly," I began.

"No, Andy," she interrupted, "I have to tell you. I know it was not fair to you. I just couldn't see you. I couldn't contact you or hear from you."

"Carly," I interrupted, seeing the difficulty she was having, "please, you don't have to explain. I am just so – *so* happy that you came. You don't know what it means to me."

"Andy!" she sobbed, "I wanted to come, I wanted to see you more than anything, to let you know that I didn't believe them," she insisted through the tears.

"I know, I know," I had not known and was overjoyed at hearing her say the words.

"The day before they arrested you our picture was in the paper, remember?" she asked.

"Yea, sure," I said, "You and Taylor and me. I have it in my cell – room."

"You do?" she asked, surprised.

"Yes," I said softly.

"Taylor's father, his biological father, Tad. He saw the picture of us and when they arrested you he tried to get custody of Taylor."

I just listened, watching the expression and intensity of her big, wet brown eyes as she spoke.

"He brought me to court and my lawyer said that if I was connected with you that it might help him to get Taylor. I was so confused and they were all saying such horrible things about you, and the Bar Association denounced you, and I was so scared that if I saw you or if you wrote to me or called me that they would find out and that the judge would take Taylor."

I began crying. I knew then that the only thing that could have kept her from me was her fear of losing Taylor, and that she stilled loved me and believed in me.

"Carly, baby," I sobbed, "Carly, it's okay. I understand. You did the right thing, you did the right thing. God, I am so happy to hear you say that. Thank you, thank you for coming and for telling me. I was so afraid that you believed what they were saying about me, and that you didn't love me."

"I never stopped," she insisted.

"I know."

"I was so afraid," she said, crying anew. "I was so scared that you would die and you would not know that. I kept seeing you there, when it happens, and you not knowing and I couldn't..."

"Thank you," I said, crying. "It'll be easier now. You make me so happy. I wish it all could have been different. I wish I had never gotten mixed up in all of this."

The guard came to the door. Our five minutes were up.

"Excuse me. Ma'am," he said, "it's time to go now."

"Can I have just a second more?" she pleaded with him.

"No, Ma'am, I'm sorry, but they're real strict. . ."

"...Just one more minute," she cried, "They're going to kill him for Christ's sake."

"Ma'am," he insisted.

"Carly," I interrupted, she turned to me.

"I will always love you," she said.

"You remind me of a ship," I began.

"Oh, God," she smiled through her tears and almost laughed.

"A magnificent sailing vessel," I continued, "when you move through a crowd, it parts like the sea, and you put all the other ships to shame."

The guard came into the room and grabbed Carly from behind.

"Take your fucking hands off of her!" I screamed, losing control. "Let her go!"

He did not relent, and he pulled her up from her seat. She did not resist, only cried.

"I love you Carly, I will *always* love you!" I yelled to her, and then she was gone.

I sat in that chair for what seemed like a very long time. I cried and I cried. Like a child I wept as loud and for as long as I could, until I had no more tears to cry. After I had finished and put my head on the table before me, Walter came in and escorted me back to my cell.

On the way back to my cell Walter told me that in all of the years that he had been a guard, I was the first man on death row that he honestly believed did not belong there. I was grateful for his confidence, but I could not respond. He brought me back and locked me in my cell, standing at the bars for a moment before shuffling down the hall. I would not see him again.

I sat listlessly for the rest of the evening, refusing to see the priest when he returned, feeling outside of myself, as though I were floating around the cell, looking down at the pitiful creature that was me, the shell of a condemned man, a cyclops nearing his end.

THIRTY-NINE

AT 11:00 P.M. THEY BEGAN PREPARING FOR MY DEATH. They dressed me in a white, cotton suit that had a flap over the veins in each of my arms. It also had bands so that they could tie my hands behind my back if necessary.

"You guys aren't going to tie me up, are you?" I asked the guard.

"Not unless you make us," he said seriously.

"Don't worry. I want it over as quickly as possible."

He did not respond.

"You don't have to shave heads anymore, right?" I asked.

"Nope," he answered coldly.

"Good," I said. "I'm quite vain about my hair, you know."

The humor was wasted on him. I suppose when your job is leading others to their deaths it would be a bad practice to begin seeing those condemned as human beings.

As soon as they had begun I really started to get nervous. Death is not an easy thing to face, regardless of how prepared you think you are for it. I asked for the priest and he immediately appeared, helping me with my Hail Mary's.

From that point forward time really began to fly by. It seemed that in no time at all we were taking the walk down the hallway, in the direction opposite that of the interview room. My heart raced as I sputtered out Hail Mary after Hail Mary. It was the way to the death chamber.

Inside of the room there was a single, metal table with a white sheet spread over the top. A man dressed all in white stood next to the table, ready to administer the lethal dosage.

"Dr. Kevorkian, I presume," I said as I walked in. I shouldn't have. There were reporters watching and listening in the ante room and it risked making me appear to be an insensitive killer who could not even take my own death seriously. I just couldn't help it. The somber looks did not change on any of the faces in that room.

One entire wall of the chamber was made of glass and in the room beyond were seated several people. I saw Amy there, winked to her, strangely comforted by the friendly, familiar face. I knew that most of the others were also from the press, there to report, first hand, my final moments. I hoped that they would not mention the Dr. Kevorkian joke. I recognized Ms. Robinson sitting in the front row. To the victor go the spoils I thought, but what possible satisfaction could she get out of seeing me put to death? I had done nothing to her. What kind of person wants to see that?

On one of the other two walls there was a large clock that read four minutes till midnight, and on a table against the opposite wall were three telephones, two of them red. I knew they would not ring.

They laid me on the table and began to strap me down. My heart rate quickened. My time had come.

"Hail Mary full of Grace, the Lord is with Thee," the Priest began.

"The initial drug is a sedative," the man in the white coat explained, though I don't know whether it was for my benefit or that of the audience. "It will be administered first and should take affect within thirty seconds."

"Blessed art Thou amongst women, and blessed is the Fruit of thy Womb, Jesus," the Priest finished.

"After the first drug takes affect, the lethal dose is administered," the white jacketed man finished.

"Holy Mary, Mother of God," I began on cue.

The man in the white jacket stuck a needle and tube in my left arm. I flinched.

"Pray for us sinners," I continued.

He moved on to the other arm.

"Now and at the hour of our deaths, Amen."

"Hail Mary full of Grace, the Lord is with Thee," the priest began anew, "blessed art Thou amongst women and blessed is the Fruit of Thy womb, Jesus."

He stuck my other arm.

"Holy Mary, mother of God, pray for us sinners, now and at the hour of our death, Amen," I continued.

"It is now one minute after midnight," the man in the white suit announced. I suddenly felt something cold going into my left arm.

"Hail Mary, full of Grace," the priest continued, his voice growing more and more distant with each syllable pronounced. I was getting sleepy.

I could no longer focus. I closed my eyes, preparing to see my Redeemer.

Suddenly, it was over. All was still and silent.

I saw a boat, Bip's boat, painted red and plying the waves of the Caribbean. My mind scanned across the vessel, starting from the stern. I saw Bip, a smile on his face and a drink in his hand, standing at the wheel. He was saying something to someone in front of him. My vision moved toward the cabin and mast, then past them to the deck in front of the cabin, the torn railing, and finally, to the most extreme point of the bow. And there, perched much like the figurine upon a Viking warship, was Bets, bare-chested, perky breasts cutting the wind as she knelt, back arched, hair flung backward, facing the coming seas. All the while a voice reigned down from the heavens, in a clear whisper, "Andy, you've done it, you are free. Goodbye, Andy Jordan. Goodbye."

I traced the voice with my mind's eye into the water, above the waves, to where Flipper was calling to me, exactly as he had done in the Lake that final day.

Suddenly he was sea creature, a porpoise, heading toward the boat, the stern, its rudder. He struck it with such force that it was nearly ripped from the bow. I saw the shock on their faces, the terror in their eyes.

Then he was Flipper again. His glowing form turned toward me and smiled. I believe I smiled back, but felt decidedly saddened as he drew away, sensing that I would not see him again in this life.

I experienced this redemption and then all was darkness and solitude save for the report of a single bell. A rapid ringing, clambering softly, somewhere in the distant reaches of my dying mind.

EPILOGUE

WELL, TO MAKE A LONG STORY SHORT, I was only unconscious when the Governor's call came in on the hot line. I awoke in the prison infirmary the next morning convinced that I had died and gone to hell, and hell was exactly like the prison I had just left. Tony had to come in and explain it all to me twice before I was truly convinced that I had not been put to death.

It seems that Bip, the great sailor that he is, veered off course, by about a hundred miles. He said his compass had gone haywire. He and Bets were picked up in Costa Rican waters as suspected drug smugglers, their boat sailing in circles, as it had been for days since something had mysteriously struck the rudder, placing them in that holding patter until they were caught. I was not surprised by the report. After all, I had seen it all occur.

Tony D'Ensina has a cousin who is an agent with the U.S. Customs Service and she called Tony the moment she learned of the fugitives' capture. Tony and J. Ryan, God bless 'em, sped to Baton Rouge in a driving rainstorm, in the middle of the night and, after nearly being arrested for pounding on the Governor's door at that hour, got him to get out of bed and make the call, only seconds before the lethal dosage was given. They put their careers and reputations on the line and saved my life.

After two days in a Costa Rican jail, Bets, the whiny little stool pigeon, broke down and told the whole story. It seems it was only a matter of time anyway. She and Bip had gotten to the point where they could hardly stand the sight of one another. Bets was convinced that Bip had tried to throw her overboard just before the Costa Rican Coast Guard intercepted them. At her trial she got ten to twenty years for cooperating, and Bip, the greedy mastermind, copped a plea for fifty. It seems that the public had tired of the whole ordeal and the District Attorney's office wanted it swept under the rug as quickly as possible. I harbor no ill feelings. I think they both got what they deserved.

The way Bets explained it, the plot had been in the making for quite some time. After several years of their both living with me, and finding out that they had so much in common, mainly greed, Bets and Bip ended up in bed one wintery evening after I had turned in early with a couple of AlkaSeltzer Plus Nighttime Cold Tablets. I suppose that was about the time she cut me off with all of her talk about weddings. She knew me well, knew that I would wait without immediately calling her bluff about marriage. All the while I was suffering, and she and Bip were getting their fill at my expense, their clandestine relationship blossoming into a full blown plot to destroy my life in the process of scamming millions of dollars.

That they ever thought they would be successful in convincing me, and much of the world, that a supposed street bum was a man from Atlantis is, in itself, incredible. That they succeeded, and made a million dollars in the process, boggles the mind. Bip had met Flipper one night while he was handling arraignments in Magistrate Court. Someone had told him about the guy's feet and he had later told Bets. Two days later Bip misplaced Flipper's paperwork and, lo-and-behold, he was back out on the street, only now he was beholden to Bip.

All Bets and Bip needed was a patsy, someone that they could feed inside information about to Flipper and manipulate the situation to make Flipper appear clairvoyant. Someone who would be kind enough not to ignore a street beggar in the first place and gullible enough to believe that he might just have some mystical power. Someone like the boy my good mother had raised; good, but not above temptation. "Hey, what about this guy sleeping in the next room while we're fucking our brains out? Surely he would never catch on. After all, he believes in bigfoot and flying saucers."

Bip ordered the equipment they needed, the tanks and underwater scooter, and had me sign for and pick some of it up. He strapped one of those bubbleless tanks beneath *The Great White* the first time that we all went out to the lake and figured Flipper just went under and breathed oxygen for fifteen minutes as they had planned. Likewise, he had dropped the tanks and scooter off of the bottom of the boat before the initial *Peepers* filming, acting as though he had lost an anchor, and Flipper had only to strap himself in and motor around the lake to convince everyone that he swam and breathed like a fish.

They planned Flipper's departure around the Regatta so that Bip would have an alibi. Only, Flipper got to know Bip and Bets a little too well and was not about to jump into that lake without knowing that Bip would be there to pick him up once the crowd had dispersed, so they painted the boat red and Bip waited offshore. Only the night before Bip bled Flipper's first tank nearly dry and filled his second tank with CO-2. Bets had gone to meet him that night, the night of Fabacher's party, and that was why Bip's car had been moved before I got home after having dropped Carly off. Flipper had obviously told her about my kissing Carly. The following day Bip waited offshore in the red boat but sailed off as soon as Flipper went under the second time. He knew that Flipper would strap himself to the underwater scooter and be weighted down to the lake's bottom forever. Perhaps I would be prosecuted for fraud, perhaps not. Flipper would never be discovered so there would be no murder charge, and Bip and Bets would just sail the seven seas and spend what was left of the million dollars that they had not blown on cars, boats, and clothes.

But then, as though some mysterious force would not allow them to get away with it, the lake had suddenly turned clear and the sea life rushed in, leading to the discovery of the tanks and scooter and exposing the plot. Looking back, knowing all that I do, it is crystal clear to me now that it was all part of the much greater picture, devised long before Bip and Bets ever dreamed up their elaborate plot. That was Flipper's reason for being here.

After their convictions, the court had a tough time deciding where the money that Bip and Bets had not spent should go, and ultimately settled with me. I got the money and promised not to sue for my imprisonment and near death experience. I attempted to split the cash with Flipper's mother, and even went to Mississippi with the check in hand. Although her house was falling down and she was in desperate need of a new car, she refused to have anything to do with the money. She was embarrassed by my offer. She cried that I would do such a thing after all that I had been through. I bought her a new car, a Cadillac, and had it delivered. The rest of the money went to establish the Flipper Club – for ecology minded youth. It's ranks are swelling, and Flipper's legacy is flourishing.

And then there is Carly. Ah, Carly. She was waiting at the gate with Taylor the day that Bets confessed and I was released. They were the most beautiful sight I have ever seen, with the possible exception of a vision in a dream that I am unable to recall. She ran up to me in tears and squeezed me until I was near the point of losing consciousness. We were married three days later and moved out of the city, north of Lake Pontchartrain, near her mother. I have a little practice there, not much. Seems that I have more pro bono clients than paying ones, but I am fulfilled. We could not be any happier and we all go visit my mom at least once a month, and we'll continue doing it, at least until we can convince her to leave her roses and move nearer to us.

Tony and J. Ryan are doing great. Business is booming and they are constantly asking me to join their practice. It seems that there are plenty of people around here who never stopped believing in me. Nonetheless, I keep politely declining their offers. Somehow the rat race and all of its so-called rewards no longer appeals to me. Tony calls me Dorothy, says I tired of Oz and snapped my heels together a few times and wound up back in the sticks. In some ways he's right. I just find happiness and success in better places now.

I didn't forget Walter either. He was with me during the most difficult period of my life, and was the only person there who bothered to treat me like a human being. I send him a turkey on Thanksgiving and a bottle of scotch every Christmas. I'm trying to get him out of that hell-hole he's working in, but it's rather hopeless. He's happy there.

I don't dream anymore. I figure I experienced the pinnacle of the phenomena and my subconscious refuses to return to the relative drabness of what it was before. My mind clouded the visions out at about the same time that the lake returned to normal, clouding itself and sending its bounty back to the sea. Biologists have attempted to explain it, but none has yet to come up with a convincing explanation and none has bothered to consult me. Still, I am left with my reward.

Carly and I are expecting our first child next month. The doctor thinks it's a girl. If so, I hope she's exactly like her mom. I haven't decided yet how I will tell her about Flipper, only that I must as soon as she is old enough to understand. He has become a part of me. I still look for him in crowds and expect to hear his voice every time I pass my old office building. Some days I find myself drawn to the lake, to the point where he last dove into the water. I listen for his calling in the wind.

For whatever reason, I was fortunate enough to have known him and have been forever changed because of it. I was lucky, had my life placed back on course. Not many people are granted such second chances.

Some days the lake looks as though it will clear again, reflecting brilliant shades of aquamarine as sunbeams rain down from between the clouds, spotlighting points on the water that I scan for Flipper's re-appearance. Driving over the Causeway Bridge from Covington on clear mornings, when the haze is still clinging to the shore, the city skyline appears as Atlantis, rising from the depths, suspended in the lake before me. It is on such days that I know Flipper is still here, in some form, somewhere amongst us, and that he and I are destined to one day meet again.

Perhaps it will be in the ocean.

Perhaps it will be as porpoises.

THE END